Shojo Beat

La Corda d'Oro

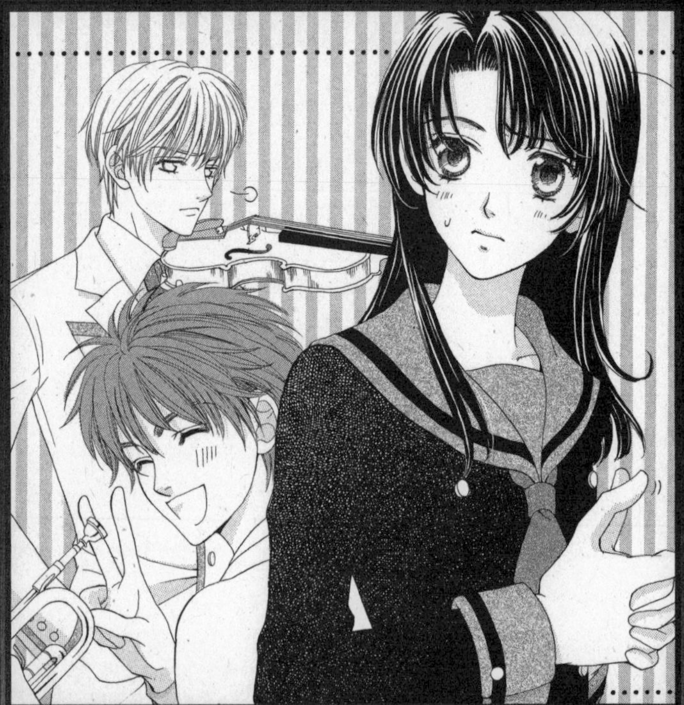

1

Story & Art by Yuki Kure

La Corda d'Oro

CONTENTS
Volume 1

Measure 1 · · · · · · · · · · · · 5

Measure 2 · · · · · · · · · · · · 57

Measure 3 · · · · · · · · · · · · 89

Measure 4 · · · · · · · · · · · · 119

Postscript · · · · · · · · · · · · 170

End Notes · · · · · · · · · · · · 184

ff

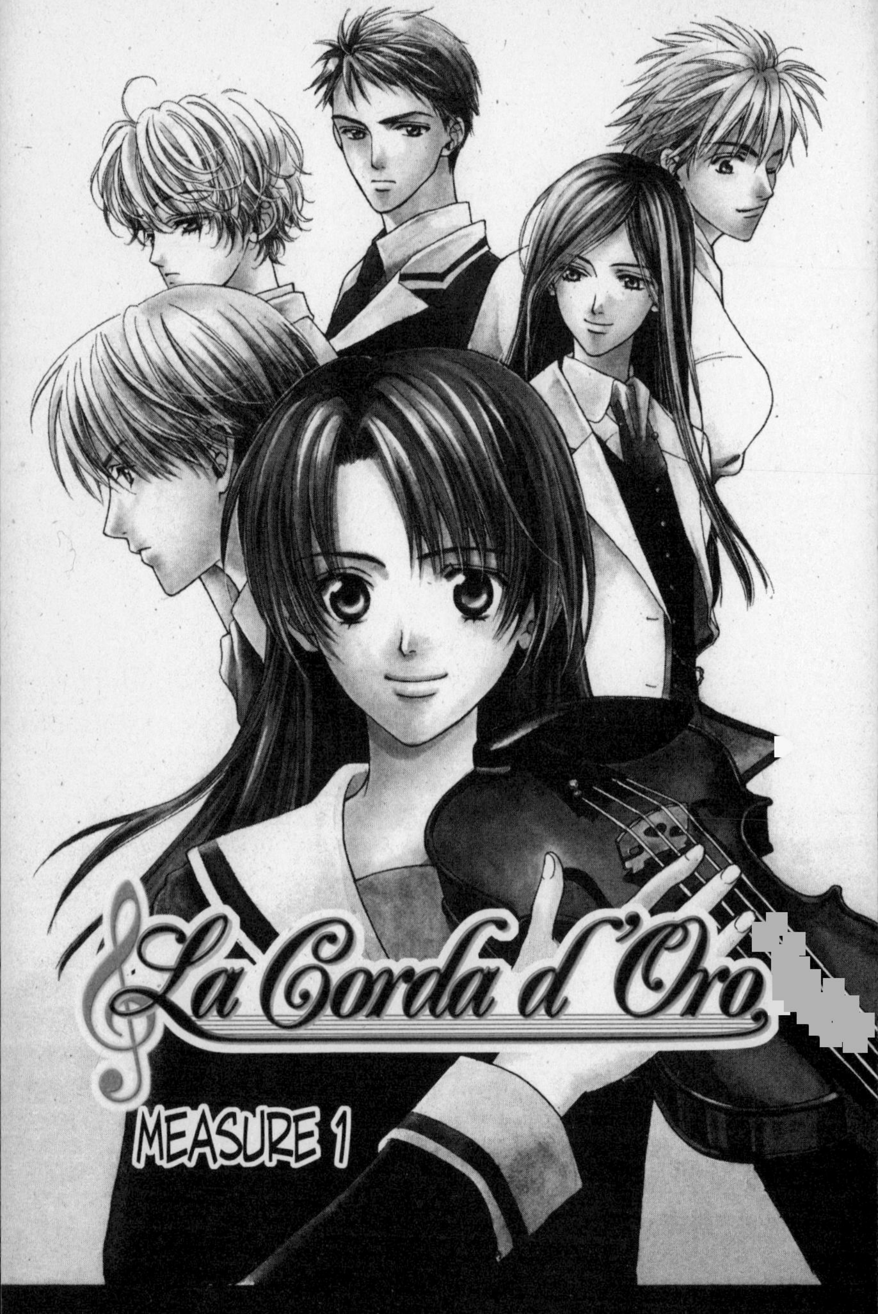
La Corda d'Oro
MEASURE 1

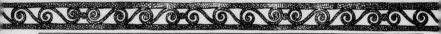

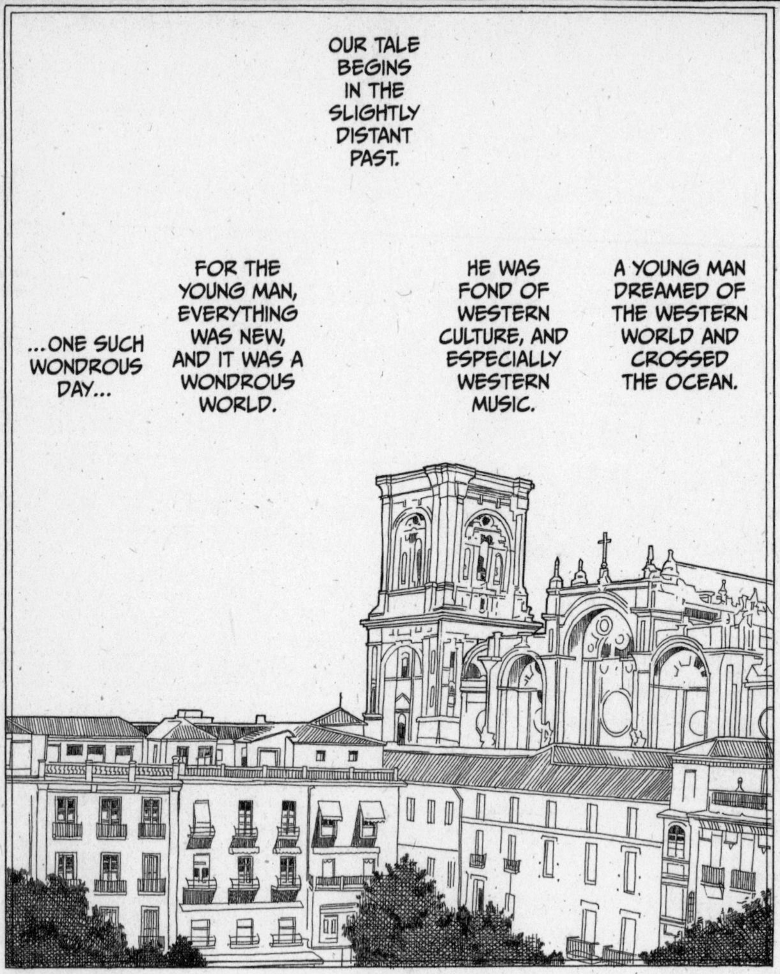
OUR TALE BEGINS IN THE SLIGHTLY DISTANT PAST.
A YOUNG MAN DREAMED OF THE WESTERN WORLD AND CROSSED THE OCEAN.
HE WAS FOND OF WESTERN CULTURE, AND ESPECIALLY WESTERN MUSIC.
FOR THE YOUNG MAN, EVERYTHING WAS NEW, AND IT WAS A WONDROUS WORLD.
...ONE SUCH WONDROUS DAY...

...HE HAD AN EXTRAORDINARY ENCOUNTER.

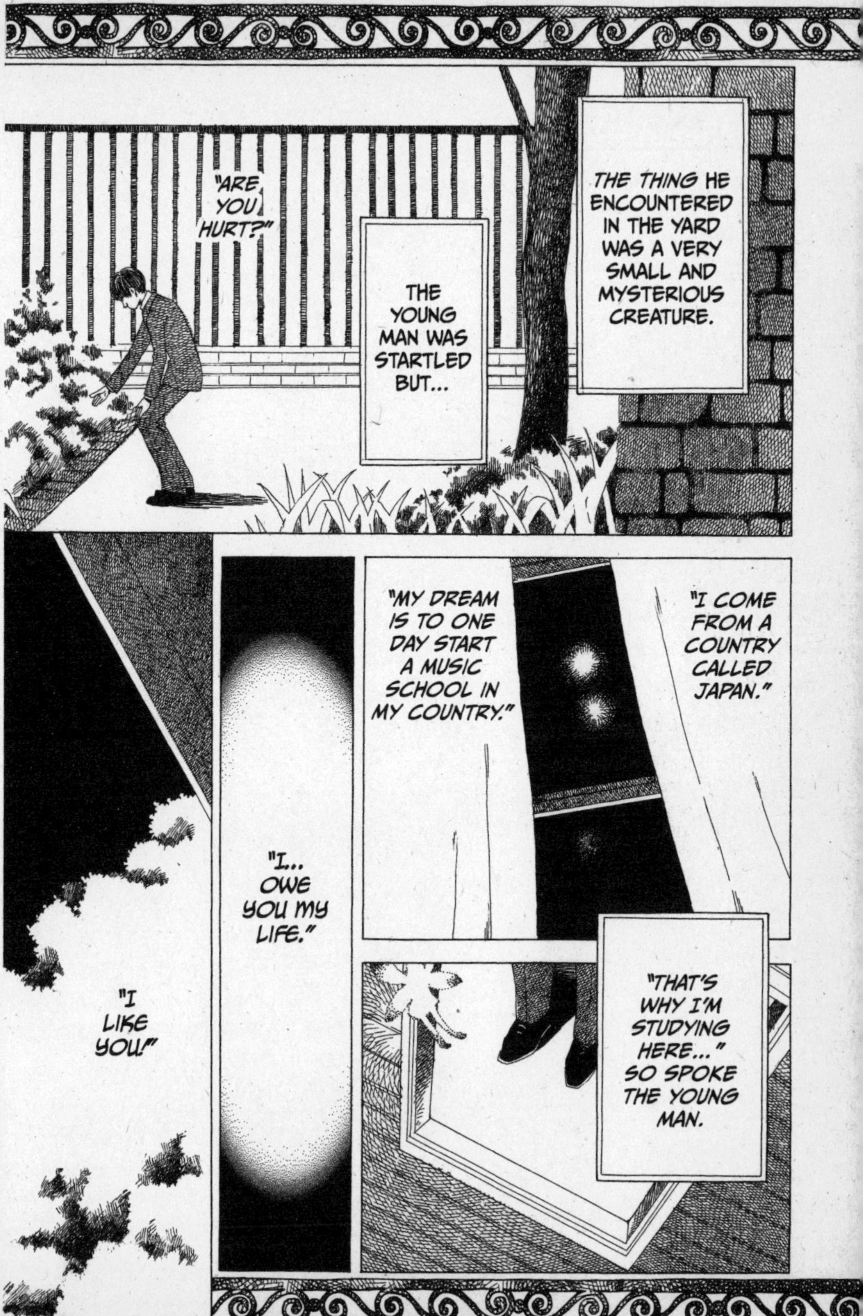
THE THING HE ENCOUNTERED IN THE YARD WAS A VERY SMALL AND MYSTERIOUS CREATURE.
THE YOUNG MAN WAS STARTLED BUT...
"ARE YOU HURT?"
"I COME FROM A COUNTRY CALLED JAPAN."
"MY DREAM IS TO ONE DAY START A MUSIC SCHOOL IN MY COUNTRY."
"THAT'S WHY I'M STUDYING HERE..." SO SPOKE THE YOUNG MAN.
"I... OWE YOU MY LIFE."
"I LIKE YOU!"

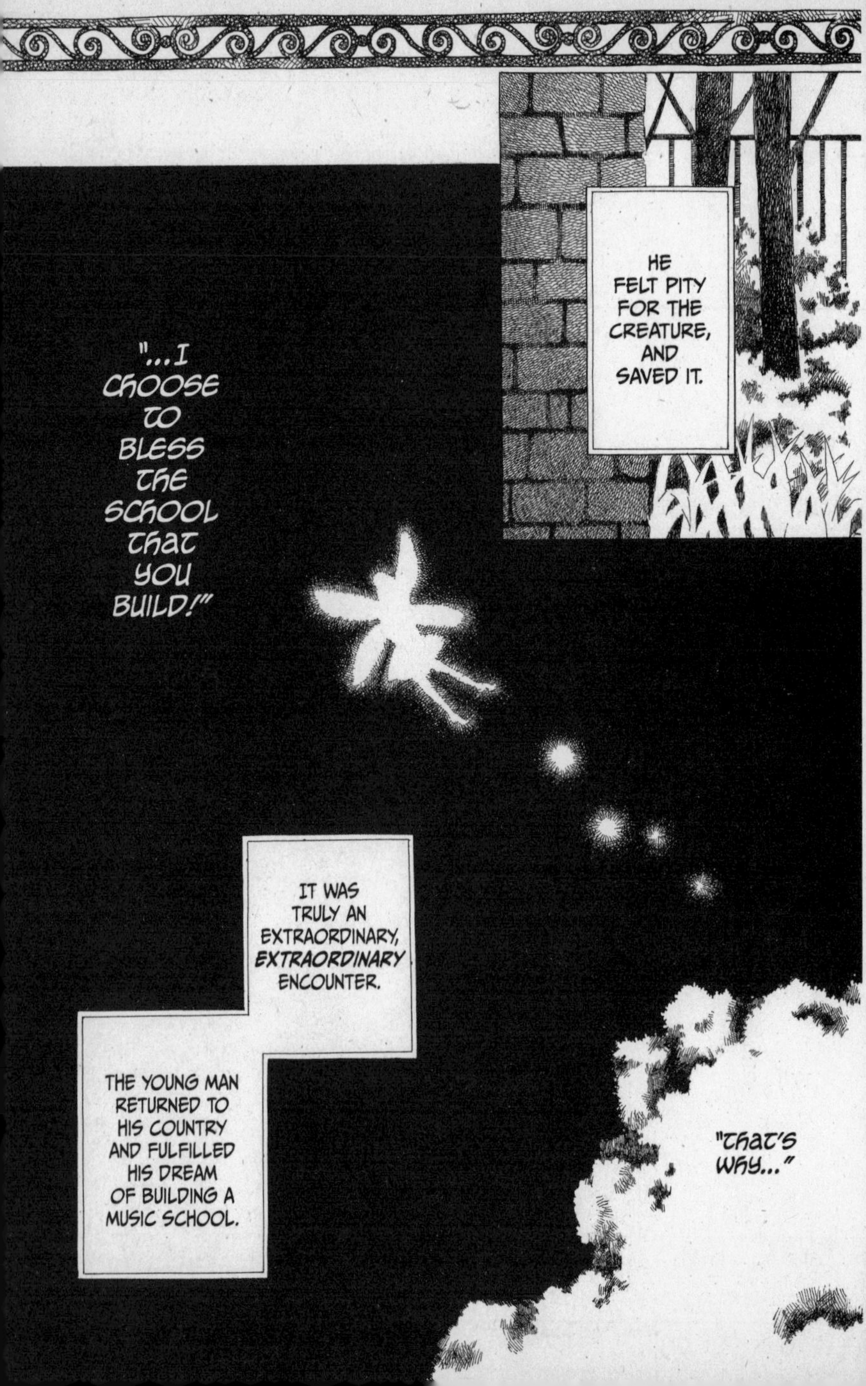
HE FELT PITY FOR THE CREATURE, AND SAVED IT.
"...I CHOOSE TO BLESS THE SCHOOL THAT YOU BUILD!"
IT WAS TRULY AN EXTRAORDINARY, *EXTRAORDINARY* ENCOUNTER.
THE YOUNG MAN RETURNED TO HIS COUNTRY AND FULFILLED HIS DREAM OF BUILDING A MUSIC SCHOOL.
"THAT'S WHY..."

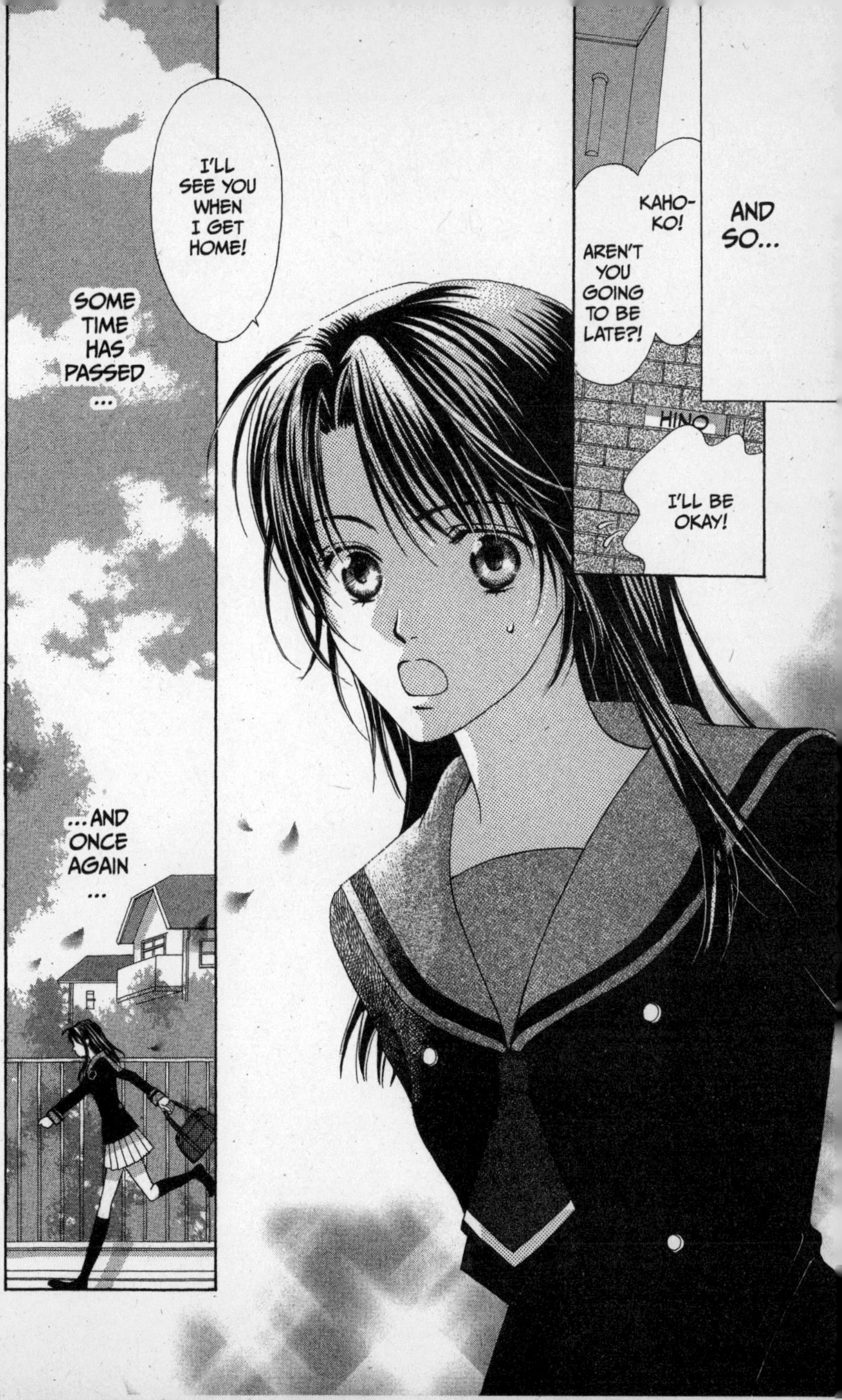
AND SO...
KAHO-KO! AREN'T YOU GOING TO BE LATE?!
HINO
I'LL BE OKAY!
I'LL SEE YOU WHEN I GET HOME!
SOME TIME HAS PASSED...
...AND ONCE AGAIN...

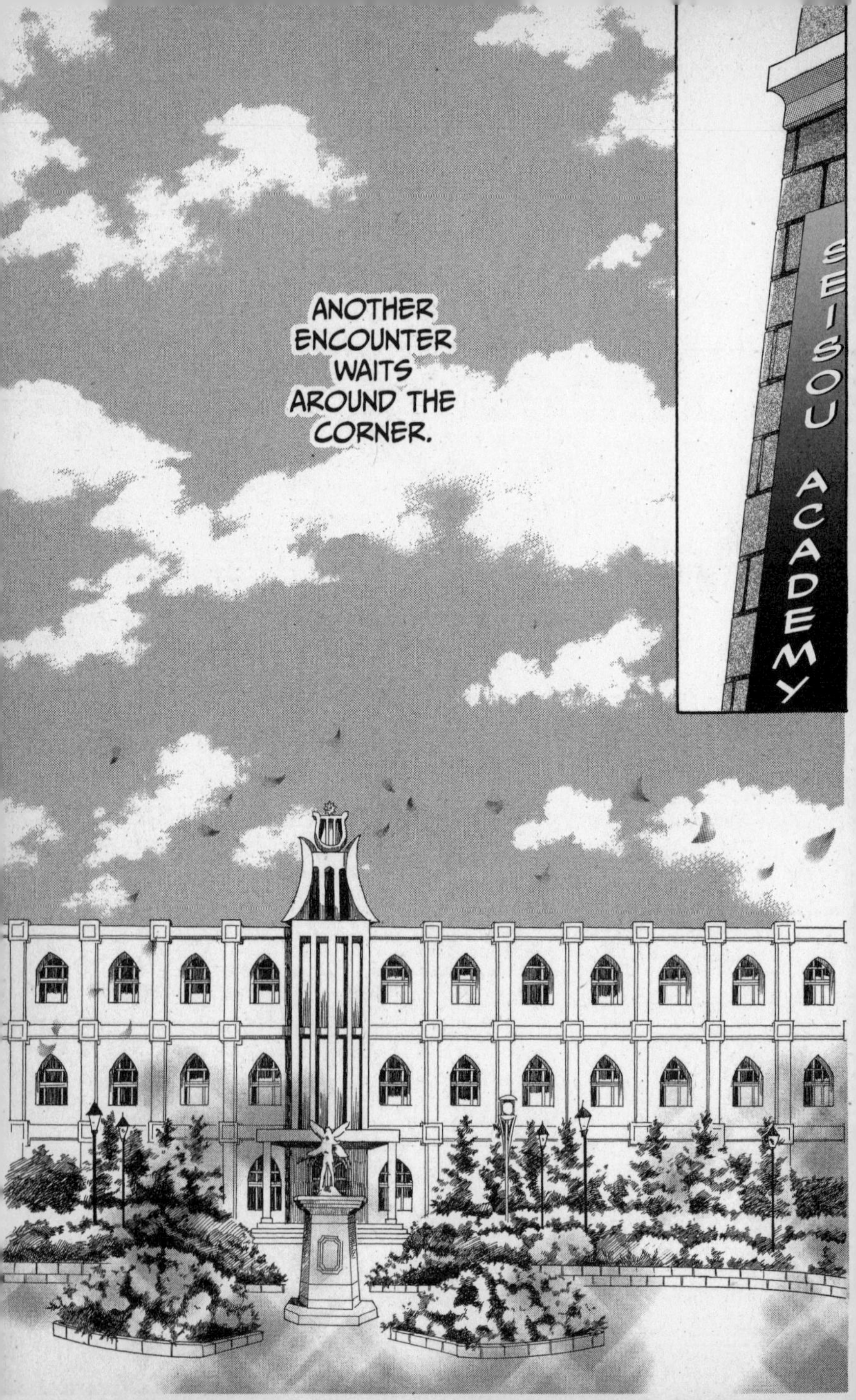
SEISOU ACADEMY
ANOTHER ENCOUNTER WAITS AROUND THE CORNER.

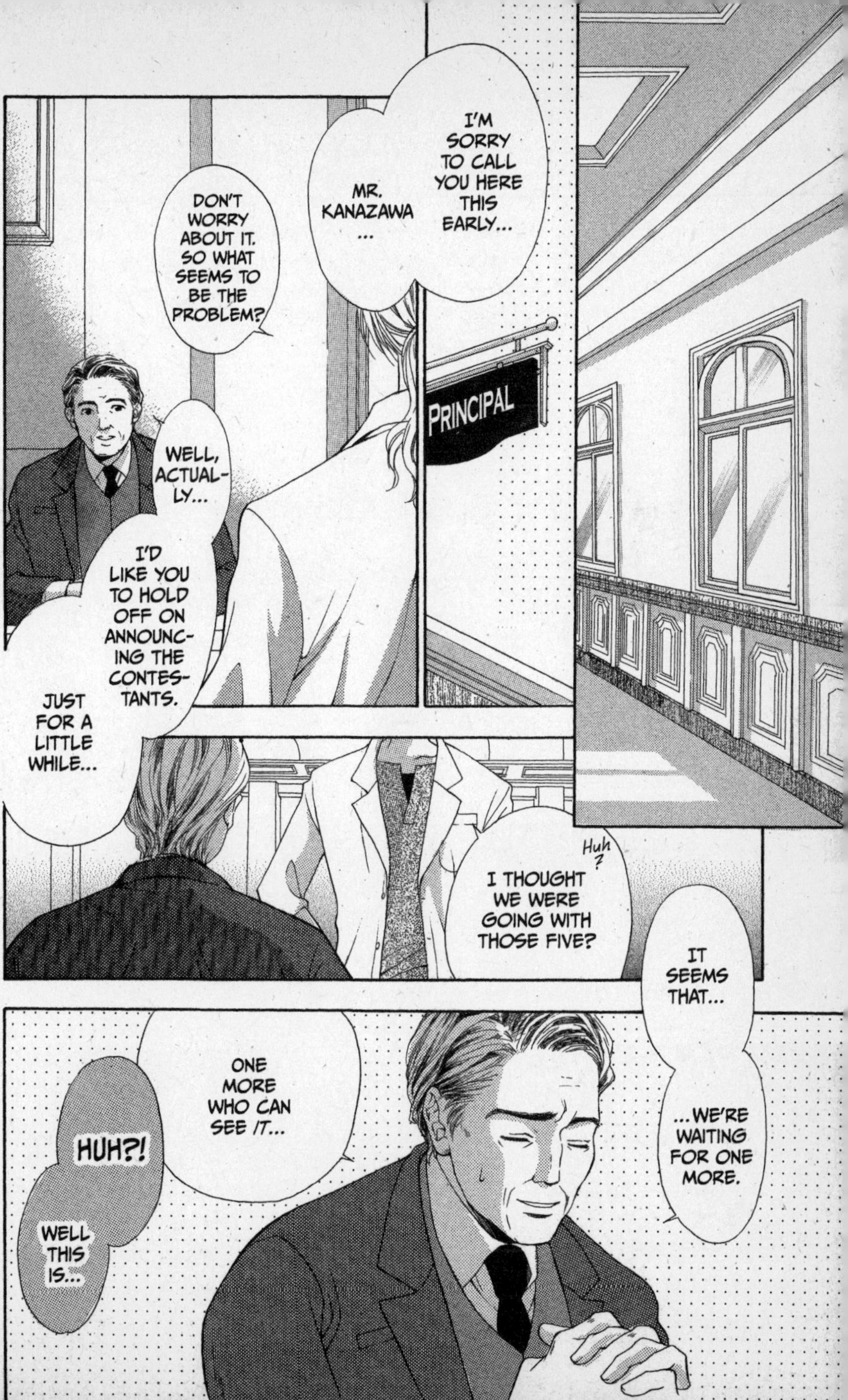

I'M SORRY TO CALL YOU HERE THIS EARLY...
MR. KANAZAWA...
DON'T WORRY ABOUT IT. SO WHAT SEEMS TO BE THE PROBLEM?
PRINCIPAL
WELL, ACTUALLY...
I'D LIKE YOU TO HOLD OFF ON ANNOUNCING THE CONTESTANTS.
JUST FOR A LITTLE WHILE...
Huh?
I THOUGHT WE WERE GOING WITH THOSE FIVE?
IT SEEMS THAT...
...WE'RE WAITING FOR ONE MORE.
ONE MORE WHO CAN SEE IT...
HUH?!
WELL THIS IS...

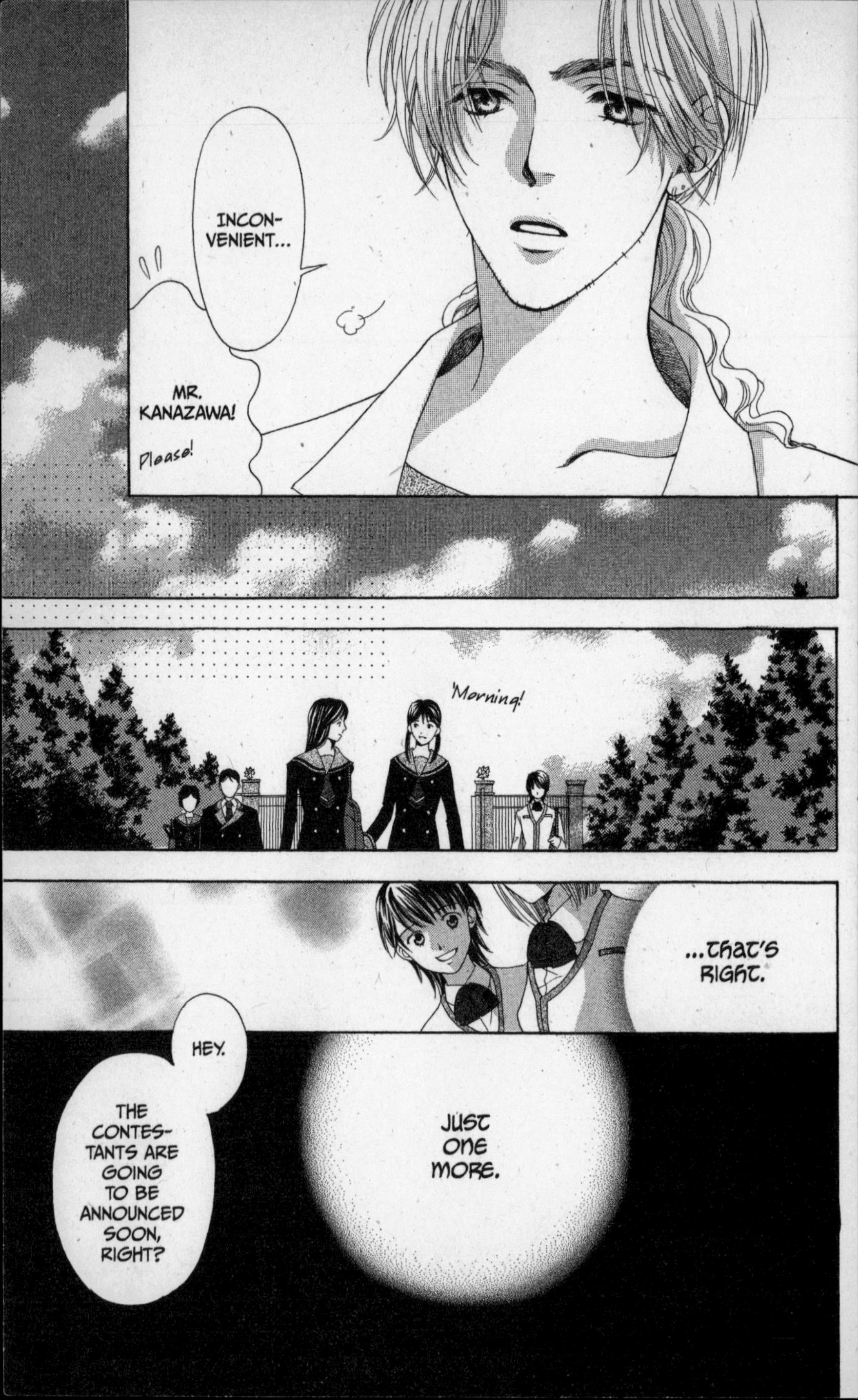
INCON-VENIENT...
MR. KANAZAWA!
Please!
'Morning!
...THAT'S RIGHT.
JUST ONE MORE.
HEY.
THE CONTES-TANTS ARE GOING TO BE ANNOUNCED SOON, RIGHT?

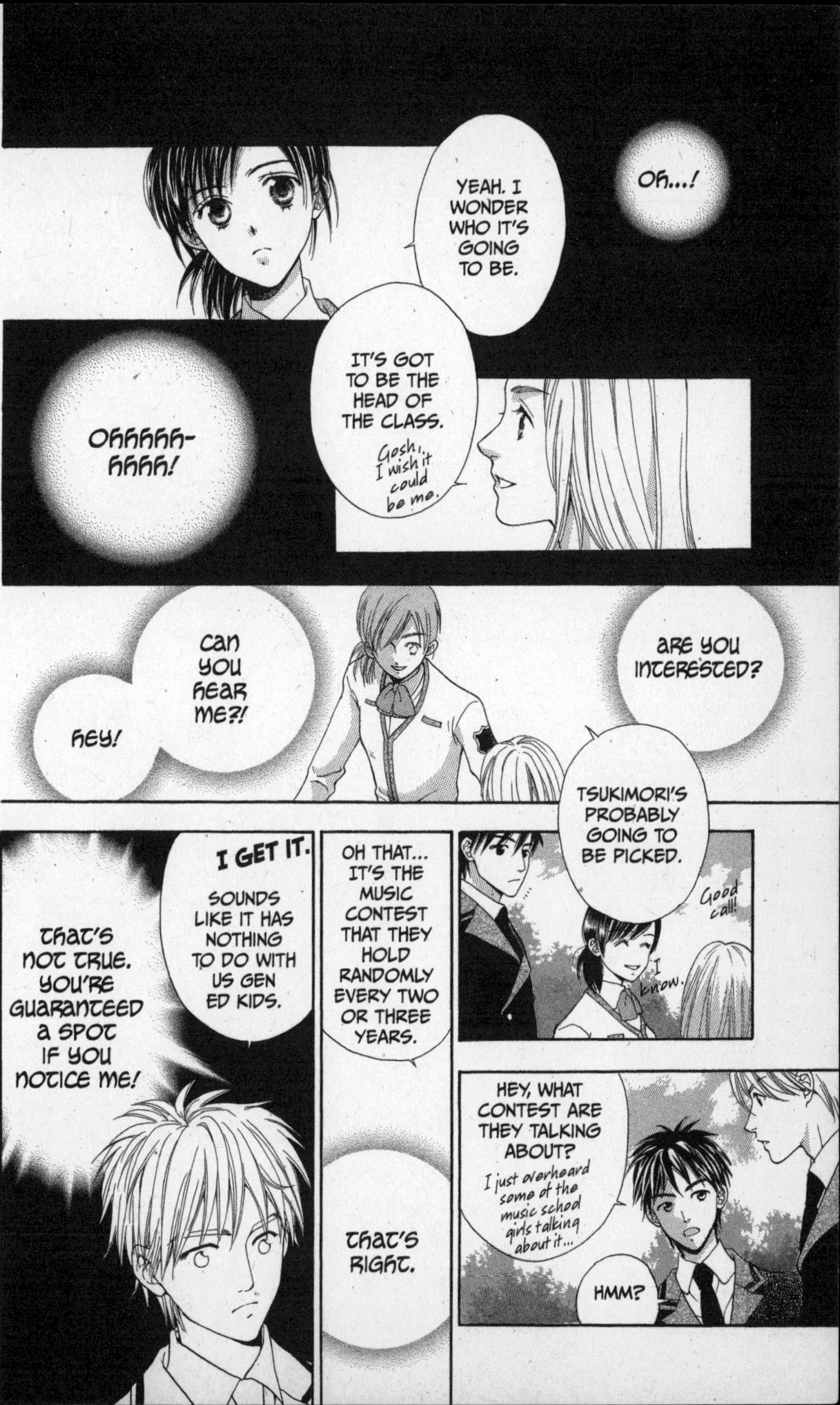

Oh...!
YEAH. I WONDER WHO IT'S GOING TO BE.
IT'S GOT TO BE THE HEAD OF THE CLASS.
Gosh, I wish it could be me.
Ohhhhh-hhhh!
are you interested?
can you hear me?!
hey!
TSUKIMORI'S PROBABLY GOING TO BE PICKED.
Good call!
I know.
HEY, WHAT CONTEST ARE THEY TALKING ABOUT?
I just overheard some of the music school girls talking about it...
HMM?
OH THAT... IT'S THE MUSIC CONTEST THAT THEY HOLD RANDOMLY EVERY TWO OR THREE YEARS.
that's right.
I GET IT.
SOUNDS LIKE IT HAS NOTHING TO DO WITH US GEN ED KIDS.
that's not true. you're guaranteed a spot if you notice me!

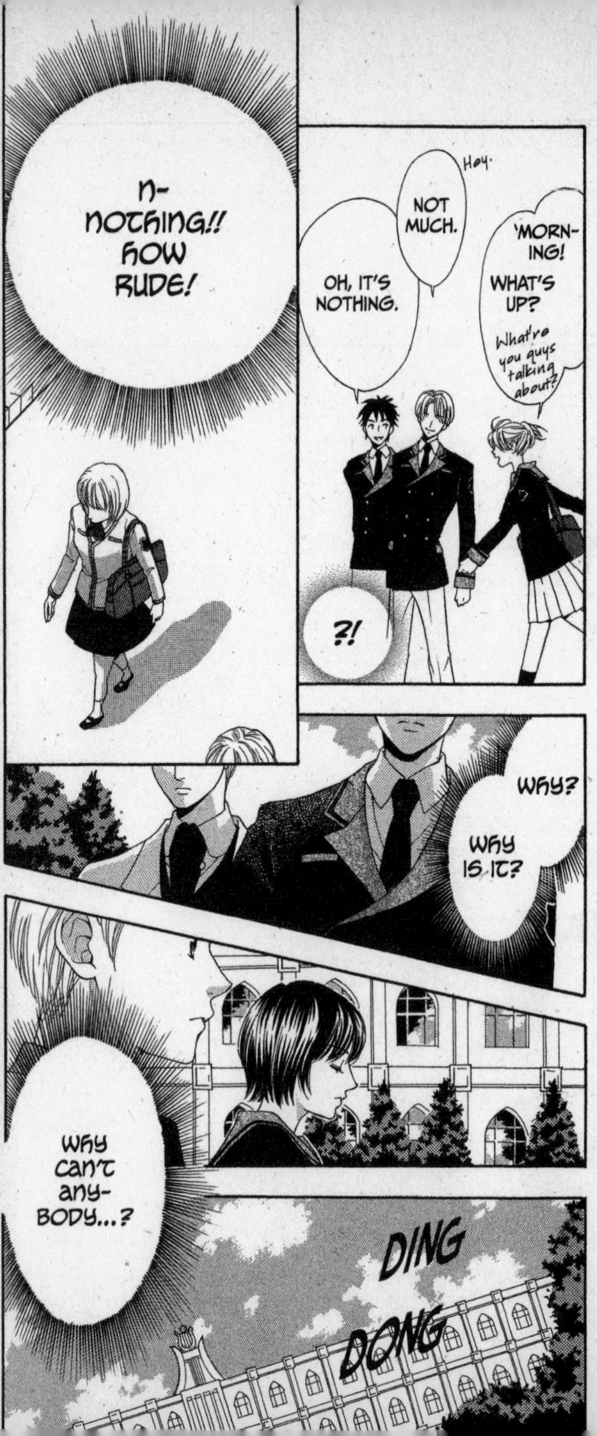
'MORNING! WHAT'S UP?
What're you guys talking about?
Hey.
NOT MUCH.
OH, IT'S NOTHING.
?!
N-NOTHING!! HOW RUDE!
WHY?
WHY IS IT?
WHY CAN'T ANY-BODY...?
DING
DONG

Greetings

Hello. It's nice to meet you. I'm Yuki Kure. I'd like to thank you for purchasing my first comic. *La Corda d'Oro* is a manga based on a video game. It's what we call a "mediamic." I hope that people who've played the game and those who haven't can both enjoy this piece.

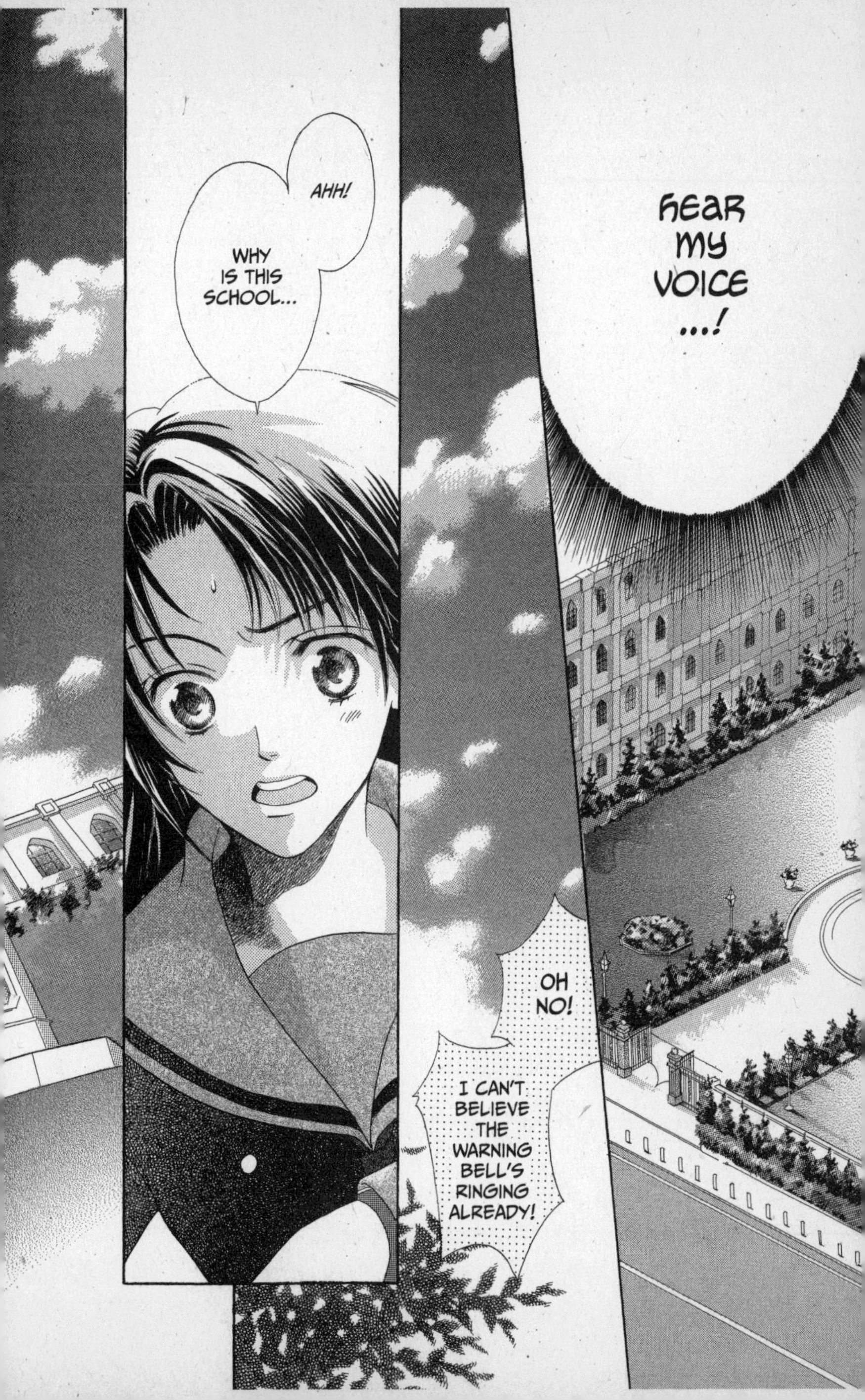
HEAR MY VOICE ...!
OH NO!
I CAN'T BELIEVE THE WARNING BELL'S RINGING ALREADY!
AHH!
WHY IS THIS SCHOOL...

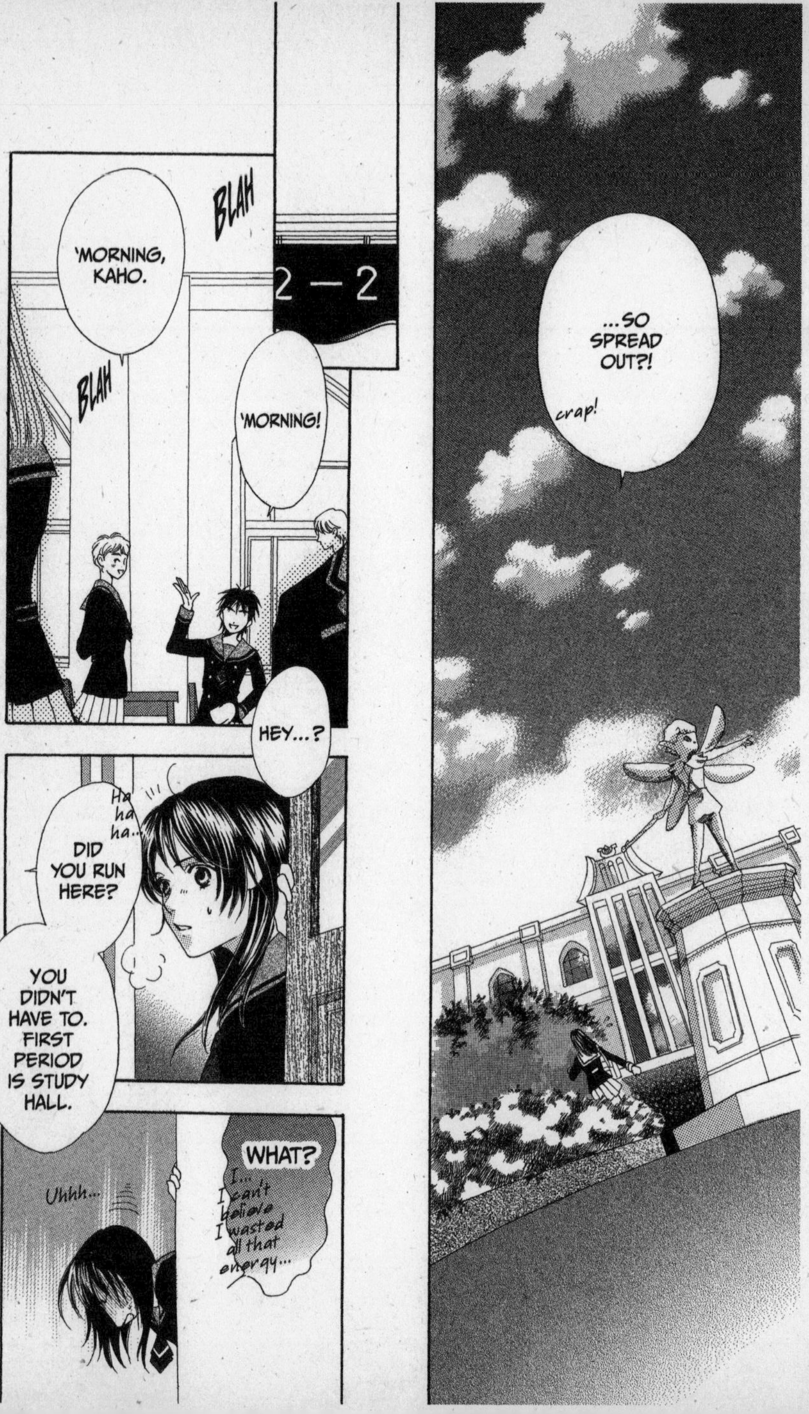
...SO SPREAD OUT?!
crap!
2—2
BLAH
'MORNING, KAHO.
BLAH
'MORNING!
HEY...?
Ha ha ha...
DID YOU RUN HERE?
YOU DIDN'T HAVE TO. FIRST PERIOD IS STUDY HALL.
WHAT?
I... I can't believe I wasted all that energy...
Uhhh...

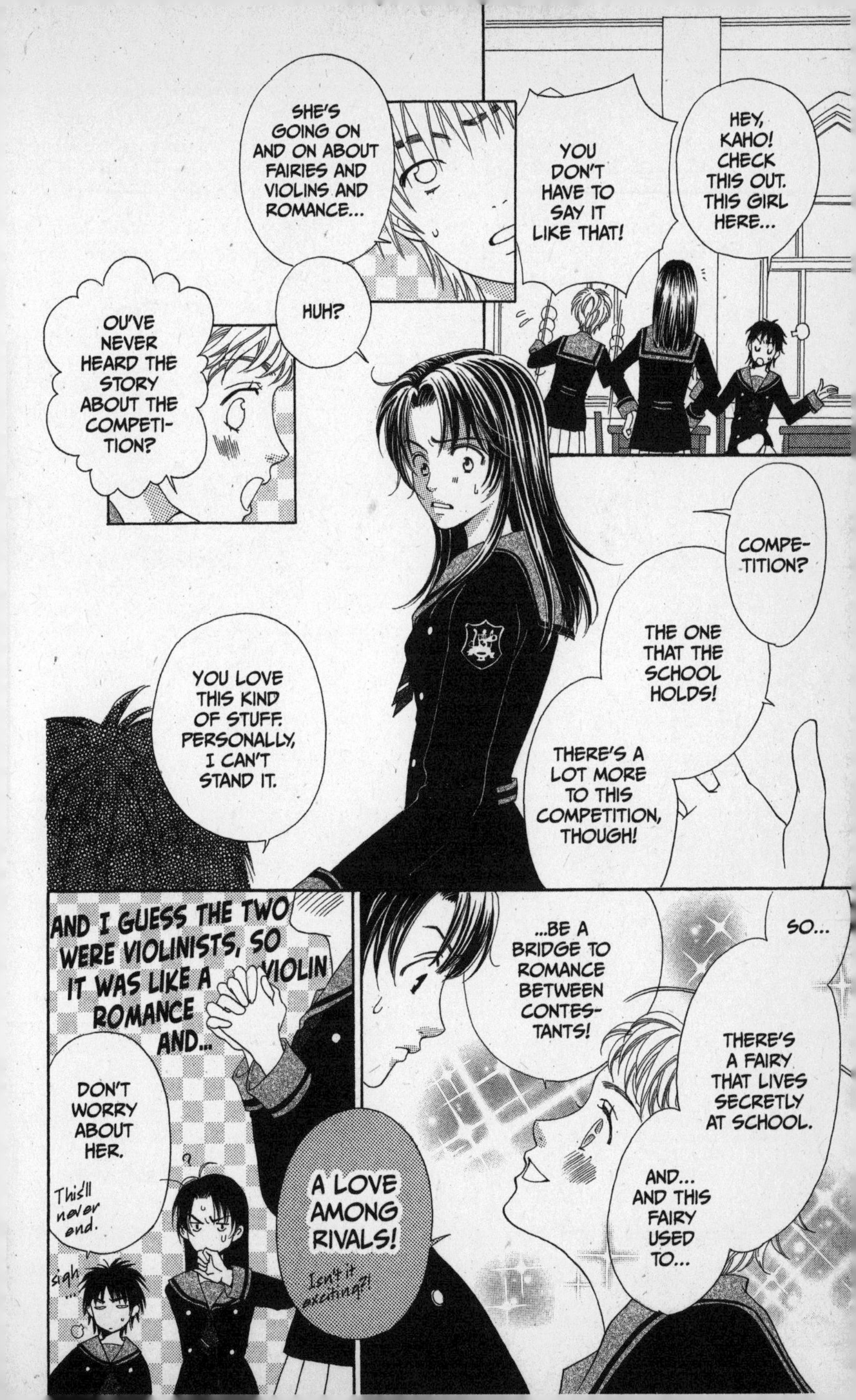
HEY, KAHO! CHECK THIS OUT. THIS GIRL HERE...
YOU DON'T HAVE TO SAY IT LIKE THAT!
SHE'S GOING ON AND ON ABOUT FAIRIES AND VIOLINS AND ROMANCE...
HUH?
OU'VE NEVER HEARD THE STORY ABOUT THE COMPETITION?
COMPETITION?
THE ONE THAT THE SCHOOL HOLDS!
THERE'S A LOT MORE TO THIS COMPETITION, THOUGH!
YOU LOVE THIS KIND OF STUFF. PERSONALLY, I CAN'T STAND IT.
SO...
THERE'S A FAIRY THAT LIVES SECRETLY AT SCHOOL.
AND... AND THIS FAIRY USED TO...
...BE A BRIDGE TO ROMANCE BETWEEN CONTESTANTS!
AND I GUESS THE TWO WERE VIOLINISTS, SO IT WAS LIKE A VIOLIN ROMANCE AND...
A LOVE AMONG RIVALS!
Isn't it exciting?!
DON'T WORRY ABOUT HER.
This'll never end.
sigh...

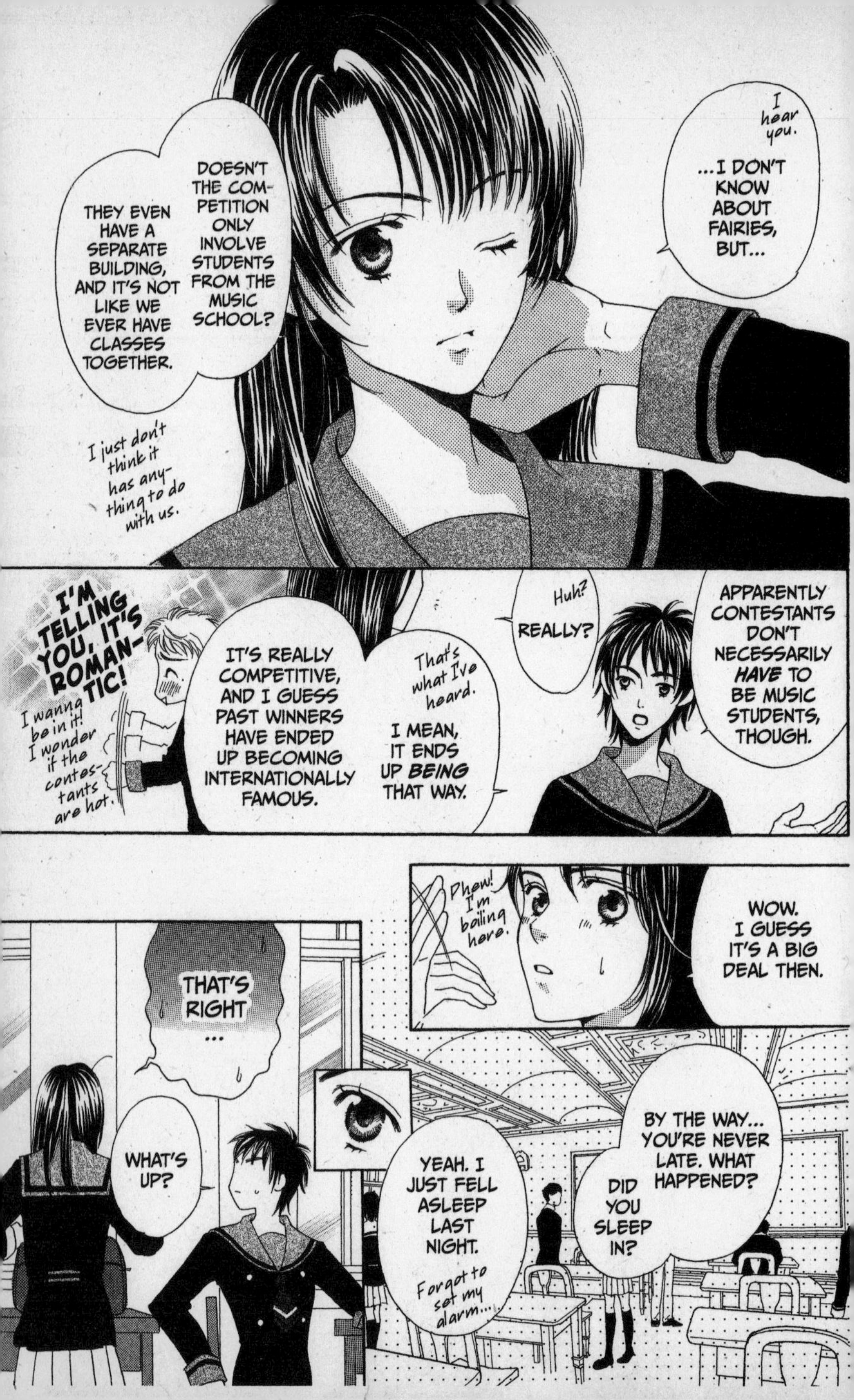
I hear you.
...I DON'T KNOW ABOUT FAIRIES, BUT...
DOESN'T THE COMPETITION ONLY INVOLVE STUDENTS FROM THE MUSIC SCHOOL?
THEY EVEN HAVE A SEPARATE BUILDING, AND IT'S NOT LIKE WE EVER HAVE CLASSES TOGETHER.
I just don't think it has anything to do with us.
APPARENTLY CONTESTANTS DON'T NECESSARILY HAVE TO BE MUSIC STUDENTS, THOUGH.
Huh? REALLY?
That's what I've heard.
I MEAN, IT ENDS UP BEING THAT WAY.
IT'S REALLY COMPETITIVE, AND I GUESS PAST WINNERS HAVE ENDED UP BECOMING INTERNATIONALLY FAMOUS.
I'M TELLING YOU, IT'S ROMANTIC!
I wanna be in it! I wonder if the contestants are hot.
WOW. I GUESS IT'S A BIG DEAL THEN.
Phew! I'm boiling here.
BY THE WAY... YOU'RE NEVER LATE. WHAT HAPPENED?
DID YOU SLEEP IN?
YEAH. I JUST FELL ASLEEP LAST NIGHT.
Forgot to set my alarm...
THAT'S RIGHT...
WHAT'S UP?

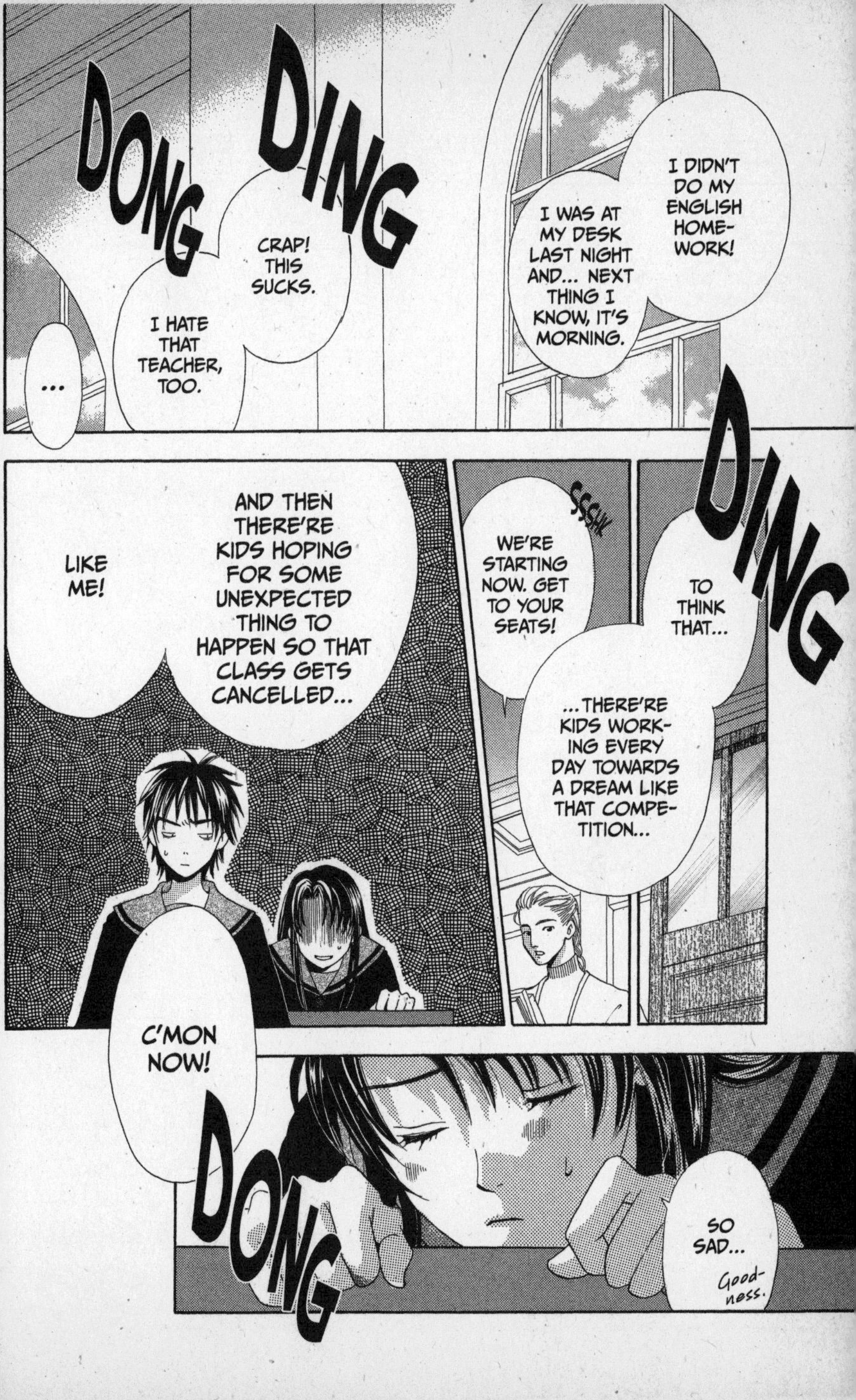
I DIDN'T DO MY ENGLISH HOME-WORK!
I WAS AT MY DESK LAST NIGHT AND... NEXT THING I KNOW, IT'S MORNING.
DING
DONG
CRAP! THIS SUCKS.
I HATE THAT TEACHER, TOO.
...
DING
TO THINK THAT...
...THERE'RE KIDS WORK-ING EVERY DAY TOWARDS A DREAM LIKE THAT COMPE-TITION...
SSSH
WE'RE STARTING NOW. GET TO YOUR SEATS!
AND THEN THERE'RE KIDS HOPING FOR SOME UNEXPECTED THING TO HAPPEN SO THAT CLASS GETS CANCELLED...
LIKE ME!
C'MON NOW!
DONG
SO SAD...
Good-ness.

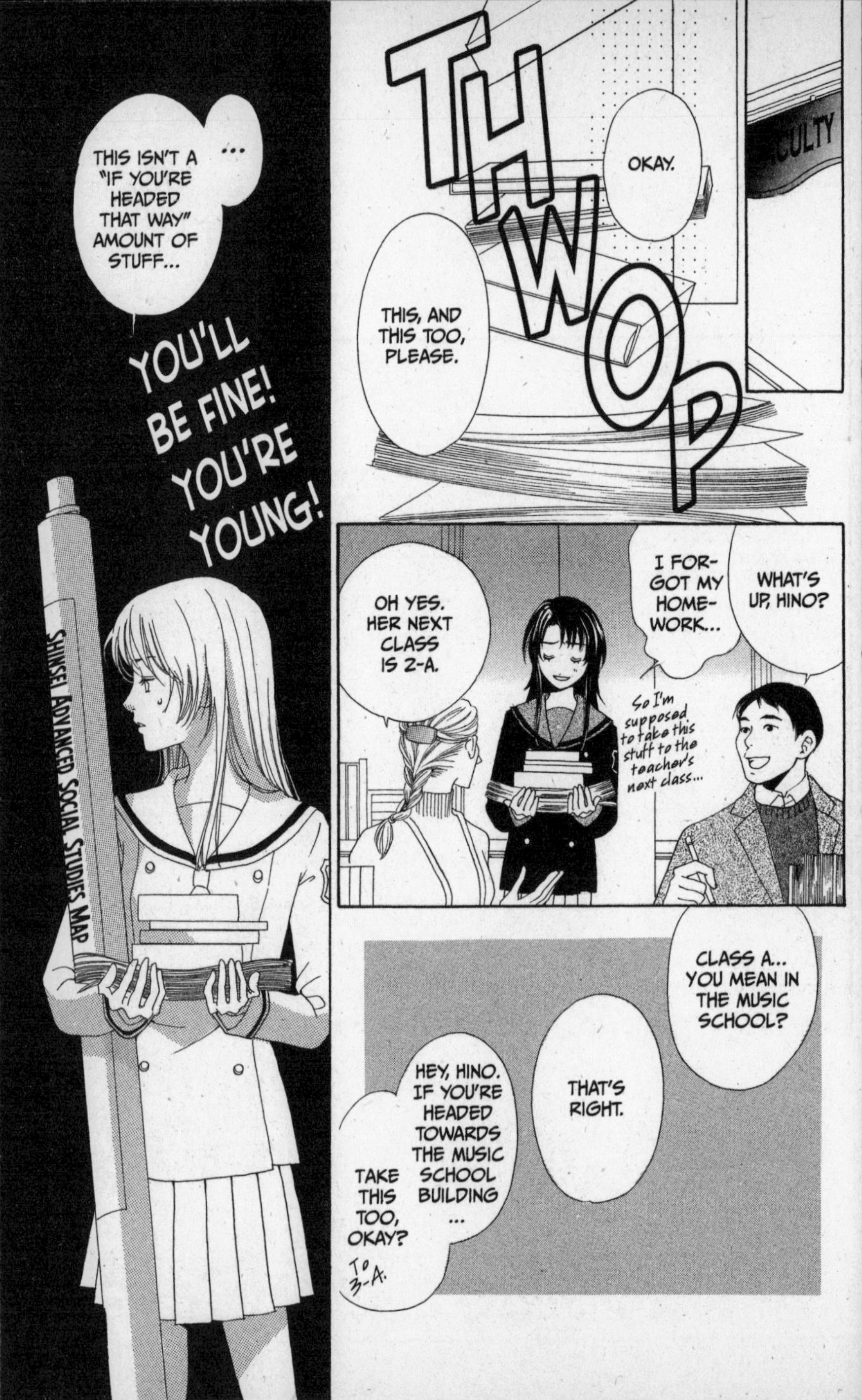
CULTY
OKAY.
THWOP
THIS, AND THIS TOO, PLEASE.
WHAT'S UP, HINO?
I FORGOT MY HOMEWORK...
So I'm supposed to take this stuff to the teacher's next class...
OH YES. HER NEXT CLASS IS 2-A.
CLASS A... YOU MEAN IN THE MUSIC SCHOOL?
THAT'S RIGHT.
HEY, HINO. IF YOU'RE HEADED TOWARDS THE MUSIC SCHOOL BUILDING...
TAKE THIS TOO, OKAY?
To 3-A.
...
THIS ISN'T A "IF YOU'RE HEADED THAT WAY" AMOUNT OF STUFF...
YOU'LL BE FINE! YOU'RE YOUNG!
SHINSEI ADVANCED SOCIAL STUDIES MAP

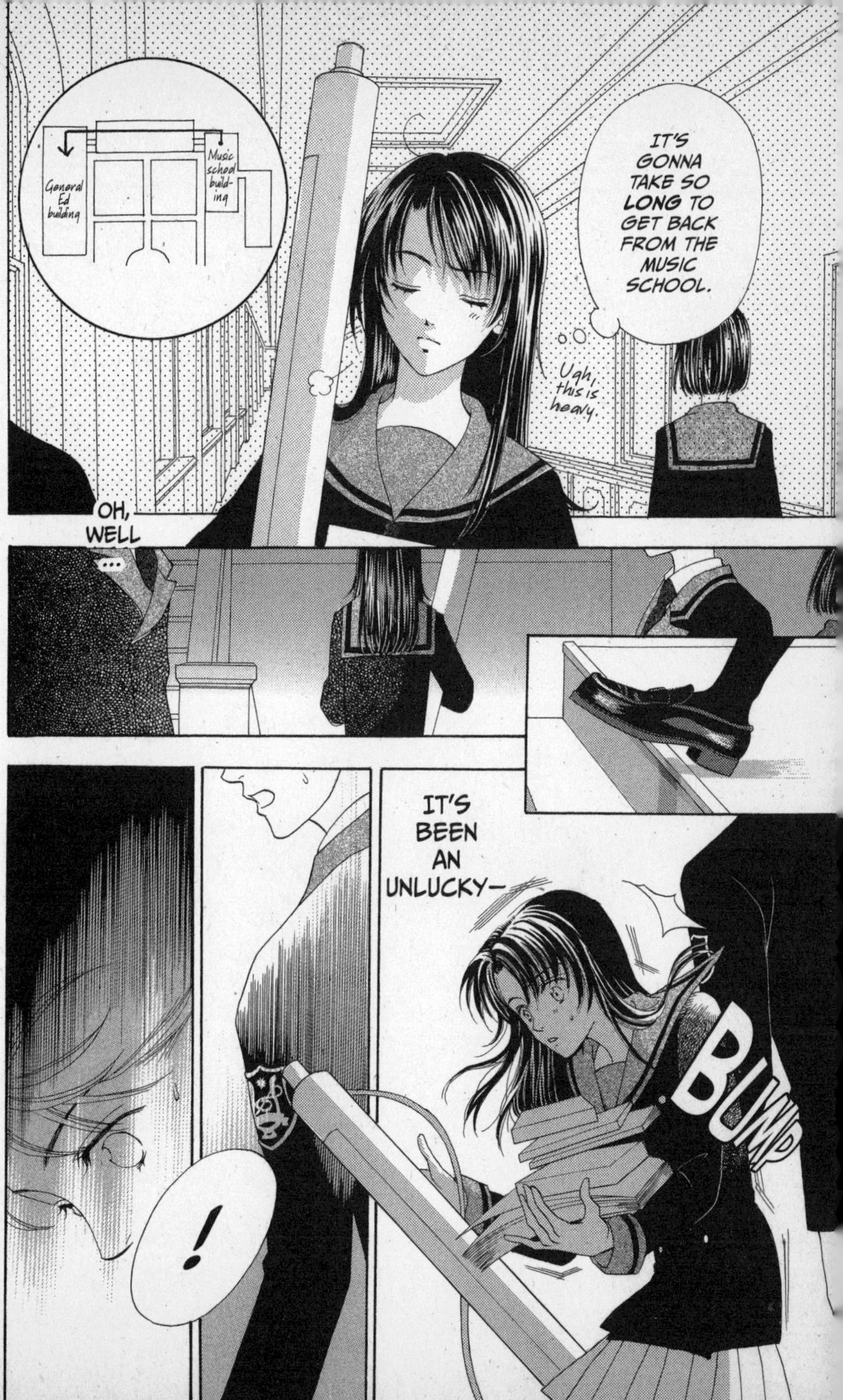
IT'S GONNA TAKE SO LONG TO GET BACK FROM THE MUSIC SCHOOL.
Ugh, this is heavy.
Music school building
General Ed building
OH, WELL...
IT'S BEEN AN UNLUCKY—
BUMP
!

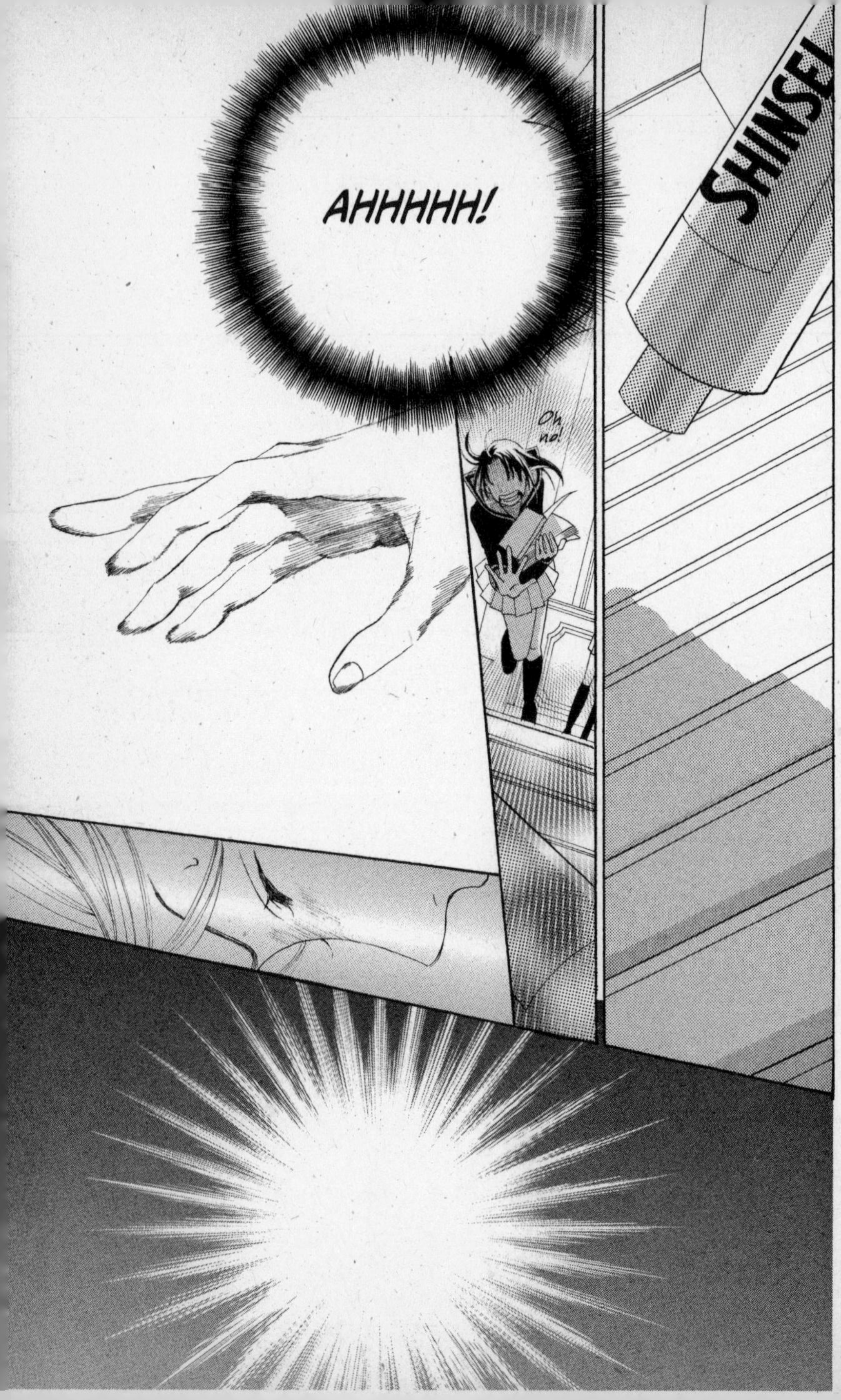
SHINSEI
Oh, no!
AHHHHH!

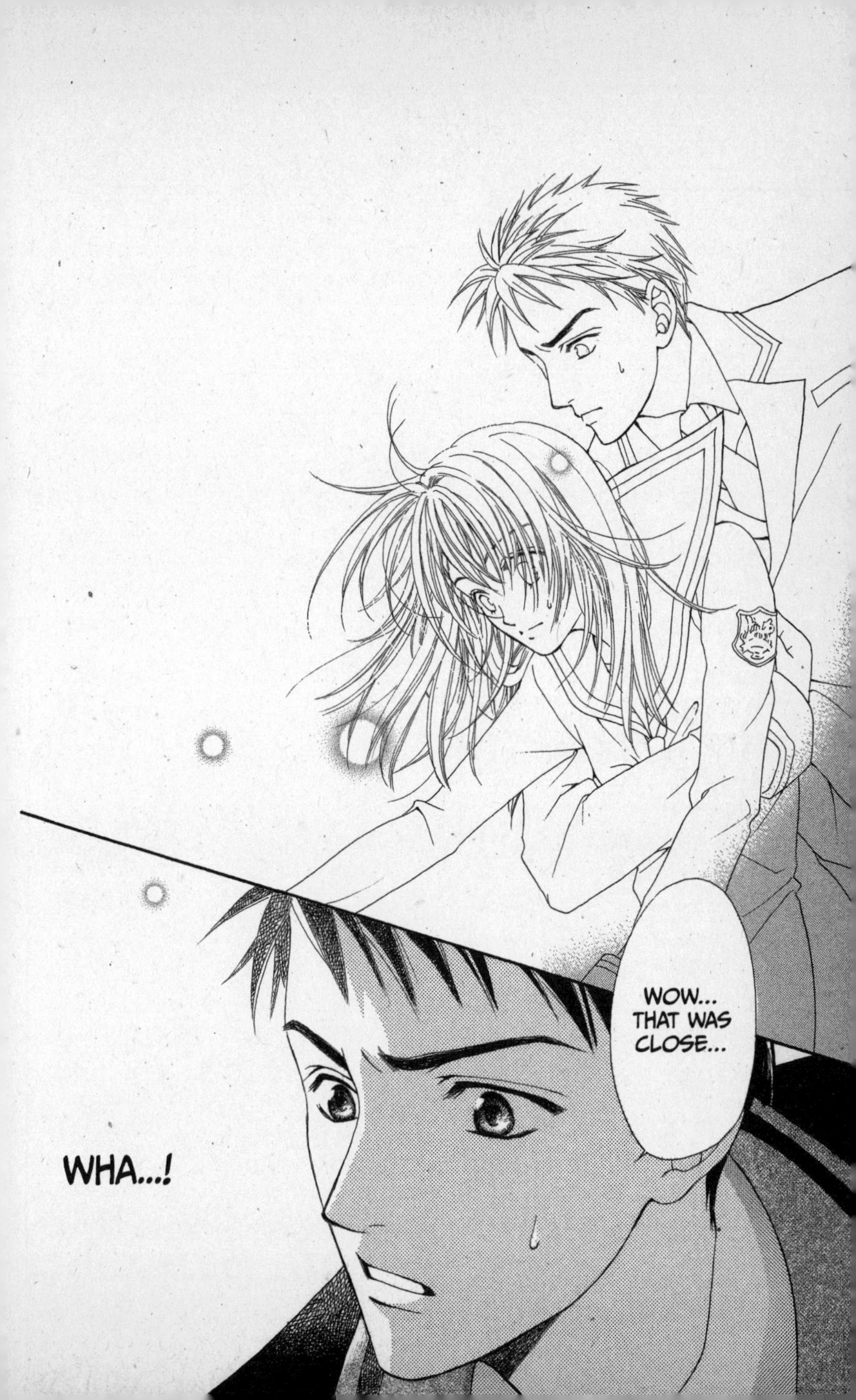
WOW... THAT WAS CLOSE...
WHA...!

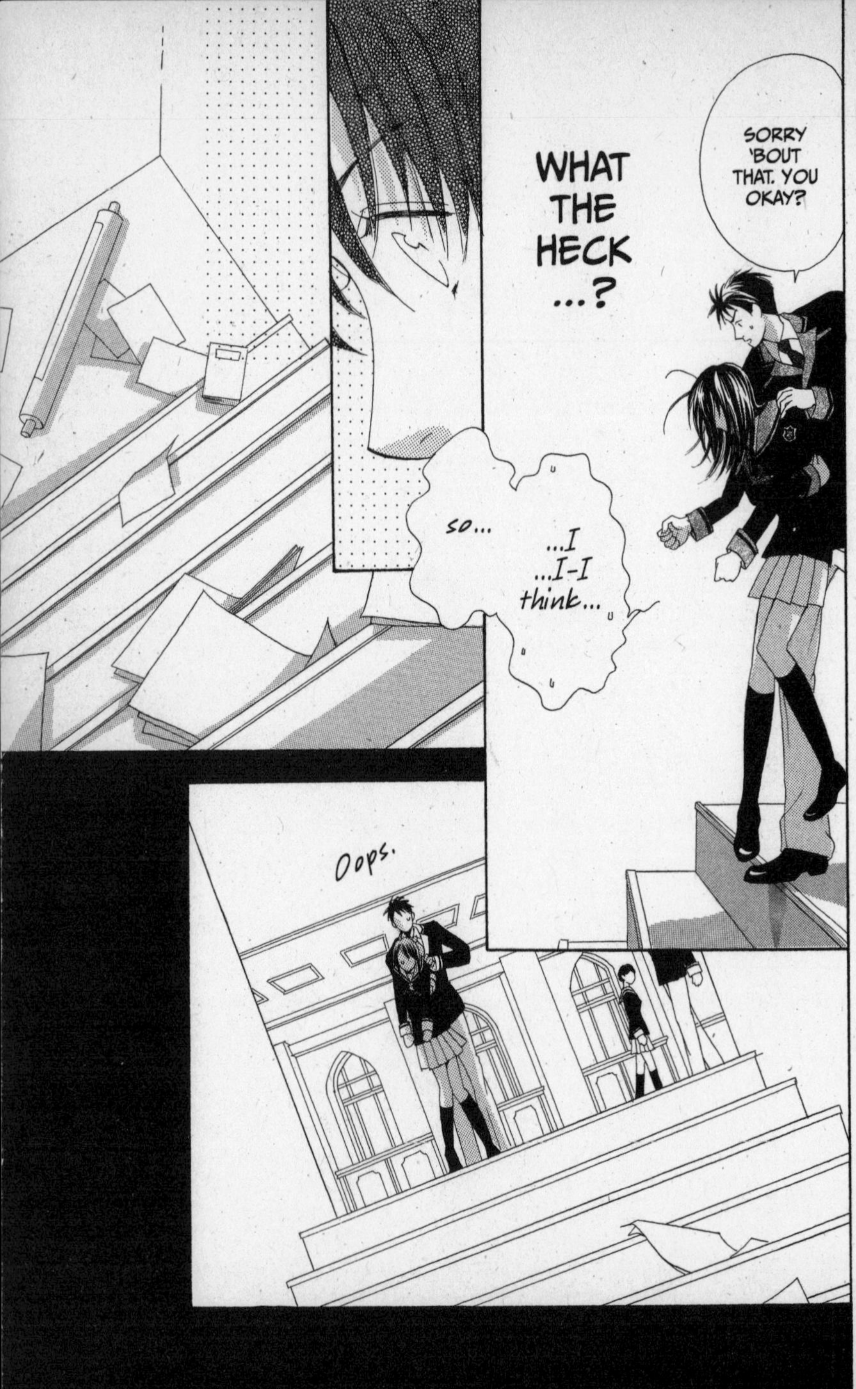
SORRY 'BOUT THAT. YOU OKAY?
WHAT THE HECK ...?
...I ...I-I think... so...
Oops.

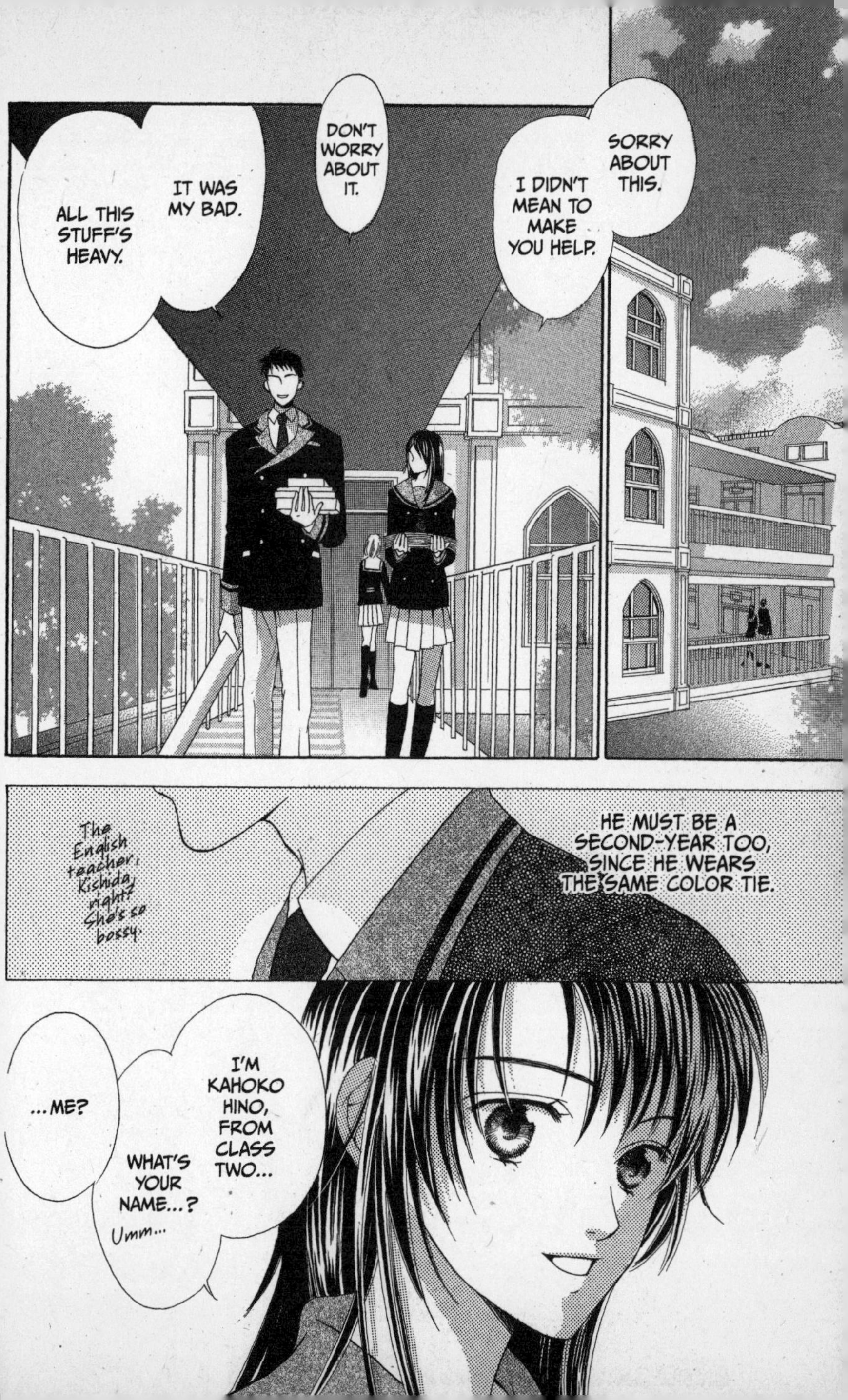
SORRY ABOUT THIS.
I DIDN'T MEAN TO MAKE YOU HELP.
DON'T WORRY ABOUT IT.
IT WAS MY BAD.
ALL THIS STUFF'S HEAVY.
HE MUST BE A SECOND-YEAR TOO, SINCE HE WEARS THE SAME COLOR TIE.
The English teacher, Kishida, right? She's so bossy.
I'M KAHOKO HINO, FROM CLASS TWO...
WHAT'S YOUR NAME...?
Umm...
...ME?

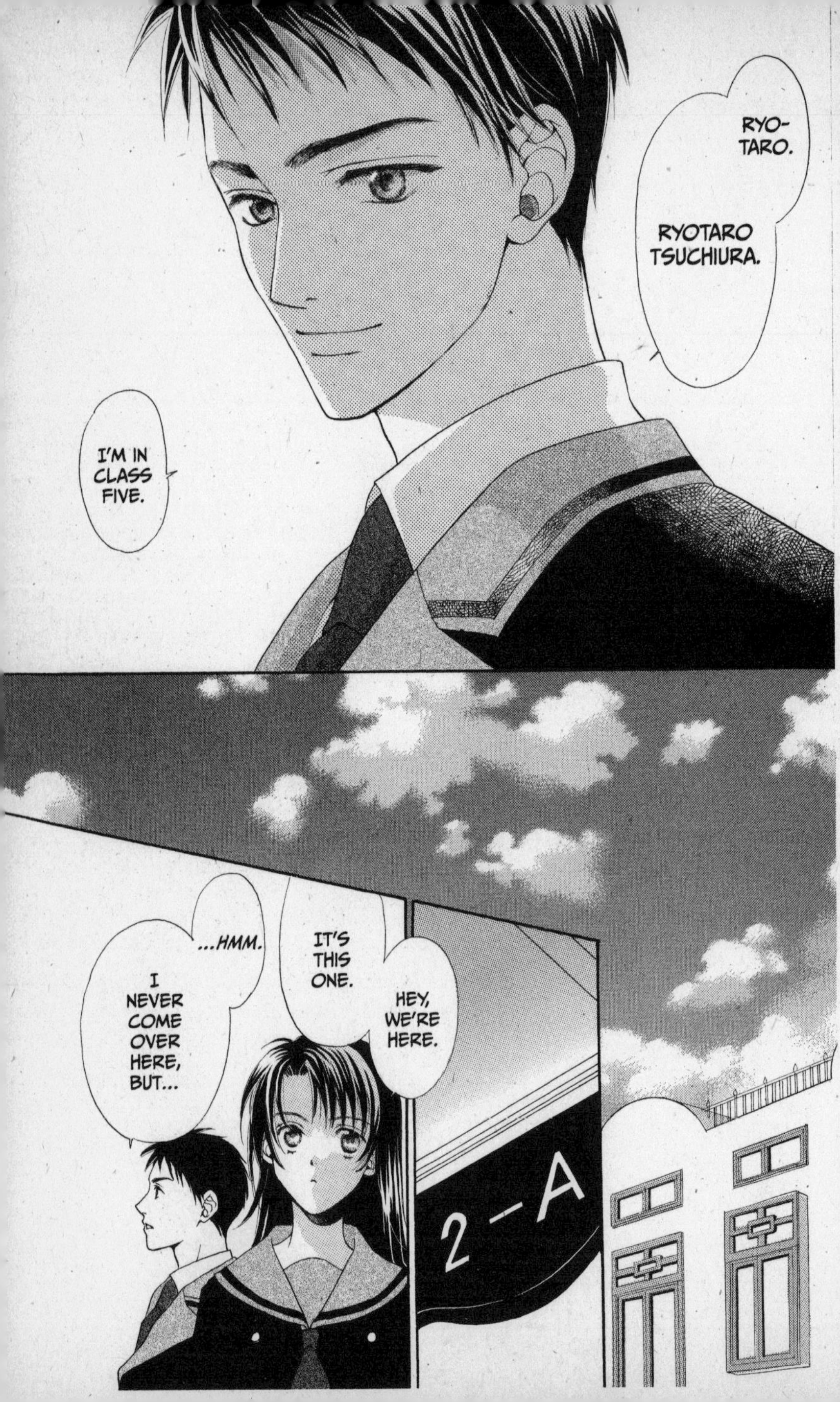
RYO-TARO.
RYOTARO TSUCHIURA.
I'M IN CLASS FIVE.
HEY, WE'RE HERE.
IT'S THIS ONE.
...HMM.
I NEVER COME OVER HERE, BUT...
2-A

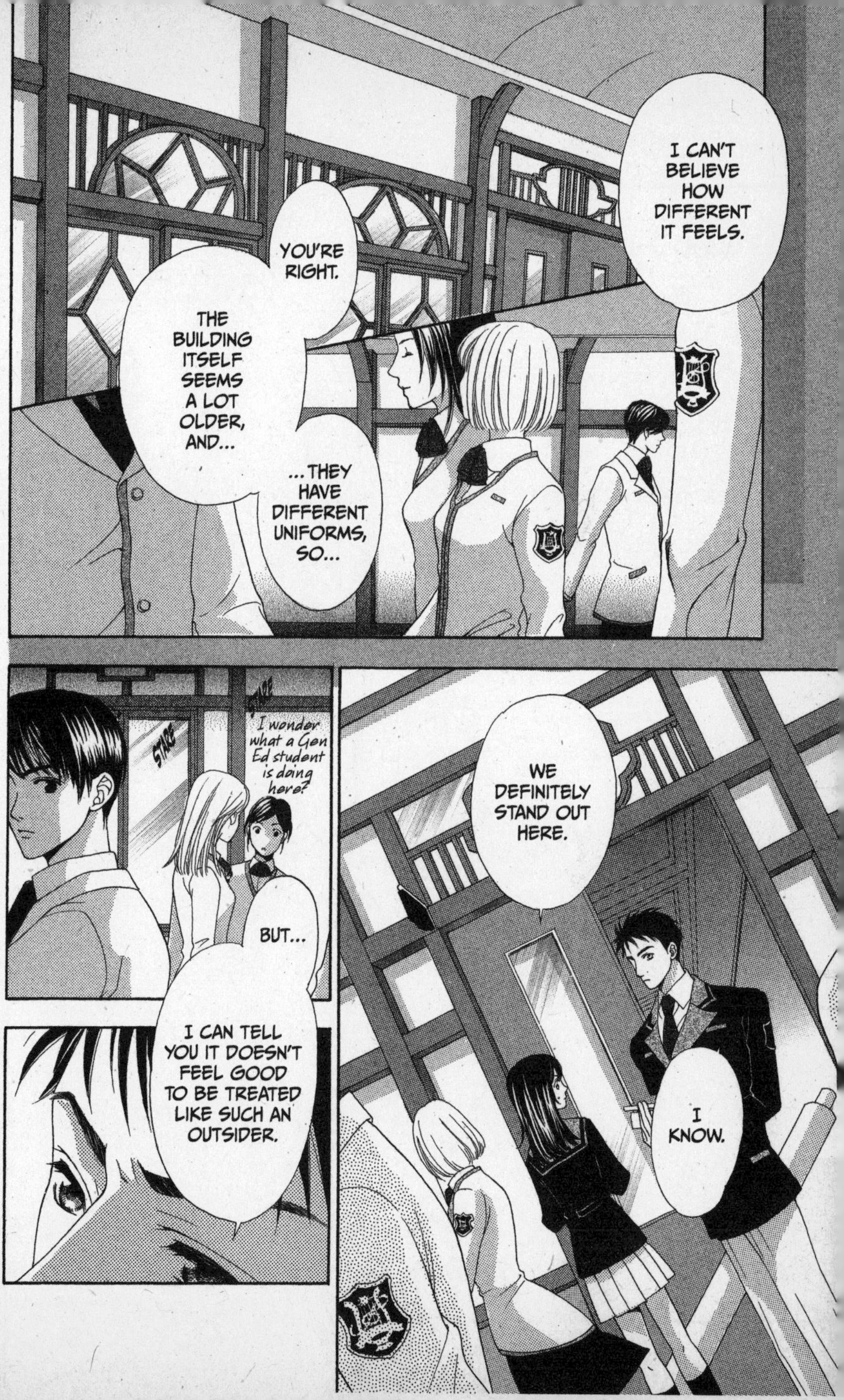
I CAN'T BELIEVE HOW DIFFERENT IT FEELS.
YOU'RE RIGHT.
THE BUILDING ITSELF SEEMS A LOT OLDER, AND...
...THEY HAVE DIFFERENT UNIFORMS, SO...
WE DEFINITELY STAND OUT HERE.
I KNOW.
STARE
STARE
I wonder what a Gen Ed student is doing here?
BUT...
I CAN TELL YOU IT DOESN'T FEEL GOOD TO BE TREATED LIKE SUCH AN OUTSIDER.

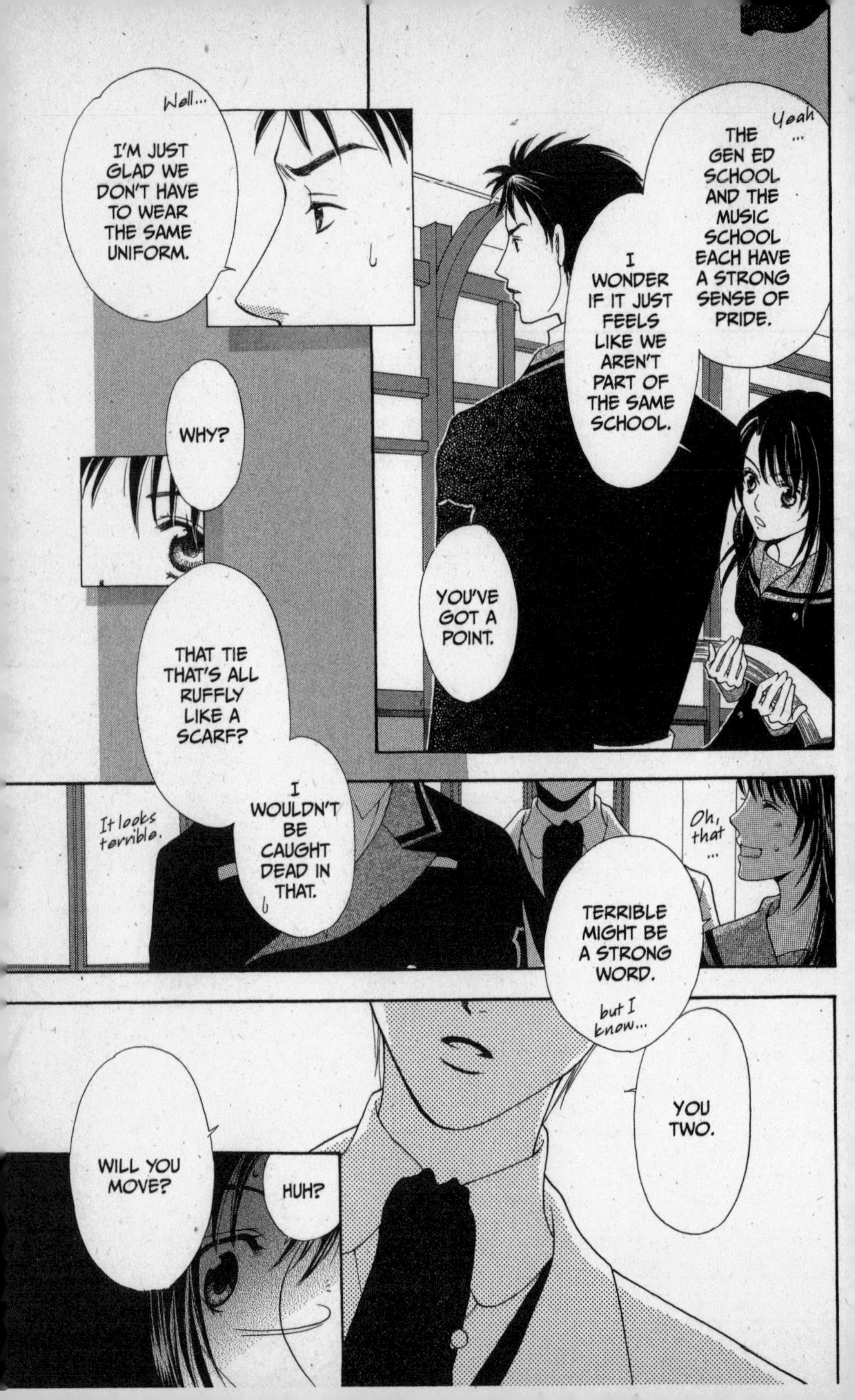

Yeah...
THE GEN ED SCHOOL AND THE MUSIC SCHOOL EACH HAVE A STRONG SENSE OF PRIDE.
I WONDER IF IT JUST FEELS LIKE WE AREN'T PART OF THE SAME SCHOOL.
YOU'VE GOT A POINT.
Well...
I'M JUST GLAD WE DON'T HAVE TO WEAR THE SAME UNIFORM.
WHY?
THAT TIE THAT'S ALL RUFFLY LIKE A SCARF?
I WOULDN'T BE CAUGHT DEAD IN THAT.
It looks terrible.
Oh, that...
TERRIBLE MIGHT BE A STRONG WORD.
but I know...
YOU TWO.
WILL YOU MOVE?
HUH?

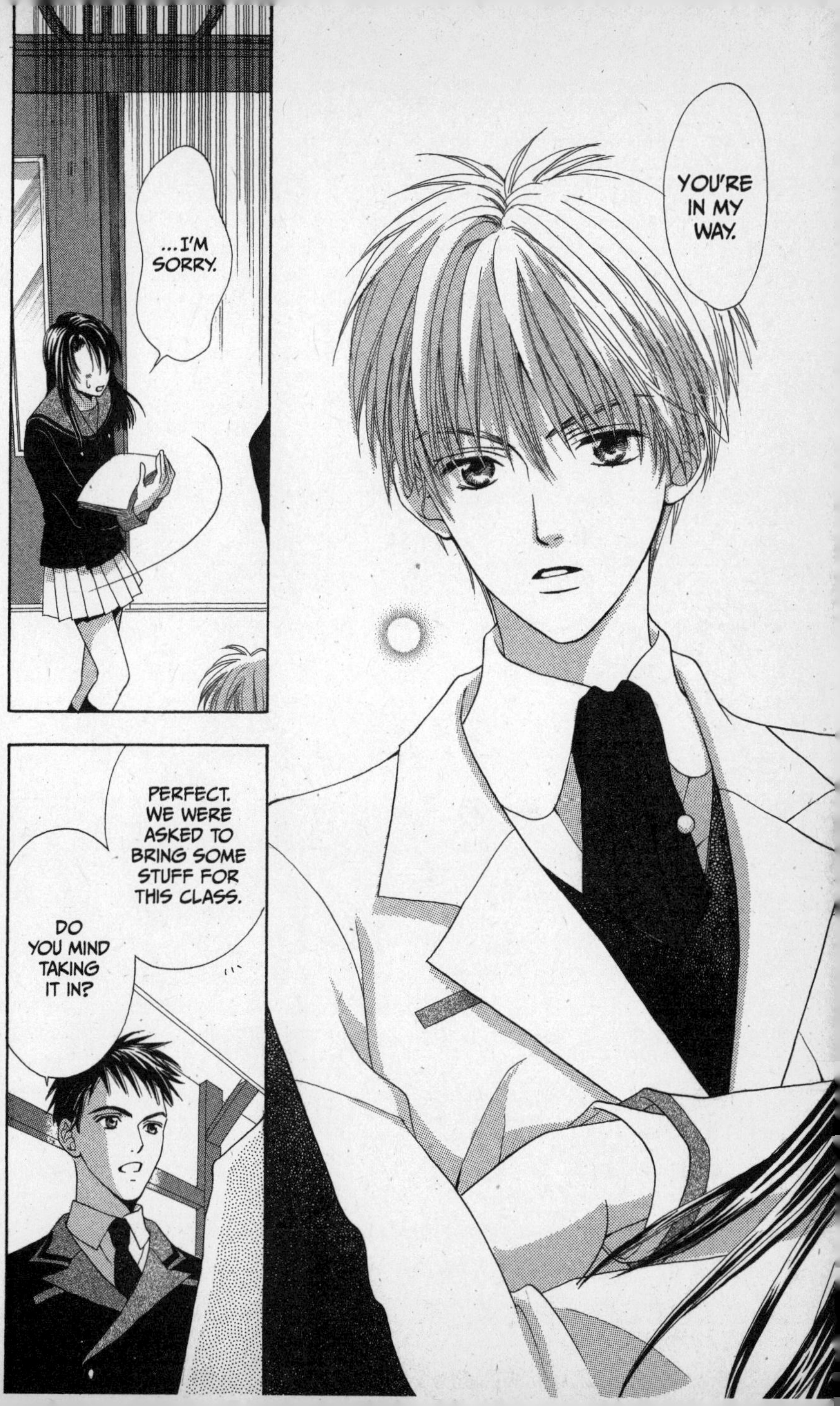
YOU'RE IN MY WAY.
...I'M SORRY.
PERFECT. WE WERE ASKED TO BRING SOME STUFF FOR THIS CLASS.
DO YOU MIND TAKING IT IN?

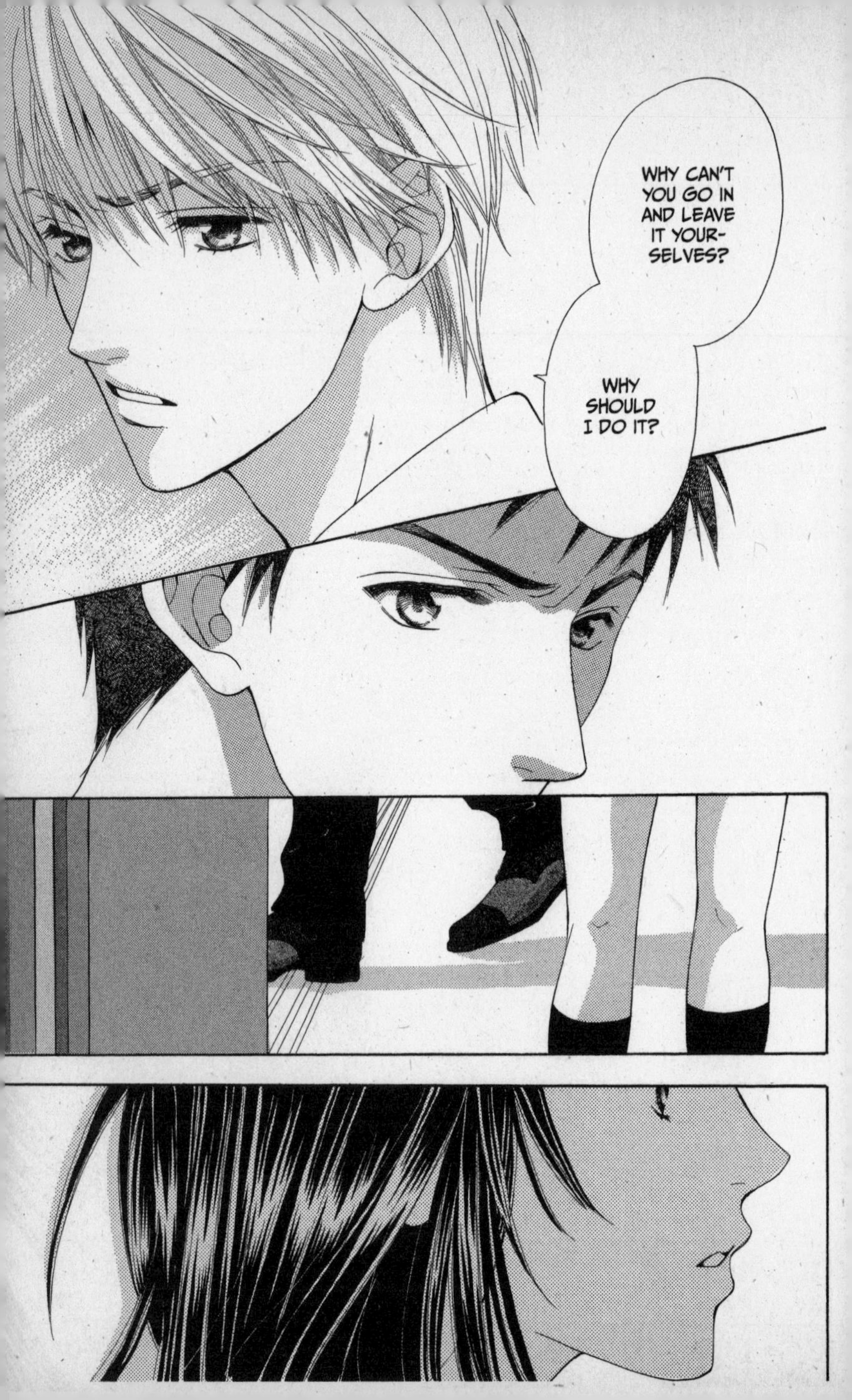
WHY CAN'T YOU GO IN AND LEAVE IT YOUR-SELVES?
WHY SHOULD I DO IT?

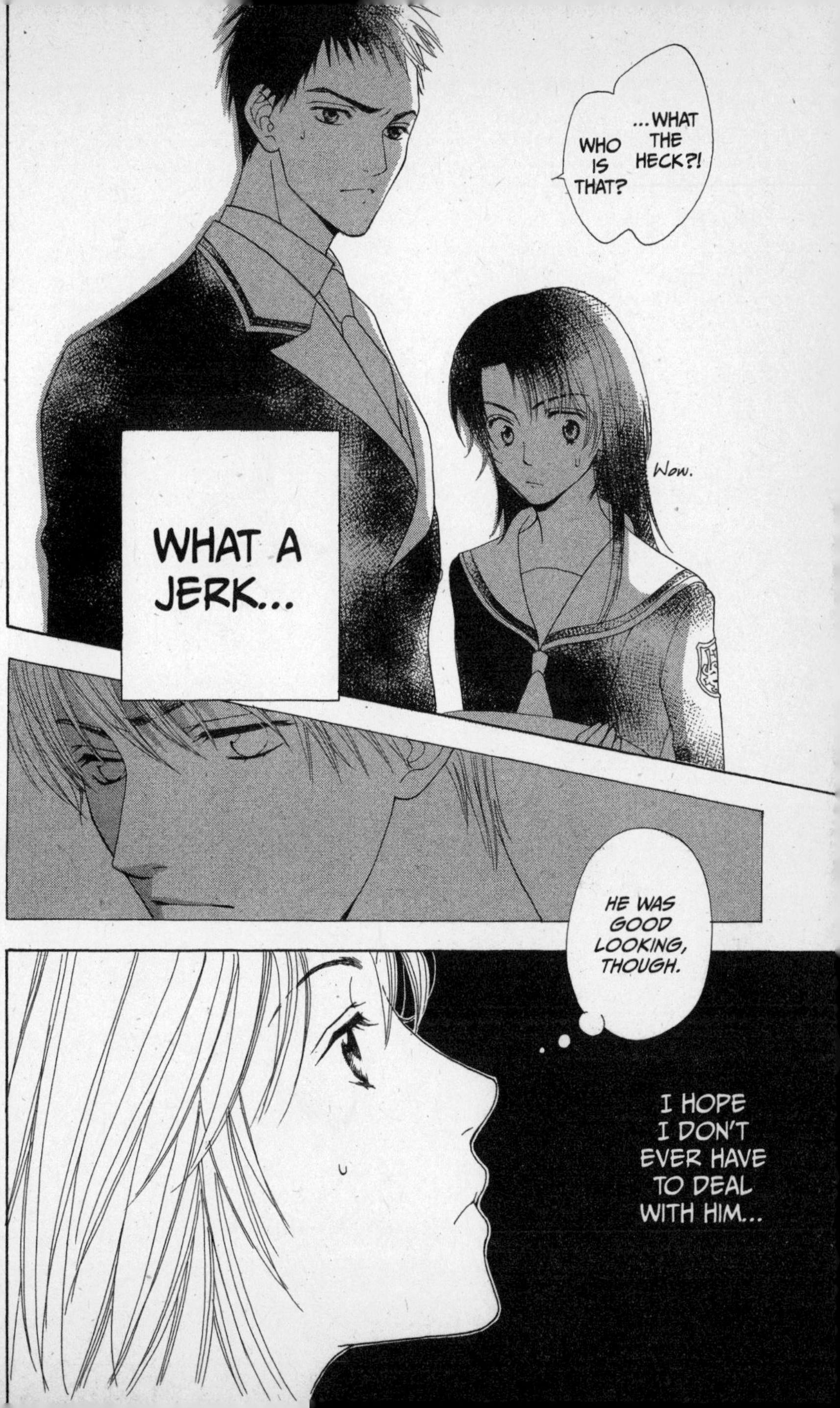
WHO IS THAT? ...WHAT THE HECK?!
Wow.
WHAT A JERK...
HE WAS GOOD LOOKING, THOUGH.
I HOPE I DON'T EVER HAVE TO DEAL WITH HIM...

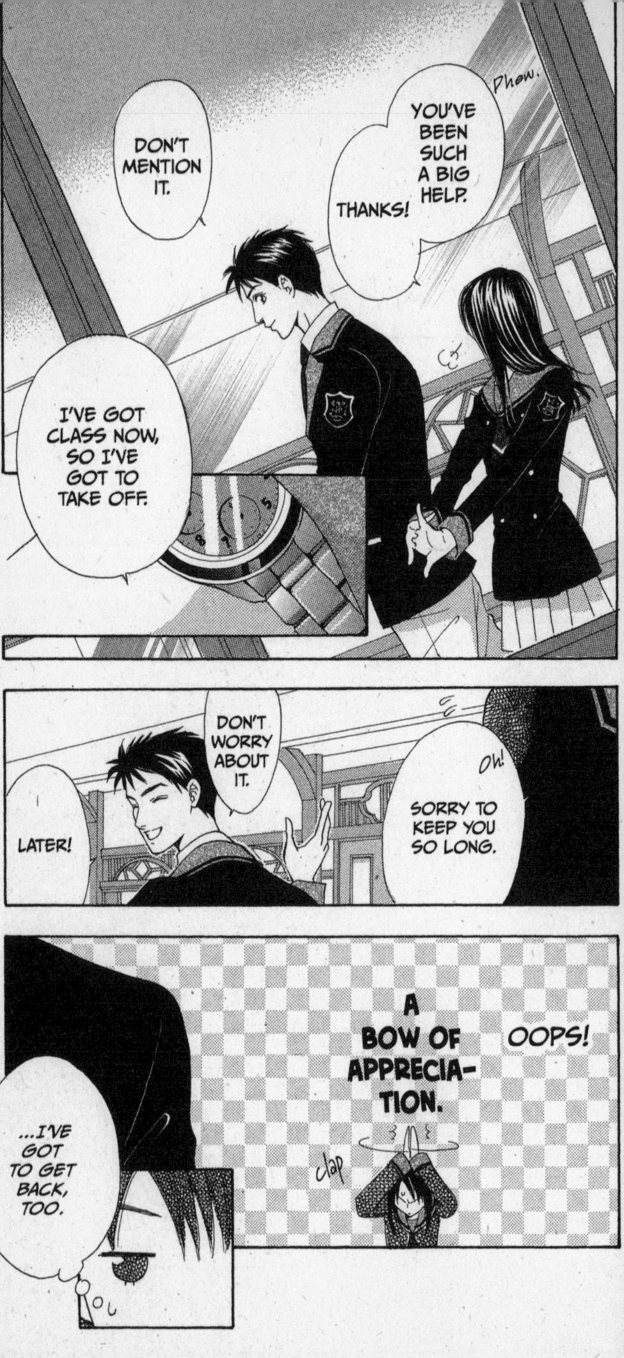
Phew.
YOU'VE BEEN SUCH A BIG HELP.
THANKS!
DON'T MENTION IT.
I'VE GOT CLASS NOW, SO I'VE GOT TO TAKE OFF.
Oh!
SORRY TO KEEP YOU SO LONG.
DON'T WORRY ABOUT IT.
LATER!
OOPS!
A BOW OF APPRECIATION.
clap
...I'VE GOT TO GET BACK, TOO.

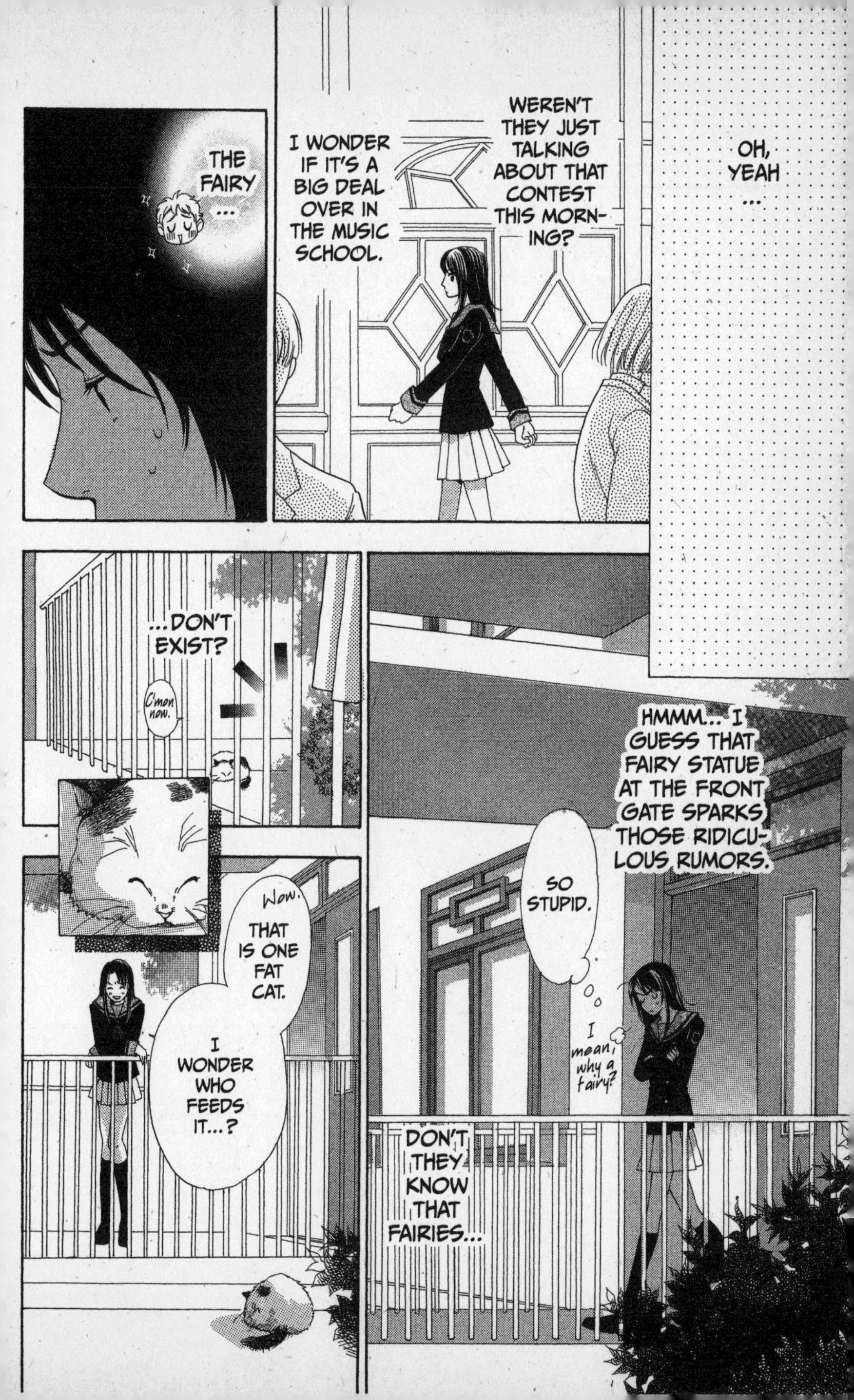
OH, YEAH ...
WEREN'T THEY JUST TALKING ABOUT THAT CONTEST THIS MORNING?
I WONDER IF IT'S A BIG DEAL OVER IN THE MUSIC SCHOOL.
THE FAIRY ...
HMMM... I GUESS THAT FAIRY STATUE AT THE FRONT GATE SPARKS THOSE RIDICULOUS RUMORS.
SO STUPID.
I mean, why a fairy?
DON'T THEY KNOW THAT FAIRIES...
...DON'T EXIST?
C'mon now.
Wow.
THAT IS ONE FAT CAT.
I WONDER WHO FEEDS IT...?

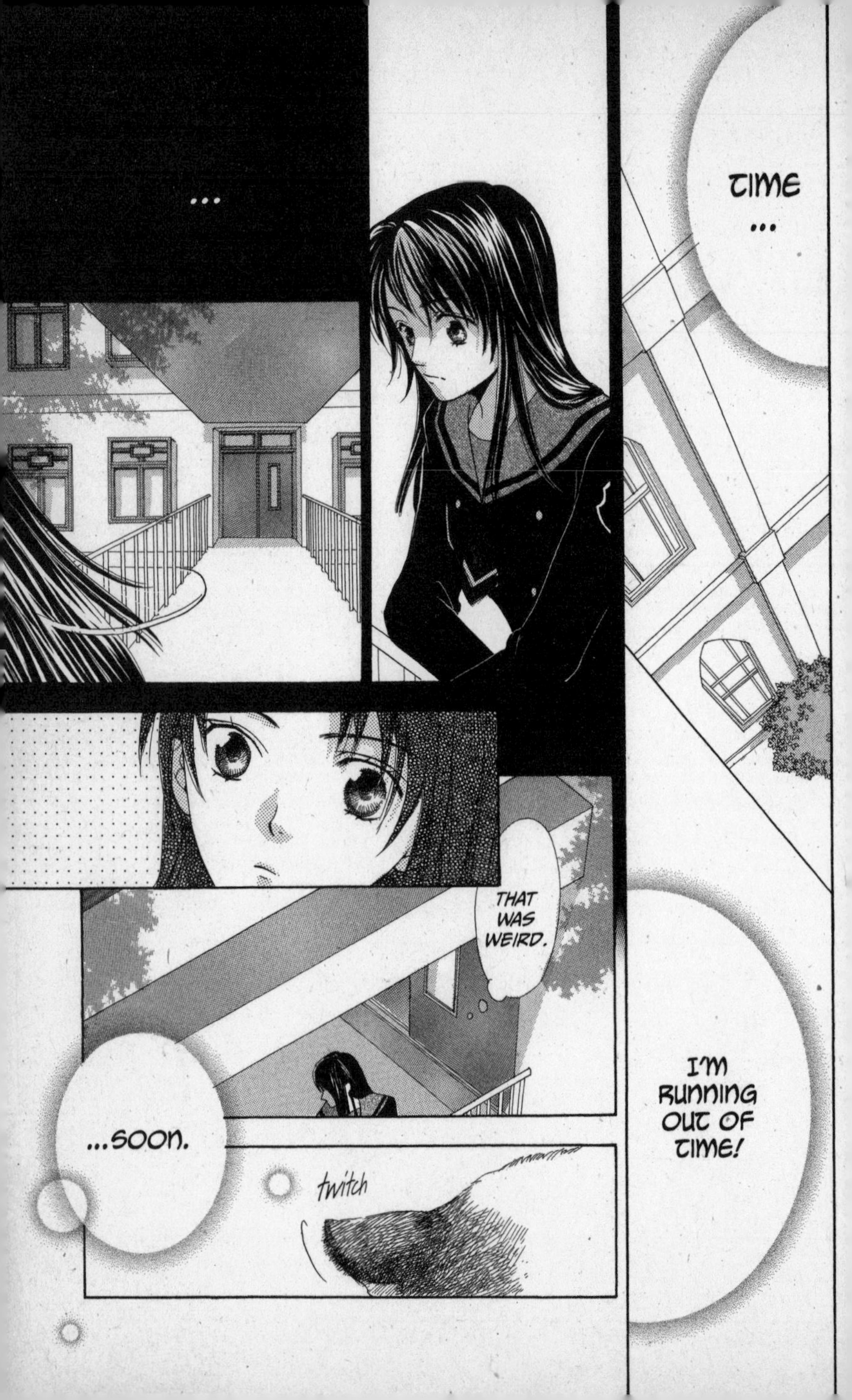
TIME ...
I'M RUNNING OUT OF TIME!
...
THAT WAS WEIRD.
...SOON.
twitch

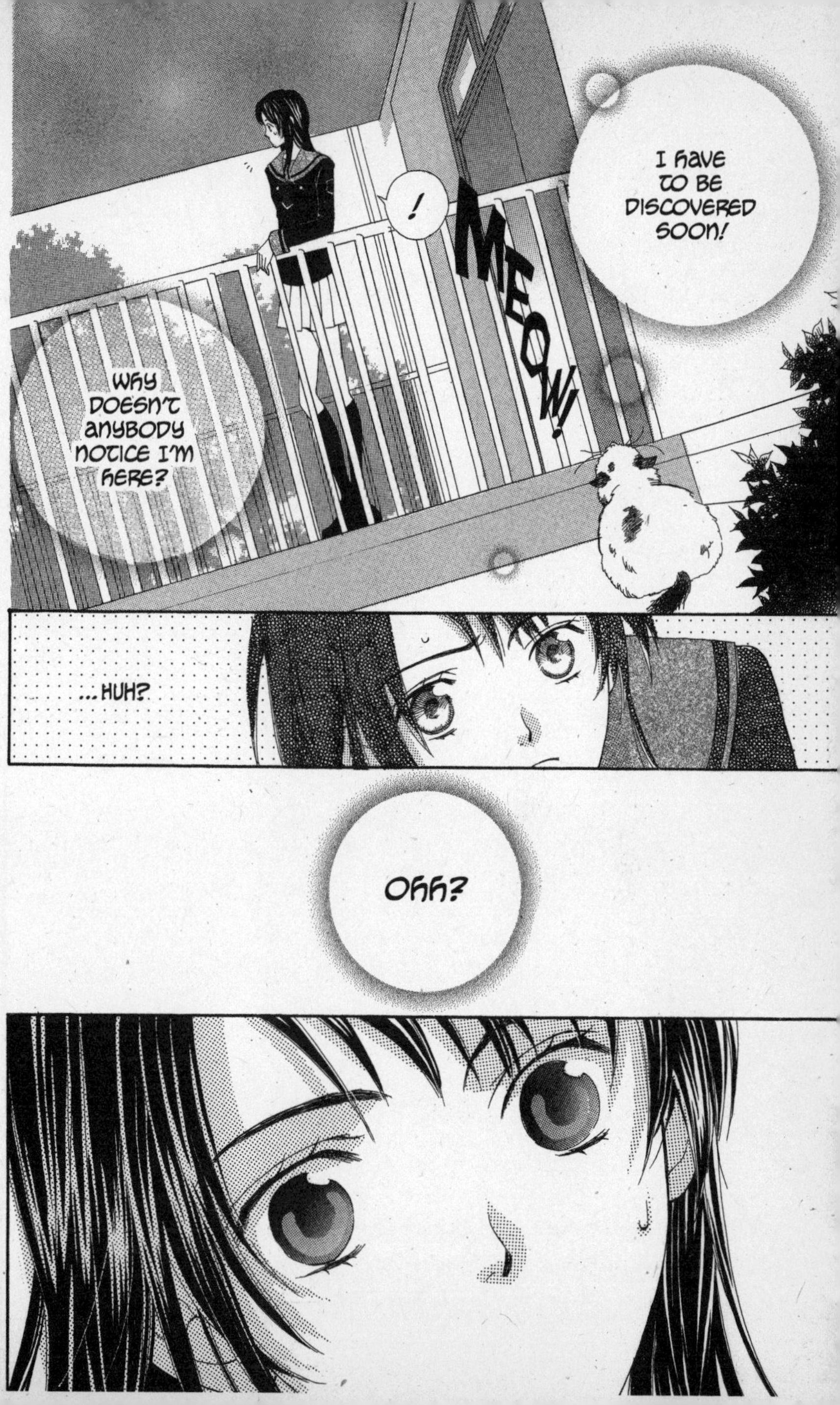
I have to be discovered soon!
!
MEOW!
Why doesn't anybody notice I'm here?
...HUH?
Ohh?

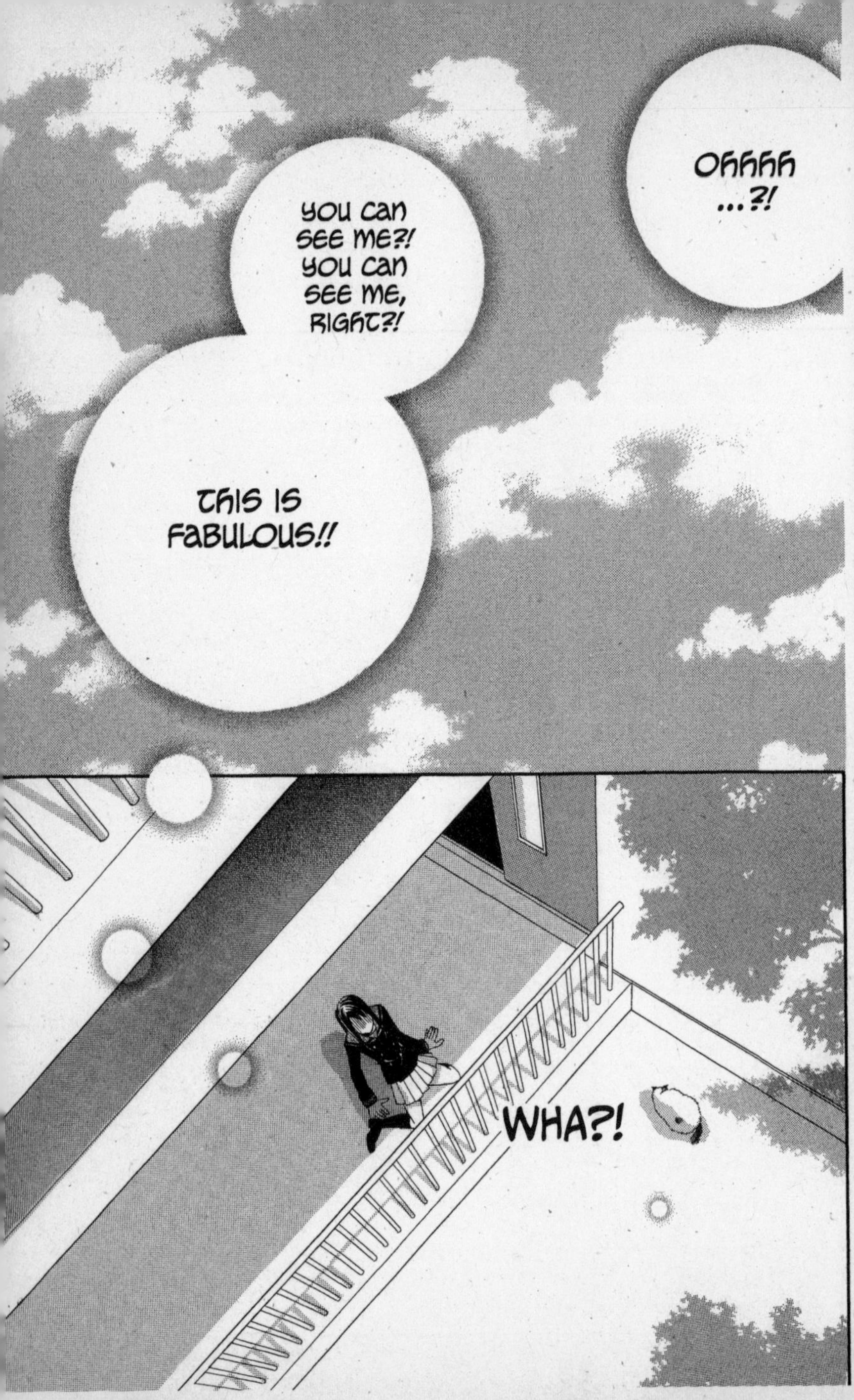
Ohhhh ...?!
You can see me?! You can see me, right?!
This is fabulous!!
WHA?!

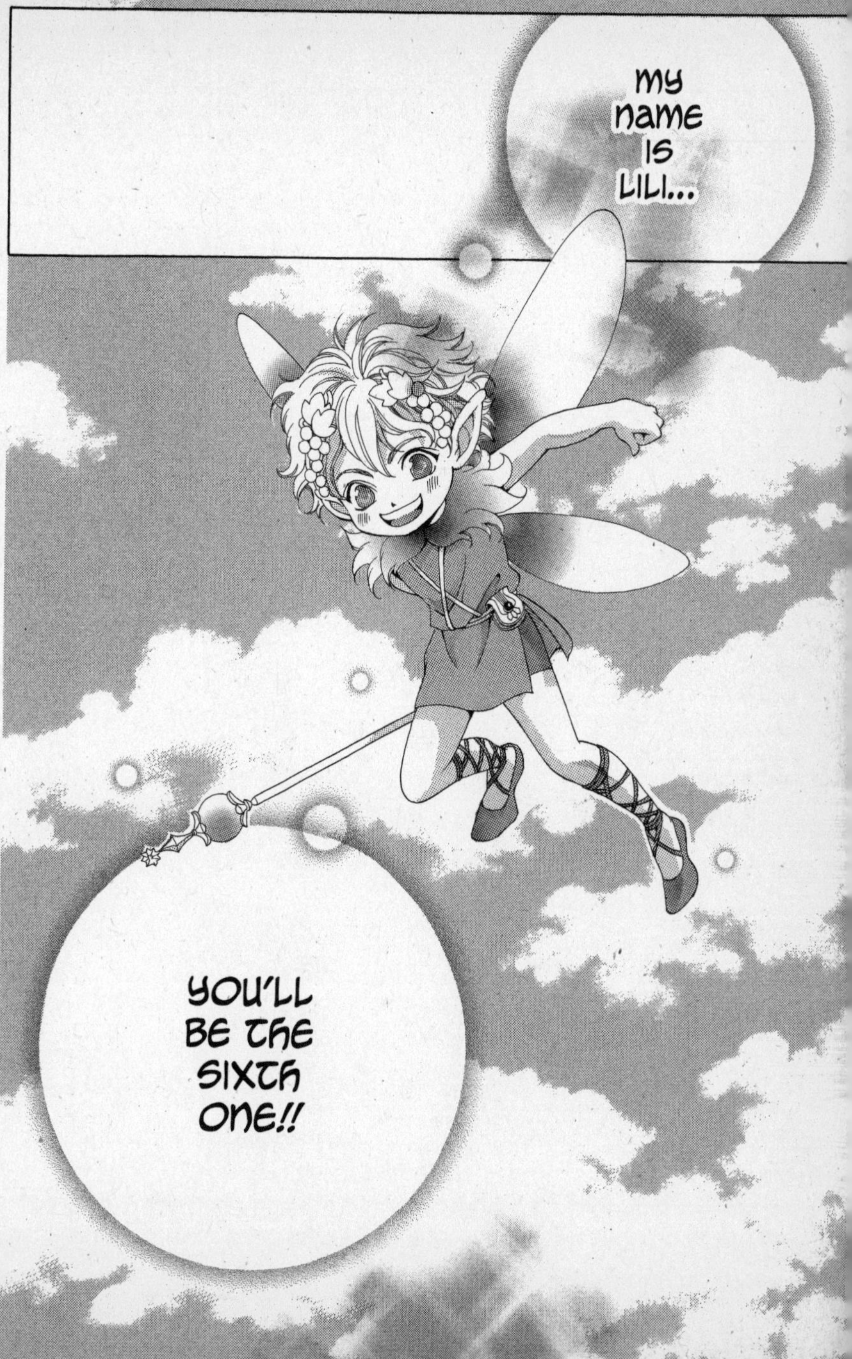
MY NAME IS LILI...
YOU'LL BE THE SIXTH ONE!!

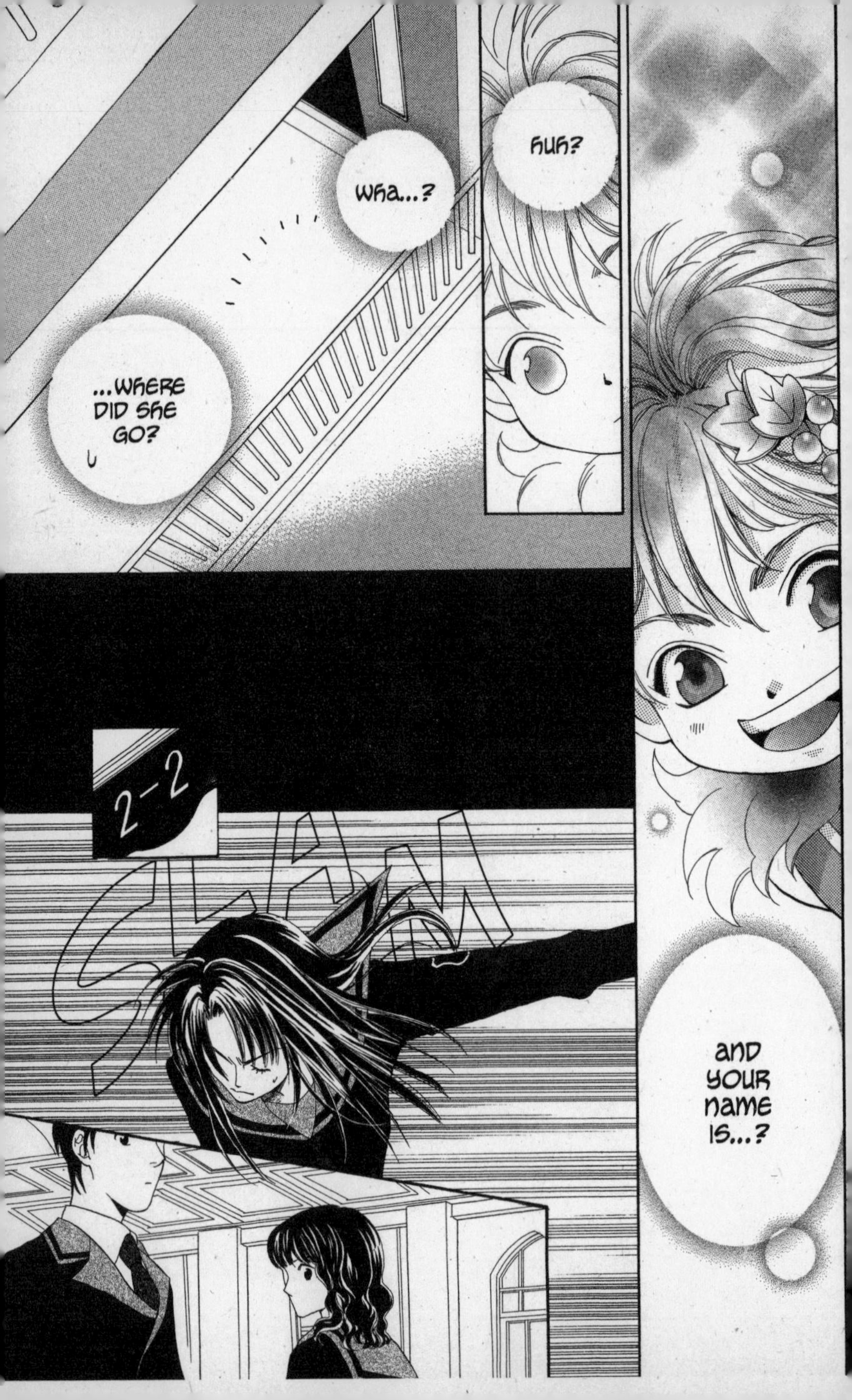
And your name is...?
Huh?
Wha...?
...Where did she go?
2-2
SLAM

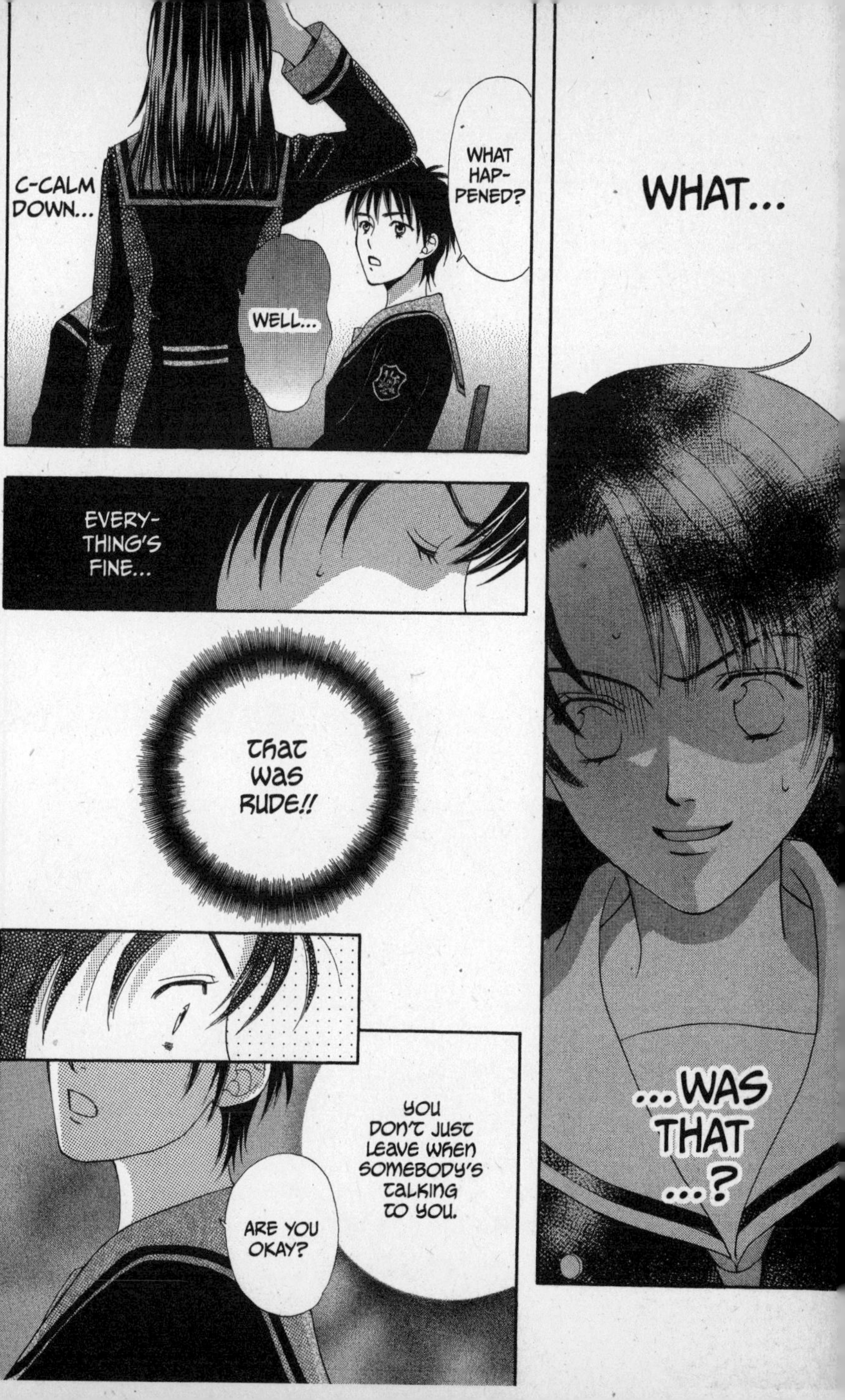
WHAT...
...WAS THAT ...?
WHAT HAP-PENED?
C-CALM DOWN...
WELL...
EVERY-THING'S FINE...
THAT WAS RUDE!!
YOU DON'T JUST LEAVE WHEN SOMEBODY'S TALKING TO YOU.
ARE YOU OKAY?

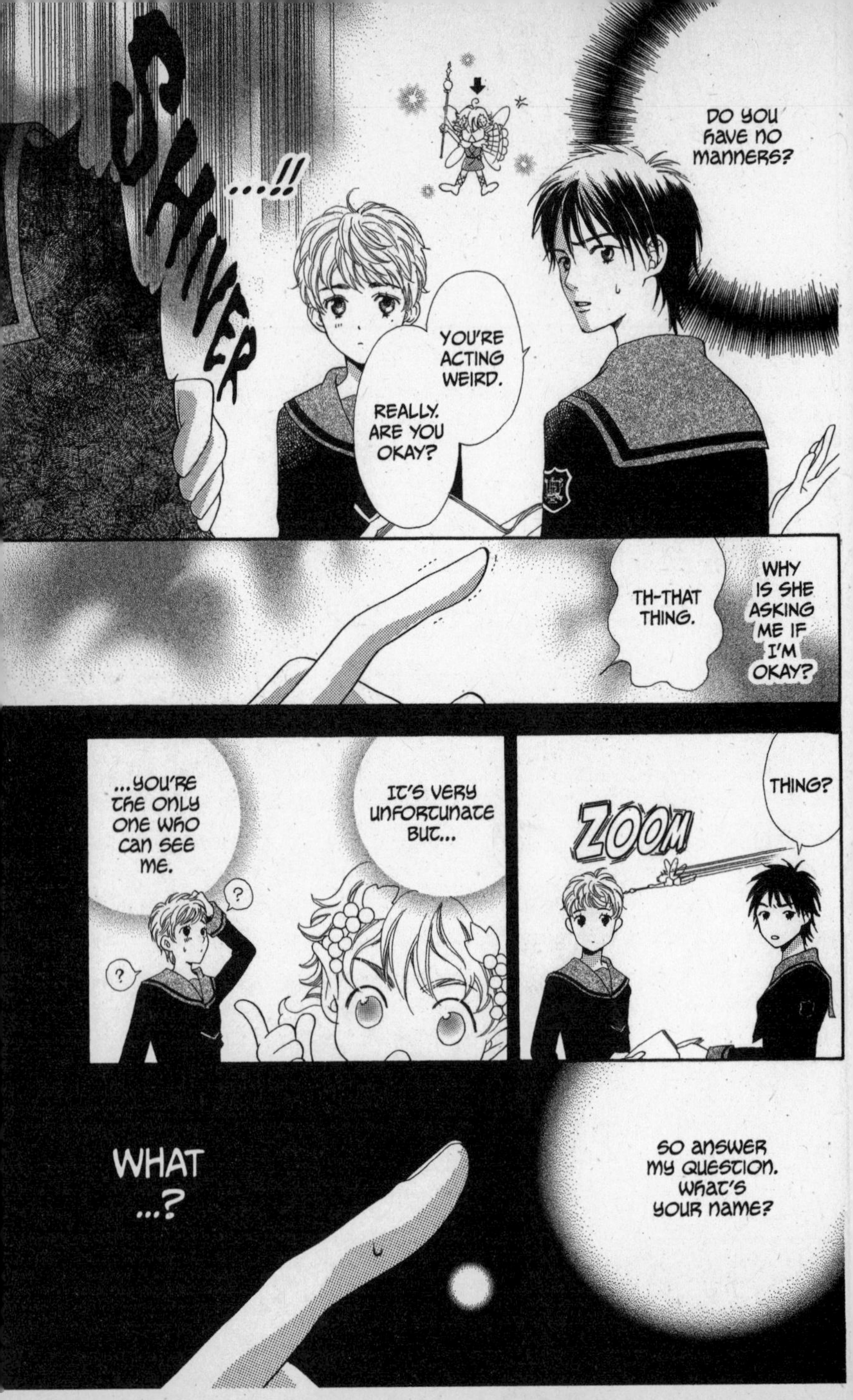
DO YOU HAVE NO MANNERS?
YOU'RE ACTING WEIRD.
REALLY. ARE YOU OKAY?
...!!
SHIVER
WHY IS SHE ASKING ME IF I'M OKAY?
TH-THAT THING.
THING?
ZOOM
IT'S VERY UNFORTUNATE BUT...
...YOU'RE THE ONLY ONE WHO CAN SEE ME.
SO ANSWER MY QUESTION. WHAT'S YOUR NAME?
WHAT ...?

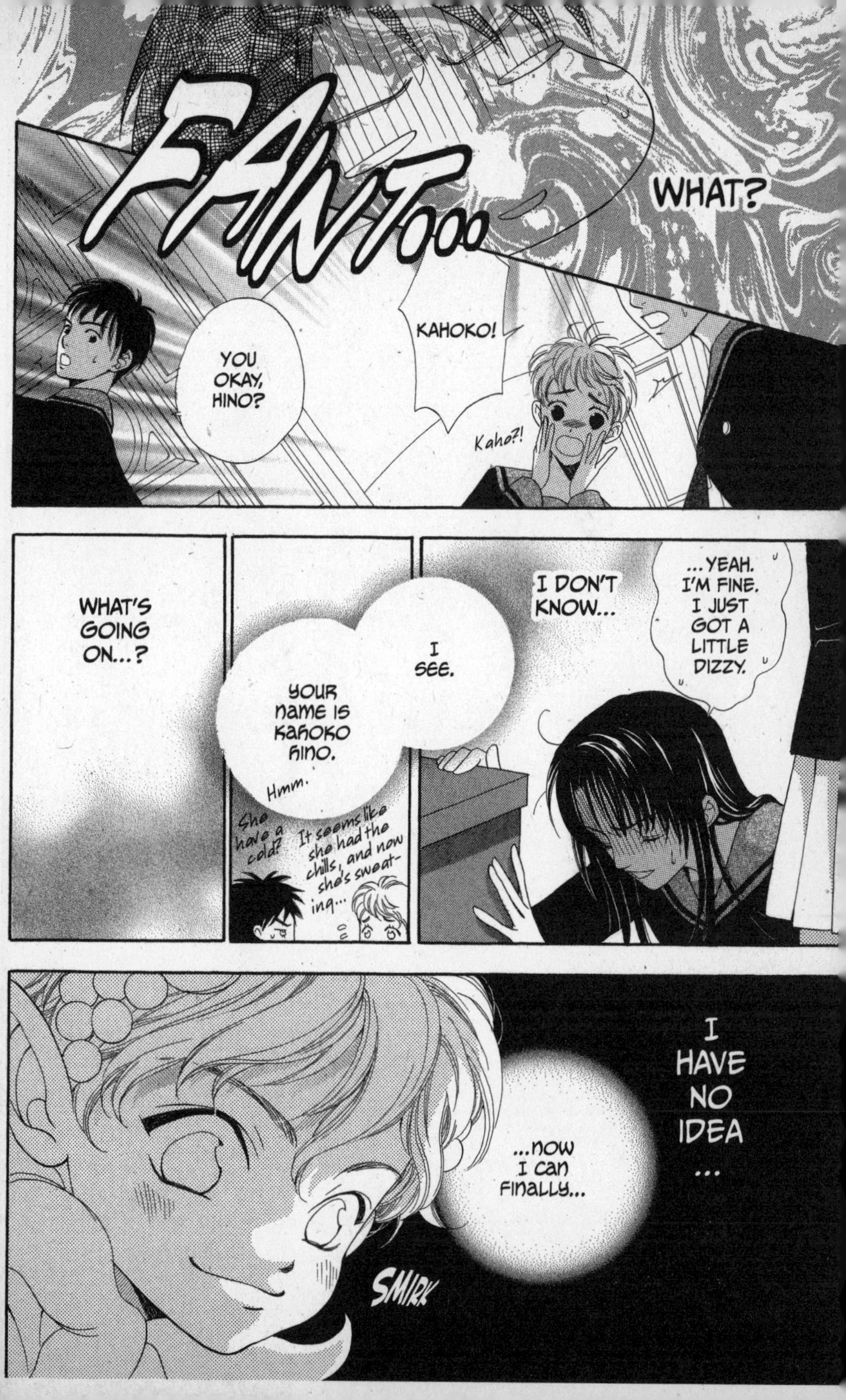
WHAT?
FAINT...
KAHOKO!
Kaho?!
YOU OKAY, HINO?
...YEAH. I'M FINE. I JUST GOT A LITTLE DIZZY.
I DON'T KNOW...
I SEE.
YOUR NAME IS KAHOKO HINO.
Hmm.
It seems like she had the chills, and now she's sweating...
She have a cold?
WHAT'S GOING ON...?
I HAVE NO IDEA ...
...now I can finally...
SMIRK

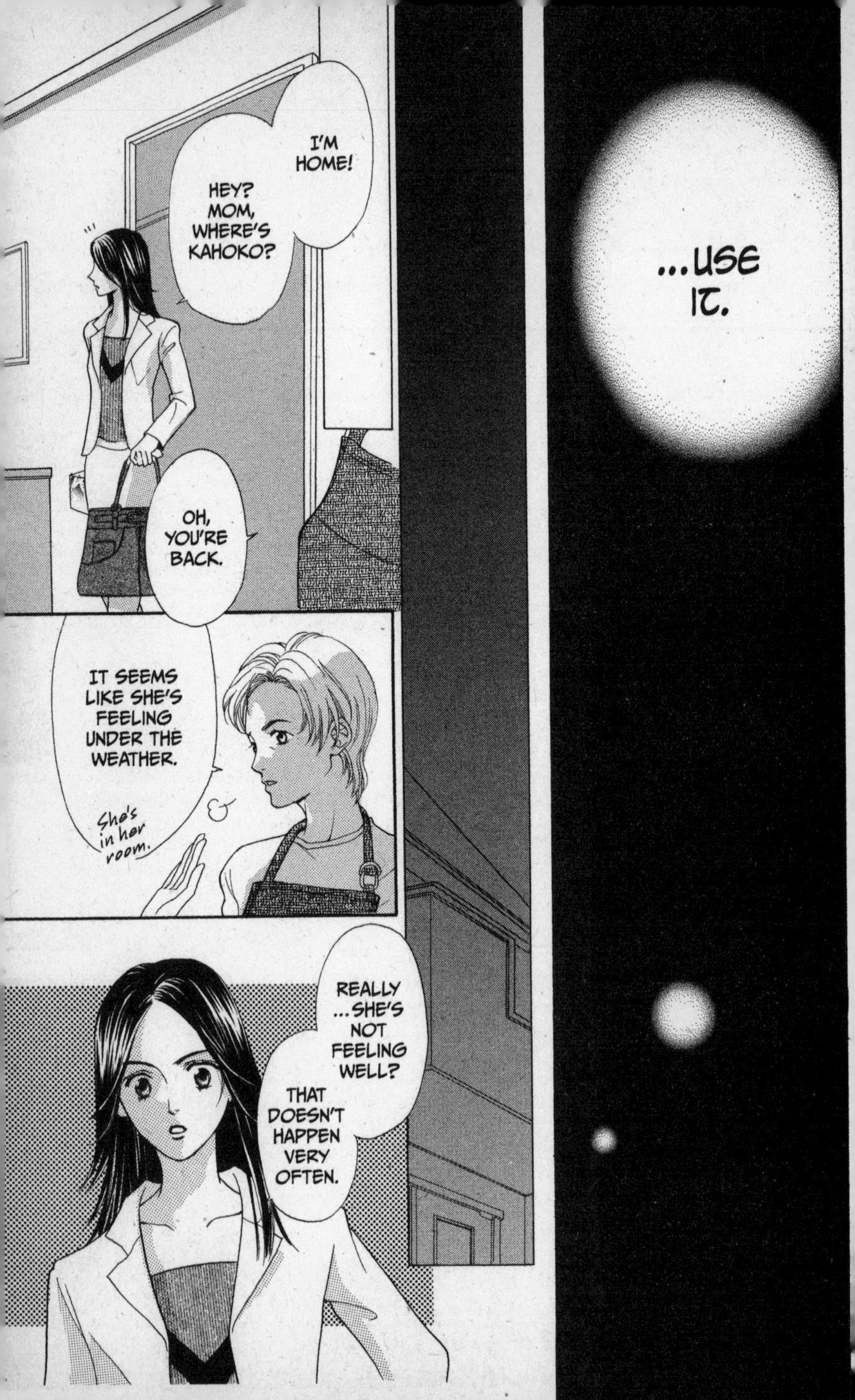
...USE IT.
I'M HOME!
HEY? MOM, WHERE'S KAHOKO?
OH, YOU'RE BACK.
IT SEEMS LIKE SHE'S FEELING UNDER THE WEATHER.
She's in her room.
REALLY ...SHE'S NOT FEELING WELL?
THAT DOESN'T HAPPEN VERY OFTEN.

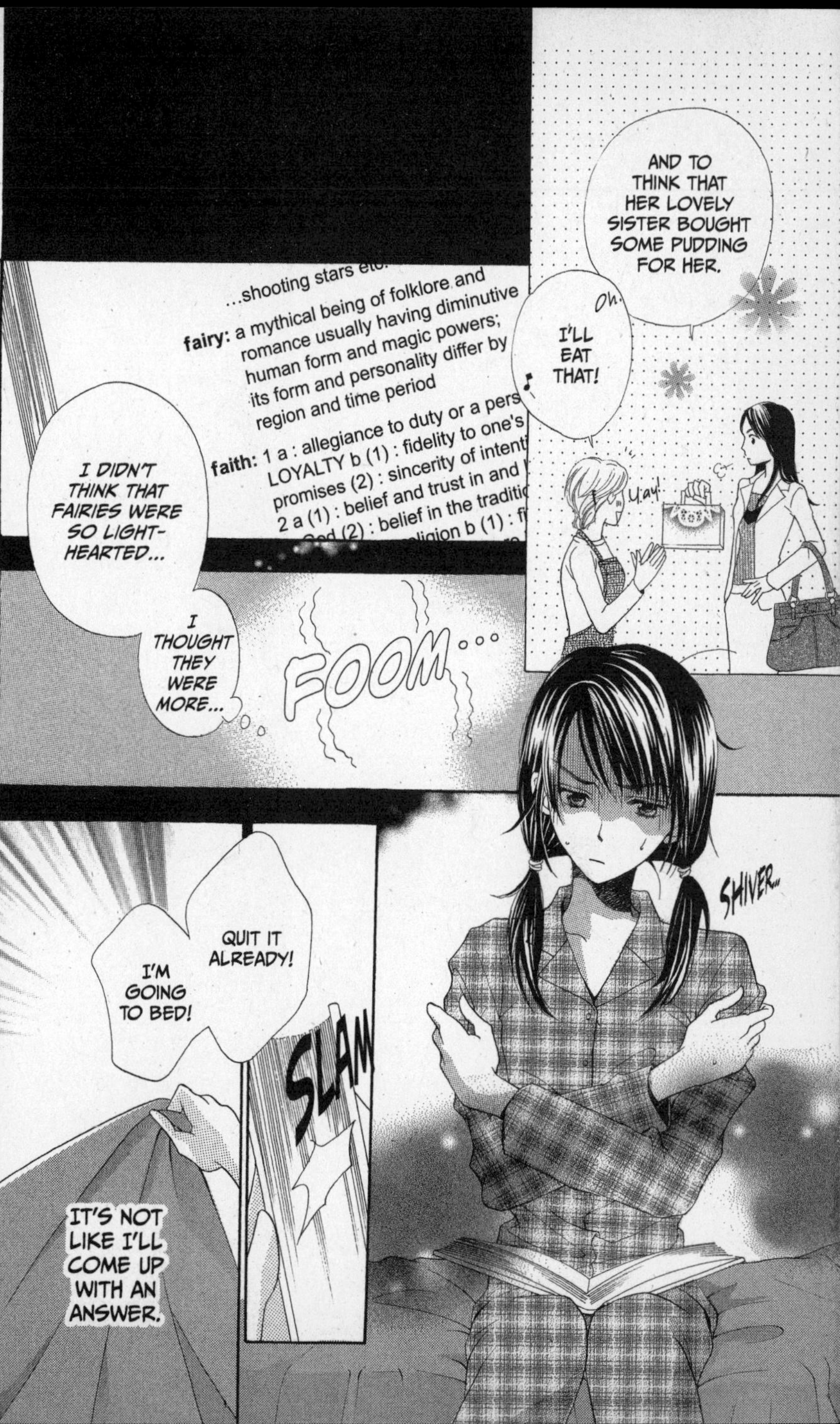
AND TO THINK THAT HER LOVELY SISTER BOUGHT SOME PUDDING FOR HER.
Oh.
I'LL EAT THAT!
Yay!
...shooting stars etc.
fairy: a mythical being of folklore and romance usually having diminutive human form and magic powers; its form and personality differ by region and time period
faith: 1 a : allegiance to duty or a pers
LOYALTY b (1) : fidelity to one's
promises (2) : sincerity of intent
2 a (1) : belief and trust in and
(2) : belief in the traditio
I DIDN'T THINK THAT FAIRIES WERE SO LIGHT-HEARTED...
I THOUGHT THEY WERE MORE...
FOOM...
SHIVER...
QUIT IT ALREADY!
I'M GOING TO BED!
SLAM
IT'S NOT LIKE I'LL COME UP WITH AN ANSWER.

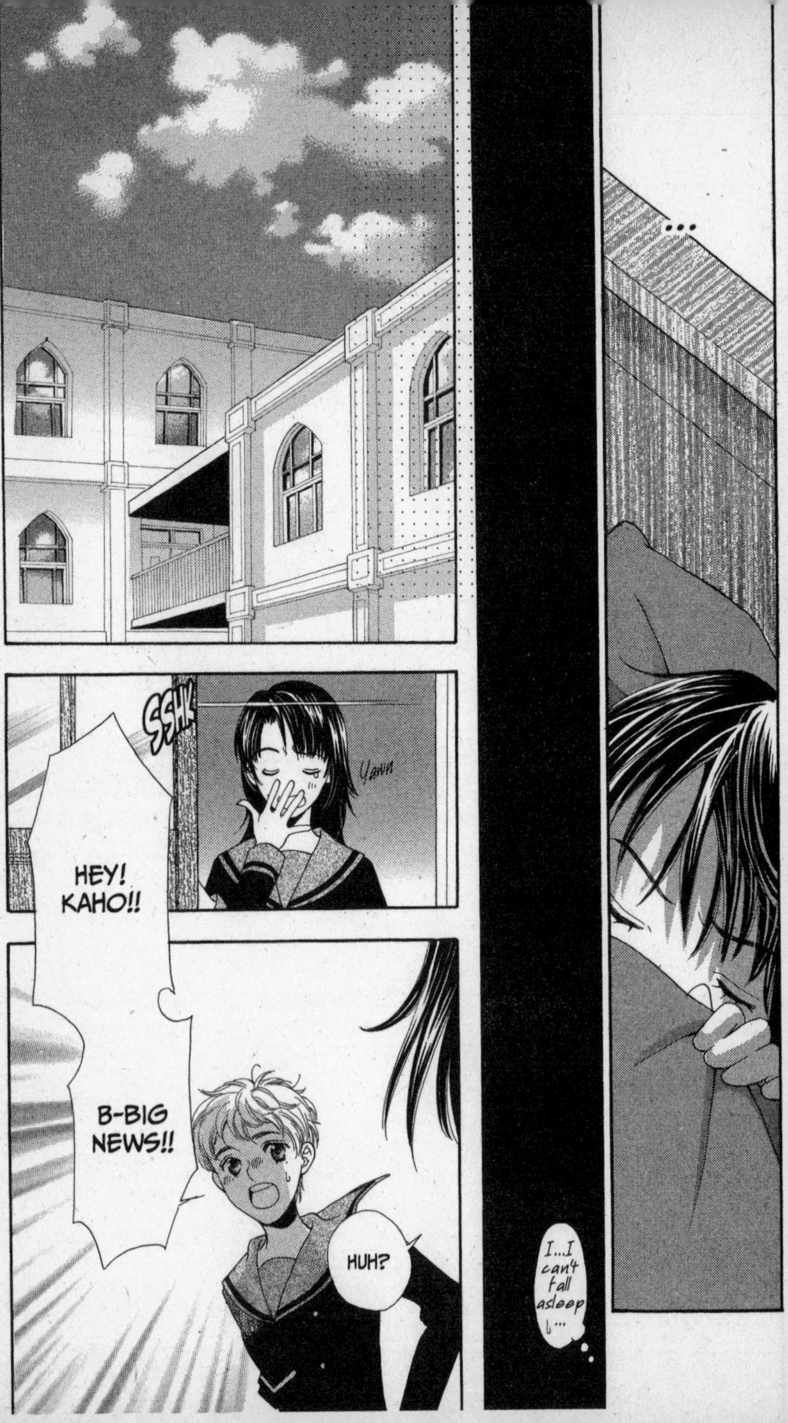
...
I...I can't fall asleep...
SSHK
Yawn
HEY! KAHO!!
B-BIG NEWS!!
HUH?

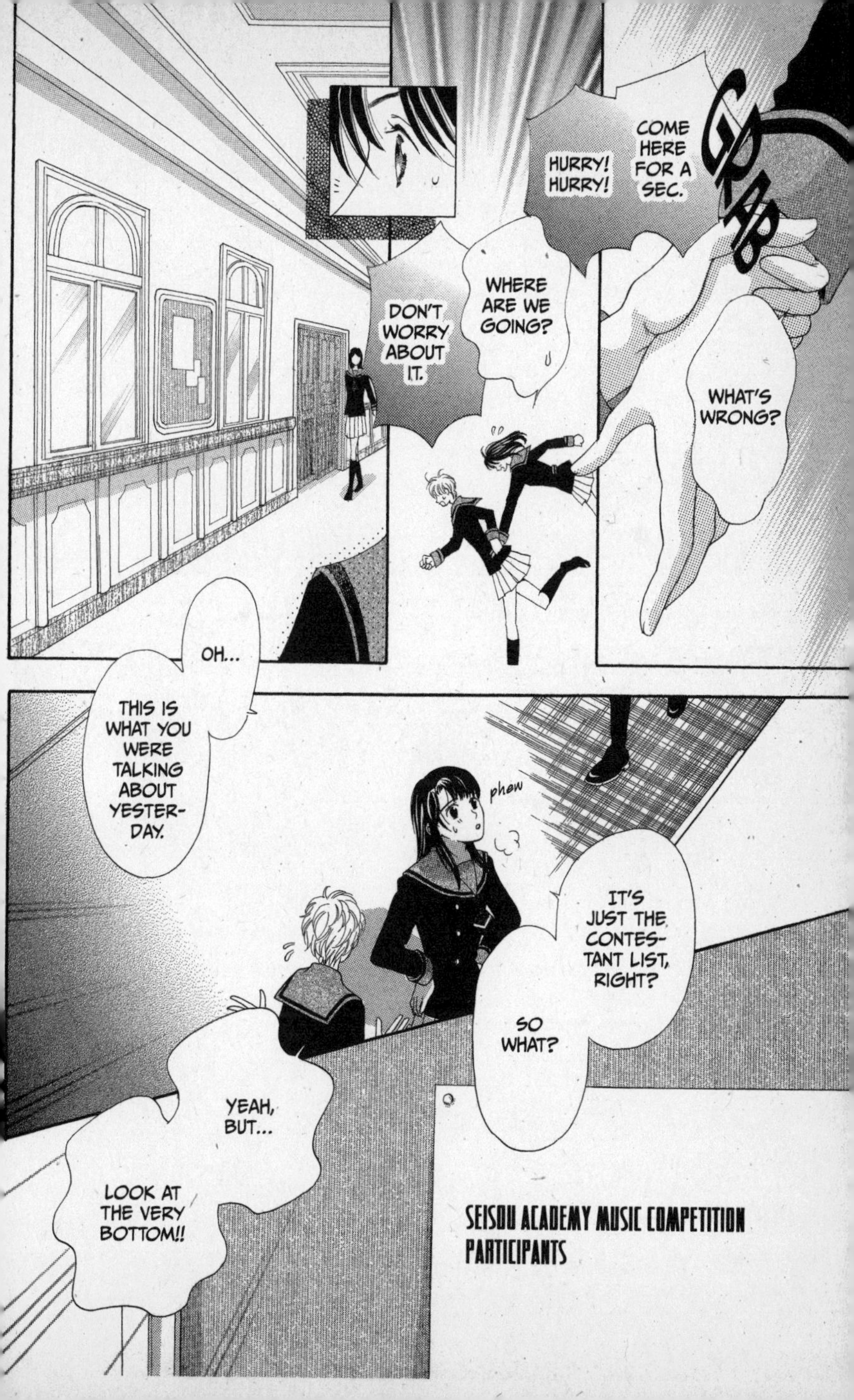
COME HERE FOR A SEC.
HURRY! HURRY!
GRAB
WHAT'S WRONG?
WHERE ARE WE GOING?
DON'T WORRY ABOUT IT.
OH...
THIS IS WHAT YOU WERE TALKING ABOUT YESTER-DAY.
phew
IT'S JUST THE CONTES-TANT LIST, RIGHT?
SO WHAT?
YEAH, BUT...
LOOK AT THE VERY BOTTOM!!
SEISOU ACADEMY MUSIC COMPETITION PARTICIPANTS

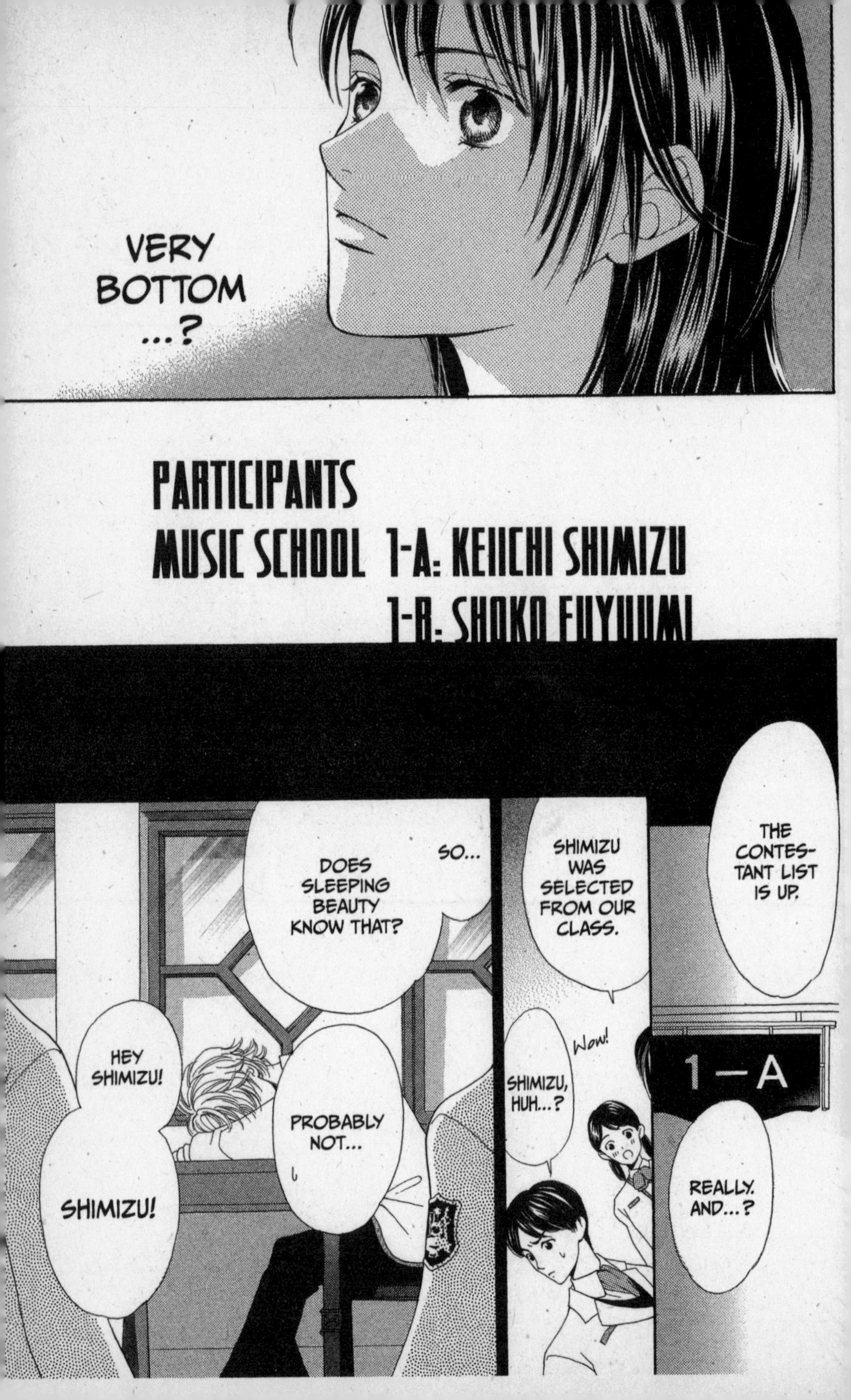
VERY BOTTOM ...?
PARTICIPANTS
MUSIC SCHOOL 1-A: KEIICHI SHIMIZU
1-B: SHOKO FUYUUMI
THE CONTES-TANT LIST IS UP.
1-A
REALLY. AND...?
SHIMIZU WAS SELECTED FROM OUR CLASS.
Wow!
SHIMIZU, HUH...?
SO...
DOES SLEEPING BEAUTY KNOW THAT?
PROBABLY NOT...
HEY SHIMIZU!
SHIMIZU!

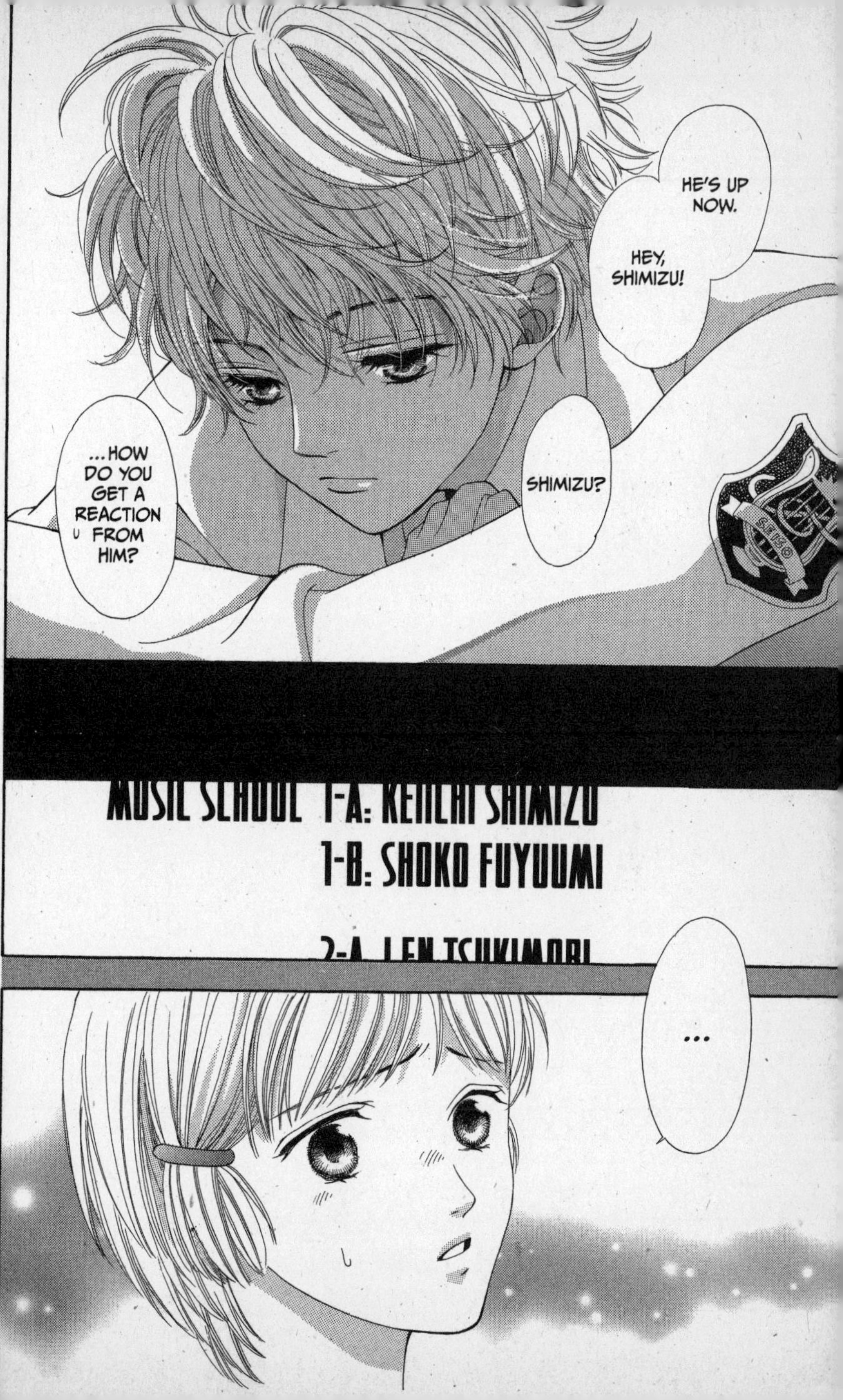
HE'S UP NOW.
HEY, SHIMIZU!
SHIMIZU?
...HOW DO YOU GET A REACTION FROM HIM?
MUSIC SCHOOL 1-A: KEIICHI SHIMIZU
1-B: SHOKO FUYUUMI
...

BLAH

BLAH

Oh...

Panic.

REN!

CONGRATU-
LATIONS.

Wow!

WELL
DONE!

2-A: LEN TSUKIMORI

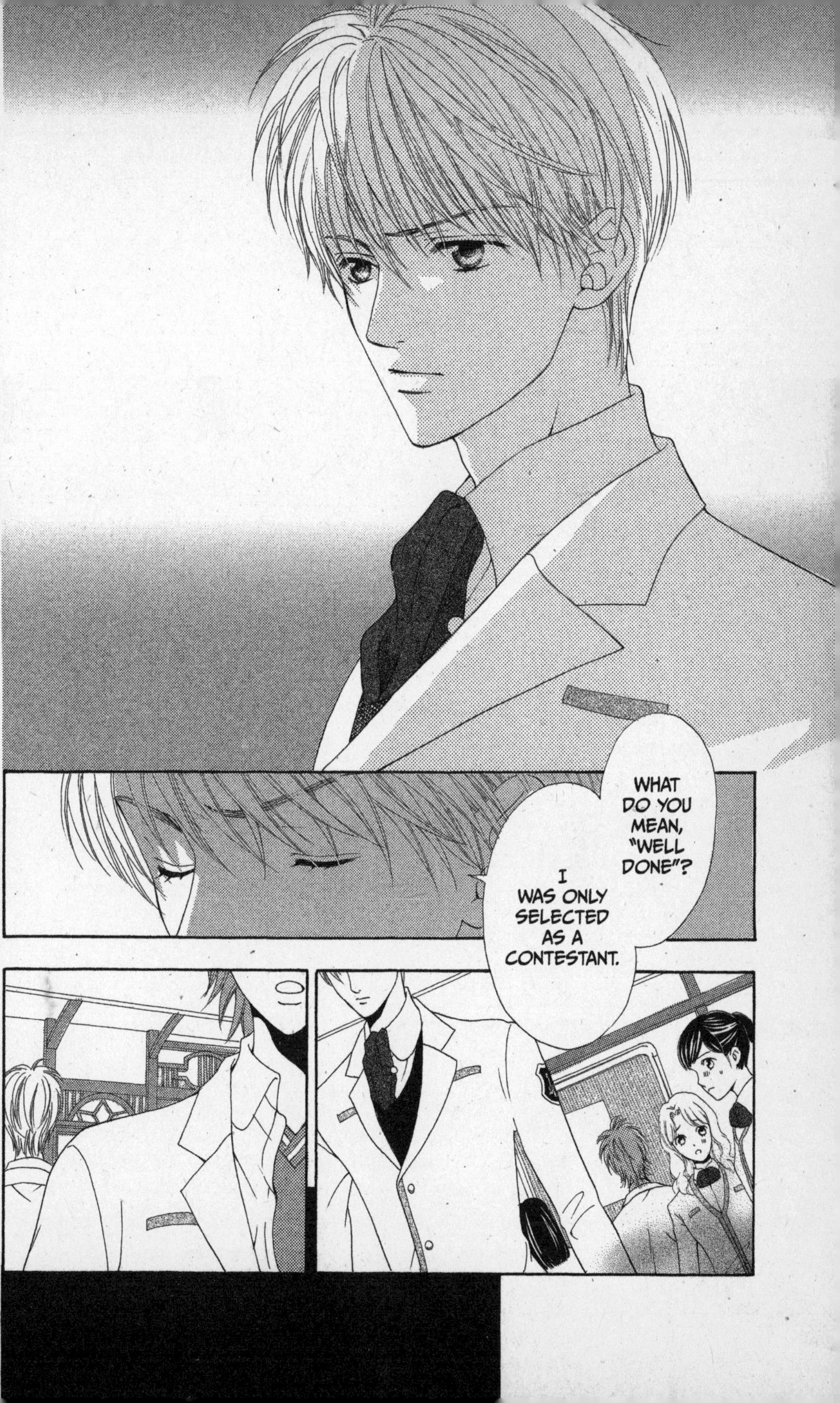
WHAT DO YOU MEAN, "WELL DONE"?
I WAS ONLY SELECTED AS A CONTESTANT.

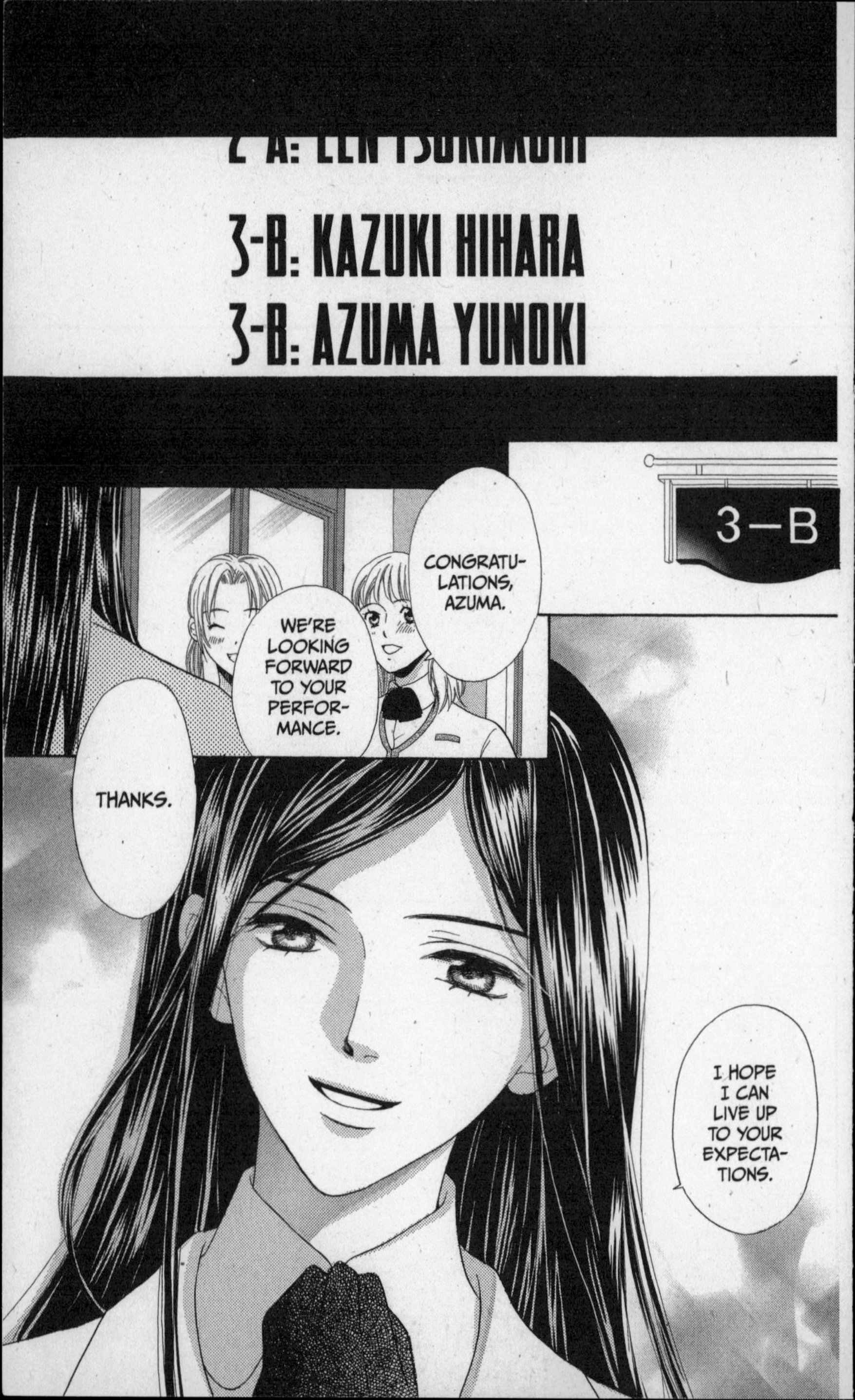
[redacted]
3-B: KAZUKI HIHARA
3-B: AZUMA YUNOKI
3-B
CONGRATU-LATIONS, AZUMA.
WE'RE LOOKING FORWARD TO YOUR PERFOR-MANCE.
THANKS.
I HOPE I CAN LIVE UP TO YOUR EXPECTA-TIONS.

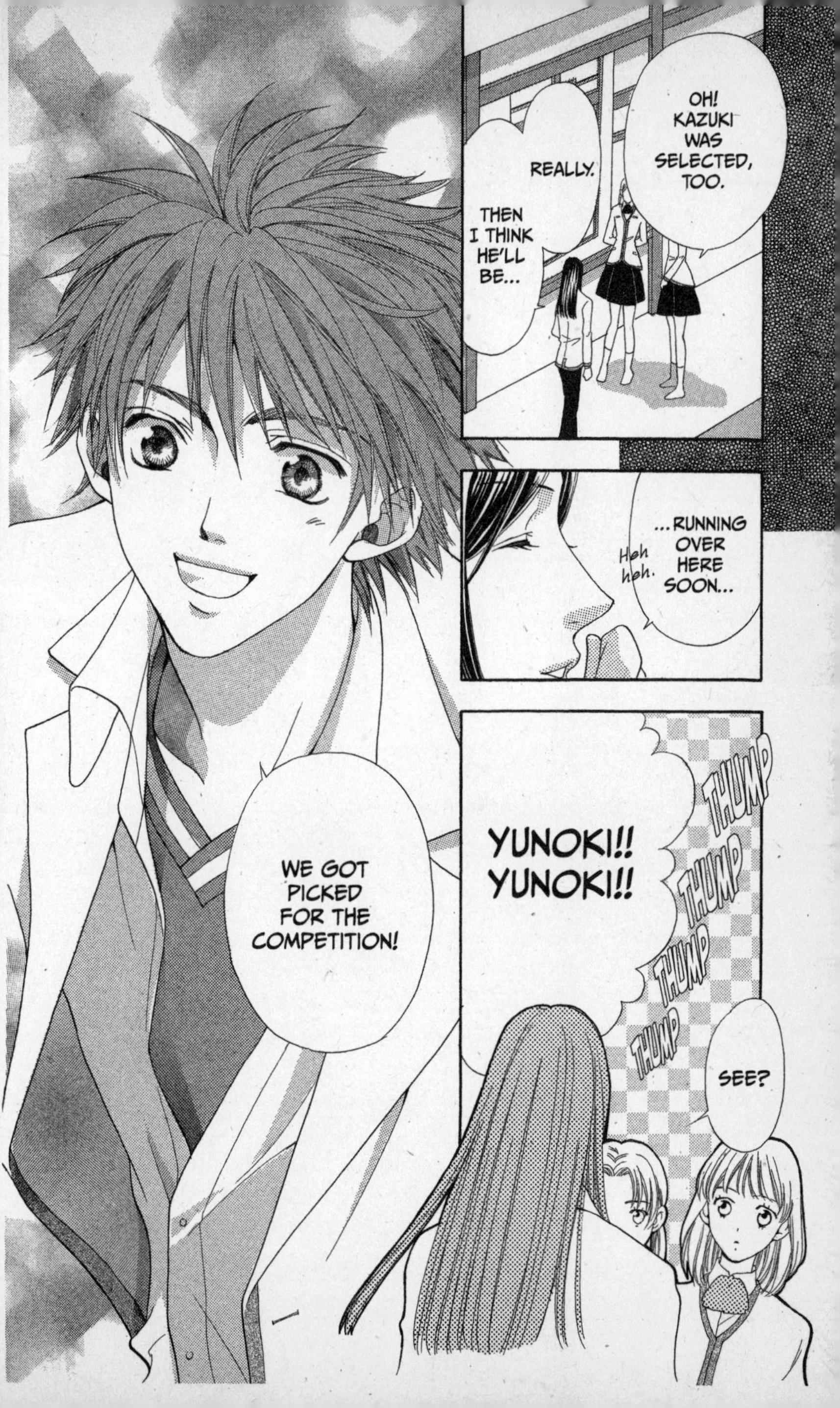
OH! KAZUKI WAS SELECTED, TOO.
REALLY.
THEN I THINK HE'LL BE...
...RUNNING OVER HERE SOON...
Heh heh.
YUNOKI!! YUNOKI!!
THUMP THUMP THUMP THUMP
SEE?
WE GOT PICKED FOR THE COMPETITION!

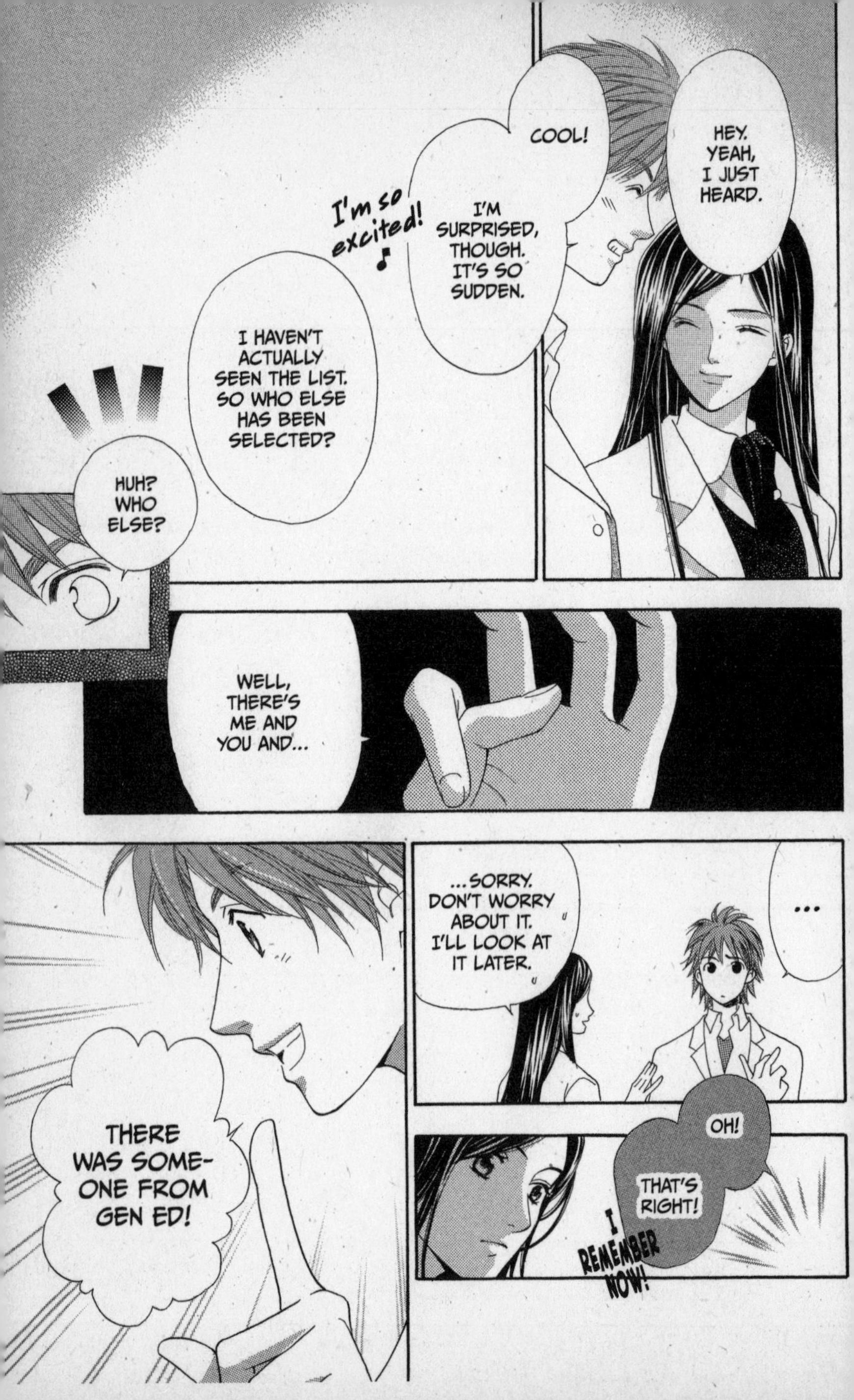
HEY. YEAH, I JUST HEARD.
COOL!
I'M SURPRISED, THOUGH. IT'S SO SUDDEN.
I'm so excited! ♪
I HAVEN'T ACTUALLY SEEN THE LIST. SO WHO ELSE HAS BEEN SELECTED?
HUH? WHO ELSE?
WELL, THERE'S ME AND YOU AND...
...
...SORRY. DON'T WORRY ABOUT IT. I'LL LOOK AT IT LATER.
OH!
THAT'S RIGHT!
I REMEMBER NOW!
THERE WAS SOME-ONE FROM GEN ED!

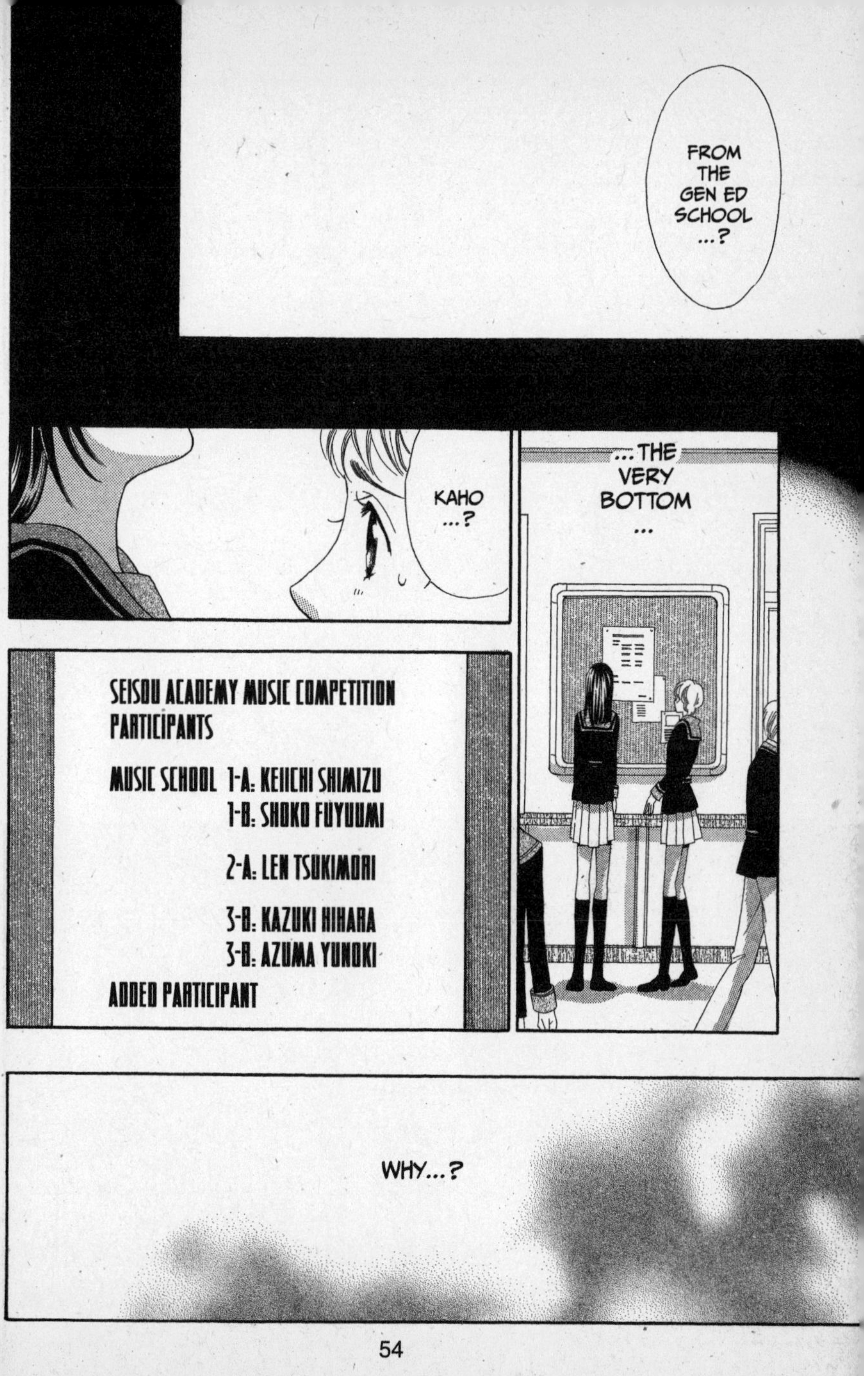
FROM THE GEN ED SCHOOL ...?
...THE VERY BOTTOM ...
KAHO ...?
SEISOU ACADEMY MUSIC COMPETITION PARTICIPANTS
MUSIC SCHOOL 1-A: KEIICHI SHIMIZU
1-B: SHOKO FUYUUMI
2-A: LEN TSUKIMORI
3-B: KAZUKI HIHARA
3-B: AZUMA YUNOKI
ADDED PARTICIPANT
WHY...?

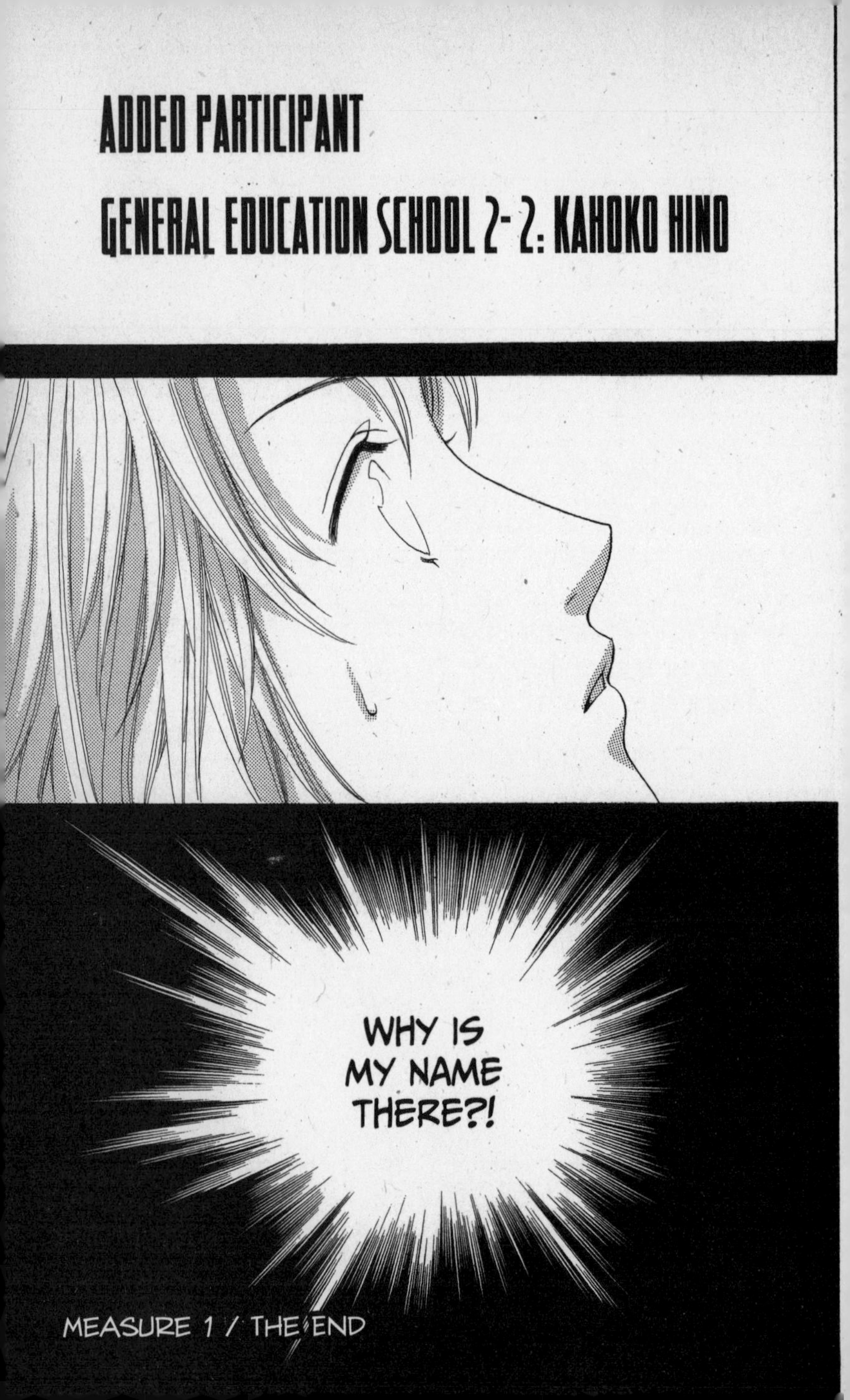
ADDED PARTICIPANT
GENERAL EDUCATION SCHOOL 2-2: KAHOKO HINO
WHY IS MY NAME THERE?!
MEASURE 1 / THE END

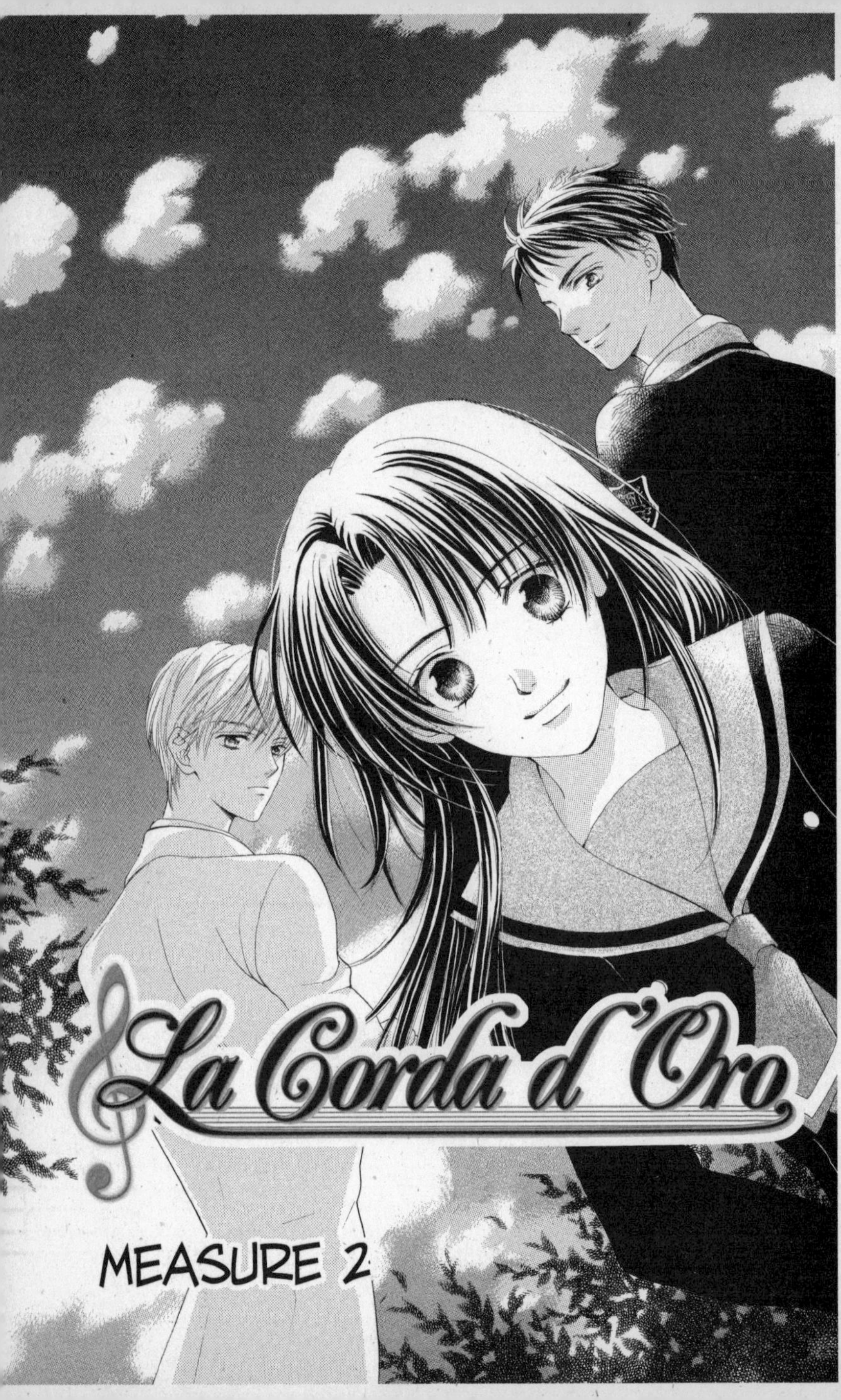
La Corda d'Oro
MEASURE 2

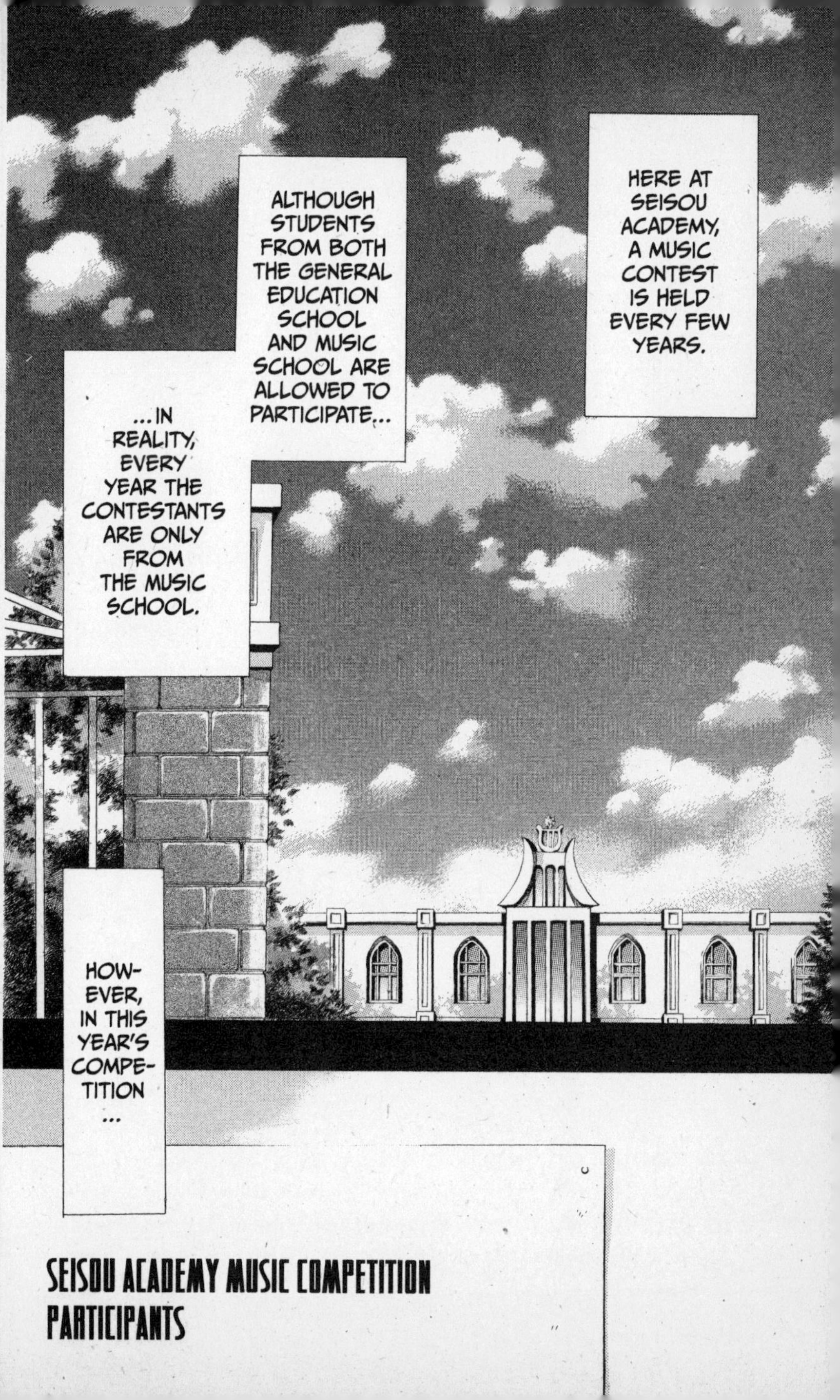
HERE AT SEISOU ACADEMY, A MUSIC CONTEST IS HELD EVERY FEW YEARS.
ALTHOUGH STUDENTS FROM BOTH THE GENERAL EDUCATION SCHOOL AND MUSIC SCHOOL ARE ALLOWED TO PARTICIPATE...
...IN REALITY, EVERY YEAR THE CONTESTANTS ARE ONLY FROM THE MUSIC SCHOOL.
HOW-EVER, IN THIS YEAR'S COMPE-TITION...
SEISOU ACADEMY MUSIC COMPETITION PARTICIPANTS

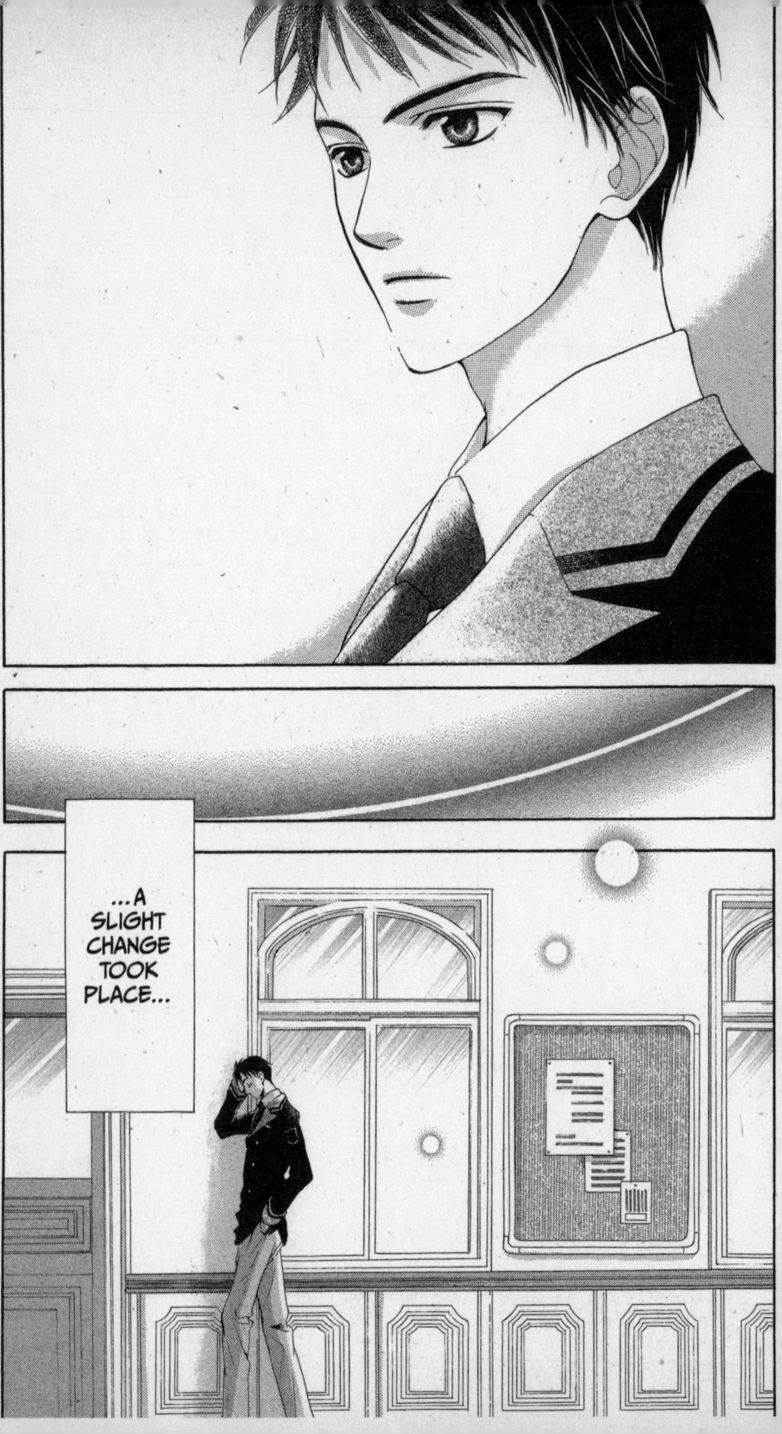
...A SLIGHT CHANGE TOOK PLACE...

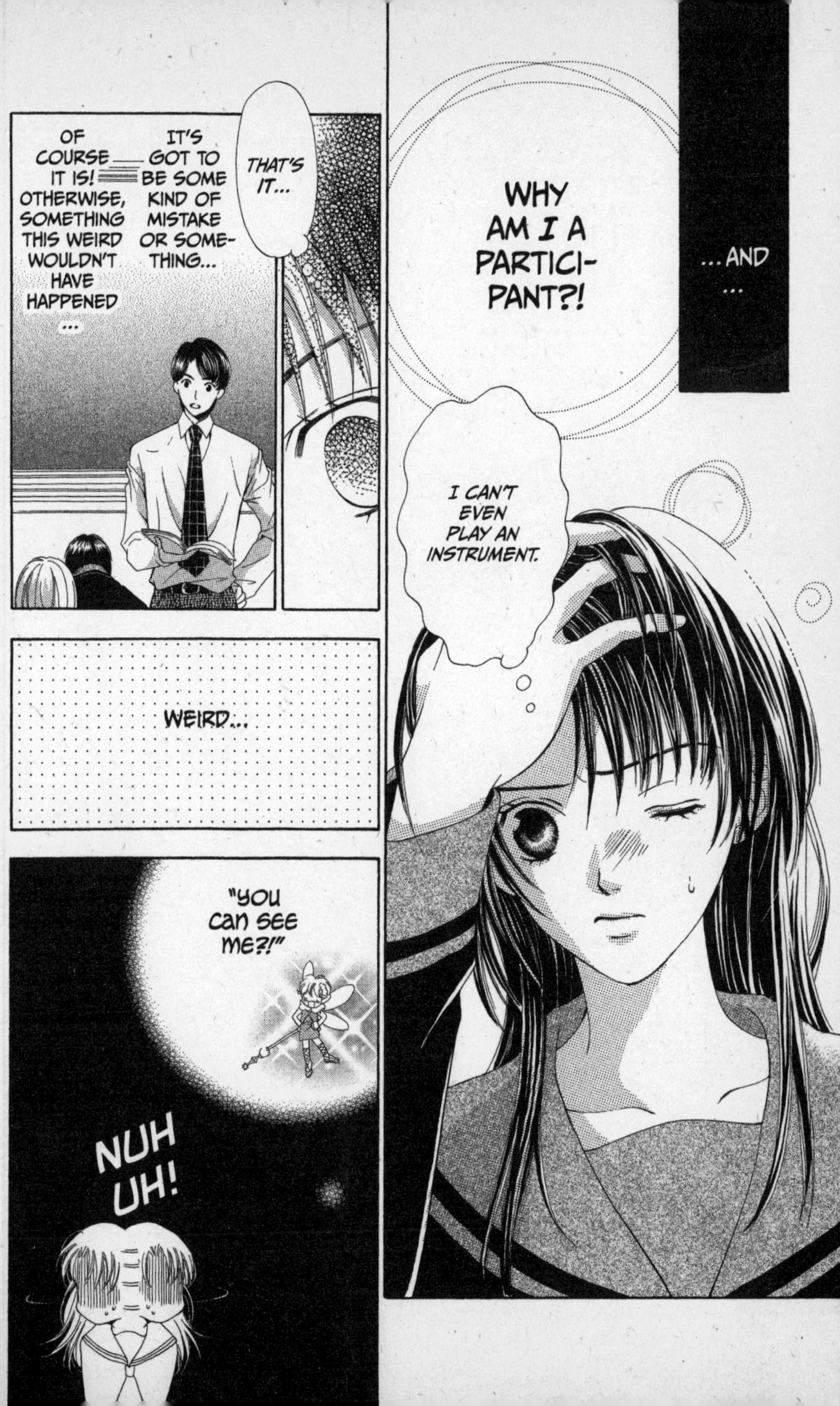
...AND ...
WHY AM I A PARTICIPANT?!
I CAN'T EVEN PLAY AN INSTRUMENT.
THAT'S IT...
IT'S GOT TO BE SOME KIND OF MISTAKE OR SOMETHING...
OF COURSE IT IS! OTHERWISE, SOMETHING THIS WEIRD WOULDN'T HAVE HAPPENED...
WEIRD...
"YOU can see me?!"
NUH UH!

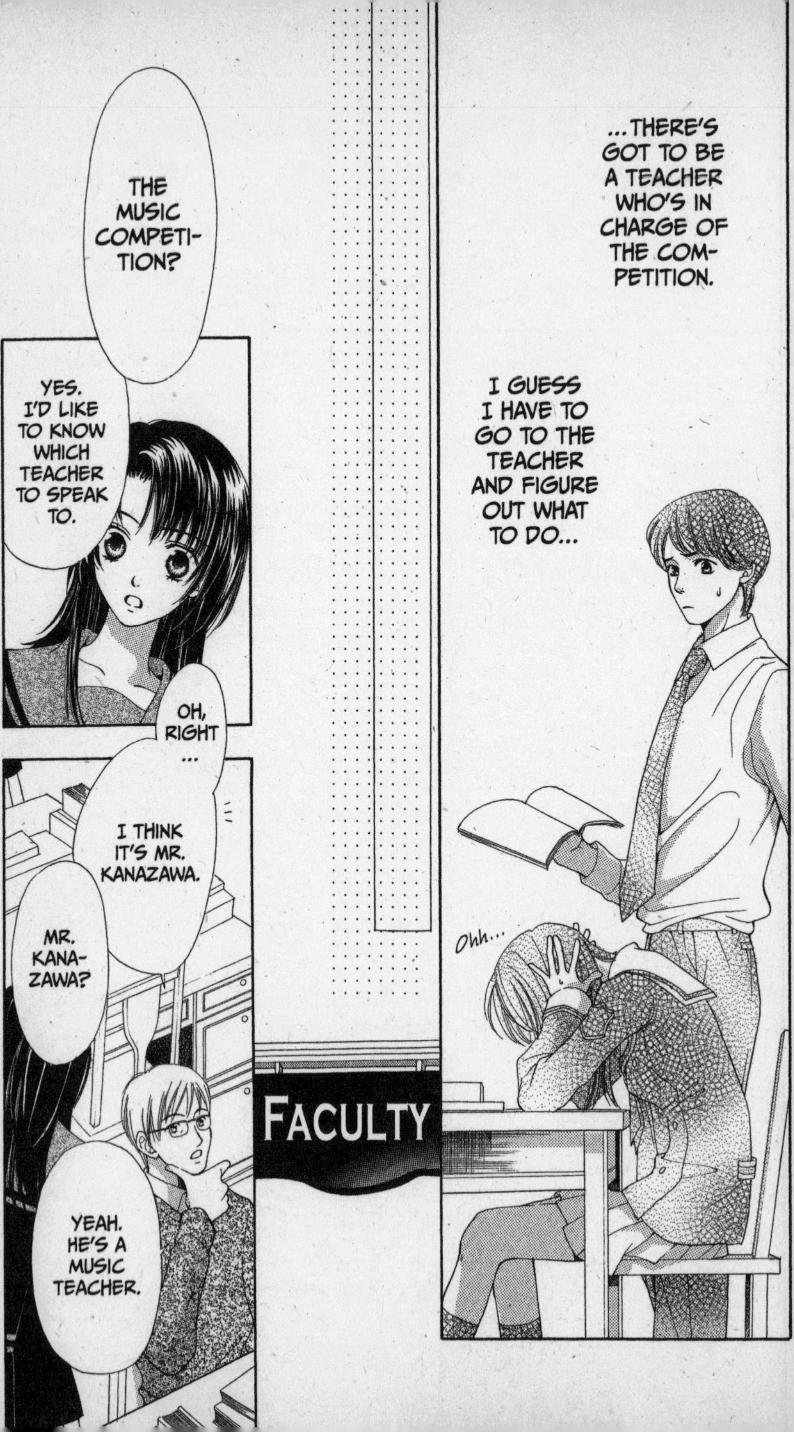
...THERE'S GOT TO BE A TEACHER WHO'S IN CHARGE OF THE COMPETITION.
I GUESS I HAVE TO GO TO THE TEACHER AND FIGURE OUT WHAT TO DO...
Ohh...
FACULTY
THE MUSIC COMPETITION?
YES. I'D LIKE TO KNOW WHICH TEACHER TO SPEAK TO.
OH, RIGHT...
I THINK IT'S MR. KANAZAWA.
MR. KANAZAWA?
YEAH. HE'S A MUSIC TEACHER.

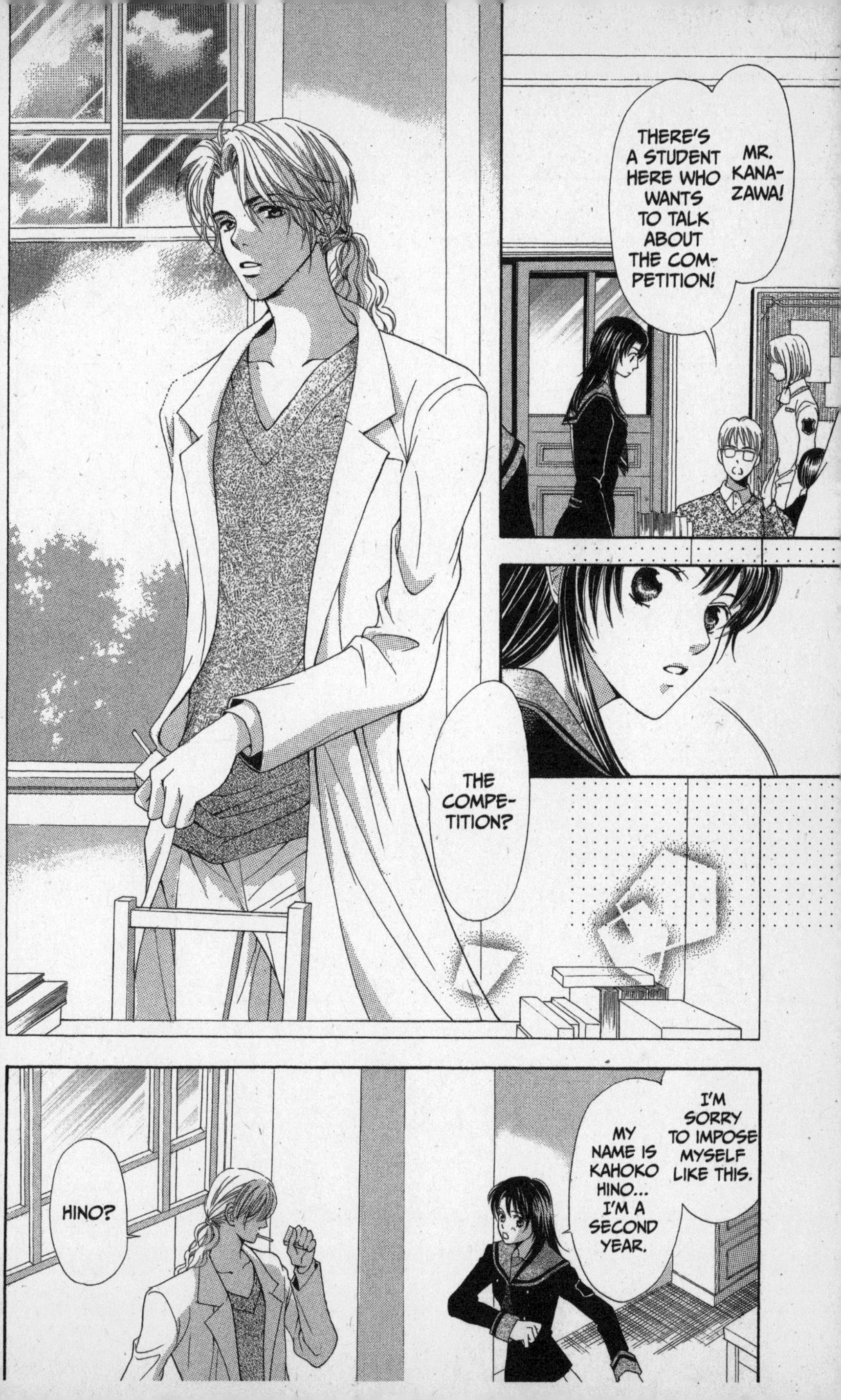
MR. KANAZAWA!
THERE'S A STUDENT HERE WHO WANTS TO TALK ABOUT THE COM-PETITION!
THE COMPE-TITION?
I'M SORRY TO IMPOSE MYSELF LIKE THIS.
MY NAME IS KAHOKO HINO... I'M A SECOND YEAR.
HINO?

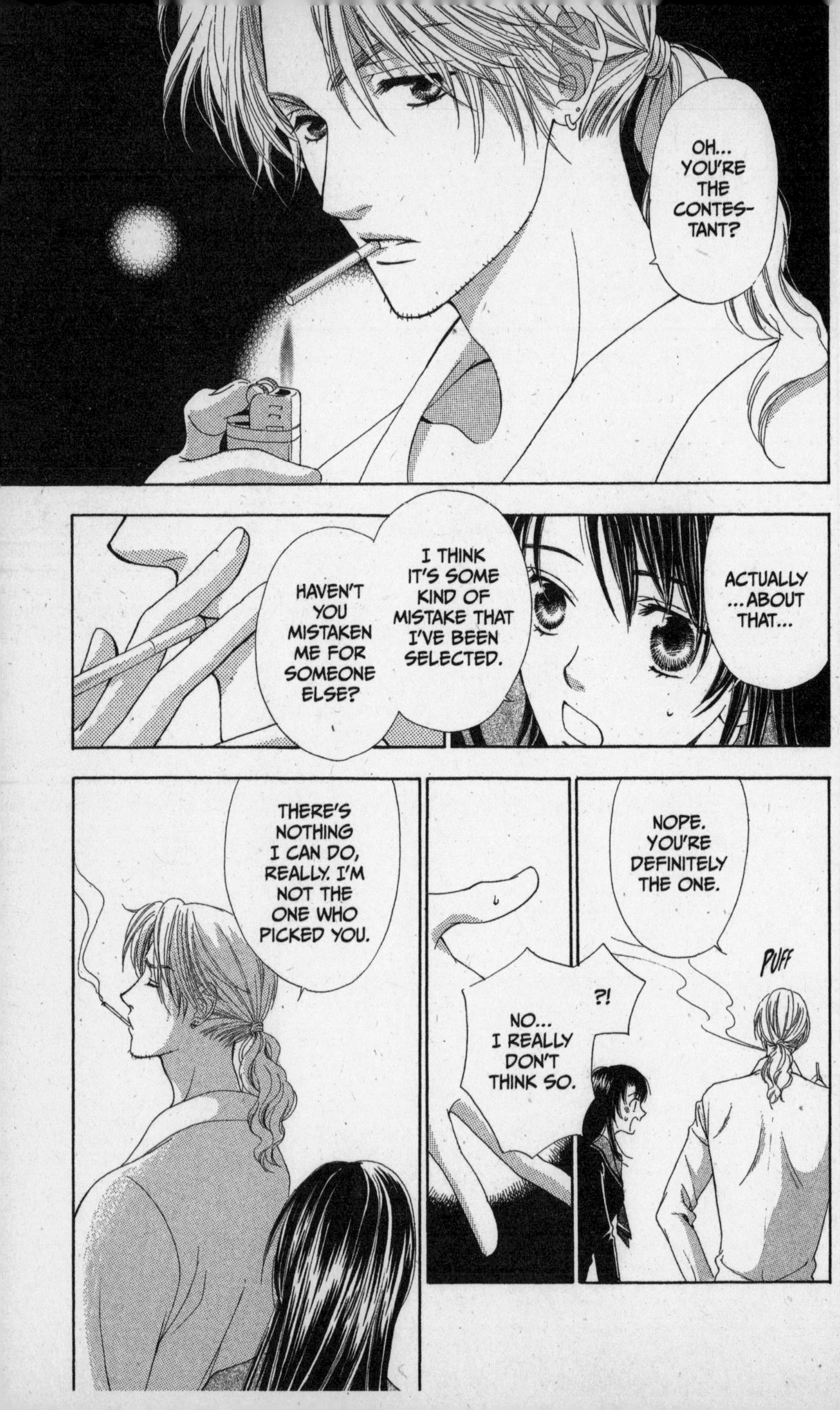
OH... YOU'RE THE CONTES-TANT?
ACTUALLY ...ABOUT THAT...
I THINK IT'S SOME KIND OF MISTAKE THAT I'VE BEEN SELECTED.
HAVEN'T YOU MISTAKEN ME FOR SOMEONE ELSE?
NOPE. YOU'RE DEFINITELY THE ONE.
PUFF
?!
NO... I REALLY DON'T THINK SO.
THERE'S NOTHING I CAN DO, REALLY. I'M NOT THE ONE WHO PICKED YOU.

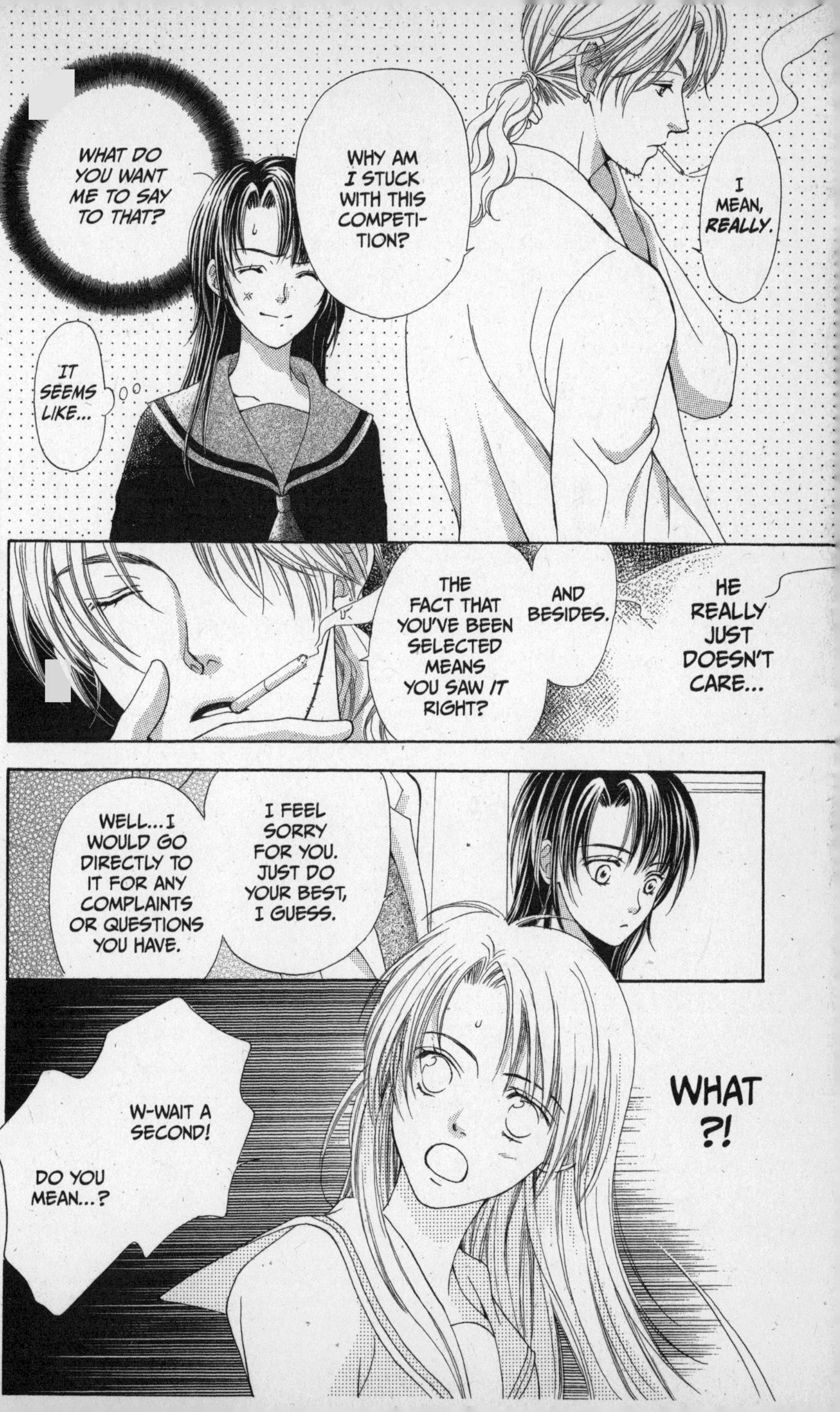
I MEAN, REALLY.
WHY AM I STUCK WITH THIS COMPETITION?
WHAT DO YOU WANT ME TO SAY TO THAT?
IT SEEMS LIKE...
HE REALLY JUST DOESN'T CARE...
AND BESIDES.
THE FACT THAT YOU'VE BEEN SELECTED MEANS YOU SAW IT RIGHT?
I FEEL SORRY FOR YOU. JUST DO YOUR BEST, I GUESS.
WELL...I WOULD GO DIRECTLY TO IT FOR ANY COMPLAINTS OR QUESTIONS YOU HAVE.
WHAT ?!
W-WAIT A SECOND!
DO YOU MEAN...?

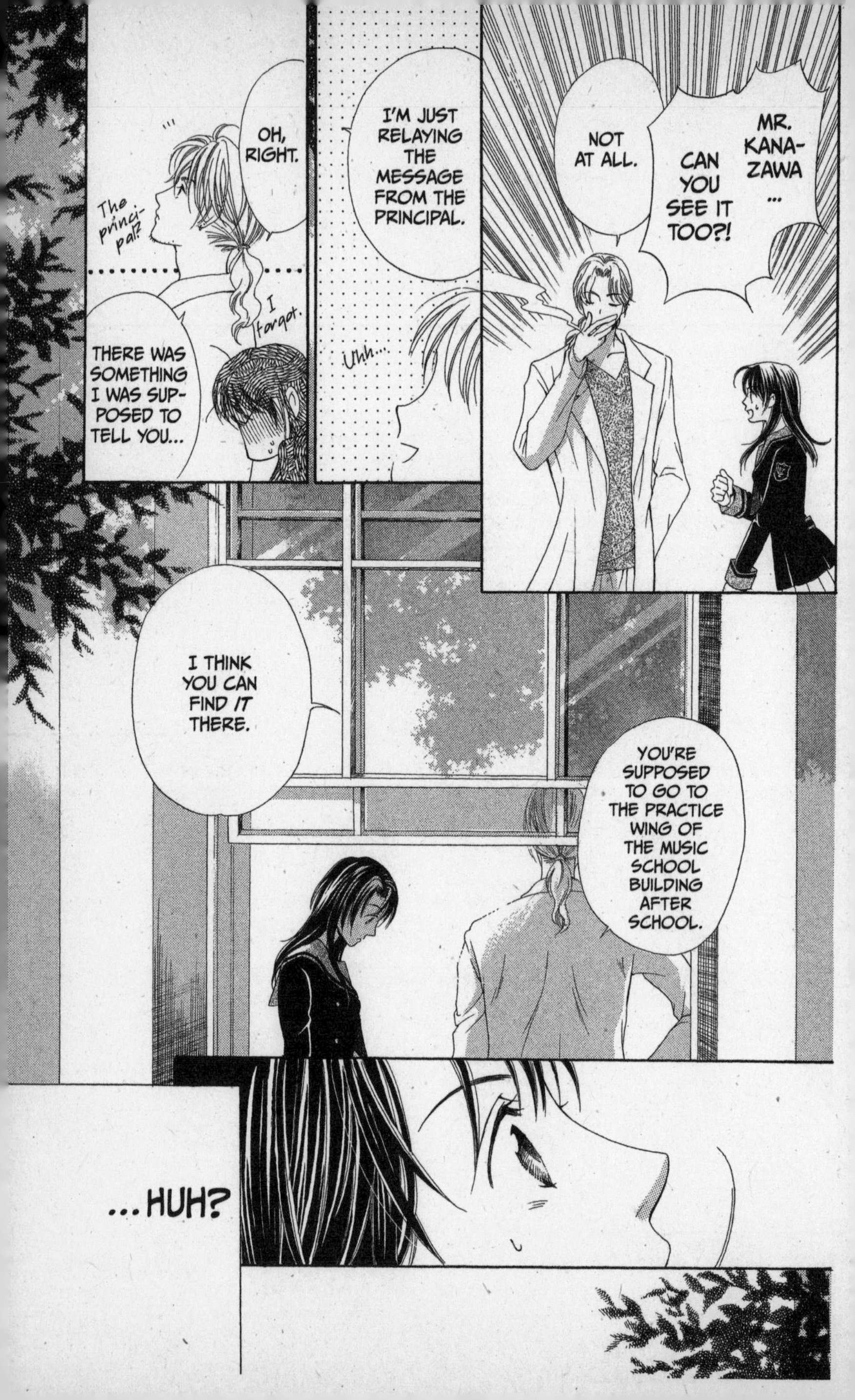
MR. KANAZAWA...
CAN YOU SEE IT TOO?!
NOT AT ALL.
I'M JUST RELAYING THE MESSAGE FROM THE PRINCIPAL.
Uhh...
OH, RIGHT.
The principal?
I forgot.
THERE WAS SOMETHING I WAS SUPPOSED TO TELL YOU...
YOU'RE SUPPOSED TO GO TO THE PRACTICE WING OF THE MUSIC SCHOOL BUILDING AFTER SCHOOL.
I THINK YOU CAN FIND *IT* THERE.
...HUH?

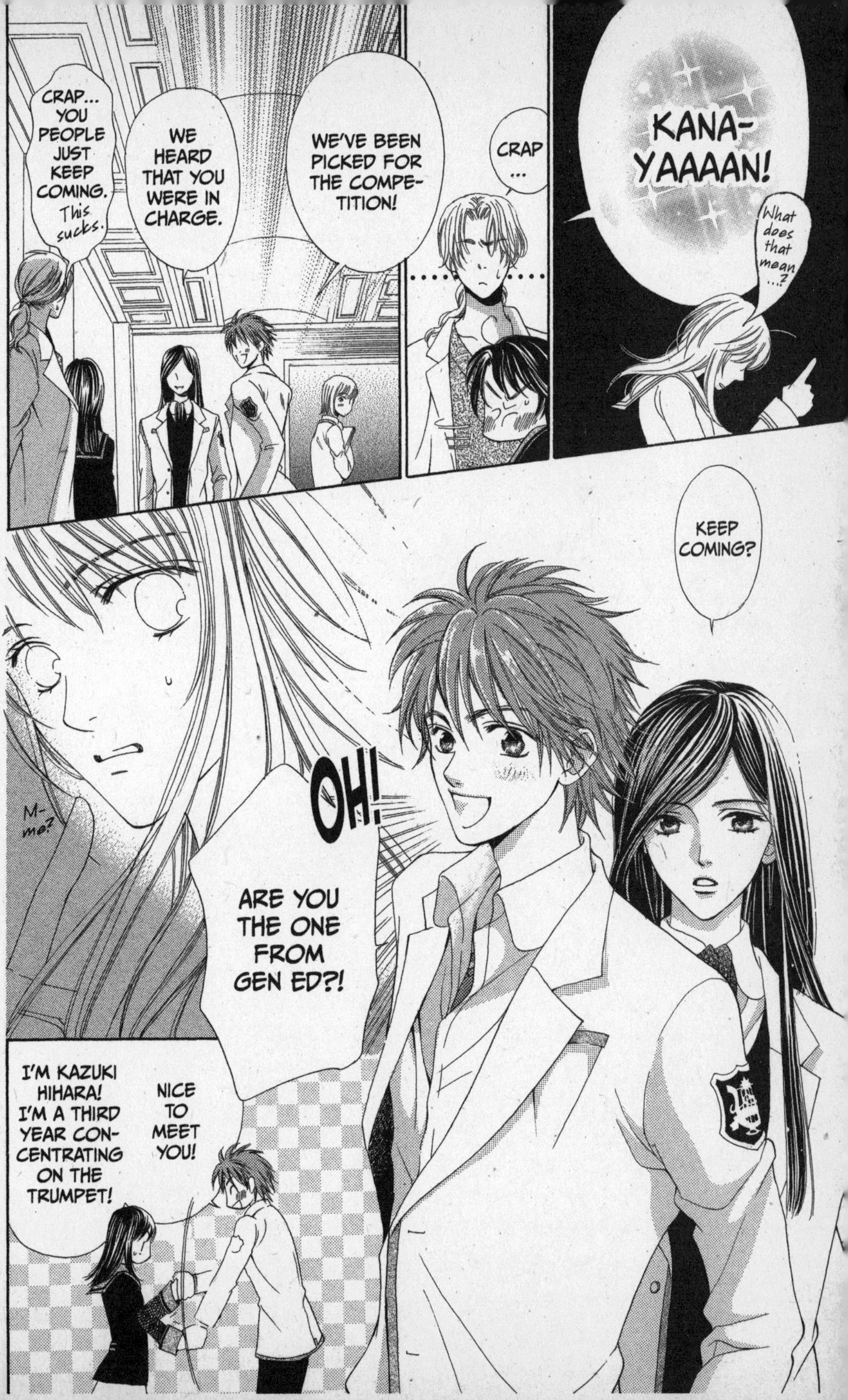
KANA-YAAAAN!
What does that mean...?
CRAP...
WE'VE BEEN PICKED FOR THE COMPETITION!
WE HEARD THAT YOU WERE IN CHARGE.
CRAP... YOU PEOPLE JUST KEEP COMING. This sucks.
KEEP COMING?
OH!
ARE YOU THE ONE FROM GEN ED?!
M-me?
NICE TO MEET YOU!
I'M KAZUKI HIHARA! I'M A THIRD YEAR CONCENTRATING ON THE TRUMPET!

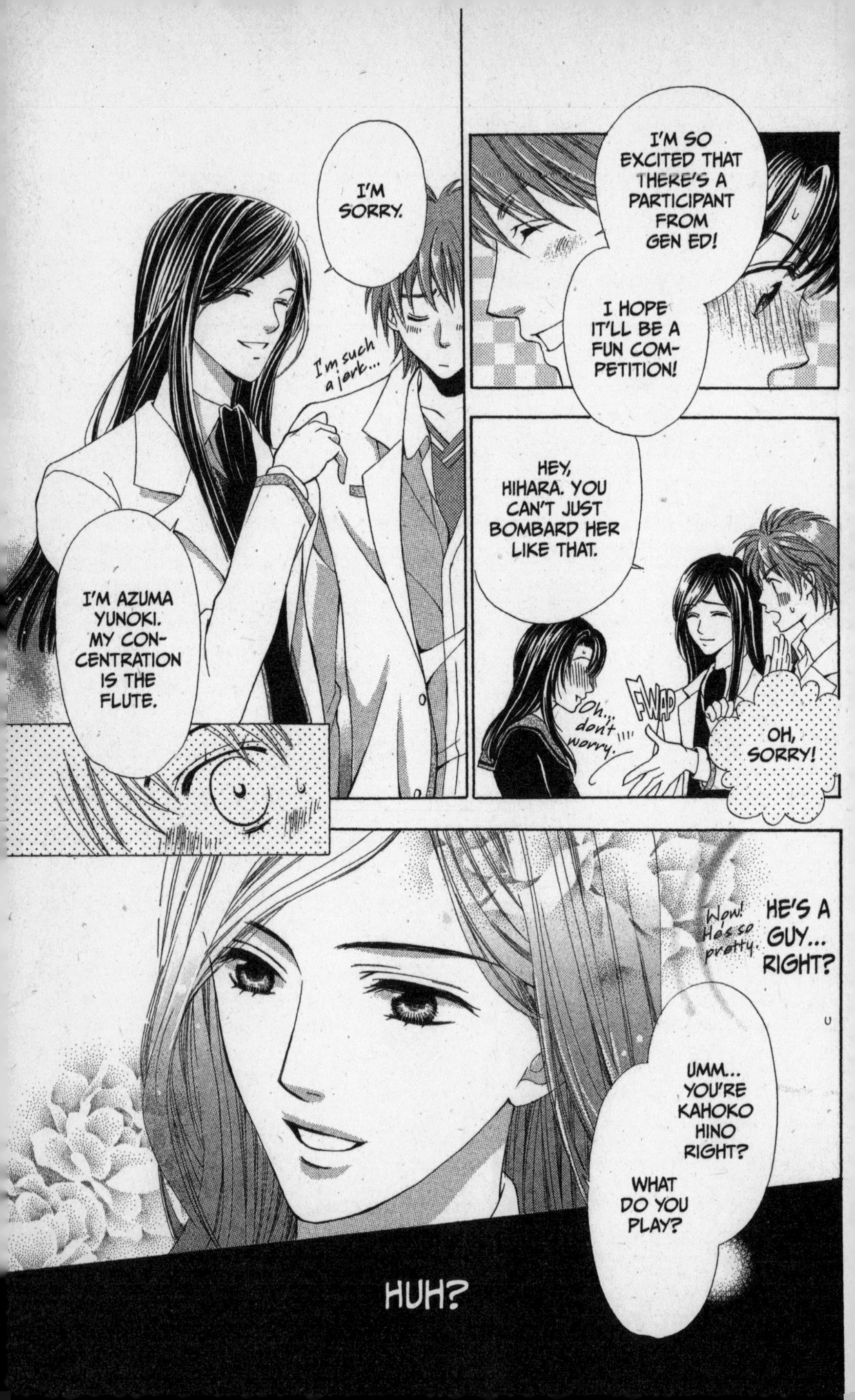
I'M SO EXCITED THAT THERE'S A PARTICIPANT FROM GEN ED!
I HOPE IT'LL BE A FUN COMPETITION!
HEY, HIHARA. YOU CAN'T JUST BOMBARD HER LIKE THAT.
FWAP
OH, SORRY!
Oh... don't worry.
I'M SORRY.
I'm such a jerk...
I'M AZUMA YUNOKI. MY CONCENTRATION IS THE FLUTE.
HE'S A GUY... RIGHT?
Wow! He's so pretty.
UMM... YOU'RE KAHOKO HINO RIGHT?
WHAT DO YOU PLAY?
HUH?

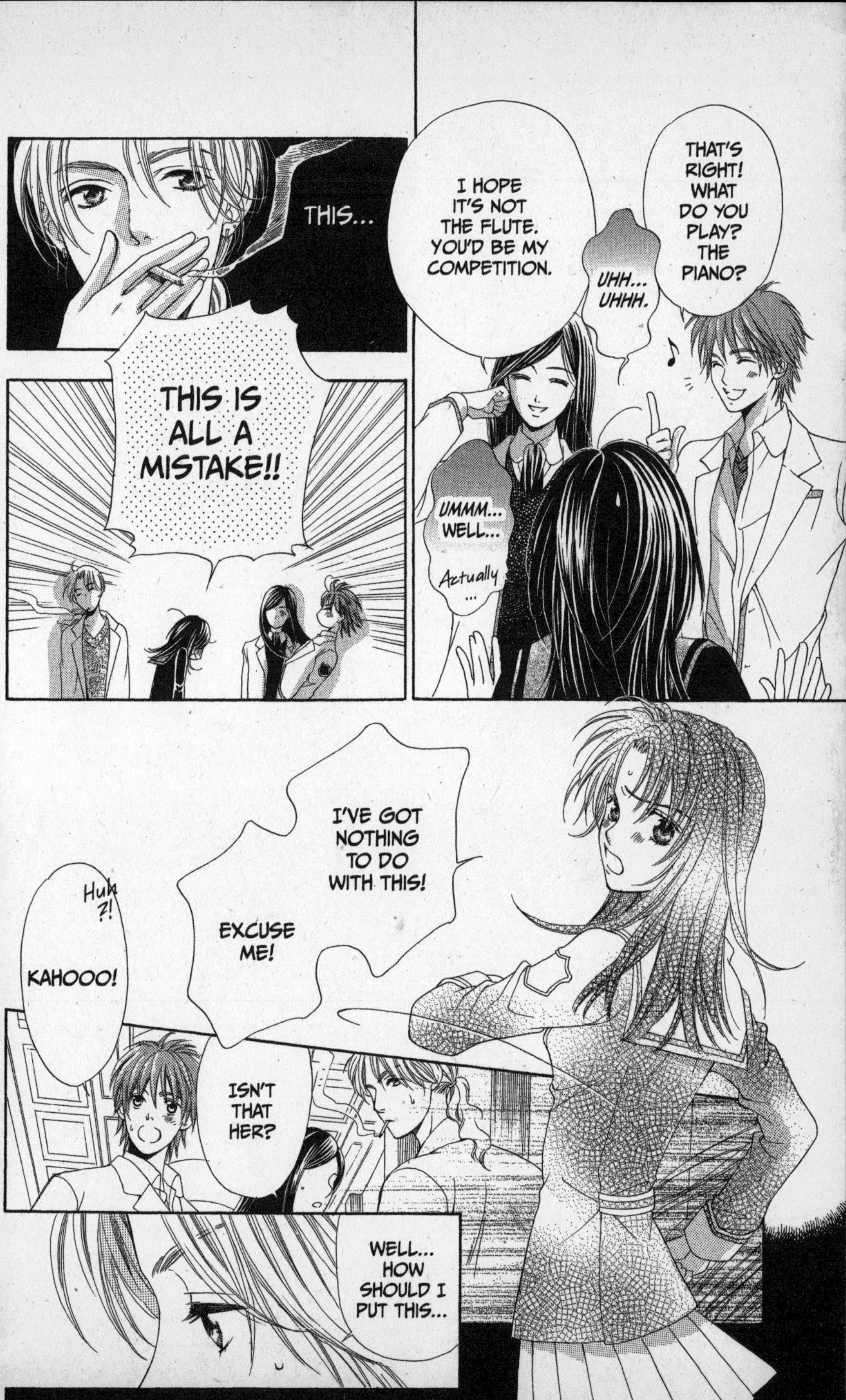
THAT'S RIGHT! WHAT DO YOU PLAY? THE PIANO?
UHH... UHHH.
I HOPE IT'S NOT THE FLUTE. YOU'D BE MY COMPETITION.
UMMM... WELL...
Actually ...
THIS...
THIS IS ALL A MISTAKE!!
I'VE GOT NOTHING TO DO WITH THIS!
EXCUSE ME!
Huh?!
KAHOOO!
ISN'T THAT HER?
WELL... HOW SHOULD I PUT THIS...

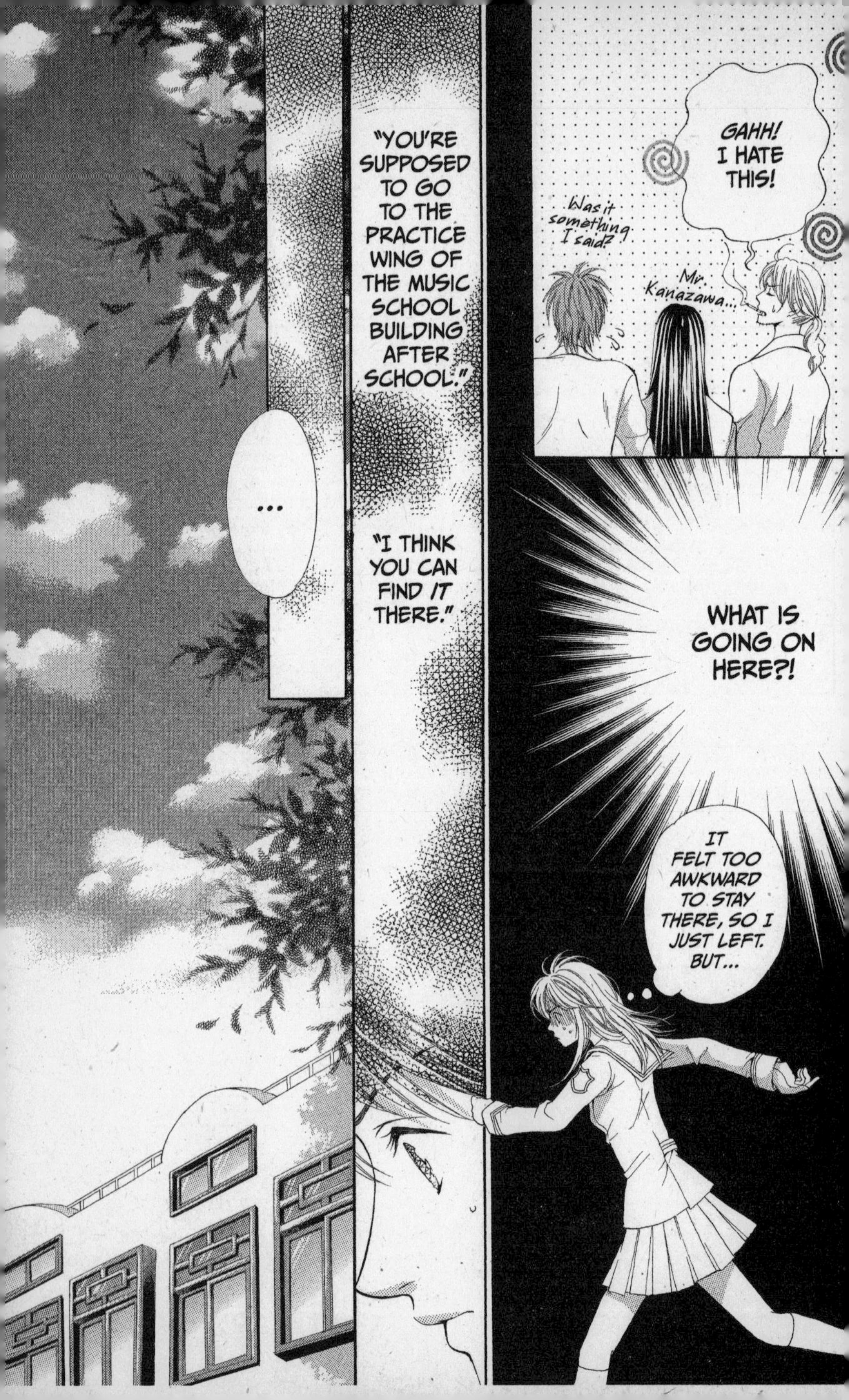
GAHH! I HATE THIS!
Mr. Kanazawa...
Was it something I said?
WHAT IS GOING ON HERE?!
IT FELT TOO AWKWARD TO STAY THERE, SO I JUST LEFT. BUT...
"YOU'RE SUPPOSED TO GO TO THE PRACTICE WING OF THE MUSIC SCHOOL BUILDING AFTER SCHOOL."
"I THINK YOU CAN FIND *IT* THERE."
...

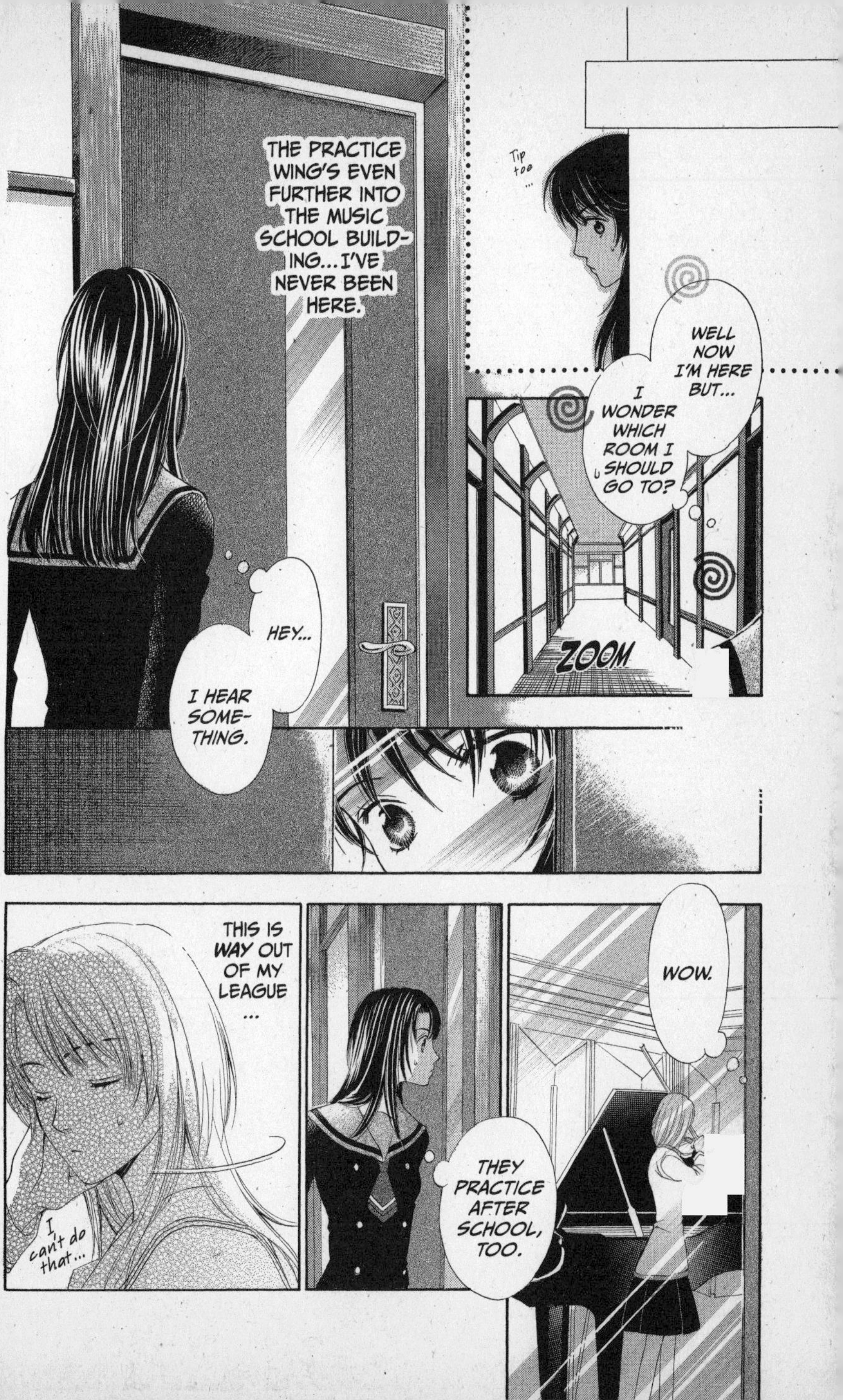
Tip toe...
THE PRACTICE WING'S EVEN FURTHER INTO THE MUSIC SCHOOL BUILDING...I'VE NEVER BEEN HERE.
WELL NOW I'M HERE BUT...
I WONDER WHICH ROOM I SHOULD GO TO?
ZOOM
HEY...
I HEAR SOMETHING.
WOW.
THEY PRACTICE AFTER SCHOOL, TOO.
THIS IS WAY OUT OF MY LEAGUE...
I can't do that...

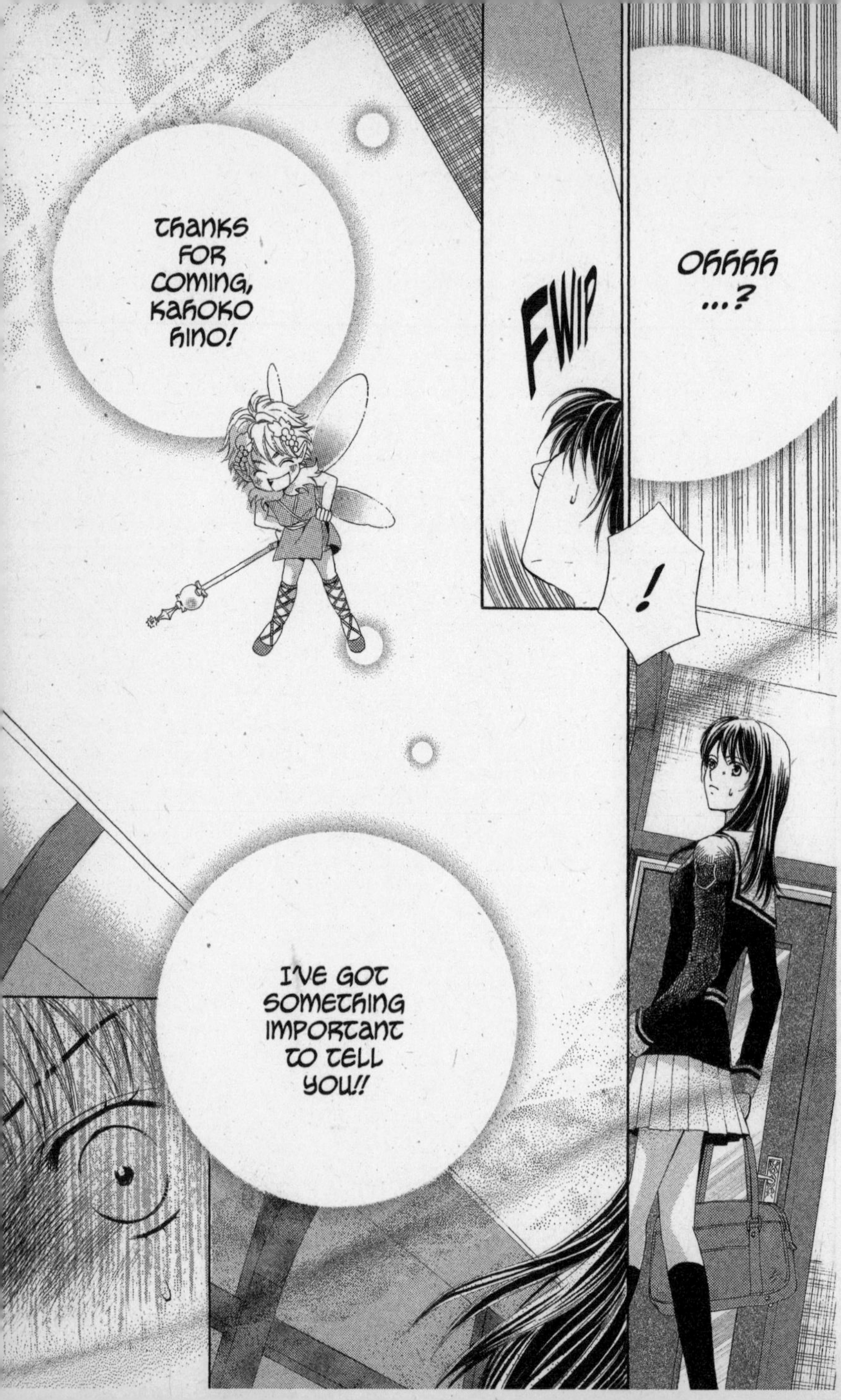
OHHHH ...?
FWIP
!
THANKS FOR COMING, KAHOKO HINO!
I'VE GOT SOMETHING IMPORTANT TO TELL YOU!!

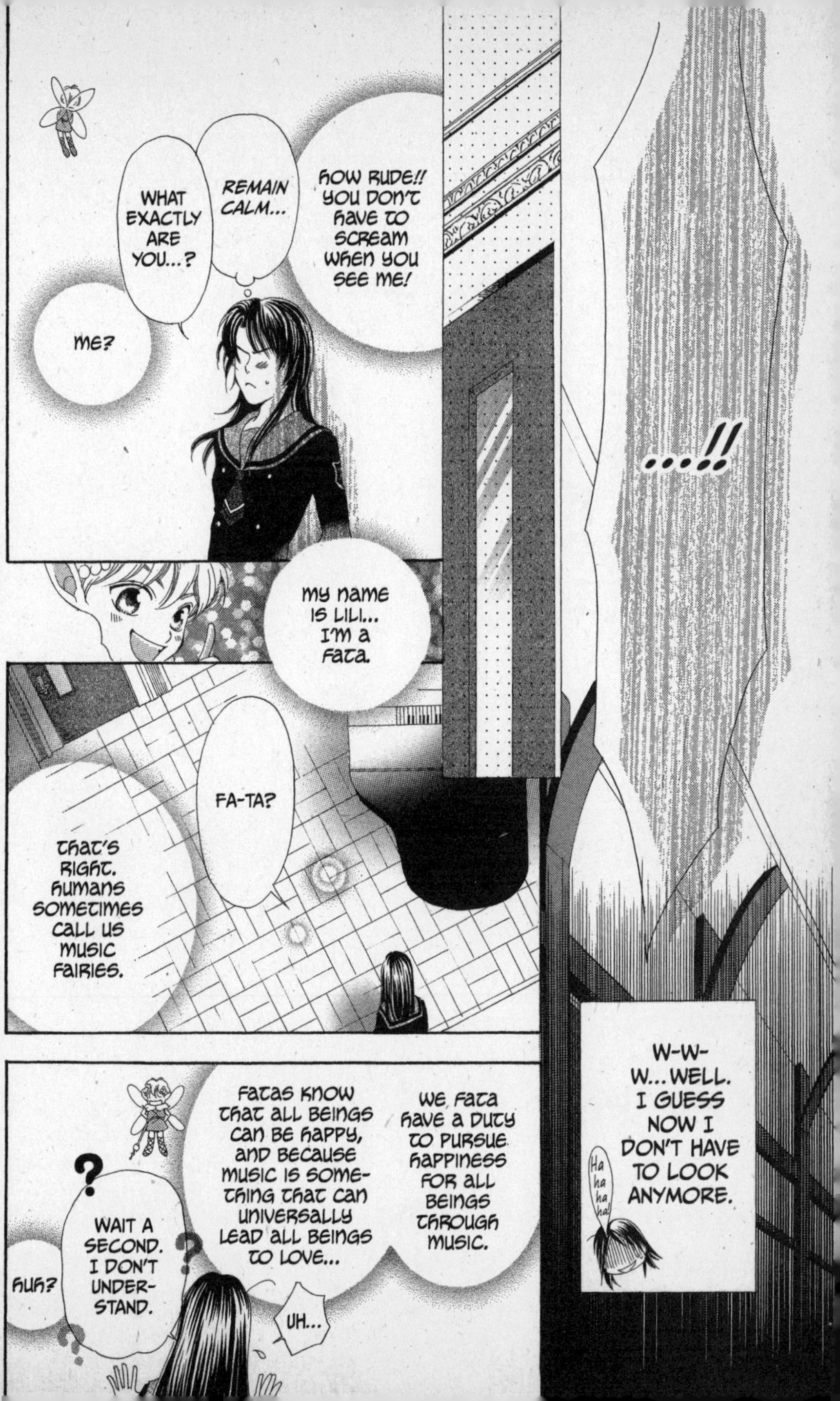
...!!
Ha ha ha!
W-W-W...WELL. I GUESS NOW I DON'T HAVE TO LOOK ANYMORE.
HOW RUDE!! YOU DON'T HAVE TO SCREAM WHEN YOU SEE ME!
REMAIN CALM...
WHAT EXACTLY ARE YOU...?
ME?
MY NAME IS LILI... I'M A FATA.
FA-TA?
THAT'S RIGHT. HUMANS SOMETIMES CALL US MUSIC FAIRIES.
WE FATA HAVE A DUTY TO PURSUE HAPPINESS FOR ALL BEINGS THROUGH MUSIC.
FATAS KNOW THAT ALL BEINGS CAN BE HAPPY, AND BECAUSE MUSIC IS SOME-THING THAT CAN UNIVERSALLY LEAD ALL BEINGS TO LOVE...
UH...
WAIT A SECOND. I DON'T UNDER-STAND.
HUH?

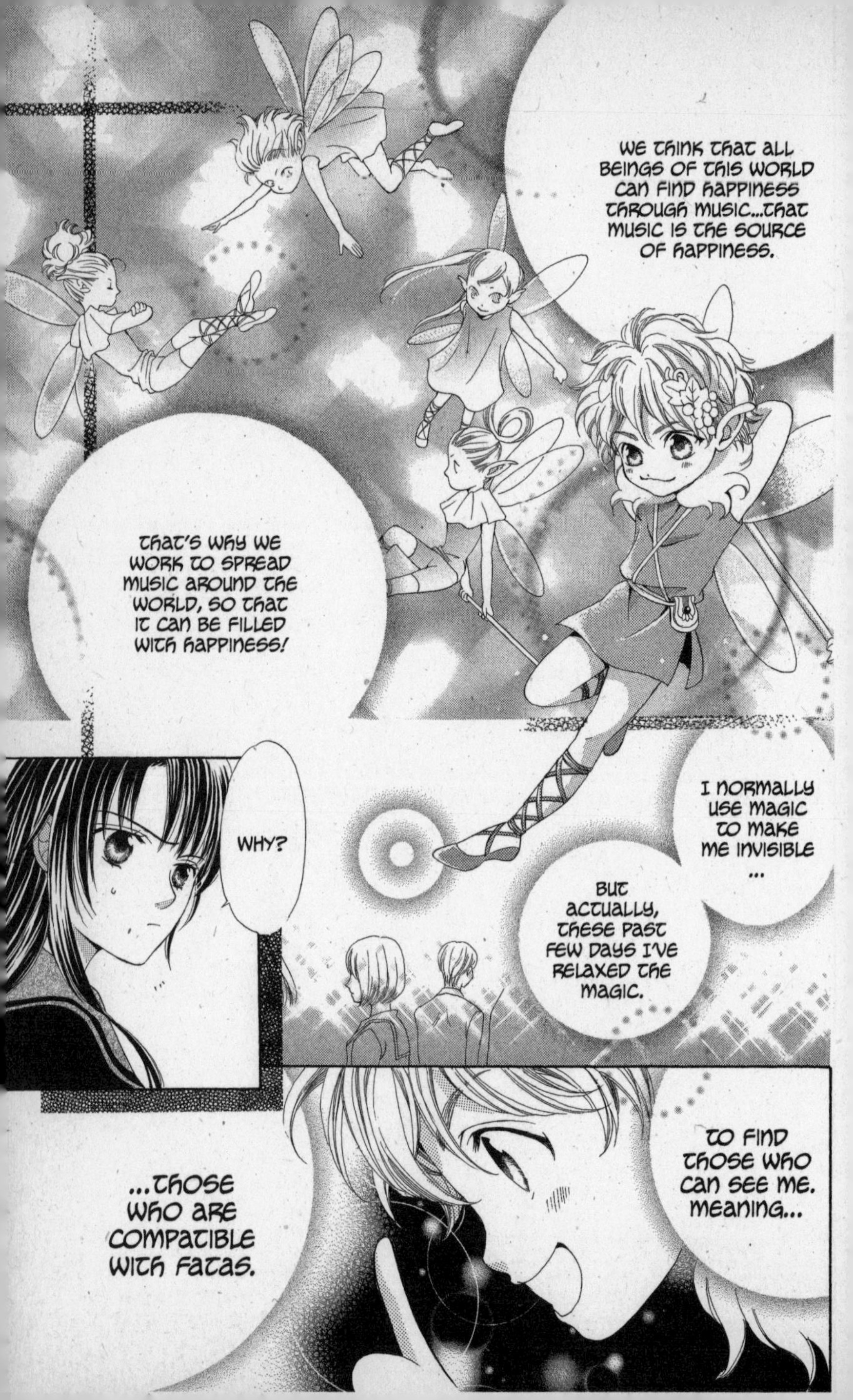
WE THINK THAT ALL BEINGS OF THIS WORLD CAN FIND HAPPINESS THROUGH MUSIC...THAT MUSIC IS THE SOURCE OF HAPPINESS.
THAT'S WHY WE WORK TO SPREAD MUSIC AROUND THE WORLD, SO THAT IT CAN BE FILLED WITH HAPPINESS!
I NORMALLY USE MAGIC TO MAKE ME INVISIBLE ...
BUT ACTUALLY, THESE PAST FEW DAYS I'VE RELAXED THE MAGIC.
WHY?
TO FIND THOSE WHO CAN SEE ME. MEANING...
...THOSE WHO ARE COMPATIBLE WITH FATAS.

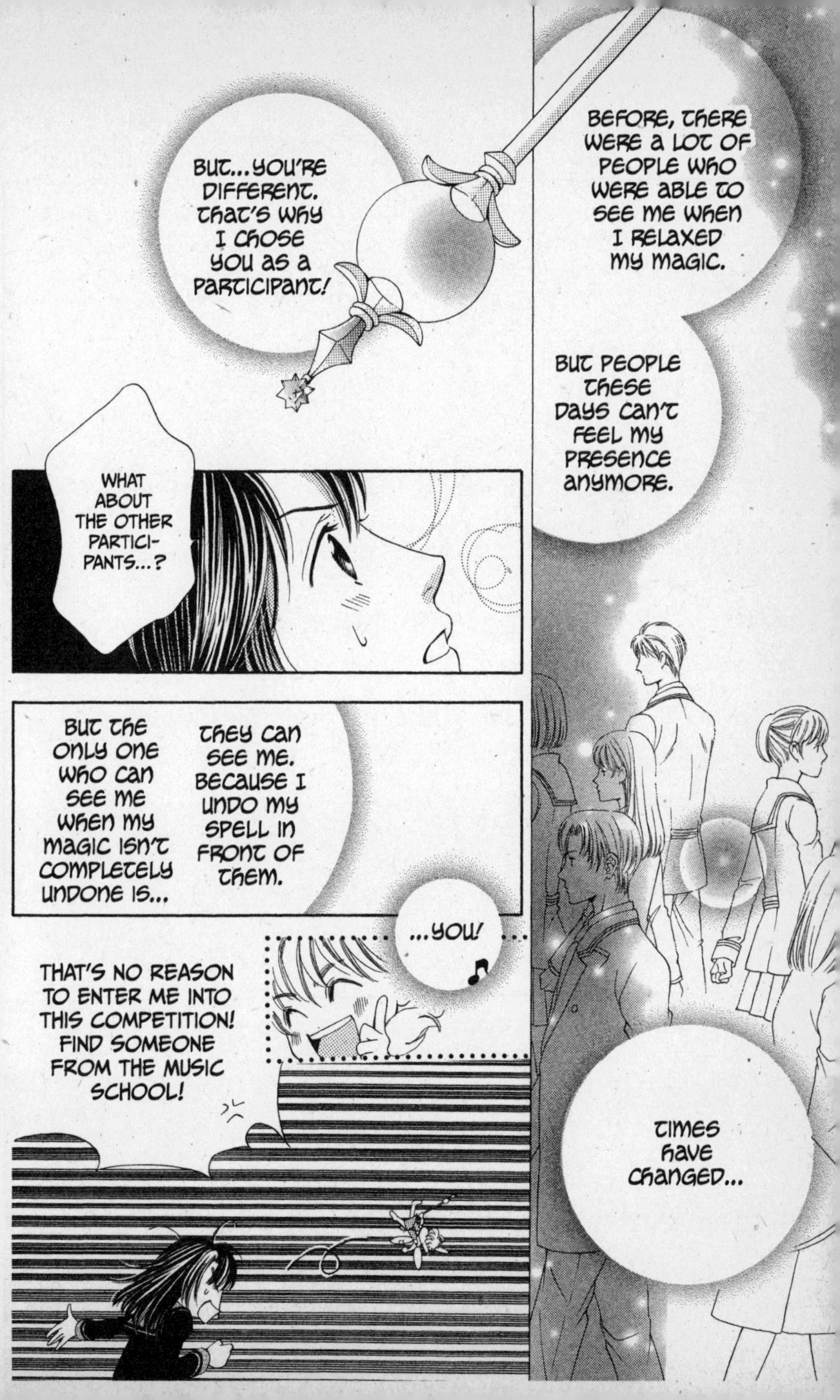

BEFORE, THERE WERE A LOT OF PEOPLE WHO WERE ABLE TO SEE ME WHEN I RELAXED MY MAGIC.
BUT PEOPLE THESE DAYS CAN'T FEEL MY PRESENCE ANYMORE.
TIMES HAVE CHANGED...
BUT...YOU'RE DIFFERENT. THAT'S WHY I CHOSE YOU AS A PARTICIPANT!
WHAT ABOUT THE OTHER PARTICI-PANTS...?
THEY CAN SEE ME. BECAUSE I UNDO MY SPELL IN FRONT OF THEM.
BUT THE ONLY ONE WHO CAN SEE ME WHEN MY MAGIC ISN'T COMPLETELY UNDONE IS...
...YOU!
THAT'S NO REASON TO ENTER ME INTO THIS COMPETITION! FIND SOMEONE FROM THE MUSIC SCHOOL!

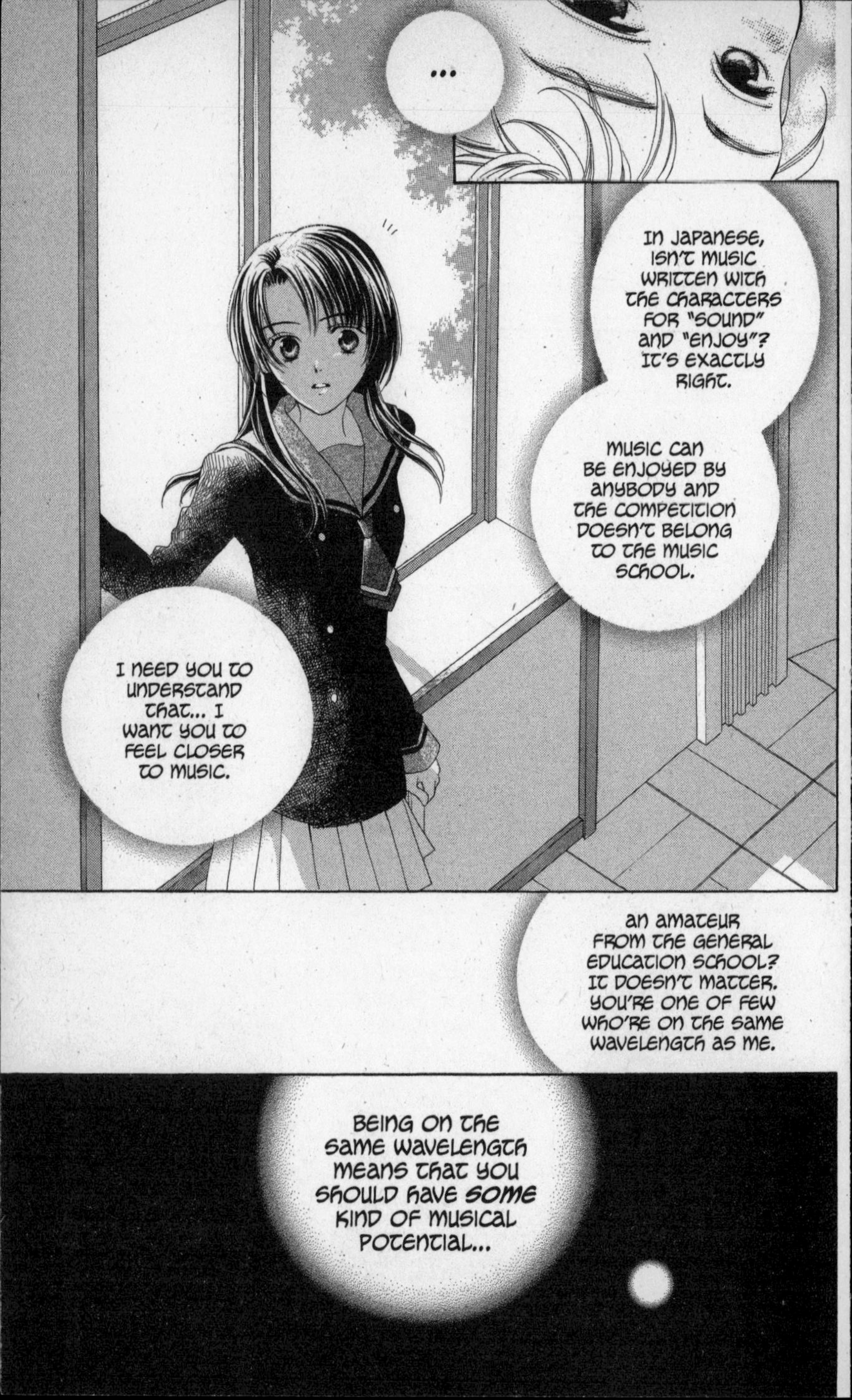
...
IN JAPANESE, ISN'T MUSIC WRITTEN WITH THE CHARACTERS FOR "SOUND" AND "ENJOY"? IT'S EXACTLY RIGHT.
MUSIC CAN BE ENJOYED BY ANYBODY AND THE COMPETITION DOESN'T BELONG TO THE MUSIC SCHOOL.
I NEED YOU TO UNDERSTAND THAT... I WANT YOU TO FEEL CLOSER TO MUSIC.
AN AMATEUR FROM THE GENERAL EDUCATION SCHOOL? IT DOESN'T MATTER. YOU'RE ONE OF FEW WHO'RE ON THE SAME WAVELENGTH AS ME.
BEING ON THE SAME WAVELENGTH MEANS THAT YOU SHOULD HAVE *SOME* KIND OF MUSICAL POTENTIAL...

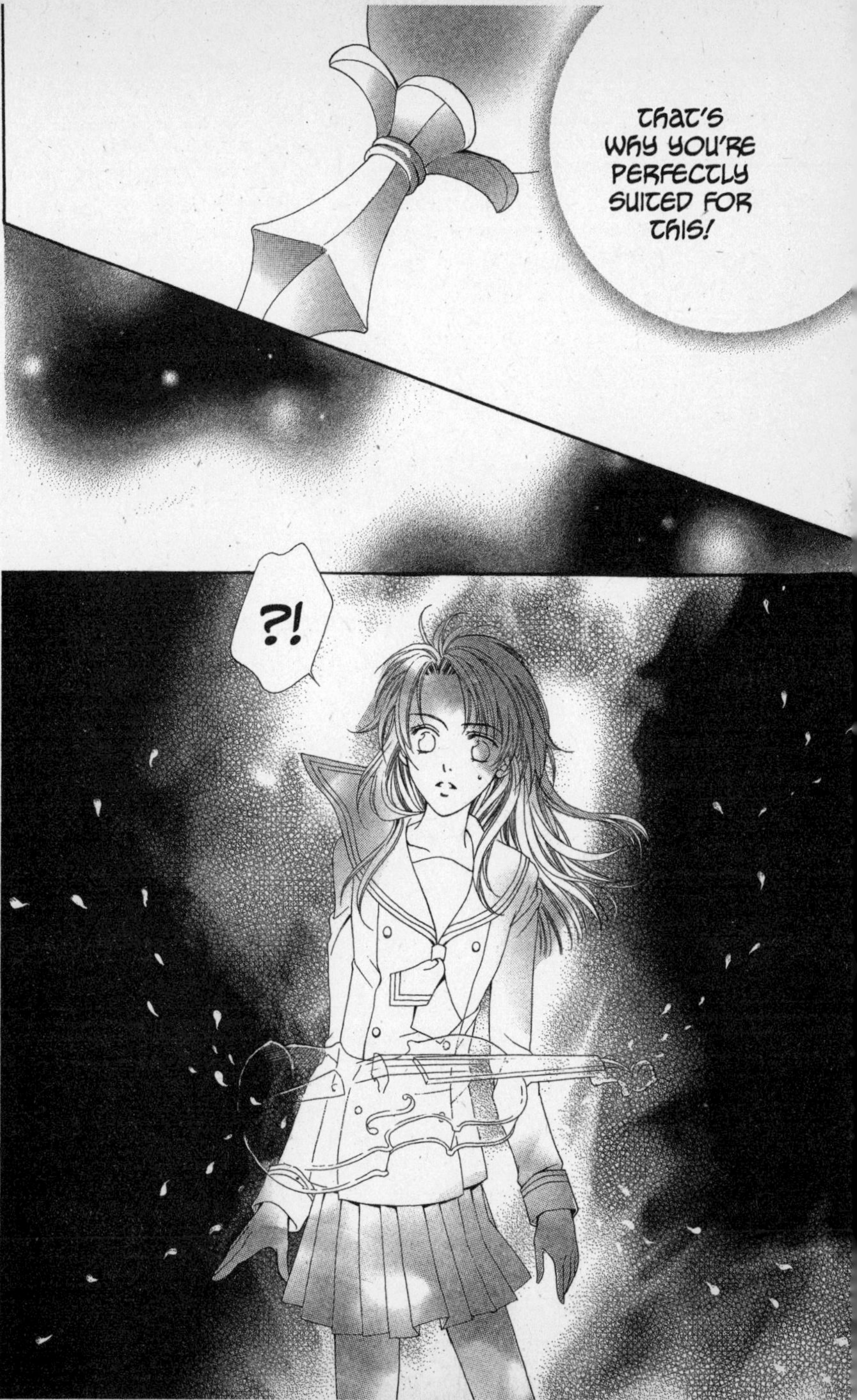
THAT'S WHY YOU'RE PERFECTLY SUITED FOR THIS!
?!

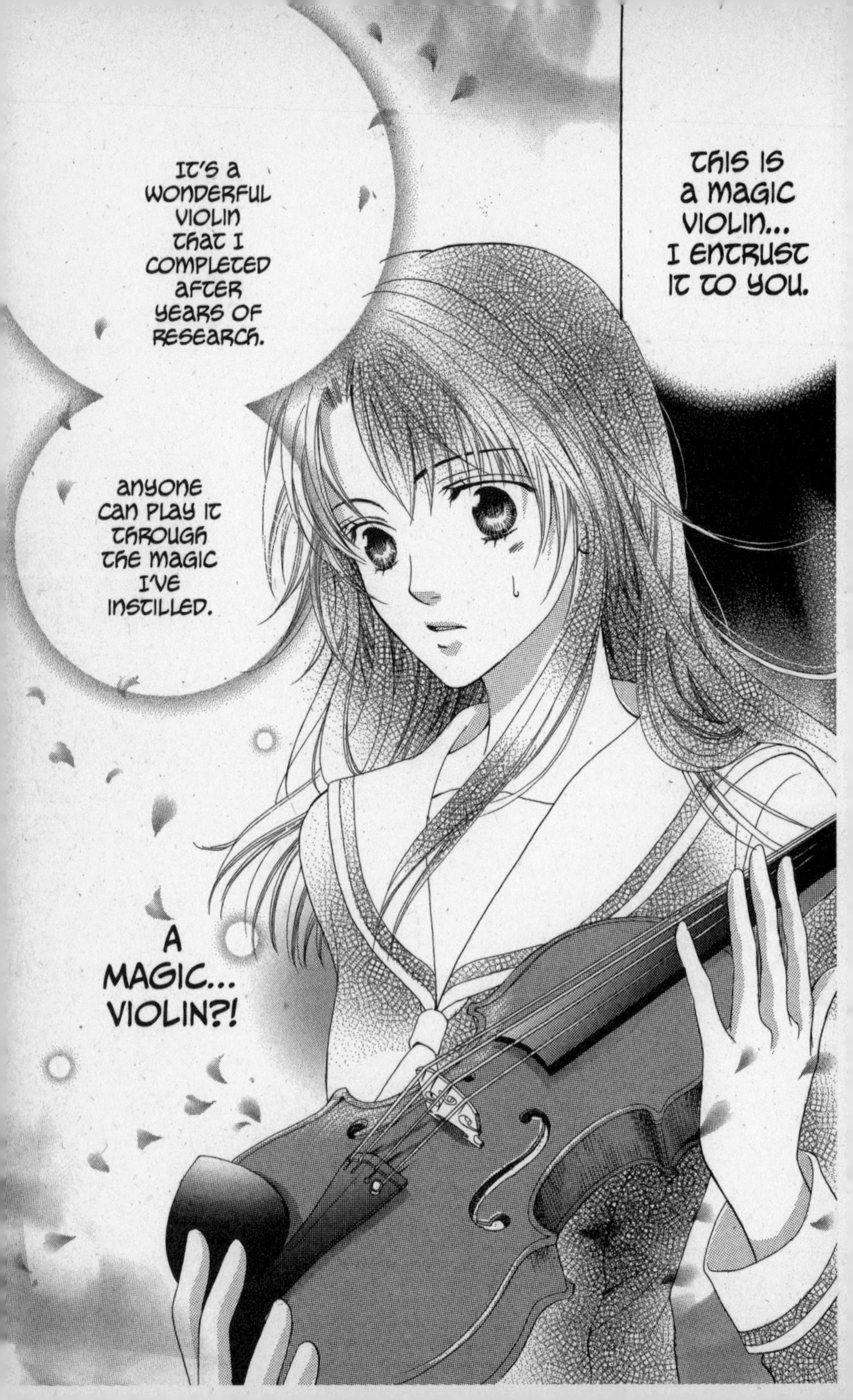
THIS IS A MAGIC VIOLIN... I ENTRUST IT TO YOU.
IT'S A WONDERFUL VIOLIN THAT I COMPLETED AFTER YEARS OF RESEARCH.
ANYONE CAN PLAY IT THROUGH THE MAGIC I'VE INSTILLED.
A MAGIC... VIOLIN?!

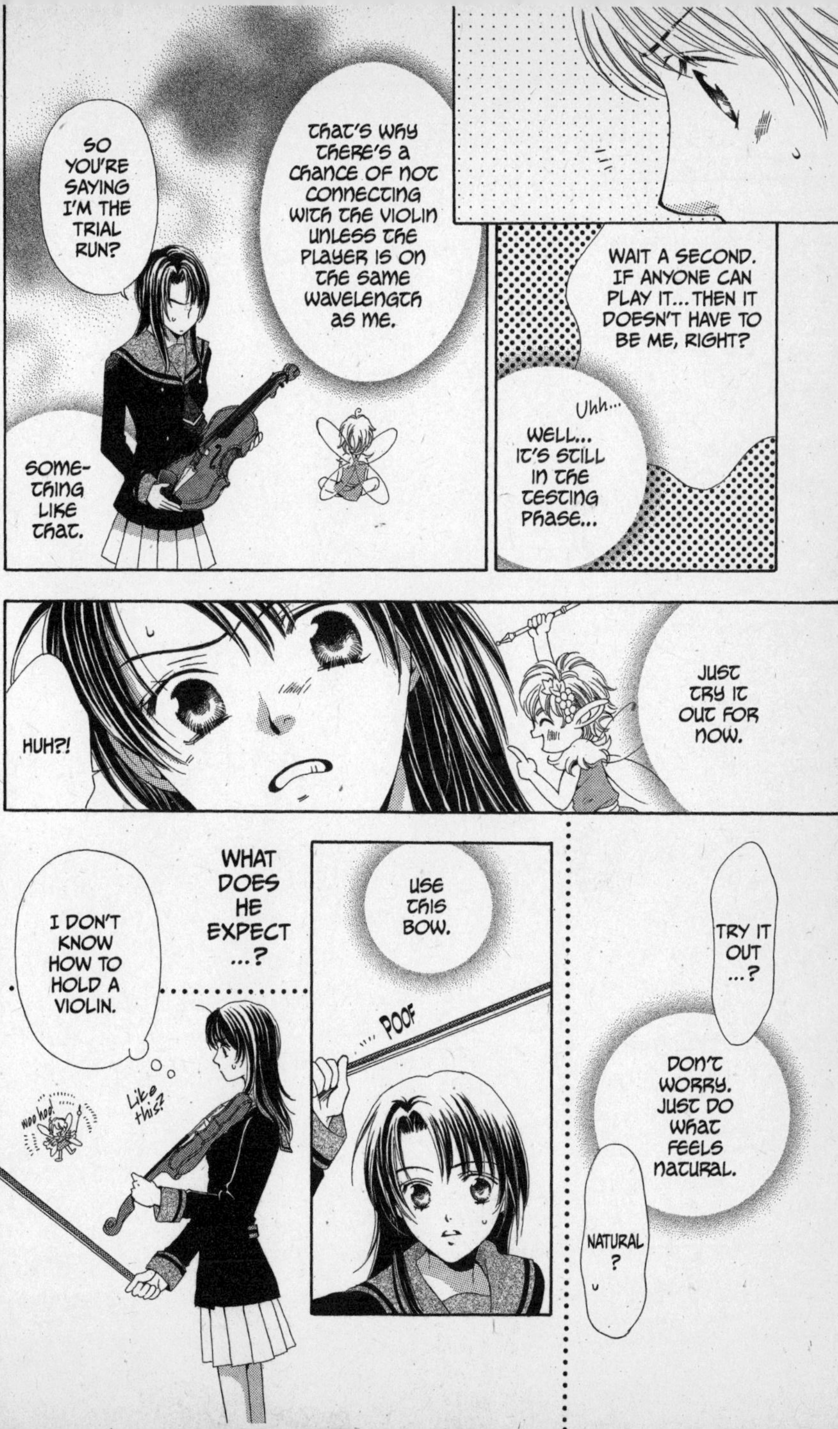
WAIT A SECOND. IF ANYONE CAN PLAY IT... THEN IT DOESN'T HAVE TO BE ME, RIGHT?
Uhh...
WELL... IT'S STILL IN THE TESTING PHASE...
THAT'S WHY THERE'S A CHANCE OF NOT CONNECTING WITH THE VIOLIN UNLESS THE PLAYER IS ON THE SAME WAVELENGTH AS ME.
SO YOU'RE SAYING I'M THE TRIAL RUN?
SOME-THING LIKE THAT.
JUST TRY IT OUT FOR NOW.
HUH?!
TRY IT OUT ...?
DON'T WORRY. JUST DO WHAT FEELS NATURAL.
NATURAL ?
USE THIS BOW.
POOF
WHAT DOES HE EXPECT ...?
I DON'T KNOW HOW TO HOLD A VIOLIN.
Like this?
woo hoo!

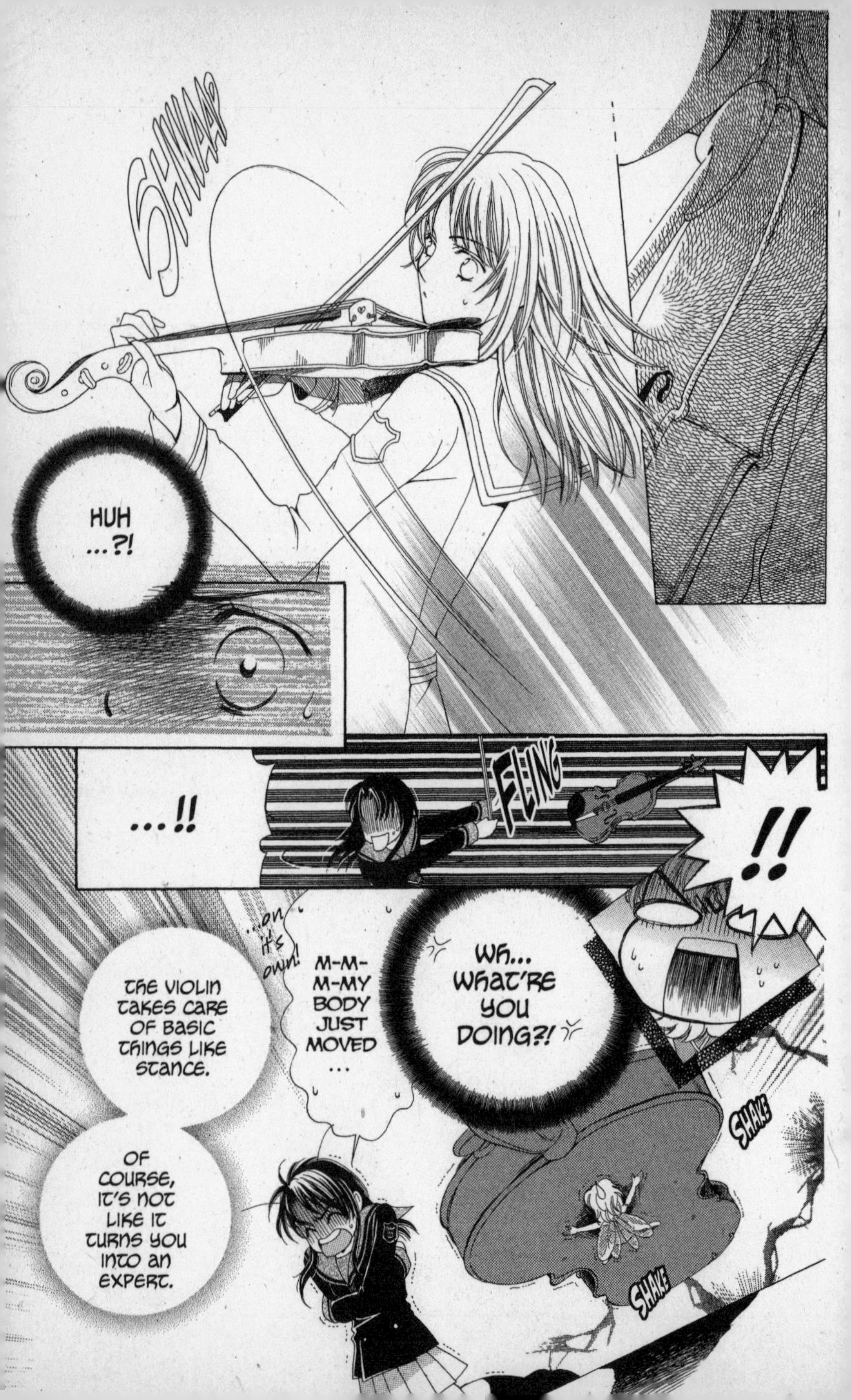
SHWAP
HUH ...?!
!!
FLING
...!!
WH... WHAT'RE YOU DOING?!
M-M-M-MY BODY JUST MOVED ...
...ON IT'S OWN!
THE VIOLIN TAKES CARE OF BASIC THINGS LIKE STANCE.
OF COURSE, IT'S NOT LIKE IT TURNS YOU INTO AN EXPERT.
SHAKE
SHAKE

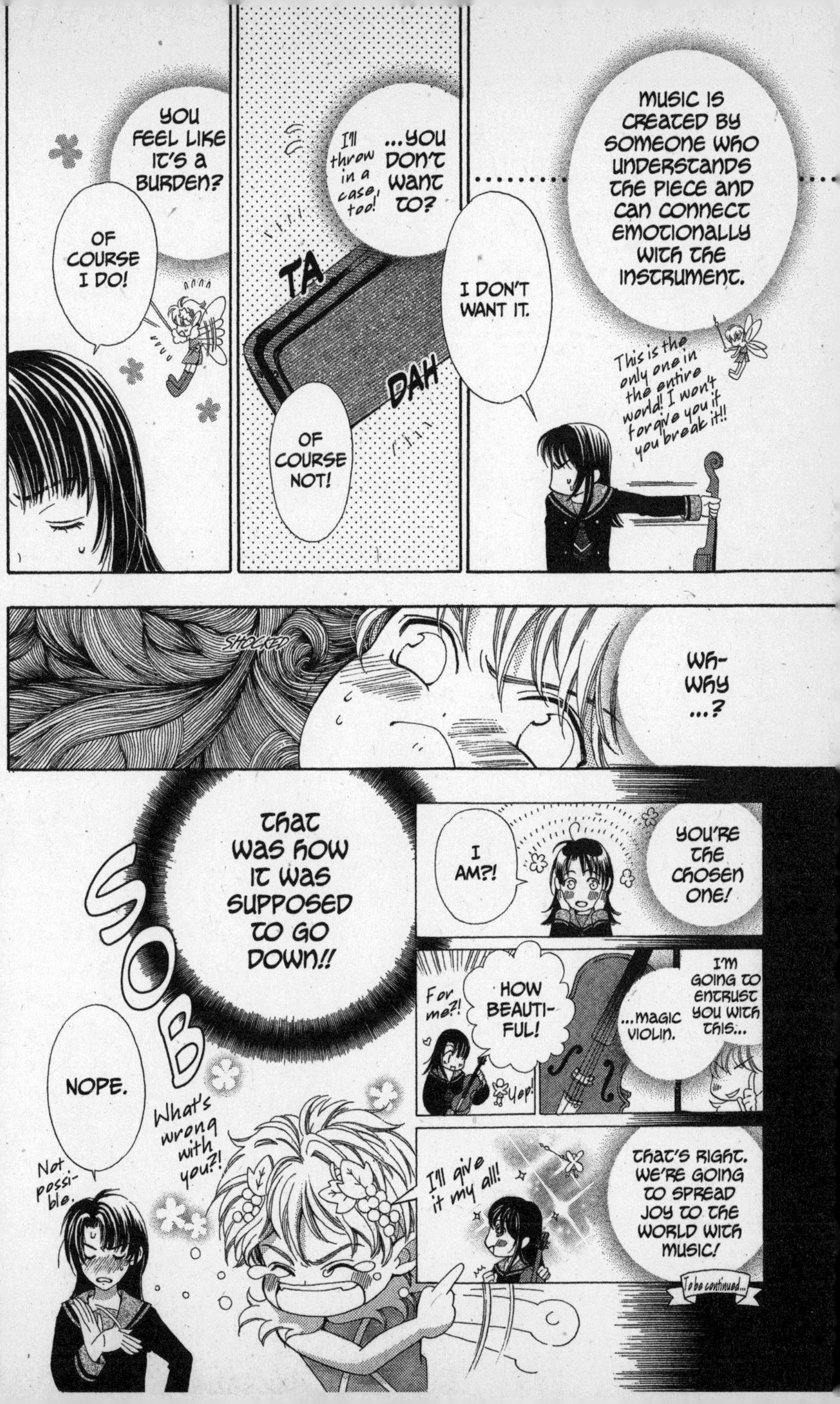
MUSIC IS CREATED BY SOMEONE WHO UNDERSTANDS THE PIECE AND CAN CONNECT EMOTIONALLY WITH THE INSTRUMENT.
I DON'T WANT IT.
This is the only one in the entire world! I won't forgive you if you break it!!
...YOU DON'T WANT TO?
I'll throw in a case, too!
TA
DAH
OF COURSE NOT!
YOU FEEL LIKE IT'S A BURDEN?
OF COURSE I DO!
SHOCKED
WH-WHY ...?
YOU'RE THE CHOSEN ONE!
I AM?!
I'M GOING TO ENTRUST YOU WITH THIS...
...MAGIC VIOLIN.
HOW BEAUTIFUL!
For me?!
Yep!
THAT'S RIGHT. WE'RE GOING TO SPREAD JOY TO THE WORLD WITH MUSIC!
I'll give it my all!
To be continued...
THAT WAS HOW IT WAS SUPPOSED TO GO DOWN!!
SOB
NOPE.
What's wrong with you?!
Not possi-ble.

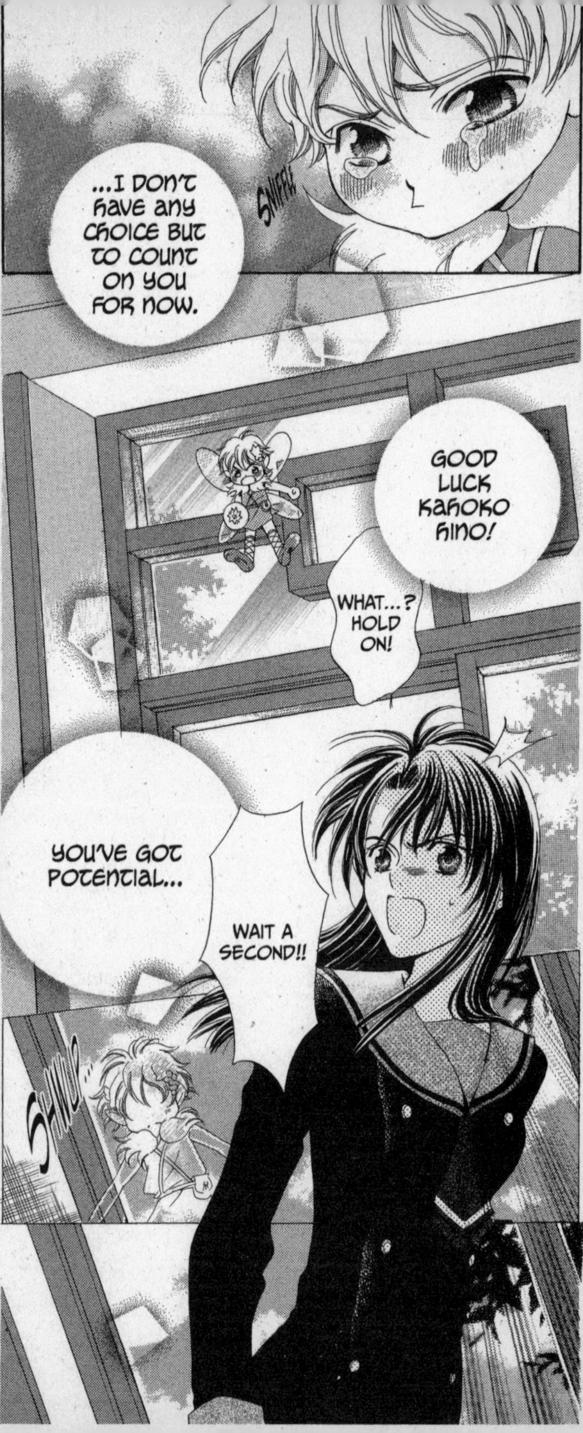
...I DON'T HAVE ANY CHOICE BUT TO COUNT ON YOU FOR NOW.
GOOD LUCK KAHOKO HINO!
WHAT...? HOLD ON!
YOU'VE GOT POTENTIAL...
WAIT A SECOND!!

Violin ①

Before the series, I went to a violin teacher to learn how to hold and play the violin. I've taken piano lessons before, but I'm pretty much music illiterate... (I've got to study...) I love the shape of the violin. I think there's something feminine about its curves... I think the wooden texture gives it a warm feel, though I admit it's difficult to draw.

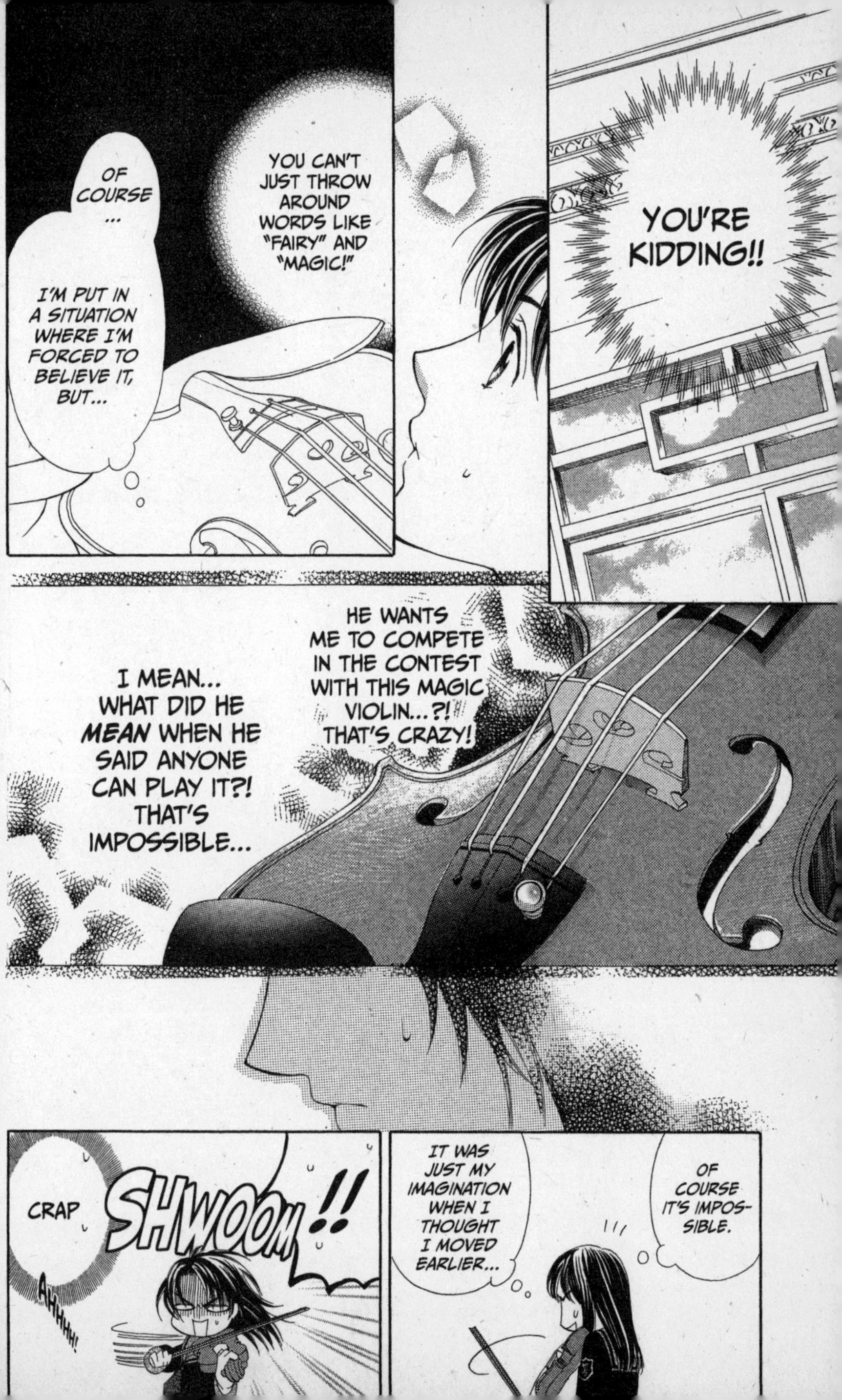
YOU'RE KIDDING!!
YOU CAN'T JUST THROW AROUND WORDS LIKE "FAIRY" AND "MAGIC!"
OF COURSE ...
I'M PUT IN A SITUATION WHERE I'M FORCED TO BELIEVE IT, BUT...
HE WANTS ME TO COMPETE IN THE CONTEST WITH THIS MAGIC VIOLIN...?! THAT'S CRAZY!
I MEAN... WHAT DID HE MEAN WHEN HE SAID ANYONE CAN PLAY IT?! THAT'S IMPOSSIBLE...
OF COURSE IT'S IMPOSSIBLE.
IT WAS JUST MY IMAGINATION WHEN I THOUGHT I MOVED EARLIER...
SHWOOM!!
CRAP
AHHHHH!

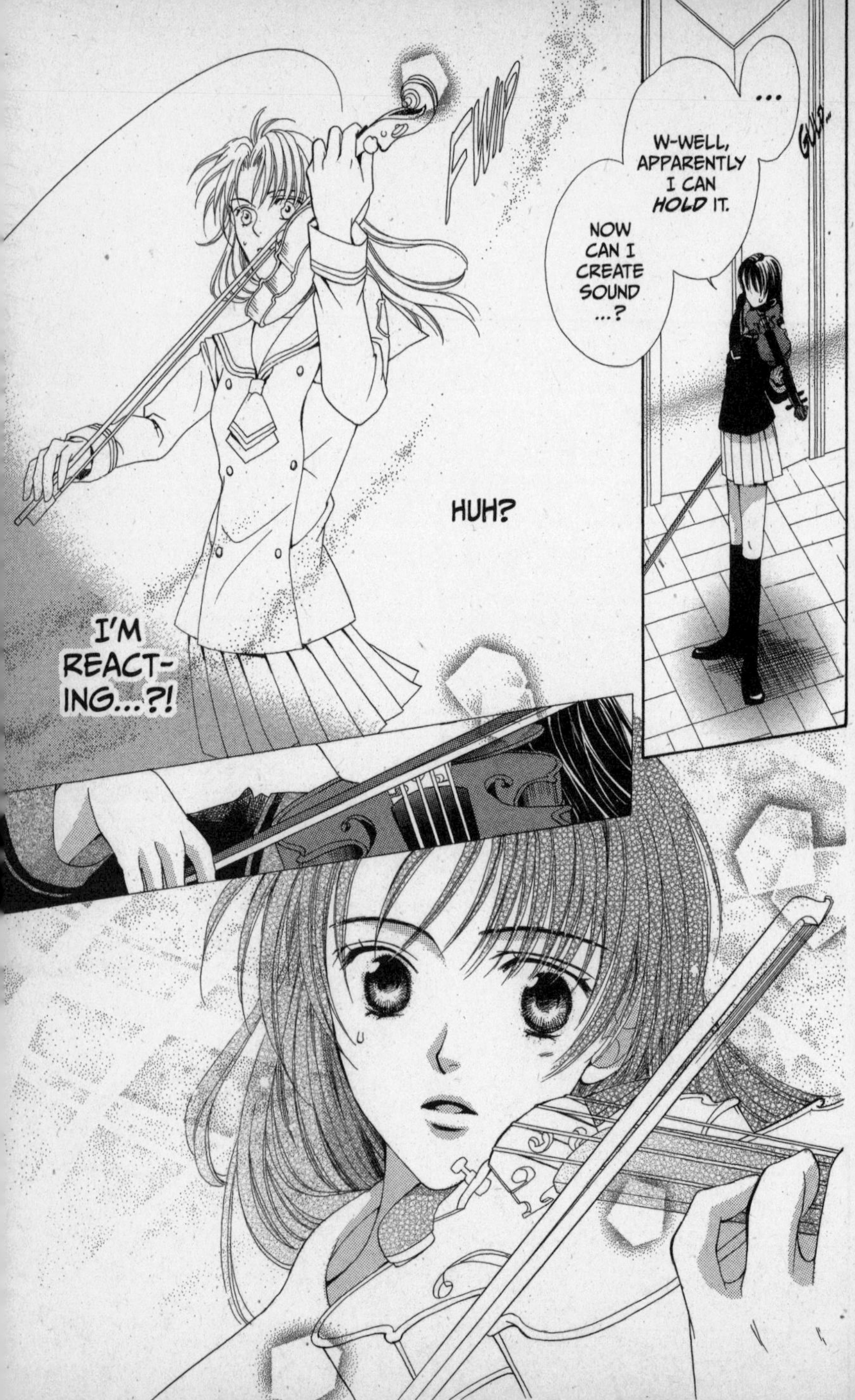
...
GULP...
W-WELL, APPARENTLY I CAN *HOLD* IT.
NOW CAN I CREATE SOUND ...?
FWIP
HUH?
I'M REACT-ING...?!

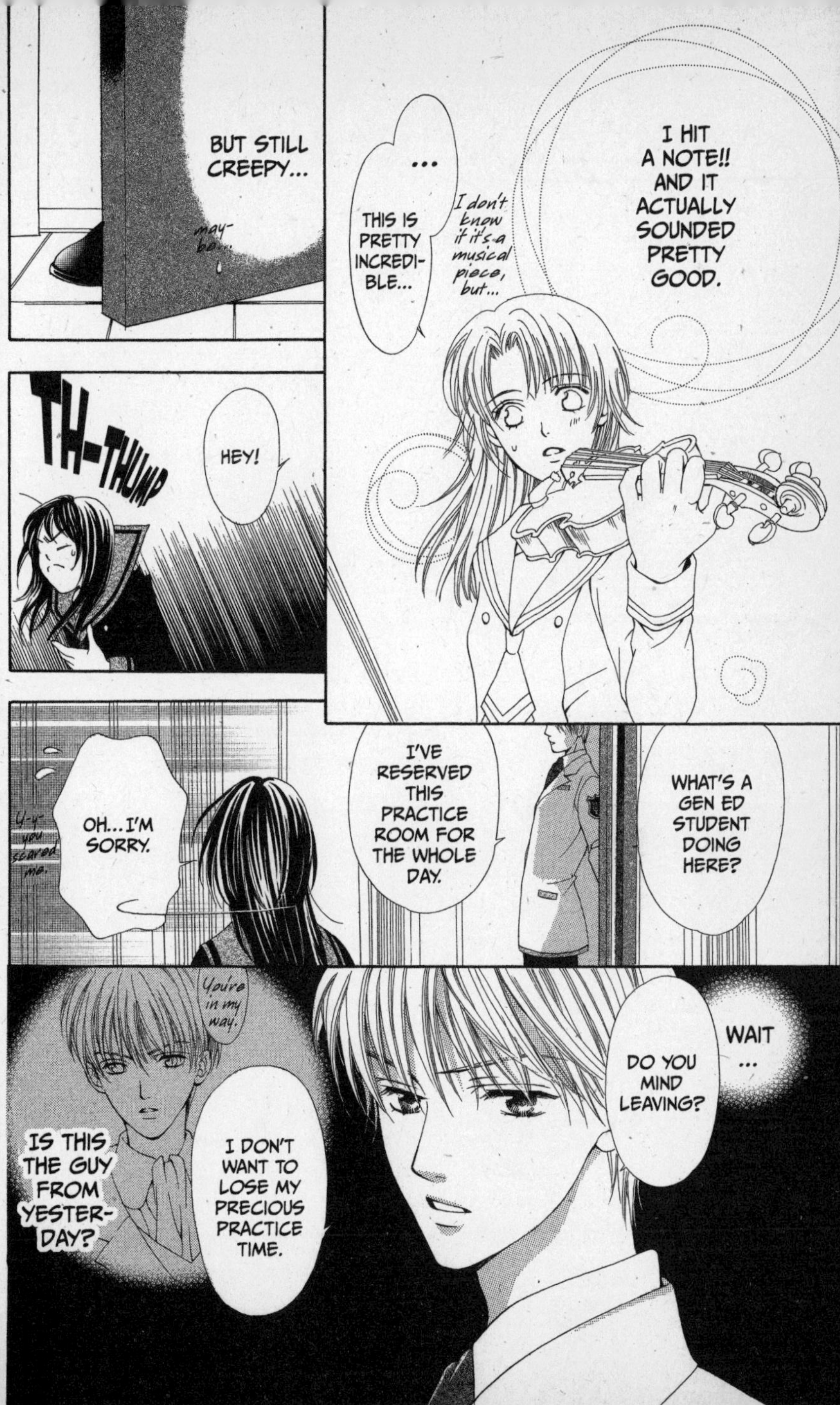
I HIT A NOTE!! AND IT ACTUALLY SOUNDED PRETTY GOOD.
I don't know if it's a musical piece, but...
... THIS IS PRETTY INCREDIBLE...
BUT STILL CREEPY...
maybe...
TH-THUMP
HEY!
WHAT'S A GEN ED STUDENT DOING HERE?
I'VE RESERVED THIS PRACTICE ROOM FOR THE WHOLE DAY.
OH...I'M SORRY.
Y-y-you scared me.
WAIT ...
DO YOU MIND LEAVING?
You're in my way.
I DON'T WANT TO LOSE MY PRECIOUS PRACTICE TIME.
IS THIS THE GUY FROM YESTERDAY?

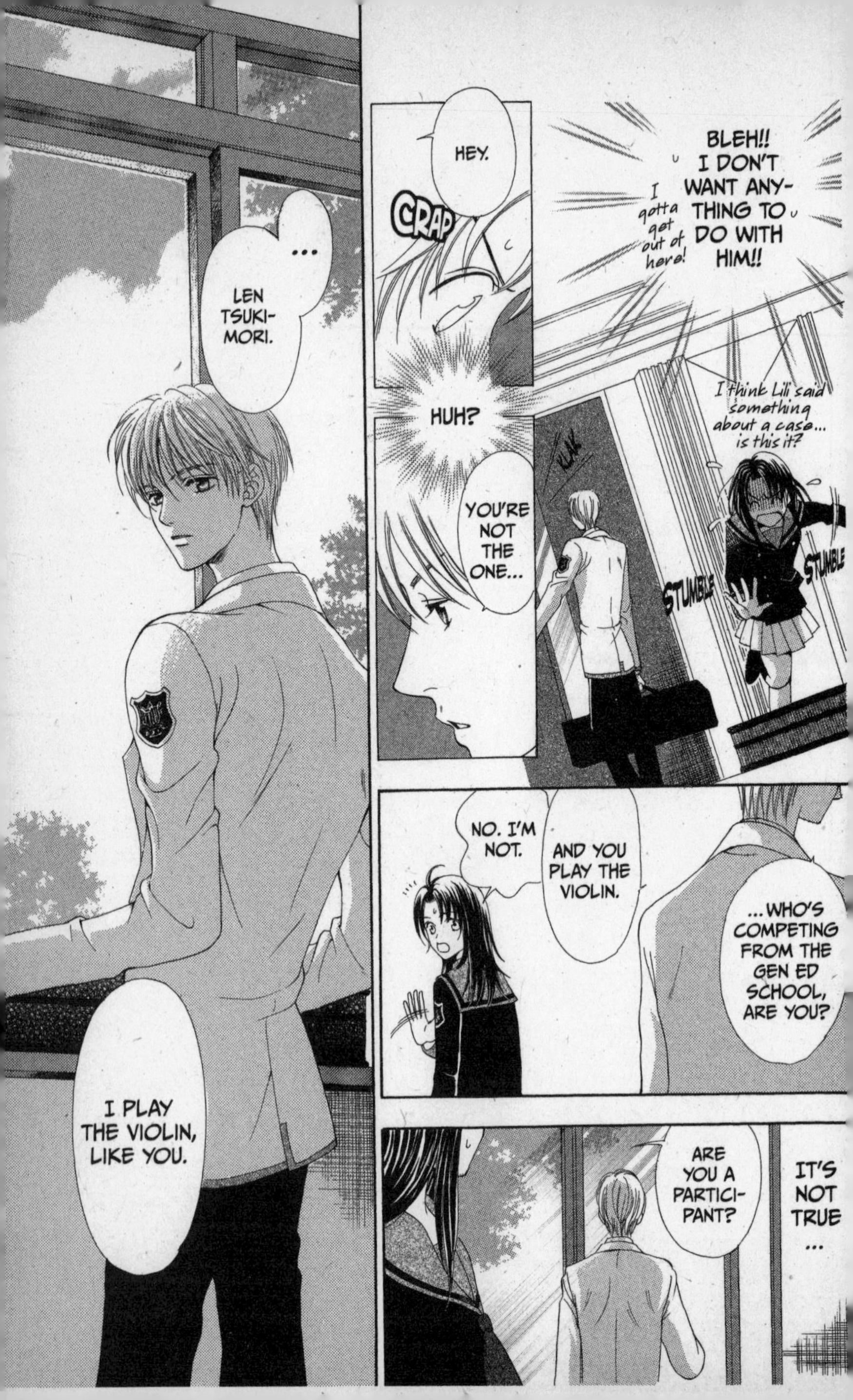
BLEH!! I DON'T WANT ANYTHING TO DO WITH HIM!!
I gotta get out of here!
I think Lili said something about a case... is this it?
KLAK
STUMBLE
STUMBLE
HEY.
CRAP
HUH?
YOU'RE NOT THE ONE...
...WHO'S COMPETING FROM THE GEN ED SCHOOL, ARE YOU?
AND YOU PLAY THE VIOLIN.
NO. I'M NOT.
IT'S NOT TRUE...
ARE YOU A PARTICIPANT?
...
LEN TSUKIMORI.
I PLAY THE VIOLIN, LIKE YOU.

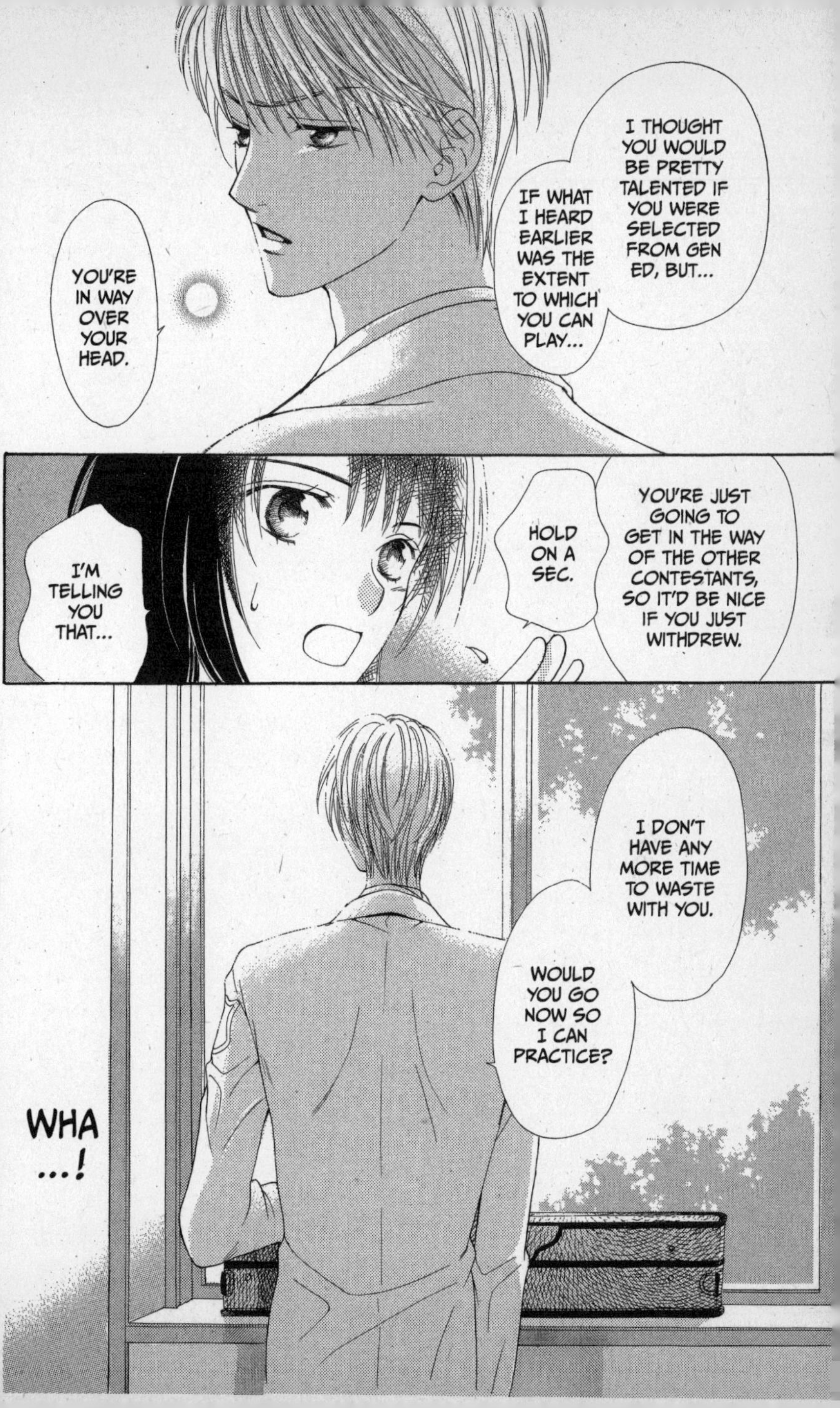
I THOUGHT YOU WOULD BE PRETTY TALENTED IF YOU WERE SELECTED FROM GEN ED, BUT...
IF WHAT I HEARD EARLIER WAS THE EXTENT TO WHICH YOU CAN PLAY...
YOU'RE IN WAY OVER YOUR HEAD.
YOU'RE JUST GOING TO GET IN THE WAY OF THE OTHER CONTESTANTS, SO IT'D BE NICE IF YOU JUST WITHDREW.
HOLD ON A SEC.
I'M TELLING YOU THAT...
I DON'T HAVE ANY MORE TIME TO WASTE WITH YOU.
WOULD YOU GO NOW SO I CAN PRACTICE?
WHA ...!

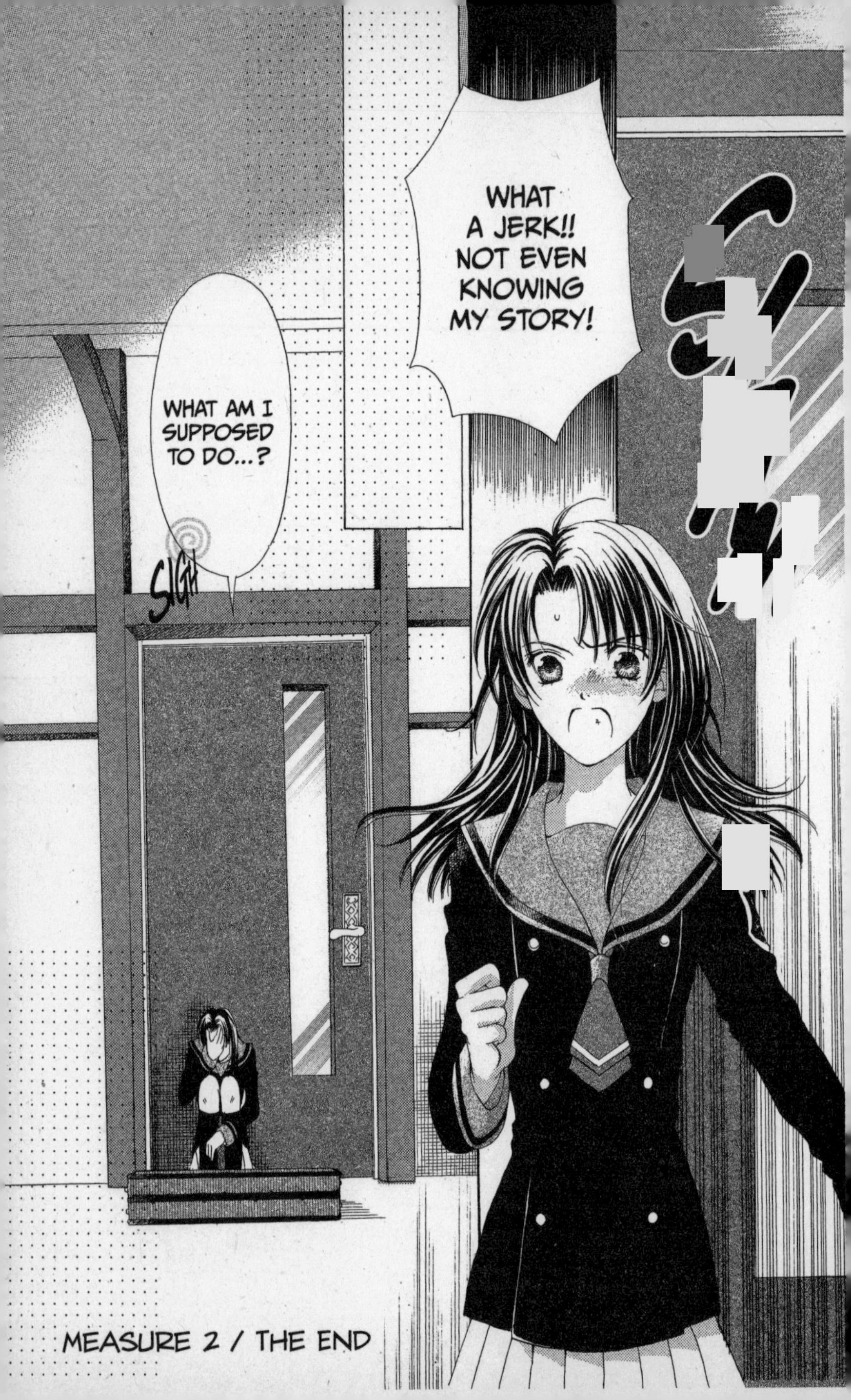
WHAT A JERK!! NOT EVEN KNOWING MY STORY!
WHAT AM I SUPPOSED TO DO...?
SIGH
MEASURE 2 / THE END

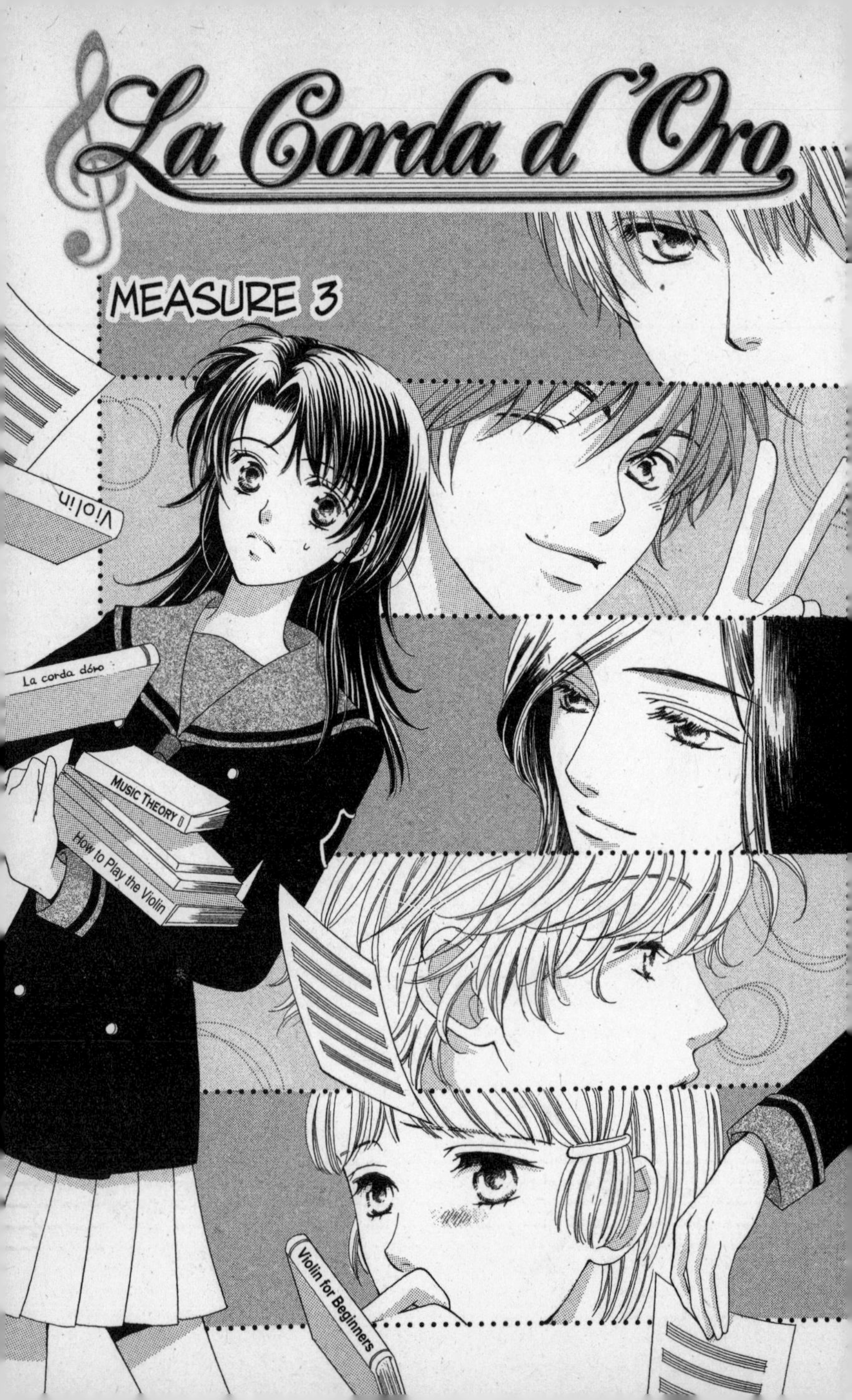
La Corda d'Oro
MEASURE 3
Violin
La corda dóro
MUSIC THEORY
How to Play the Violin
Violin for Beginners

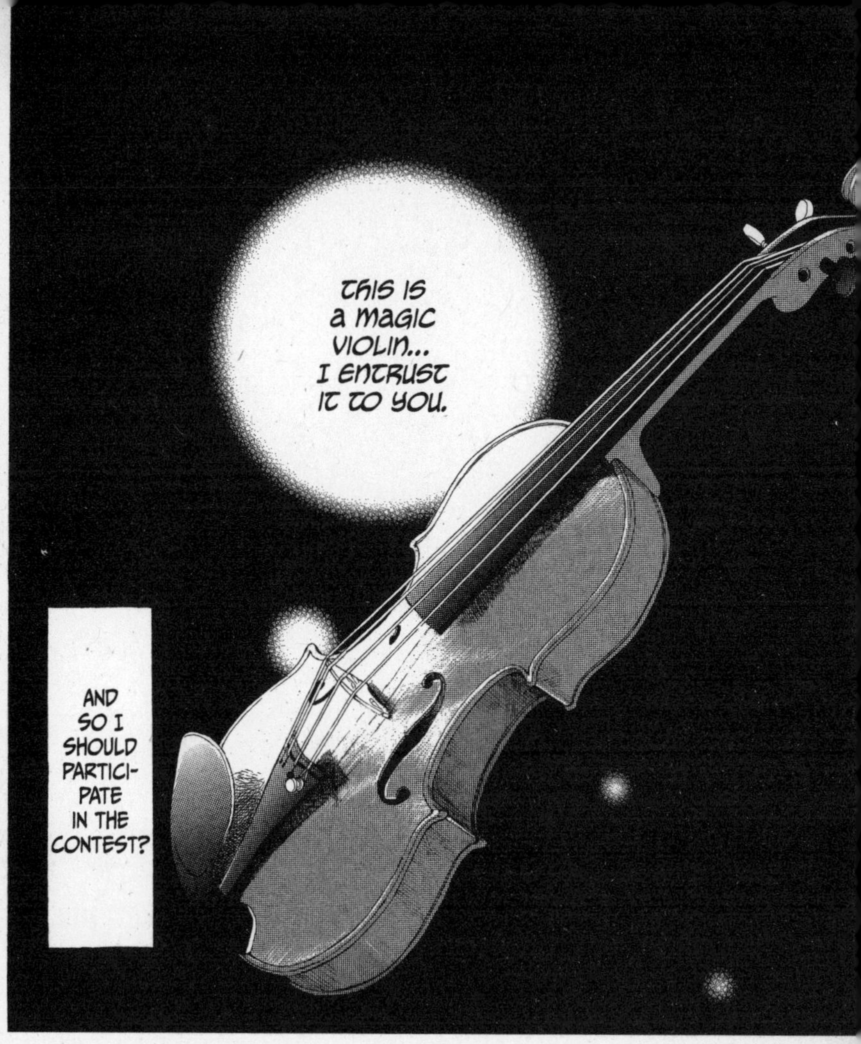
THIS IS a MAGIC VIOLIN... I ENTRUST IT TO YOU.
AND SO I SHOULD PARTICI-PATE IN THE CONTEST?
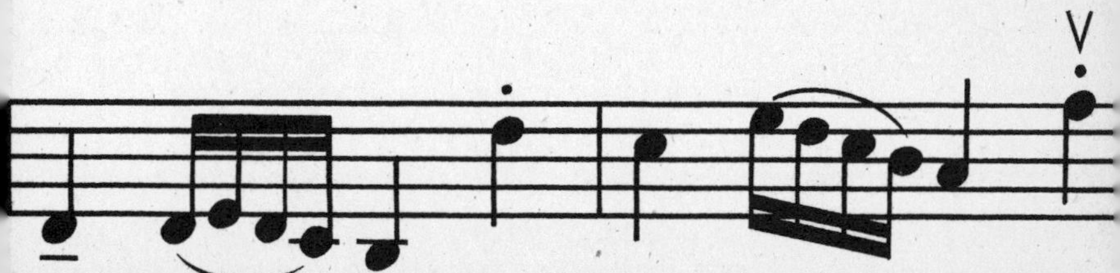

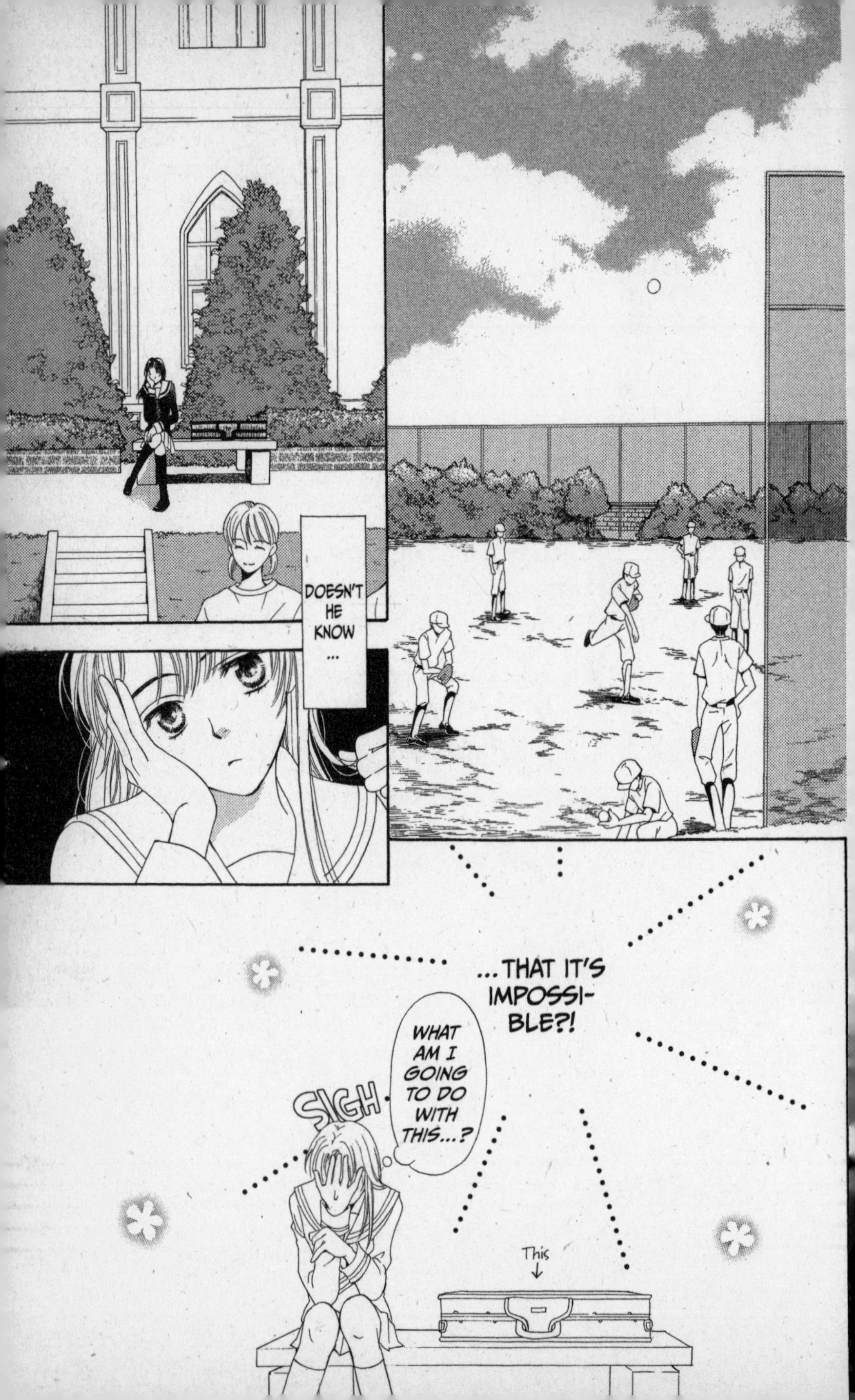
DOESN'T HE KNOW ...
...THAT IT'S IMPOSSI-BLE?!
WHAT AM I GOING TO DO WITH THIS...?
SIGH
This

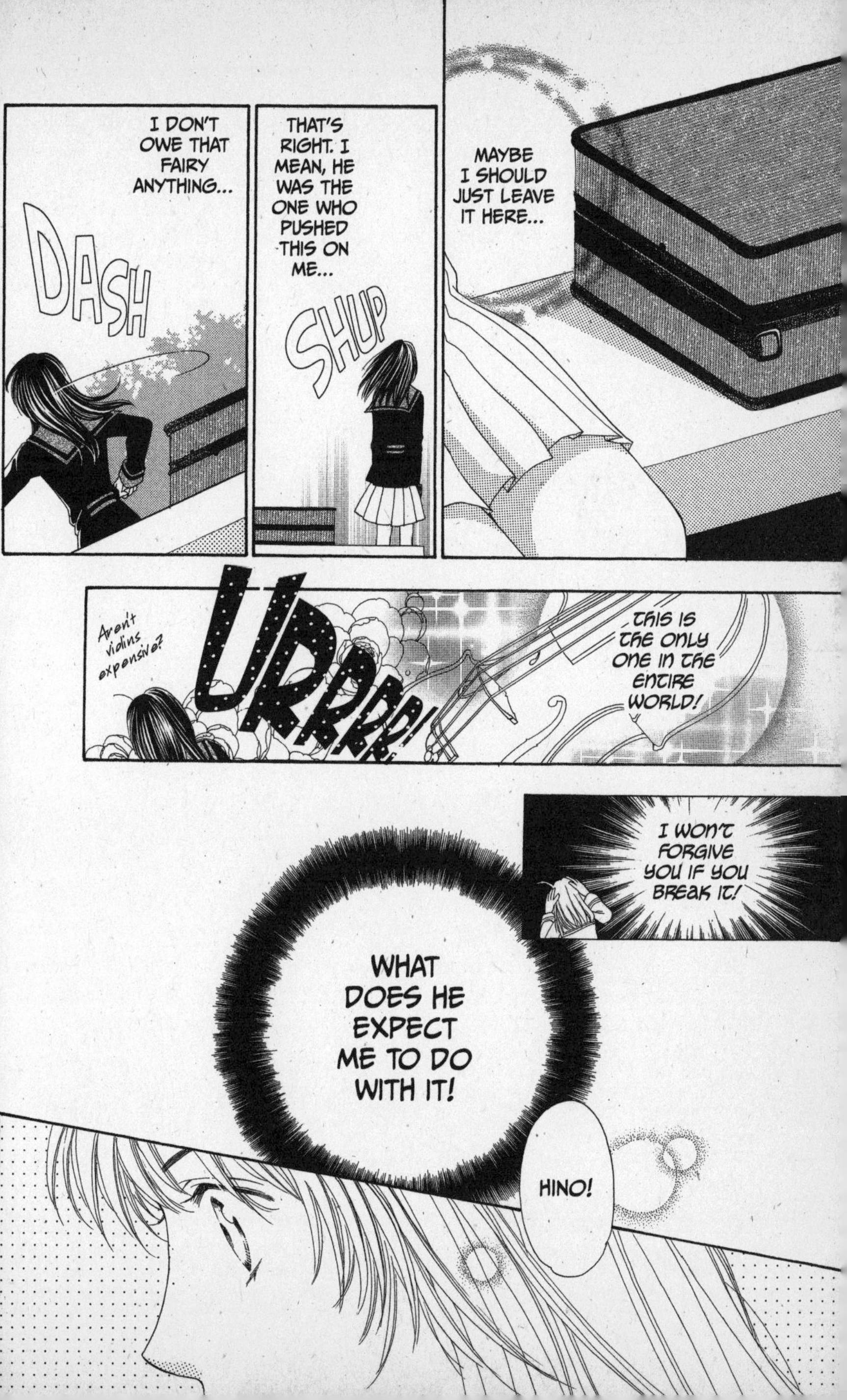
MAYBE I SHOULD JUST LEAVE IT HERE...
THAT'S RIGHT. I MEAN, HE WAS THE ONE WHO PUSHED THIS ON ME...
SHUP
I DON'T OWE THAT FAIRY ANYTHING...
DASH
THIS IS THE ONLY ONE IN THE ENTIRE WORLD!
URRRR!
Aren't violins expensive?
I WON'T FORGIVE YOU IF YOU BREAK IT!
WHAT DOES HE EXPECT ME TO DO WITH IT!
HINO!

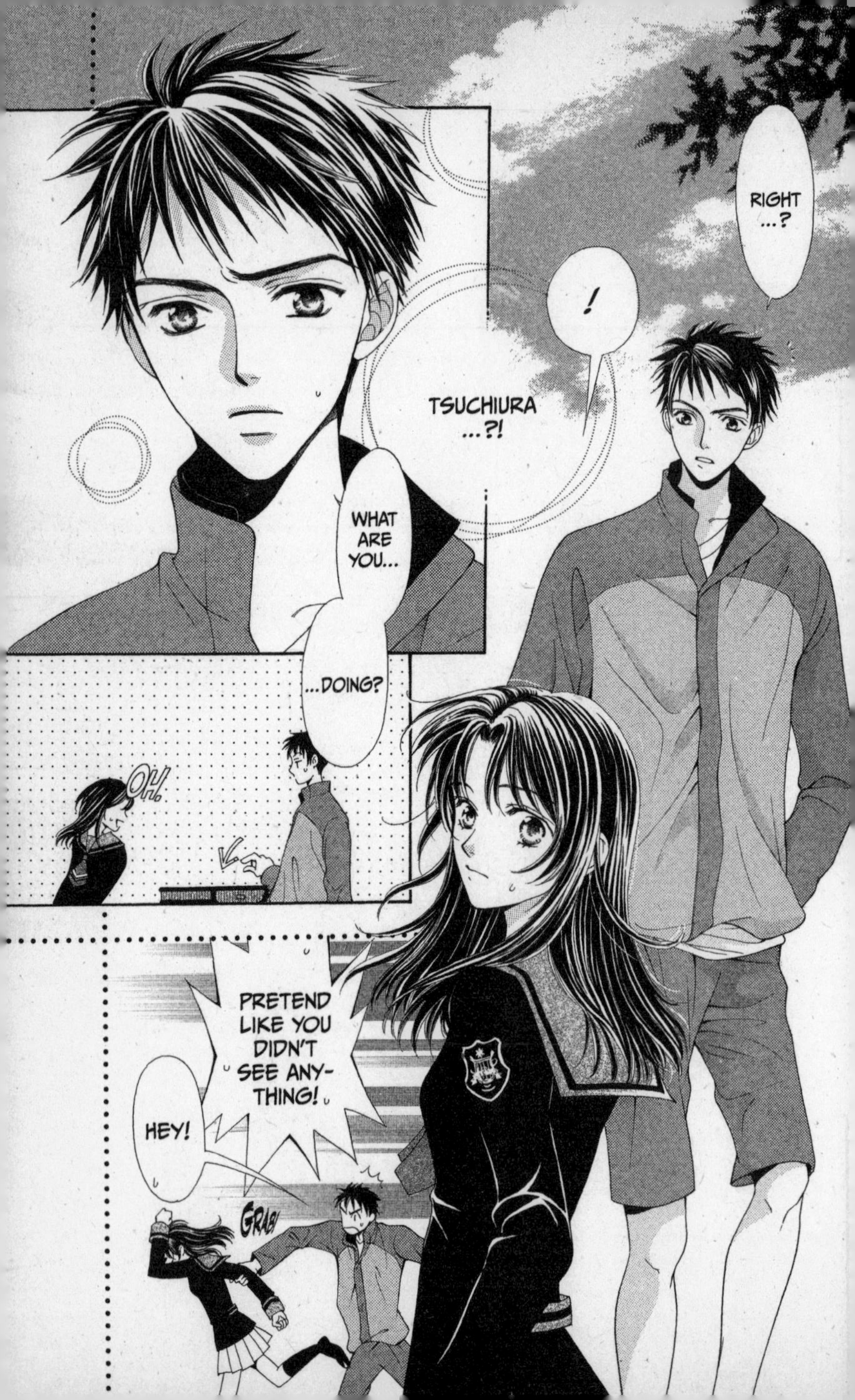
RIGHT ...?
!
TSUCHIURA ...?!
WHAT ARE YOU...
...DOING?
OH.
PRETEND LIKE YOU DIDN'T SEE ANY-THING!
HEY!
GRAB!

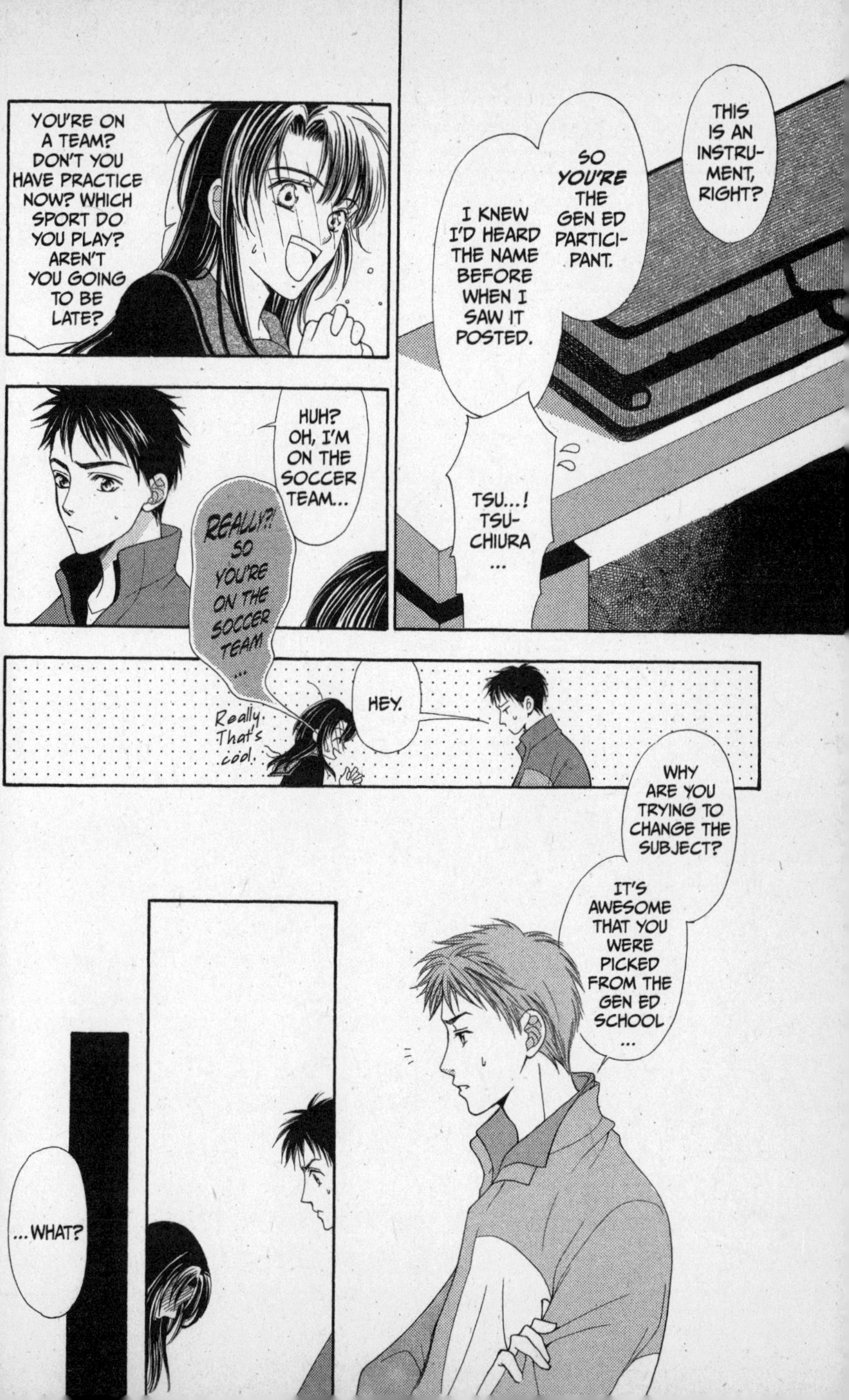
THIS IS AN INSTRUMENT, RIGHT?
SO *YOU'RE* THE GEN ED PARTICIPANT.
I KNEW I'D HEARD THE NAME BEFORE WHEN I SAW IT POSTED.
TSU...! TSU-CHIURA ...
YOU'RE ON A TEAM? DON'T YOU HAVE PRACTICE NOW? WHICH SPORT DO YOU PLAY? AREN'T YOU GOING TO BE LATE?
HUH? OH, I'M ON THE SOCCER TEAM...
REALLY?! SO YOU'RE ON THE SOCCER TEAM ...
Really. That's cool.
HEY.
WHY ARE YOU TRYING TO CHANGE THE SUBJECT?
IT'S AWESOME THAT YOU WERE PICKED FROM THE GEN ED SCHOOL ...
...WHAT?

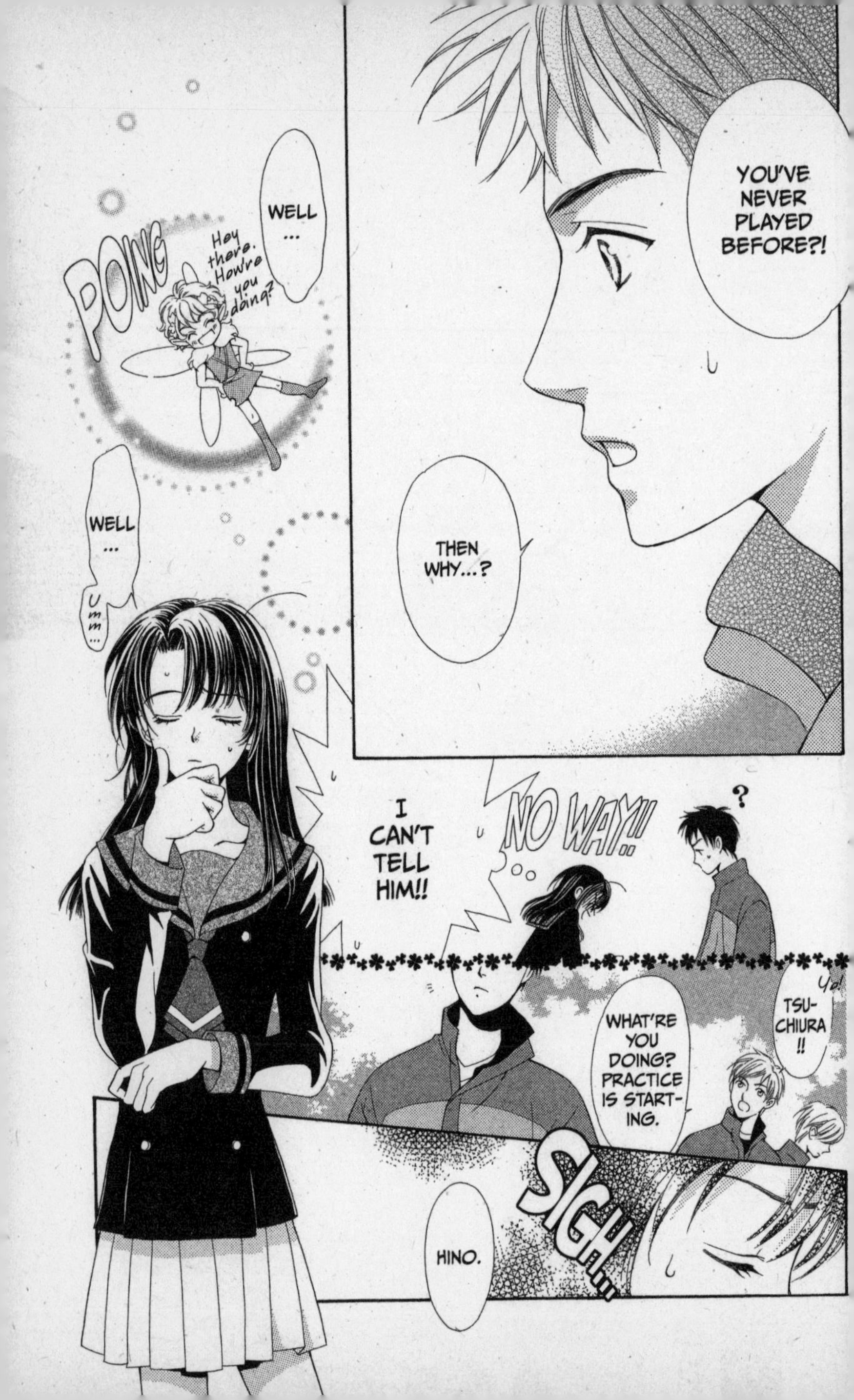
YOU'VE NEVER PLAYED BEFORE?!
THEN WHY...?
WELL ...
POING
Hey there. How're you doing?
WELL ...
Umm...
I CAN'T TELL HIM!!
NO WAY!!
Yo!
TSU-CHIURA !!
WHAT'RE YOU DOING? PRACTICE IS START-ING.
SIGH...
HINO.

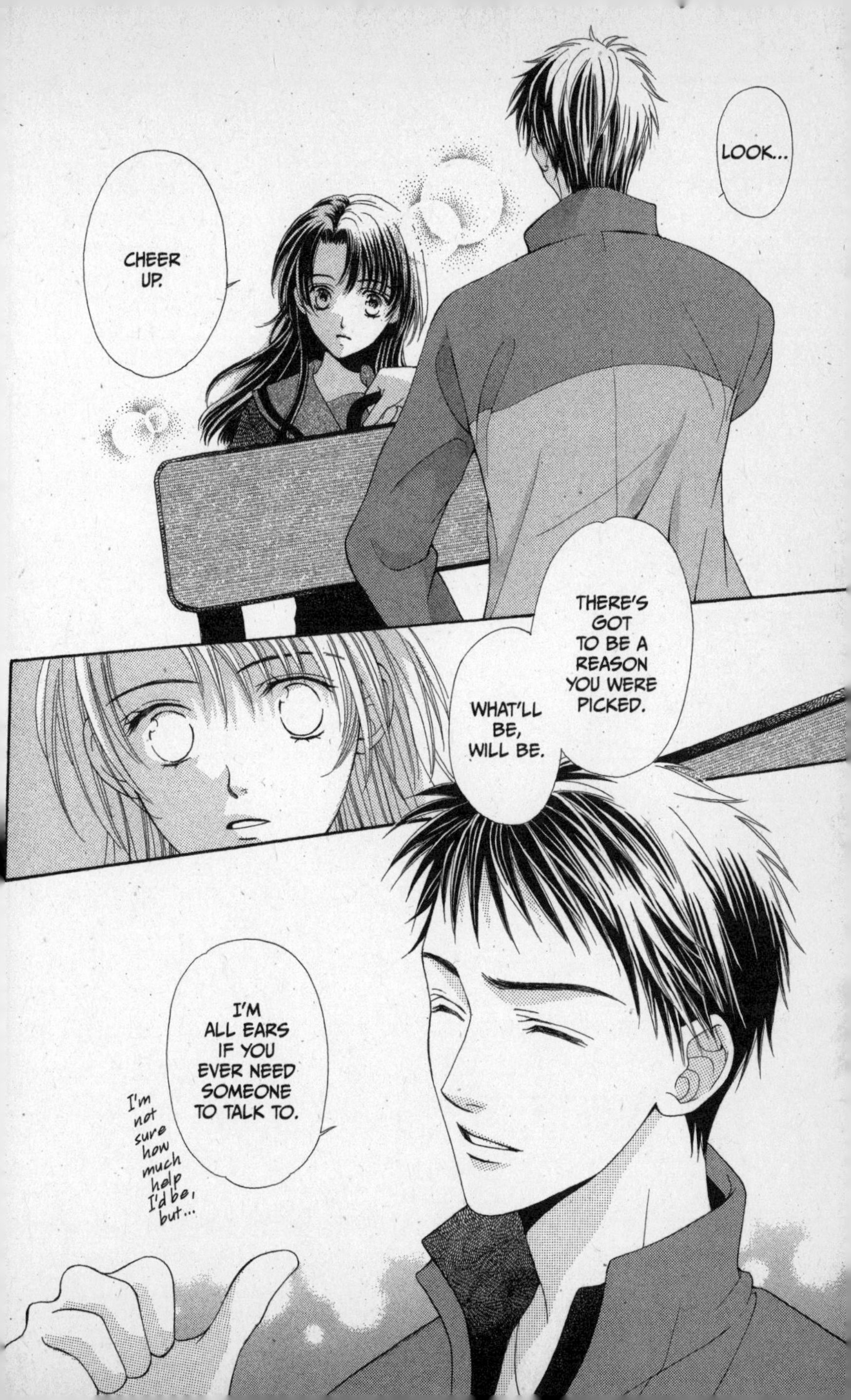
LOOK...
CHEER UP.
THERE'S GOT TO BE A REASON YOU WERE PICKED.
WHAT'LL BE, WILL BE.
I'M ALL EARS IF YOU EVER NEED SOMEONE TO TALK TO.
I'm not sure how much help I'd be, but...

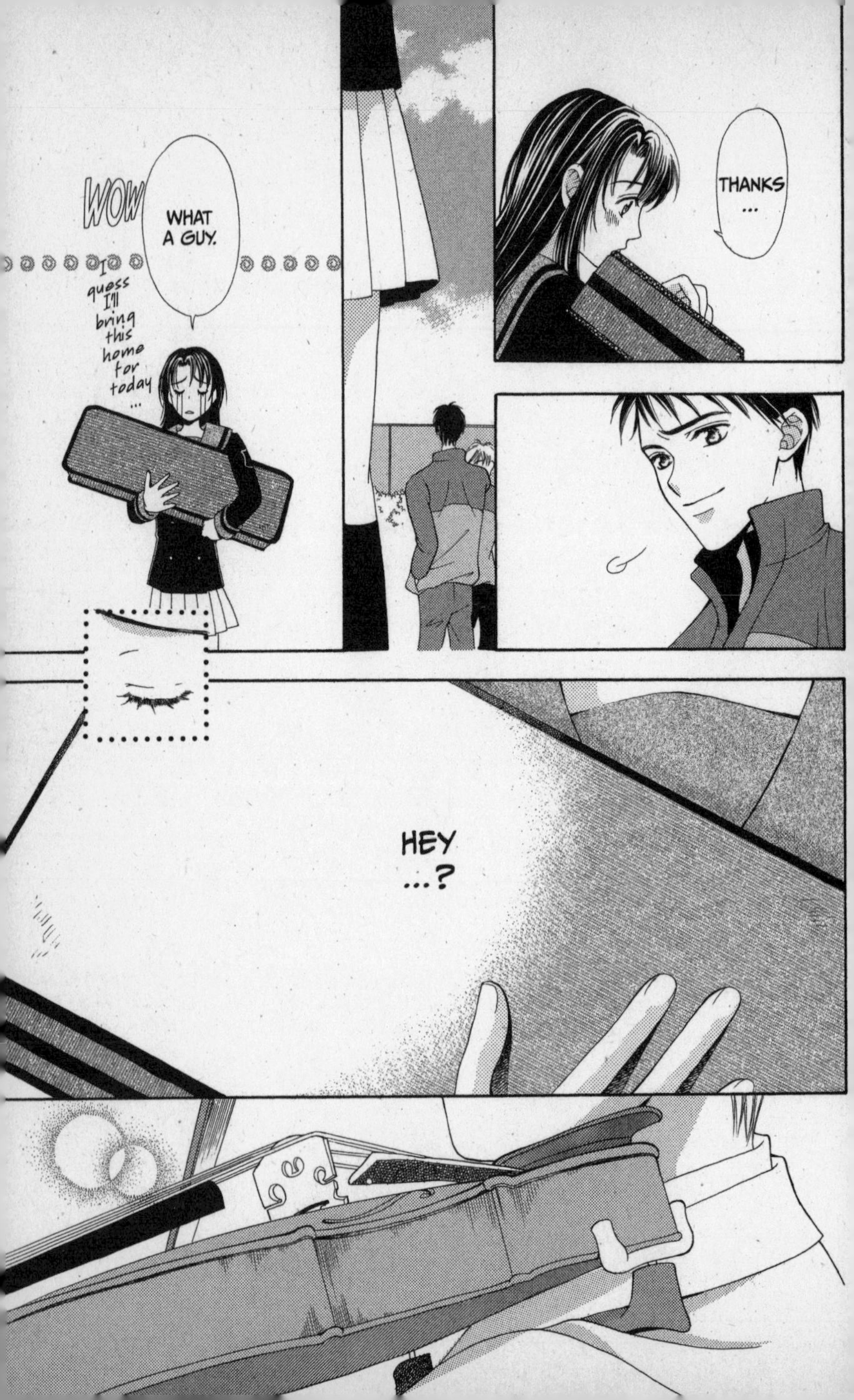
THANKS ...
WOW
WHAT A GUY.
I guess I'll bring this home for today ...
HEY ...?

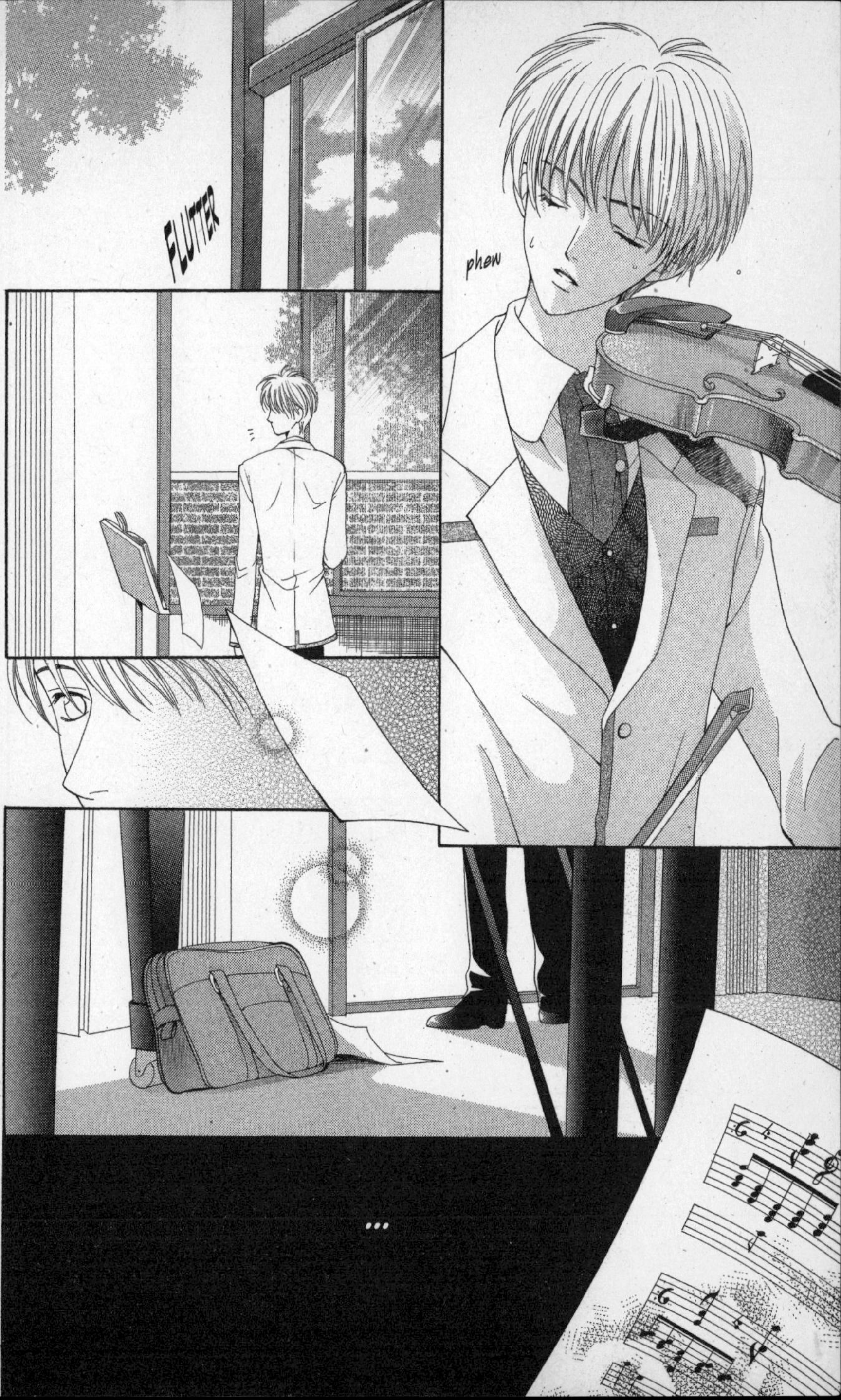
phew
FLUTTER
...

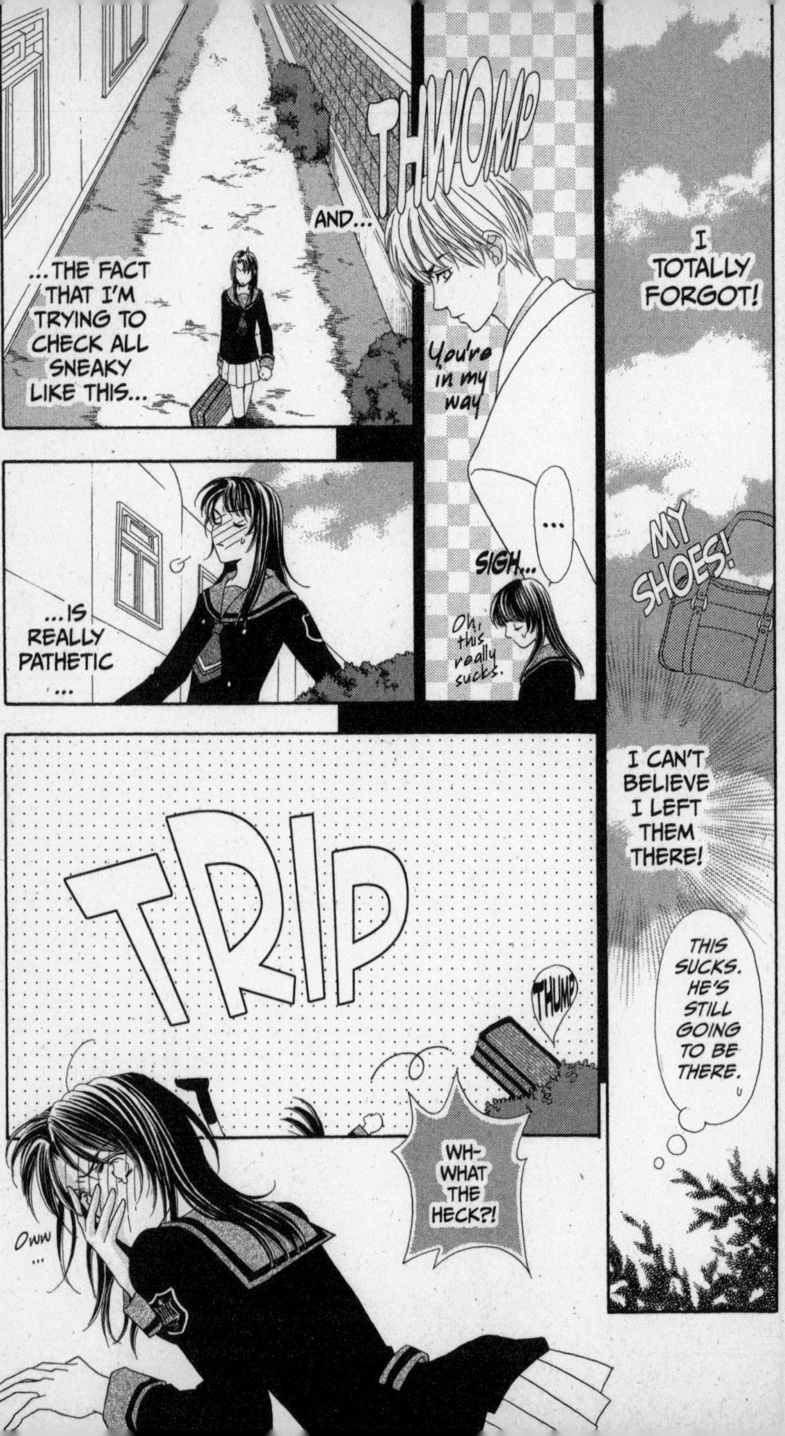
I TOTALLY FORGOT!
MY SHOES!
I CAN'T BELIEVE I LEFT THEM THERE!
THIS SUCKS. HE'S STILL GOING TO BE THERE.
THWOMP
AND...
You're in my way
...
SIGH...
Oh, this really sucks.
...THE FACT THAT I'M TRYING TO CHECK ALL SNEAKY LIKE THIS...
...IS REALLY PATHETIC...
TRIP
THUMP
WH- WHAT THE HECK?!
Oww ...

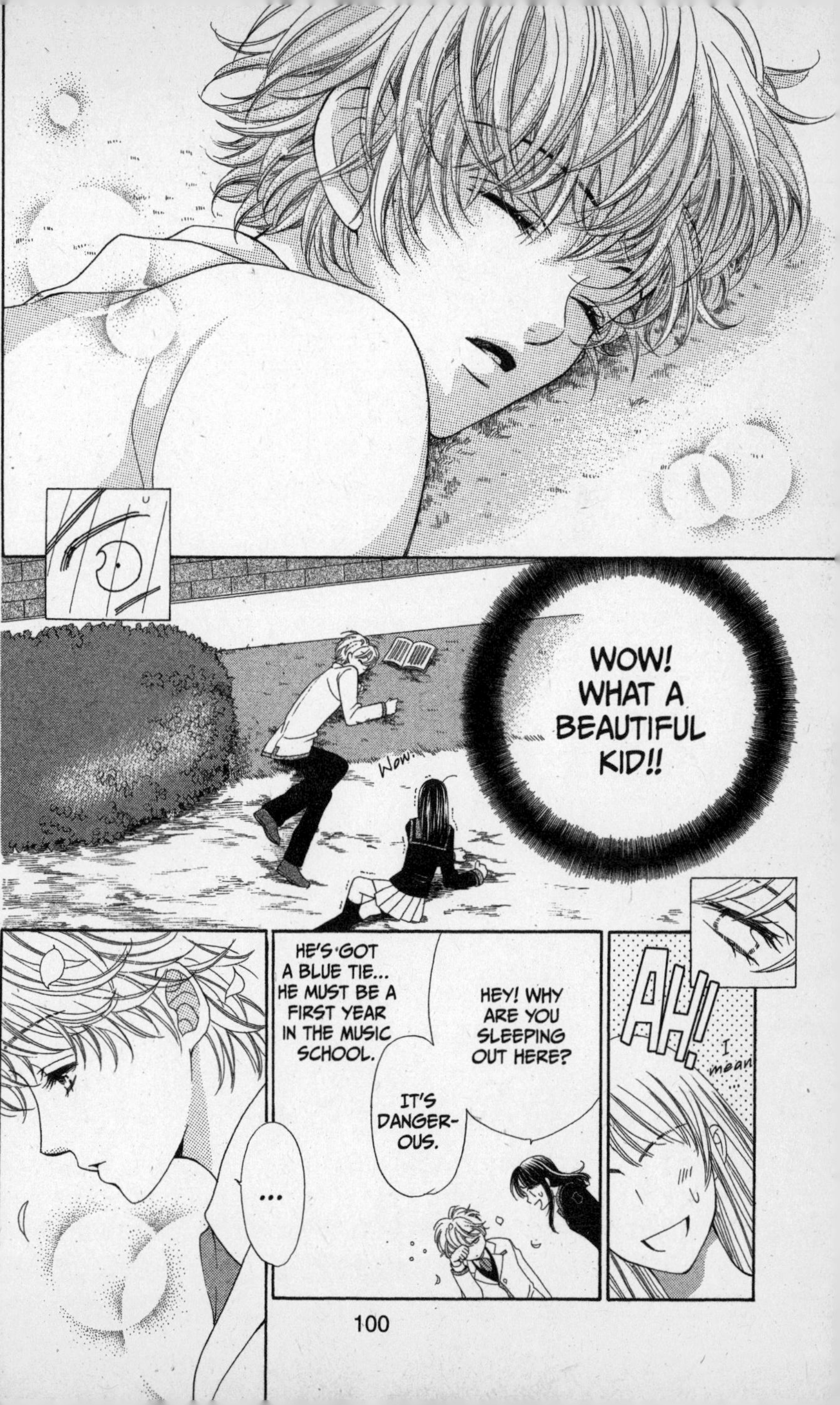
WOW! WHAT A BEAUTIFUL KID!!
Wow!
AH!
I mean
HEY! WHY ARE YOU SLEEPING OUT HERE?
IT'S DANGEROUS.
HE'S GOT A BLUE TIE... HE MUST BE A FIRST YEAR IN THE MUSIC SCHOOL.
...

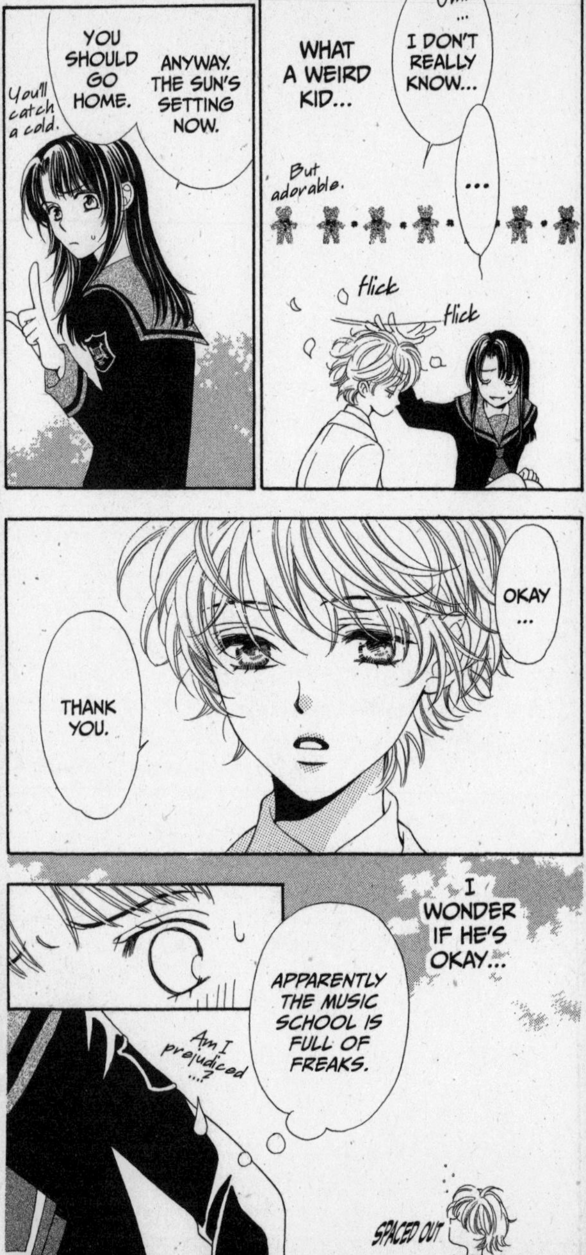
Umm ... I DON'T REALLY KNOW...
...
WHAT A WEIRD KID...
But adorable.
flick
flick
ANYWAY. THE SUN'S SETTING NOW.
YOU SHOULD GO HOME.
You'll catch a cold.
OKAY ...
THANK YOU.
I WONDER IF HE'S OKAY...
APPARENTLY THE MUSIC SCHOOL IS FULL OF FREAKS.
Am I prejudiced ...?
SPACED OUT

Violin ②

And my impression... It's difficult... Extremely. (Of course.) I couldn't even hold the bow properly, so I had a problem even before trying to make a sound. It was exhausting, and I woke up sore the next day. My arms and my lower back ached, along with my right finger...for whatever reason. I'm totally out of shape and it's really quite pathetic. Yes, I know that health is essential... But I had a great time. Sensei, thank you so much.

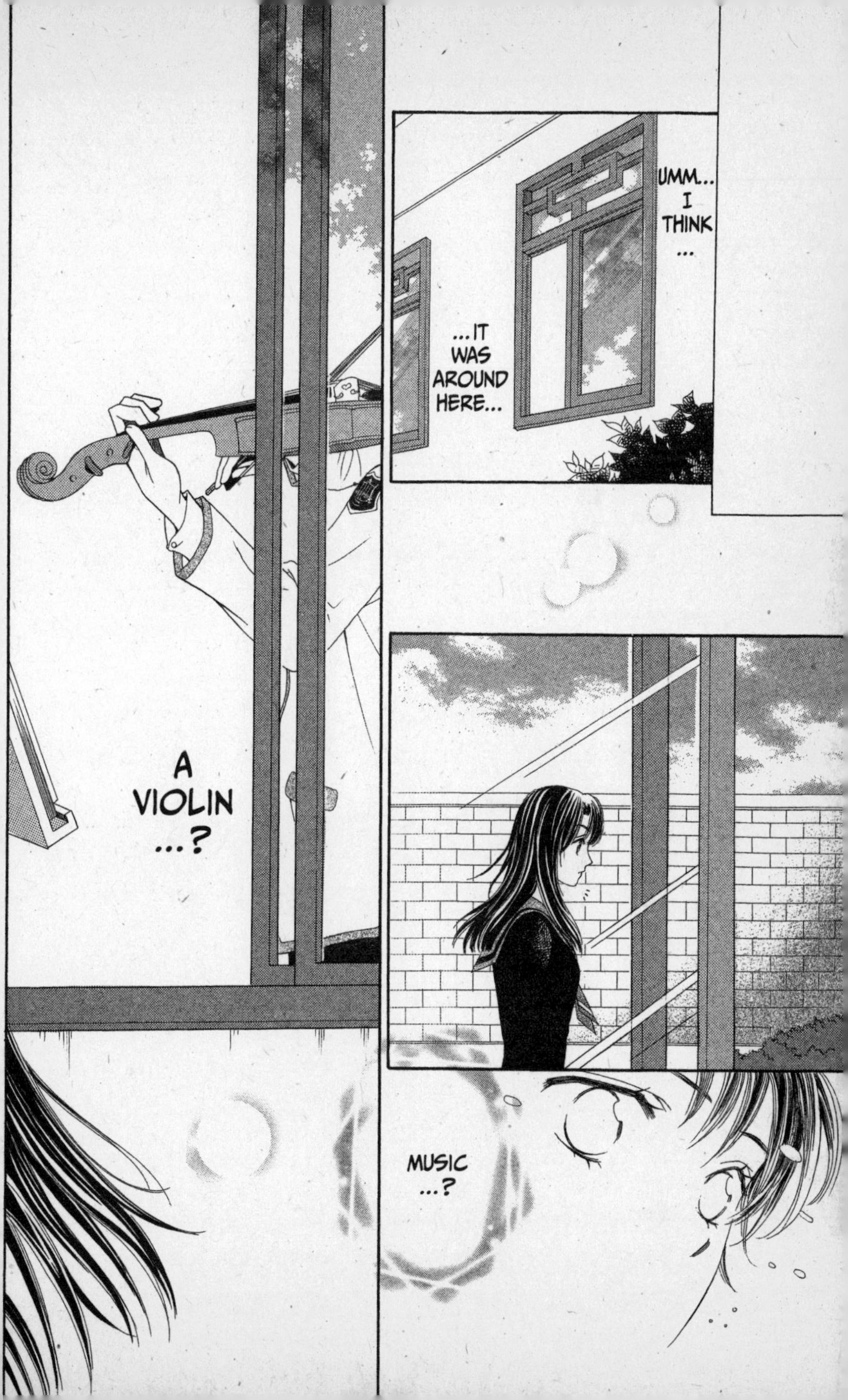
UMM... I THINK...
...IT WAS AROUND HERE...
A VIOLIN ...?
MUSIC ...?

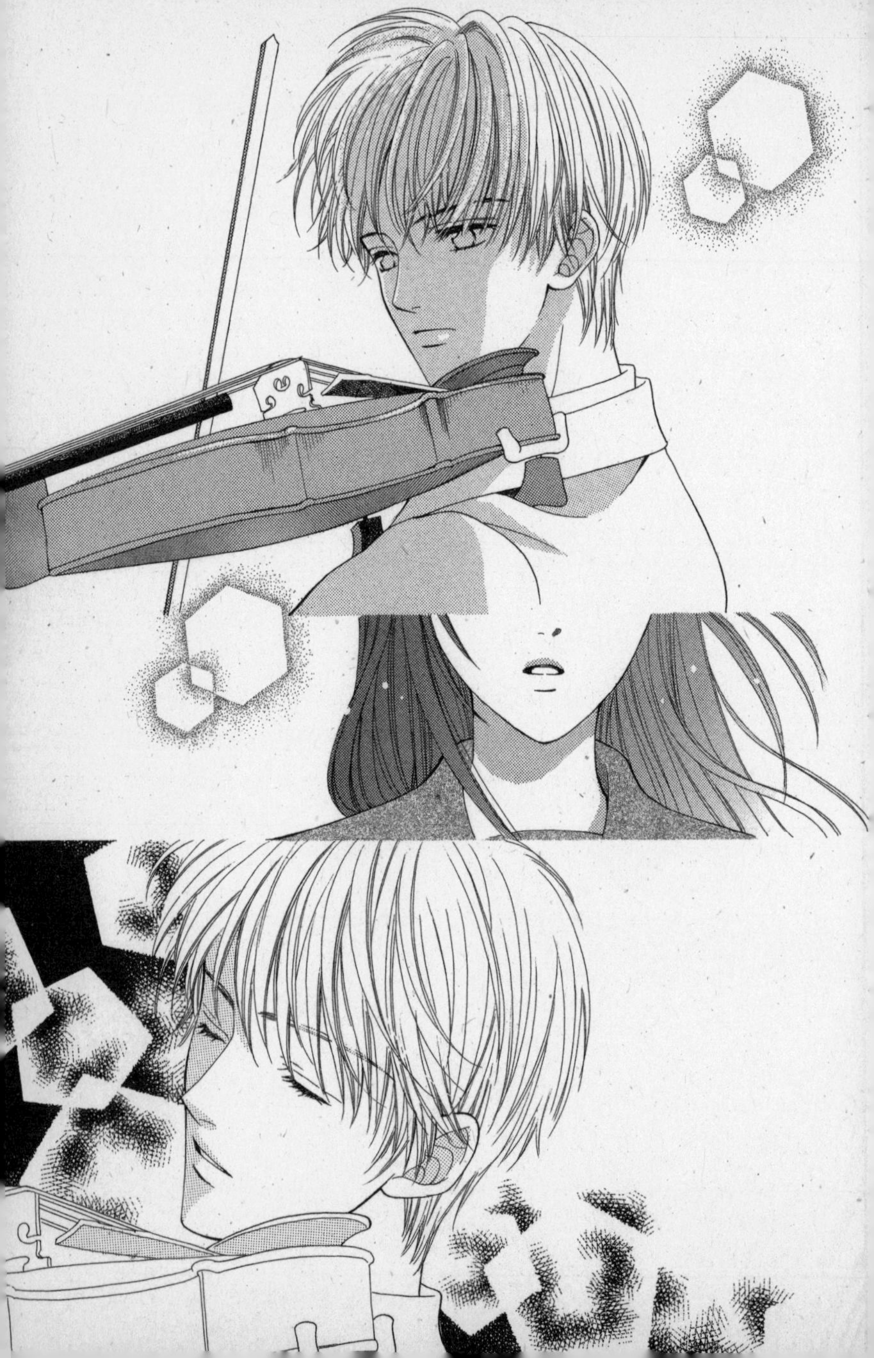

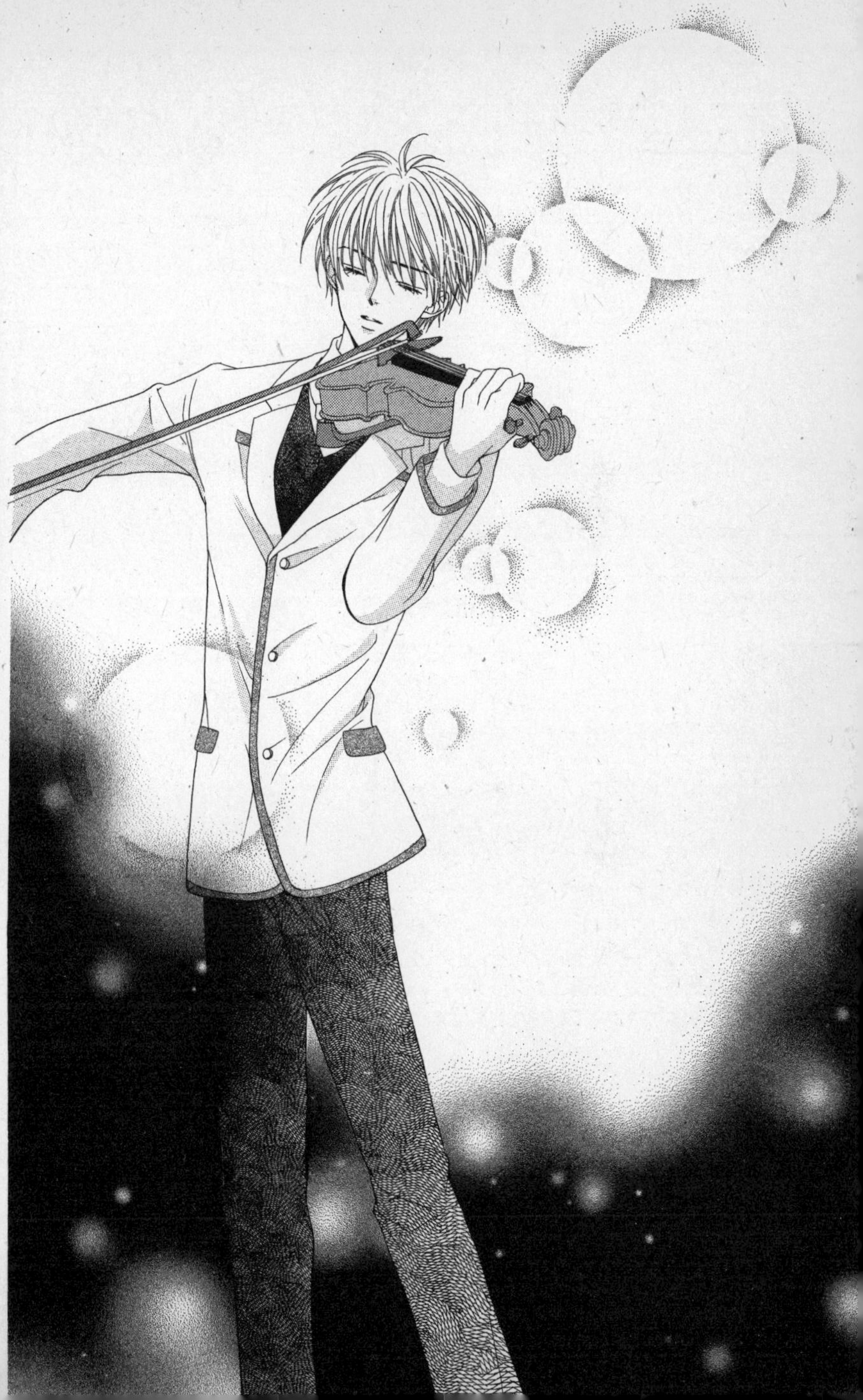

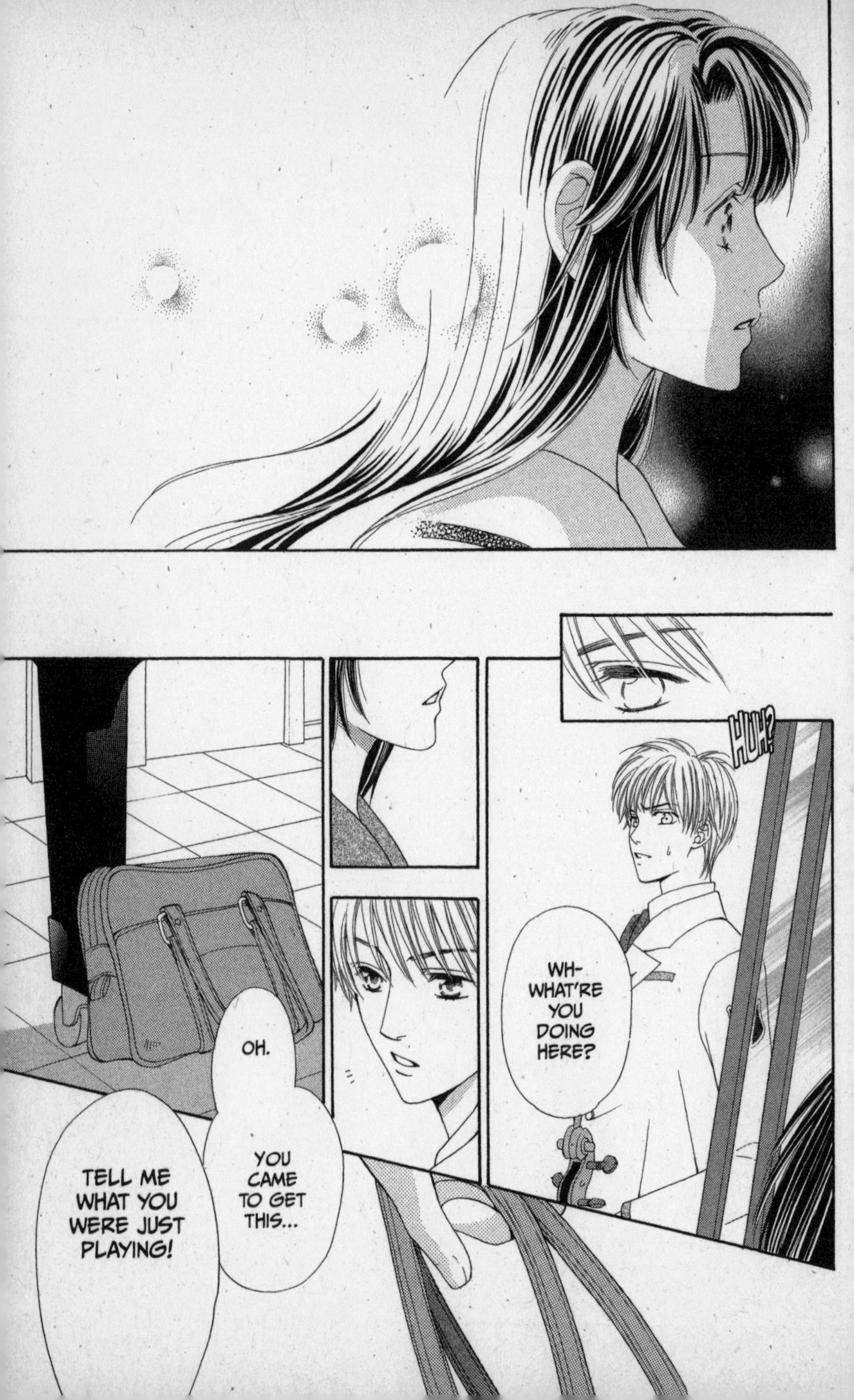
HUH?
WH- WHAT'RE YOU DOING HERE?
OH.
YOU CAME TO GET THIS...
TELL ME WHAT YOU WERE JUST PLAYING!

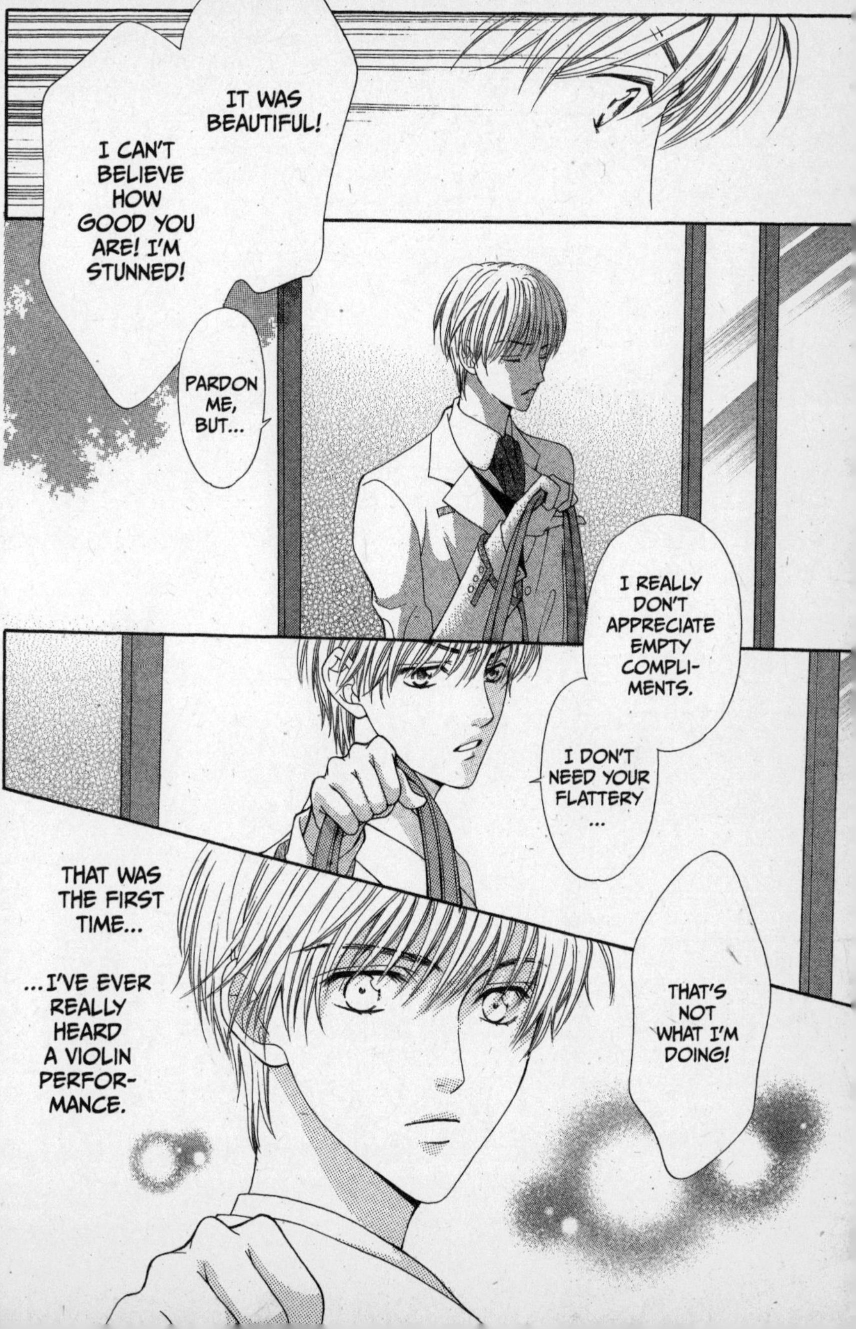
IT WAS BEAUTIFUL! I CAN'T BELIEVE HOW GOOD YOU ARE! I'M STUNNED!
PARDON ME, BUT...
I REALLY DON'T APPRECIATE EMPTY COMPLI- MENTS.
I DON'T NEED YOUR FLATTERY ...
THAT'S NOT WHAT I'M DOING!
THAT WAS THE FIRST TIME...
...I'VE EVER REALLY HEARD A VIOLIN PERFOR- MANCE.

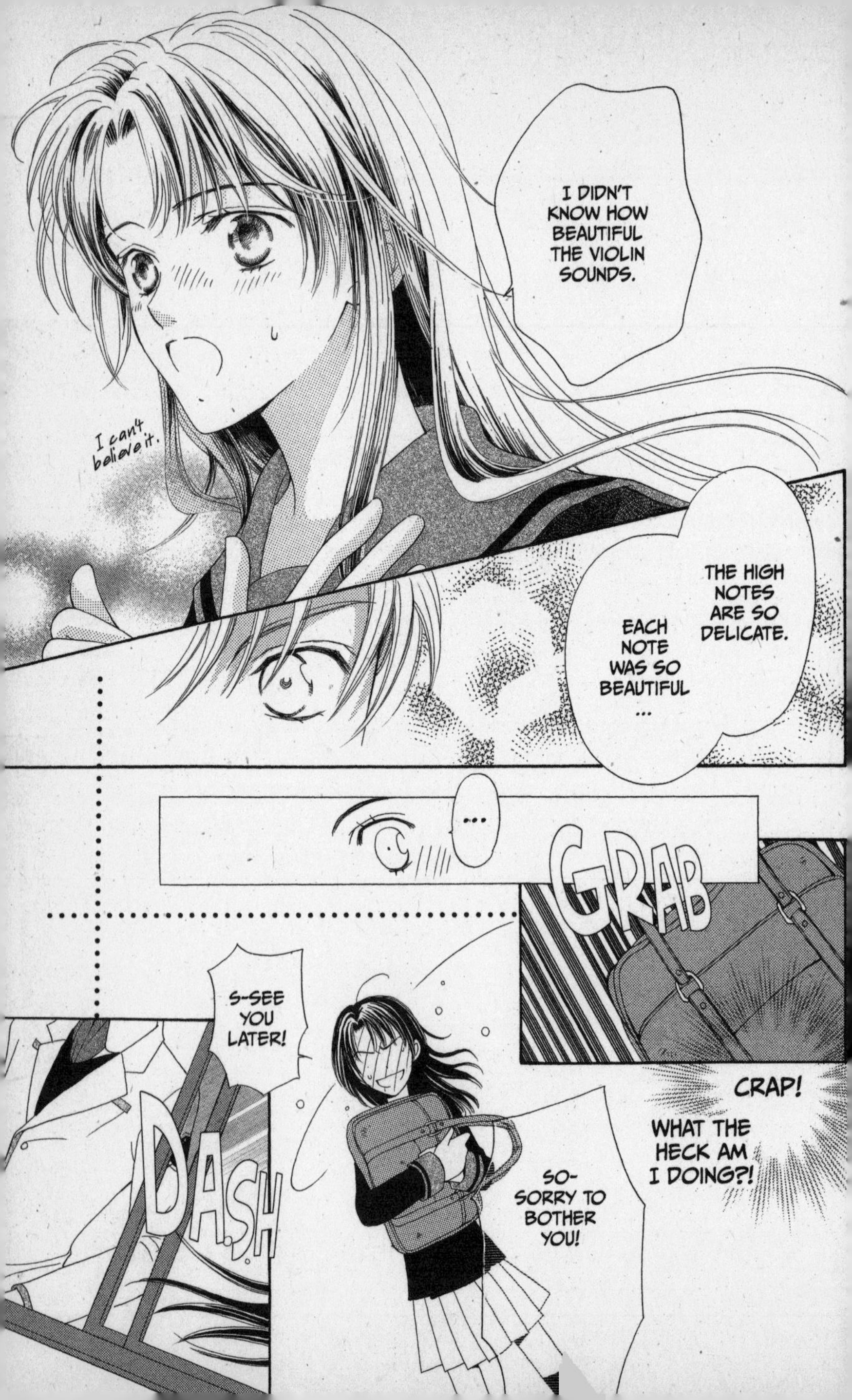

I DIDN'T KNOW HOW BEAUTIFUL THE VIOLIN SOUNDS.
I can't believe it.
THE HIGH NOTES ARE SO DELICATE.
EACH NOTE WAS SO BEAUTIFUL ...
...
GRAB
CRAP!
WHAT THE HECK AM I DOING?!
SO-SORRY TO BOTHER YOU!
S-SEE YOU LATER!
DASH

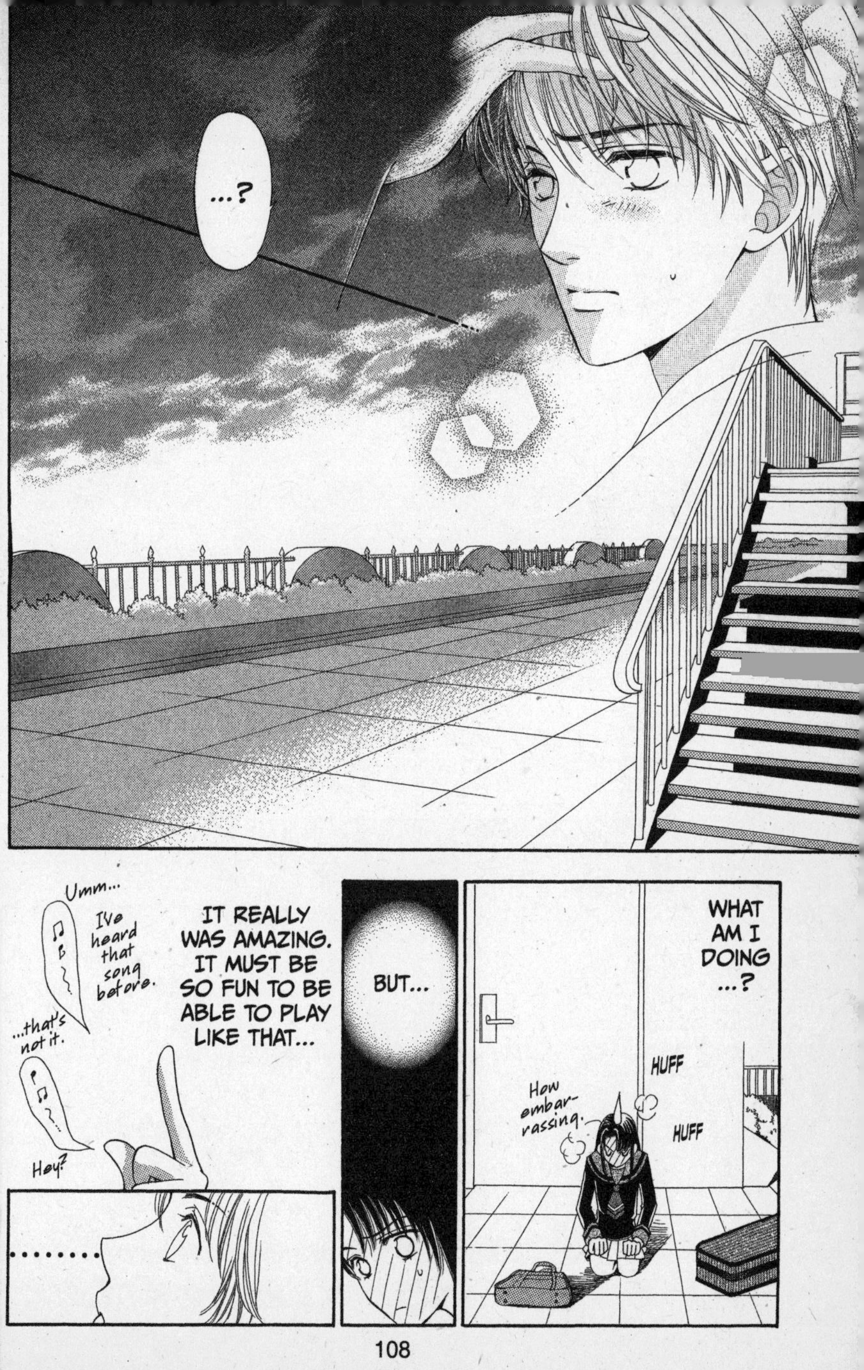
...?
WHAT AM I DOING ...?
HUFF
HUFF
How embarrassing.
BUT...
IT REALLY WAS AMAZING. IT MUST BE SO FUN TO BE ABLE TO PLAY LIKE THAT...
Umm... I've heard that song before.
...that's not it.
Hey?
....

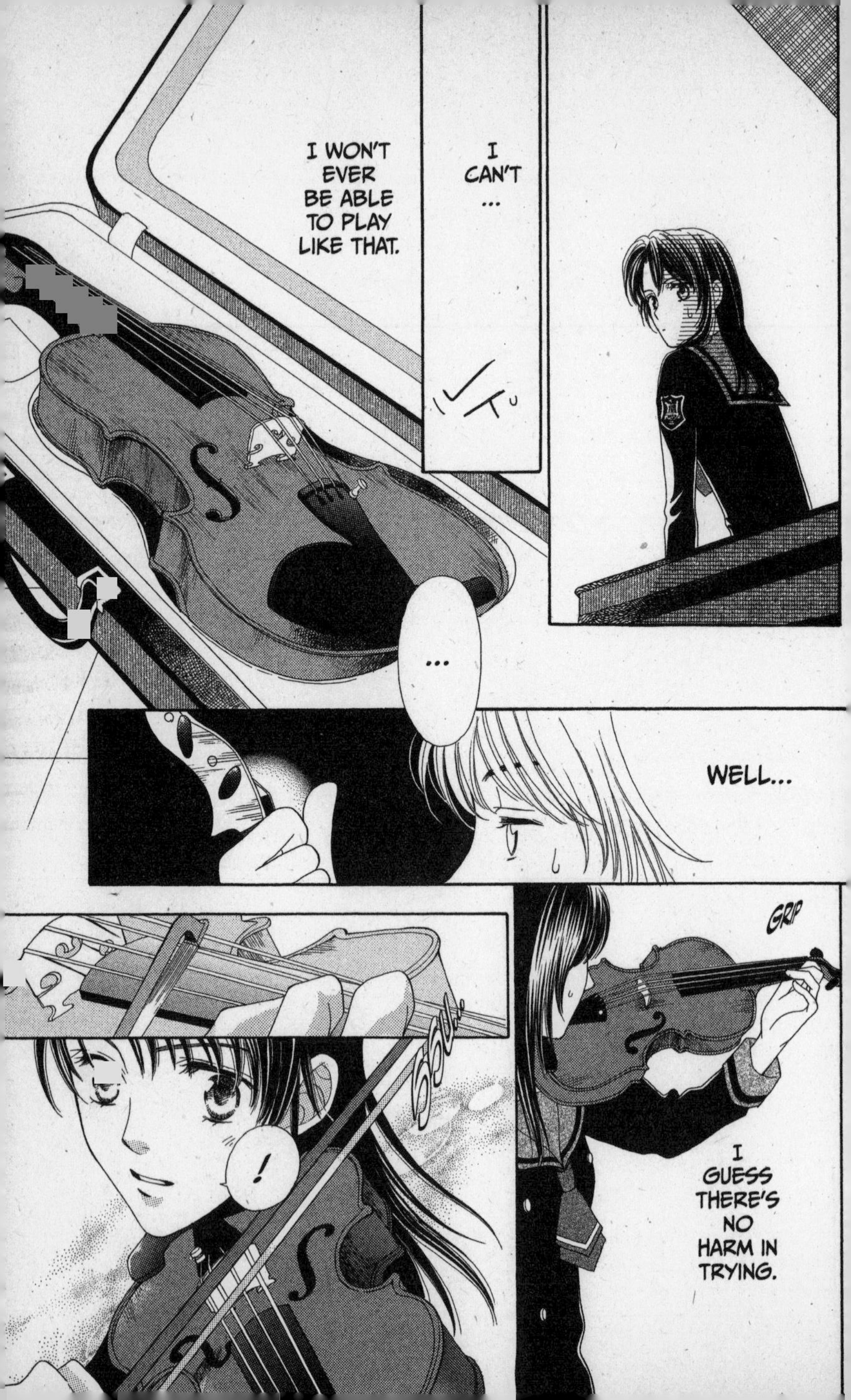
I CAN'T ...
I WON'T EVER BE ABLE TO PLAY LIKE THAT.
...
WELL...
GRIP
I GUESS THERE'S NO HARM IN TRYING.
!

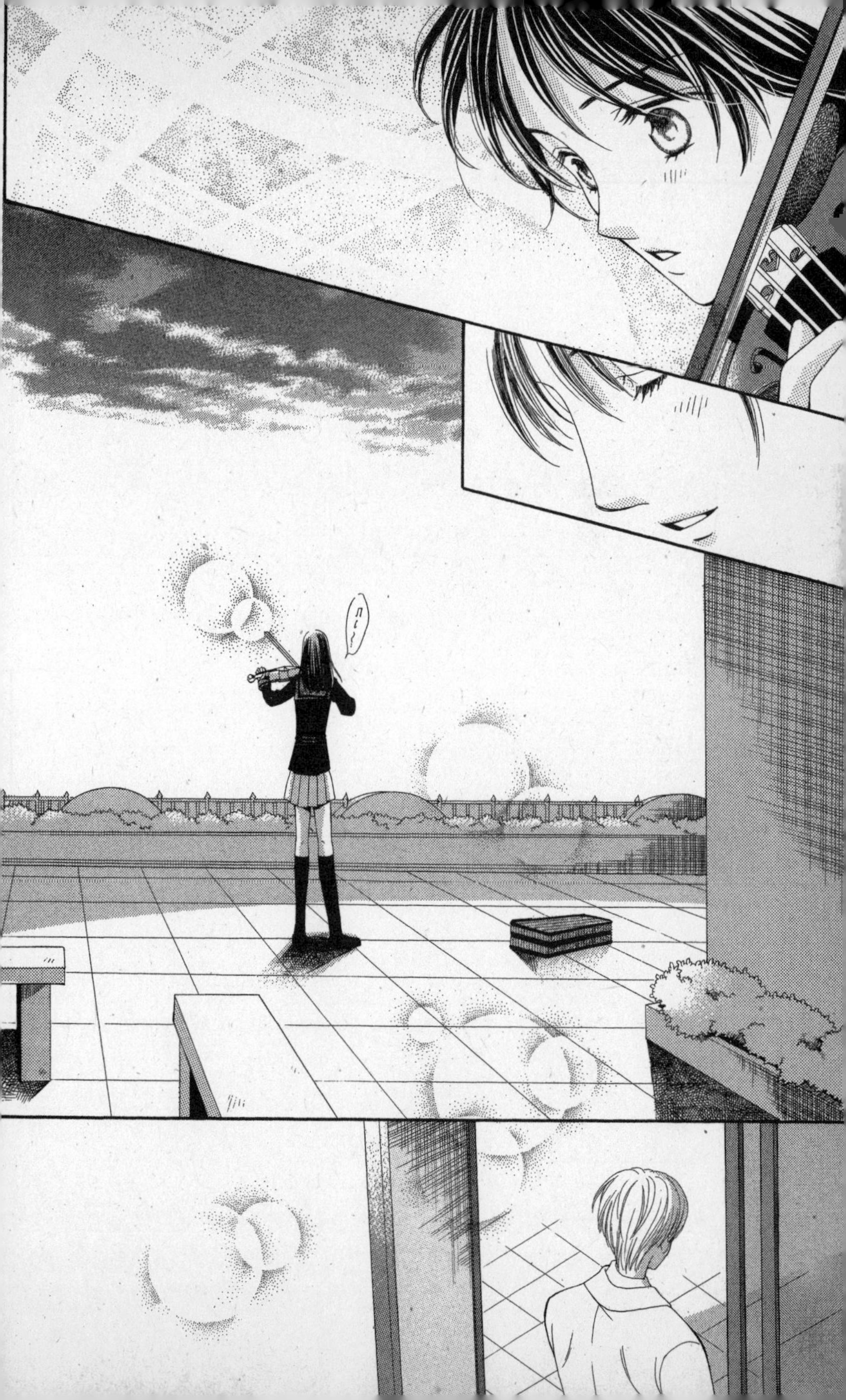

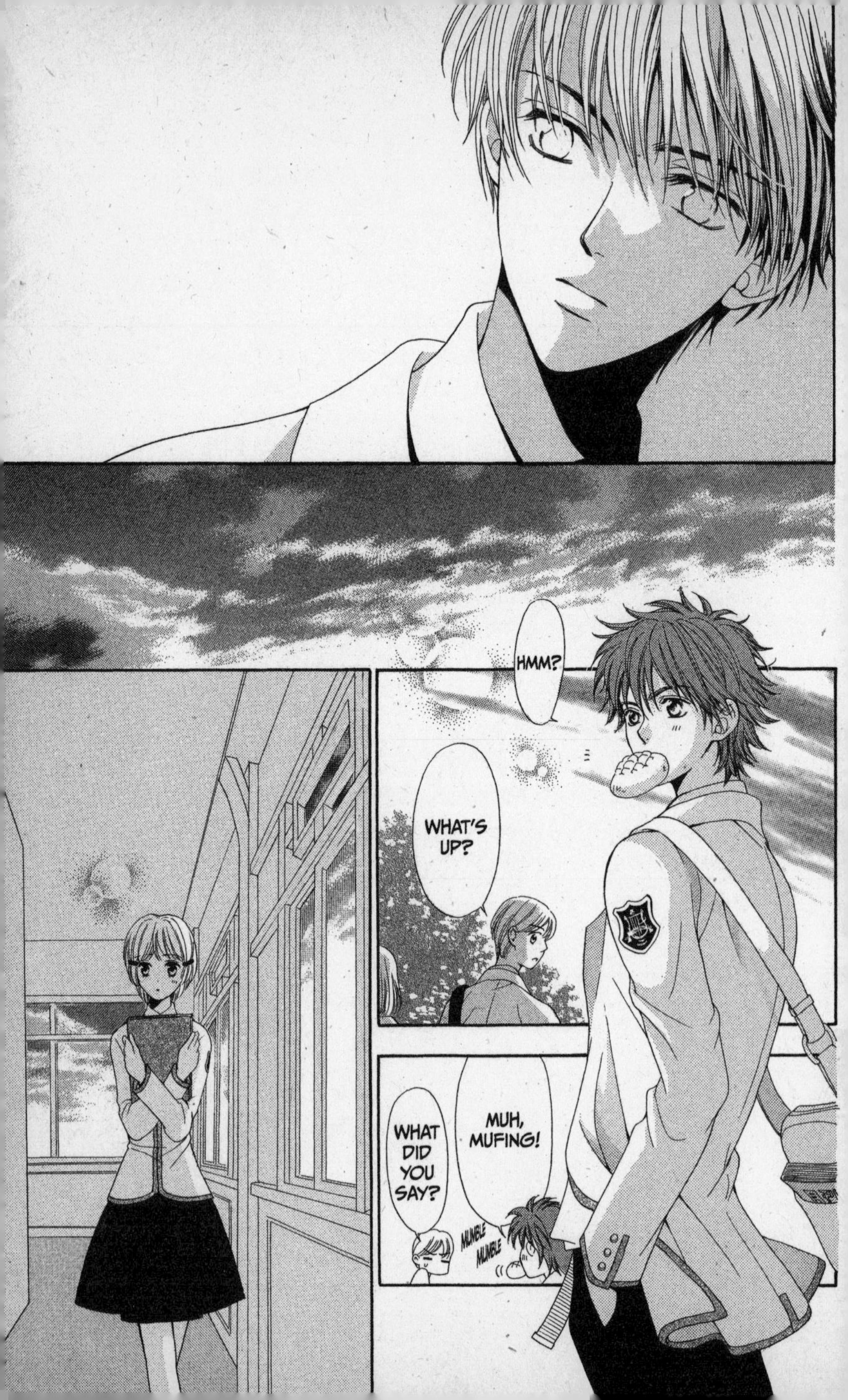
HMM?
WHAT'S UP?
MUH, MUFING!
WHAT DID YOU SAY?
MUMBLE MUMBLE

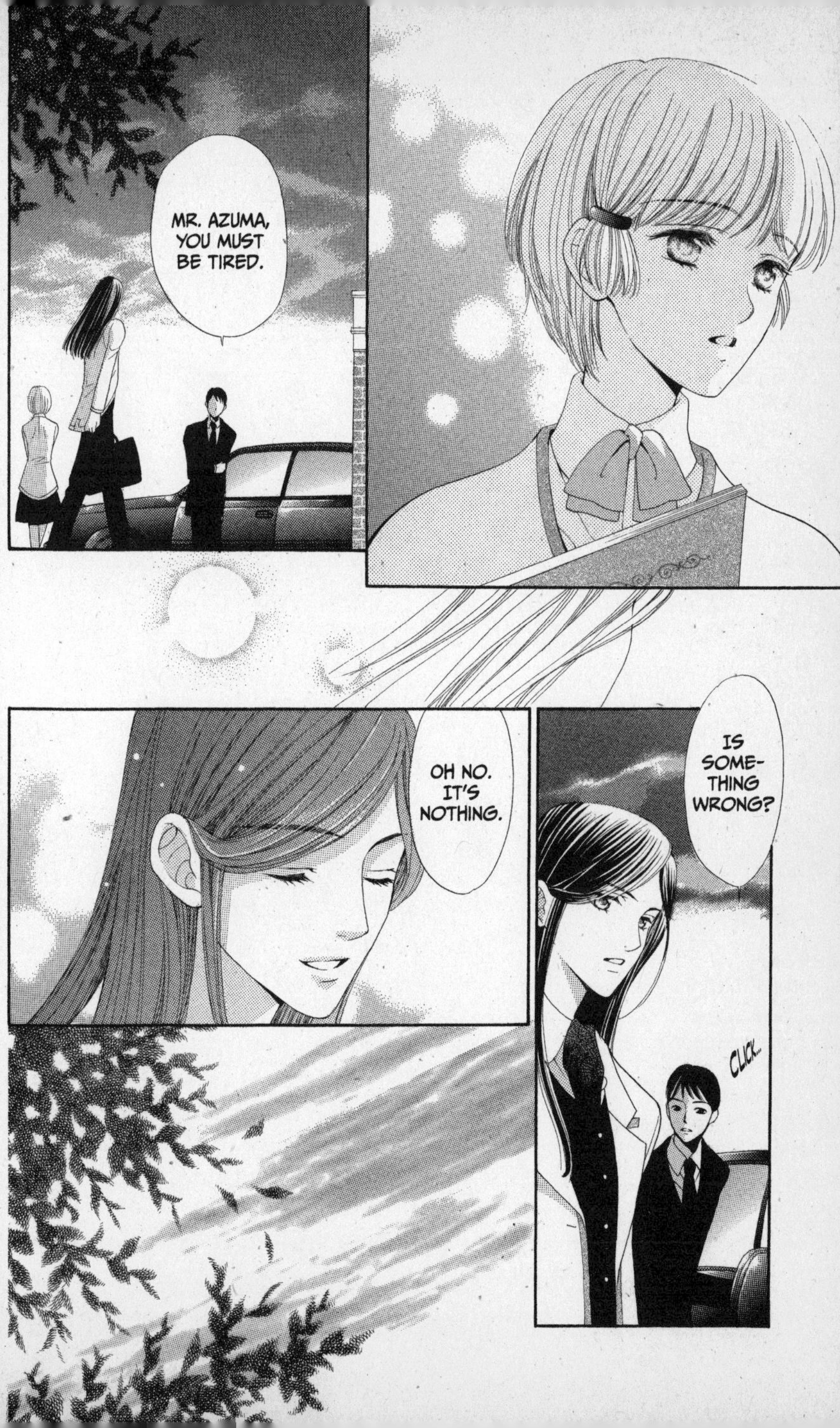
MR. AZUMA, YOU MUST BE TIRED.
IS SOMETHING WRONG?
CLICK...
OH NO. IT'S NOTHING.

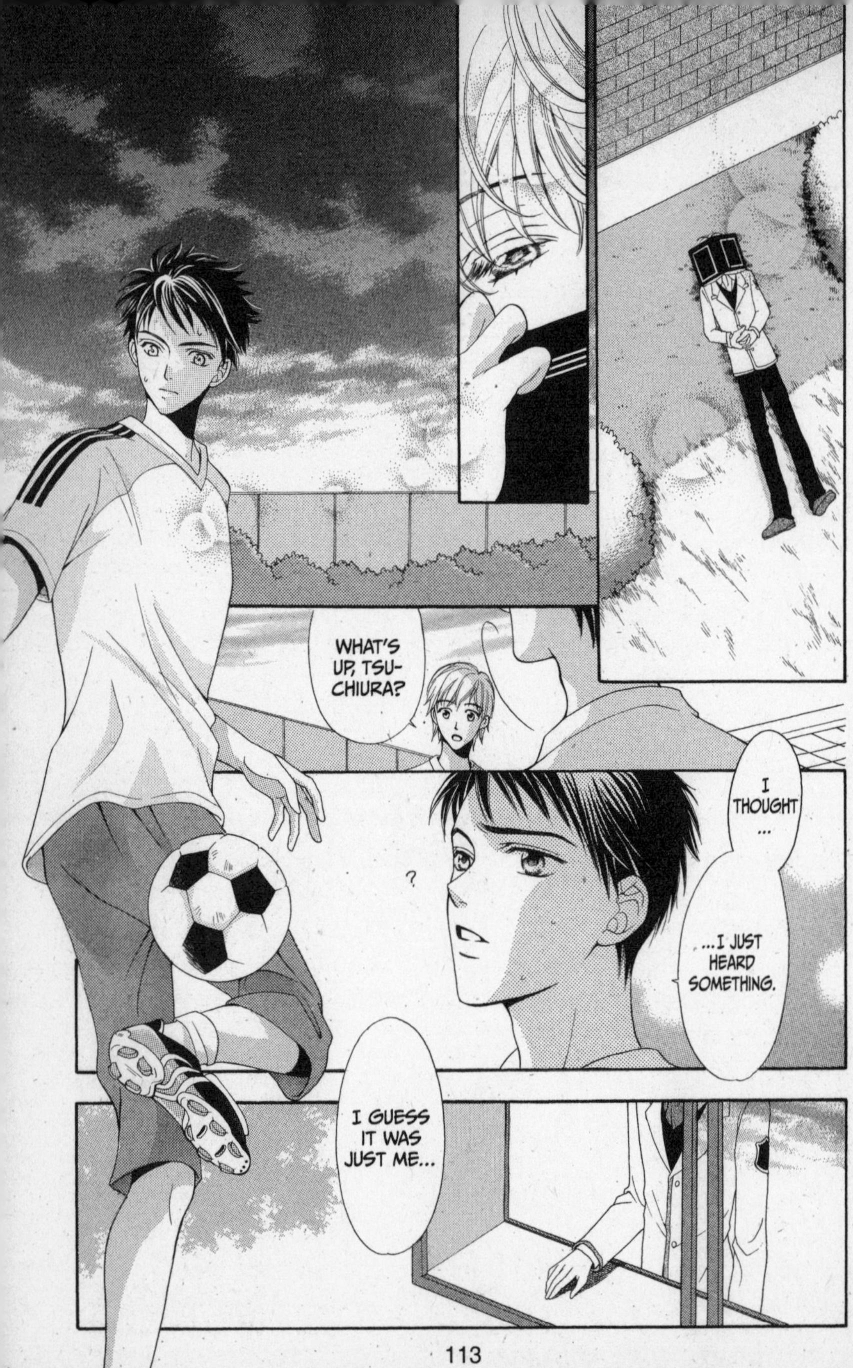
WHAT'S UP, TSU-CHIURA?
I THOUGHT...
?
...I JUST HEARD SOMETHING.
I GUESS IT WAS JUST ME...

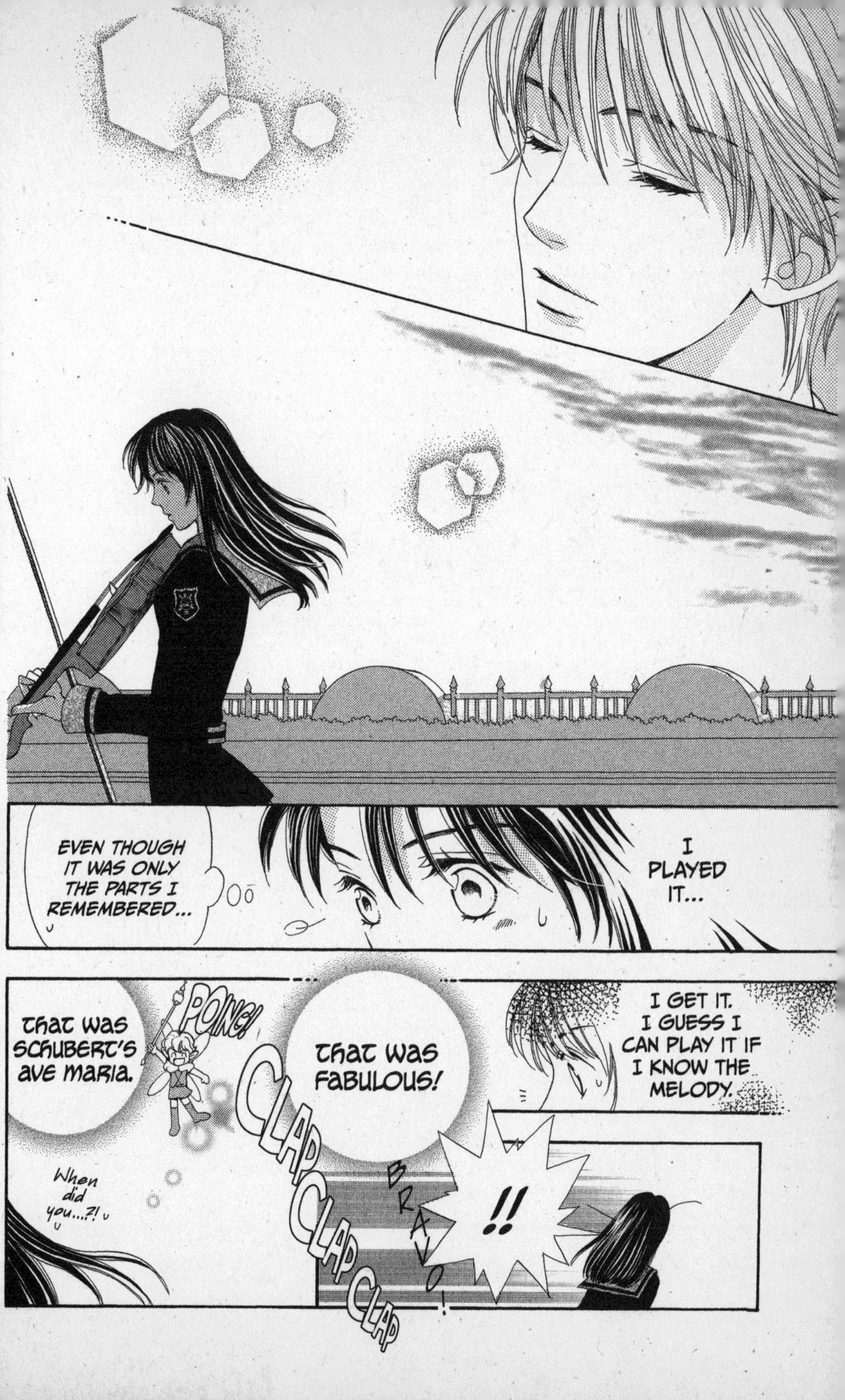
I PLAYED IT...
EVEN THOUGH IT WAS ONLY THE PARTS I REMEMBERED...
I GET IT. I GUESS I CAN PLAY IT IF I KNOW THE MELODY.
BRAVO!
!!
That was fabulous!
CLAP CLAP CLAP CLAP
POING!
That was Schubert's Ave Maria.
When did you...?!

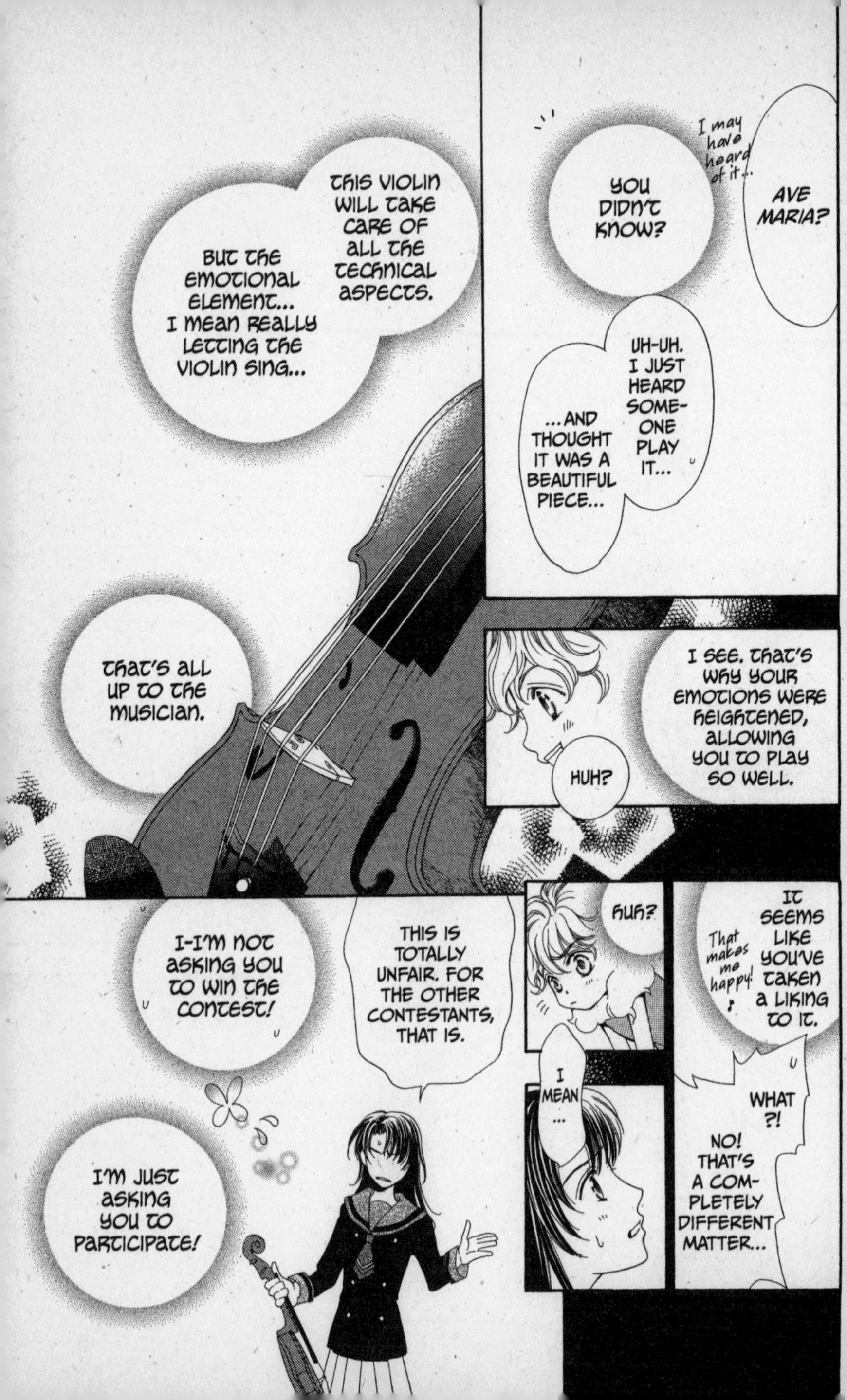
AVE MARIA?
I may have heard of it...
YOU DIDN'T KNOW?
UH-UH. I JUST HEARD SOME-ONE PLAY IT...
...AND THOUGHT IT WAS A BEAUTIFUL PIECE...
I SEE. THAT'S WHY YOUR EMOTIONS WERE HEIGHTENED, ALLOWING YOU TO PLAY SO WELL.
HUH?
THIS VIOLIN WILL TAKE CARE OF ALL THE TECHNICAL ASPECTS.
BUT THE EMOTIONAL ELEMENT... I MEAN REALLY LETTING THE VIOLIN SING...
THAT'S ALL UP TO THE MUSICIAN.
IT SEEMS LIKE YOU'VE TAKEN A LIKING TO IT.
That makes me happy!
WHAT?!
NO! THAT'S A COM-PLETELY DIFFERENT MATTER...
HUH?
I MEAN...
THIS IS TOTALLY UNFAIR. FOR THE OTHER CONTESTANTS, THAT IS.
I-I'M NOT ASKING YOU TO WIN THE CONTEST!
I'M JUST ASKING YOU TO PARTICIPATE!

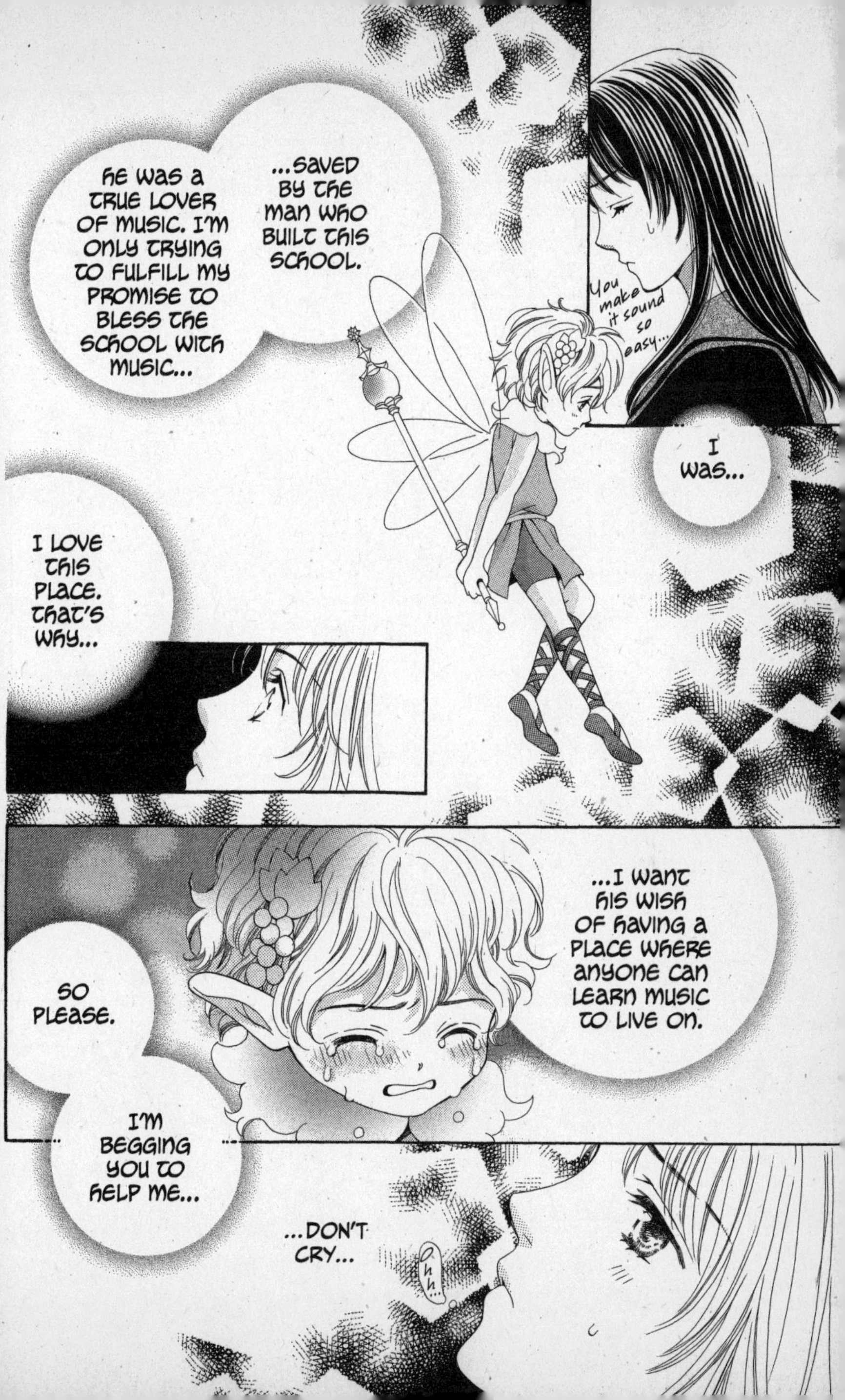

You make it sound so easy...
I was...
...SAVED BY THE MAN WHO BUILT THIS SCHOOL.
HE WAS A TRUE LOVER OF MUSIC. I'M ONLY TRYING TO FULFILL MY PROMISE TO BLESS THE SCHOOL WITH MUSIC...
I LOVE THIS PLACE. THAT'S WHY...
...I WANT HIS WISH OF HAVING A PLACE WHERE ANYONE CAN LEARN MUSIC TO LIVE ON.
SO PLEASE.
I'M BEGGING YOU TO HELP ME...
...DON'T CRY...
Nh...

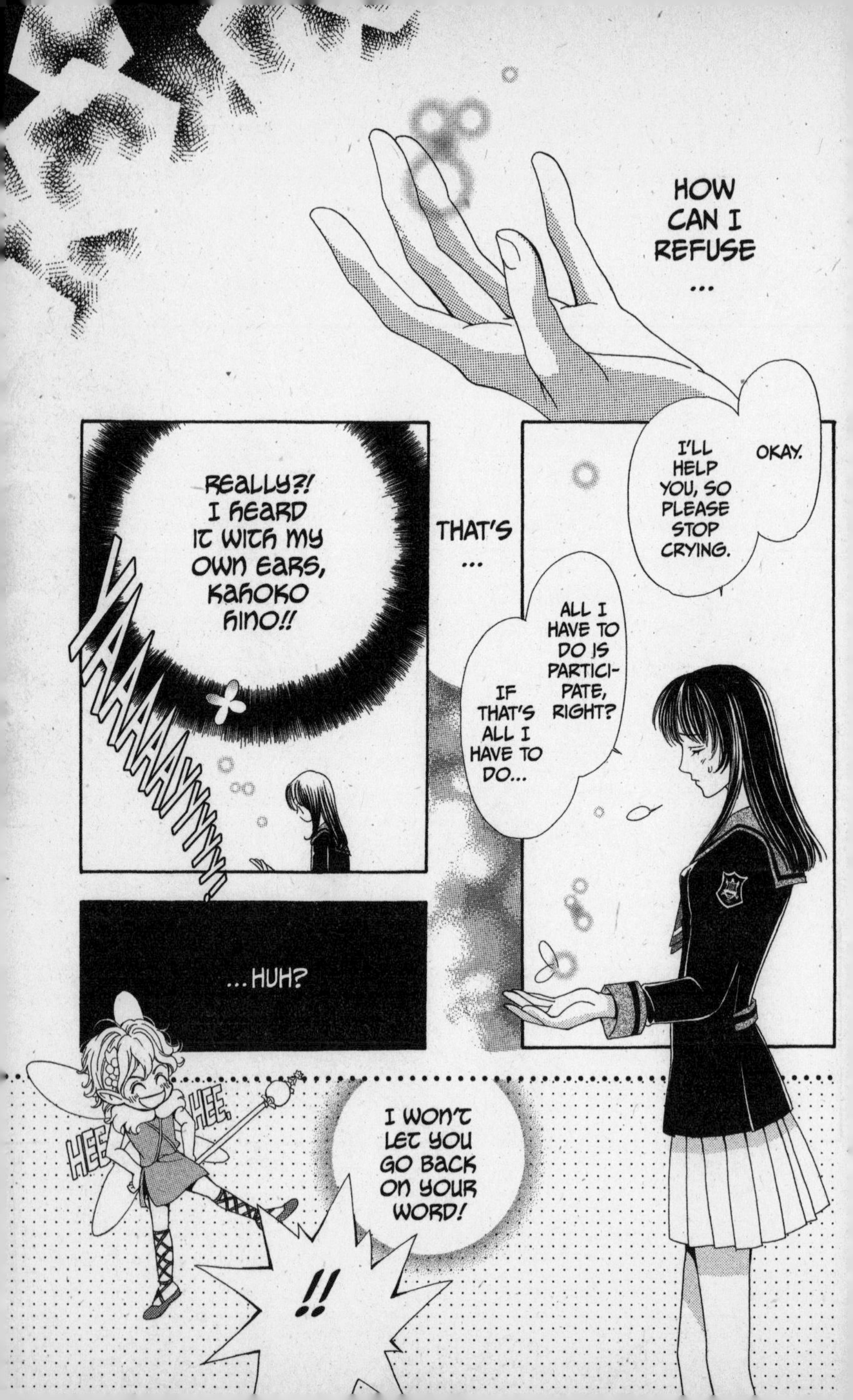
HOW CAN I REFUSE ...
OKAY.
I'LL HELP YOU, SO PLEASE STOP CRYING.
ALL I HAVE TO DO IS PARTICIPATE, RIGHT?
IF THAT'S ALL I HAVE TO DO...
THAT'S ...
REALLY?! I HEARD IT WITH MY OWN EARS, KAHOKO HINO!!
YAAAAAYYYYY!
...HUH?
I WON'T LET YOU GO BACK ON YOUR WORD!
HEE HEE.
!!

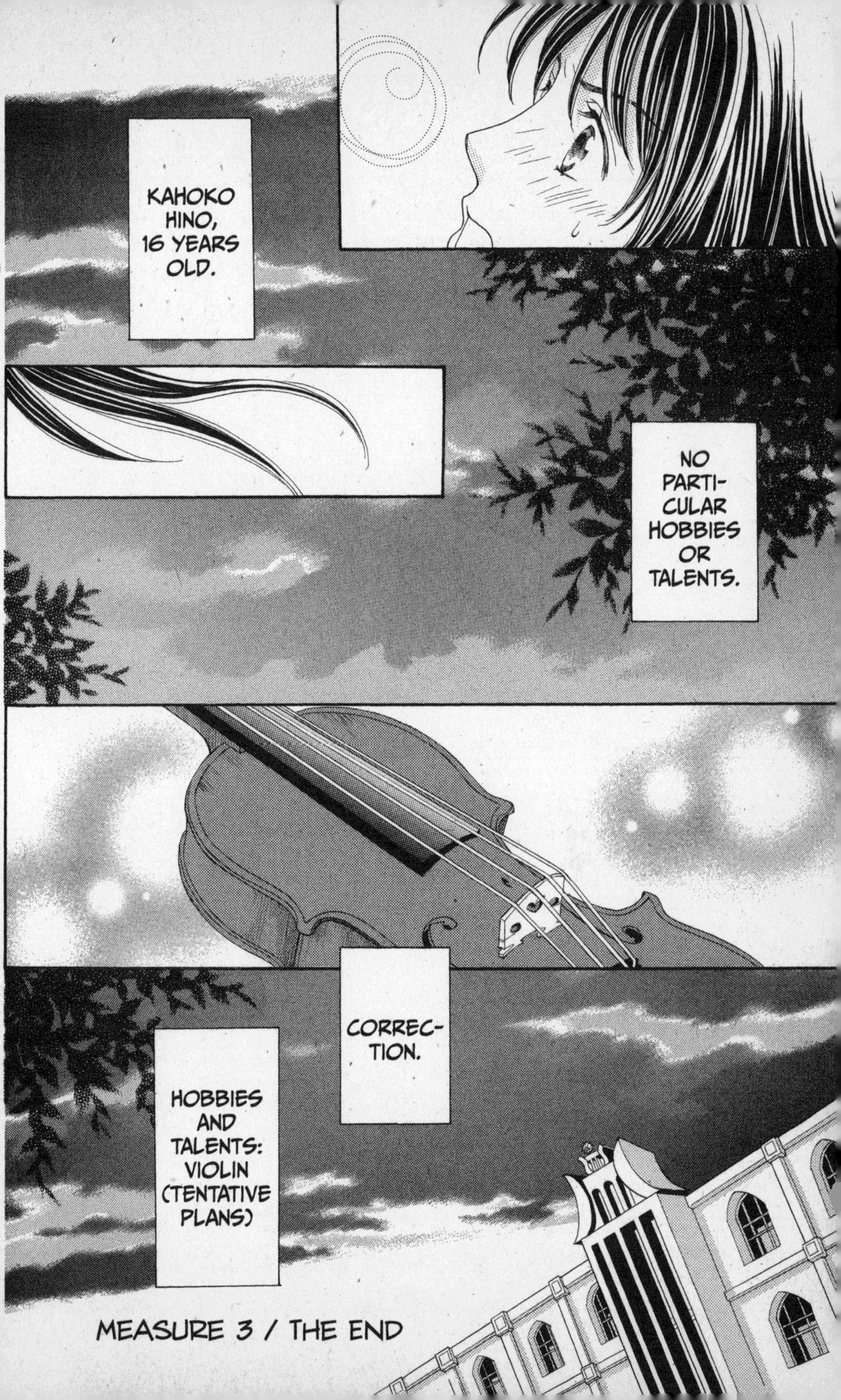
KAHOKO HINO, 16 YEARS OLD.
NO PARTI- CULAR HOBBIES OR TALENTS.
CORREC- TION.
HOBBIES AND TALENTS: VIOLIN (TENTATIVE PLANS)
MEASURE 3 / THE END

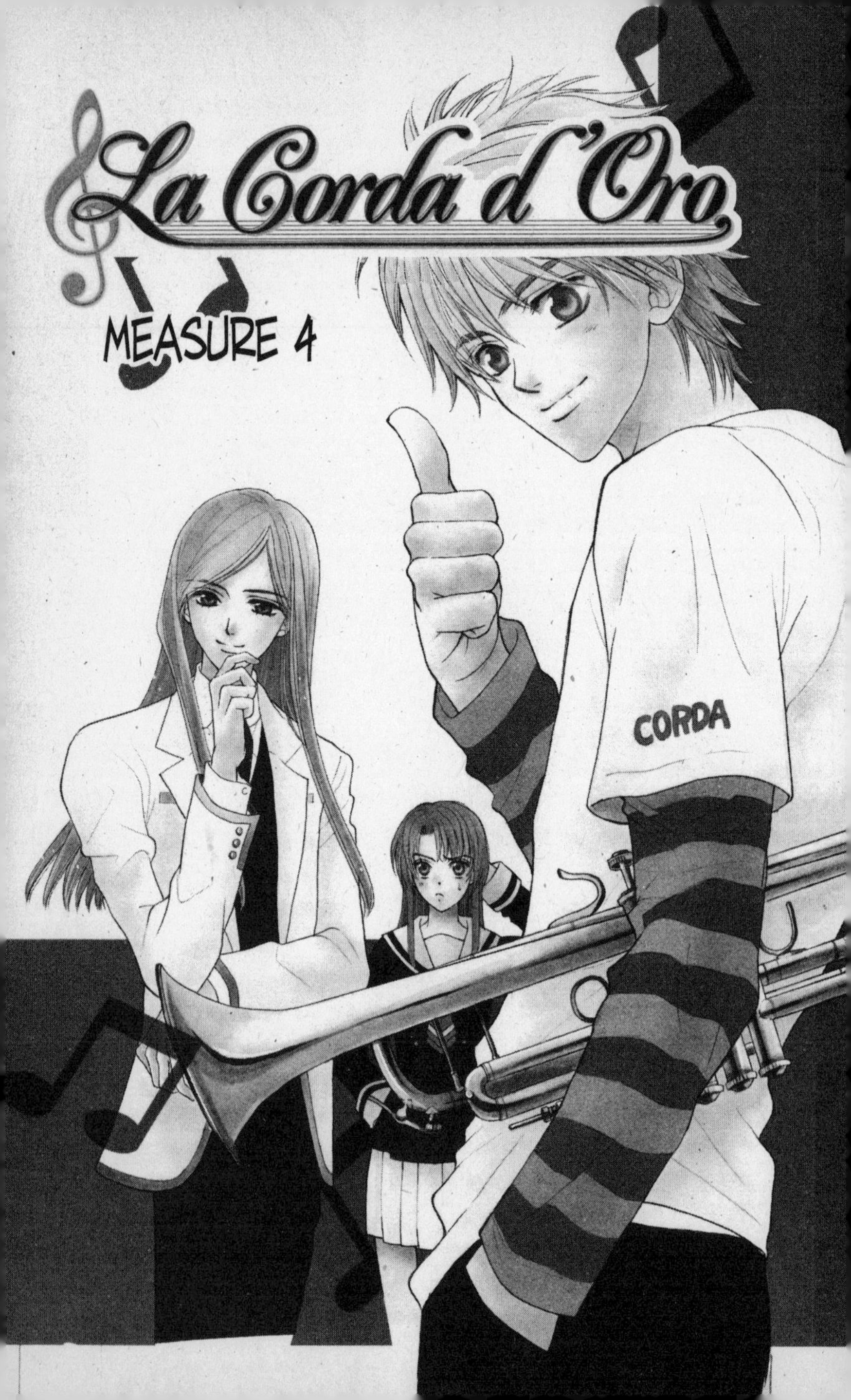
La Corda d'Oro
MEASURE 4
CORDA

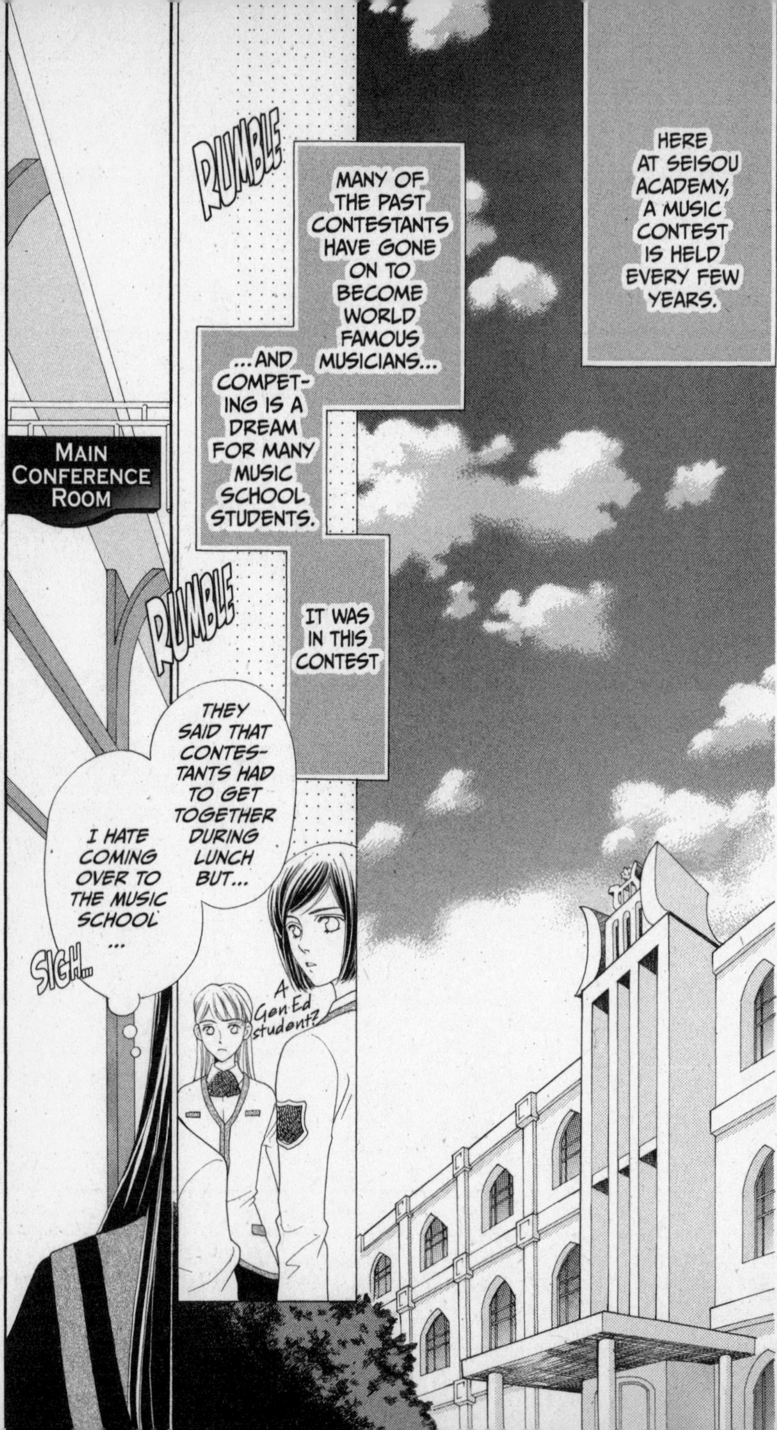
HERE AT SEISOU ACADEMY, A MUSIC CONTEST IS HELD EVERY FEW YEARS.
MANY OF THE PAST CONTESTANTS HAVE GONE ON TO BECOME WORLD FAMOUS MUSICIANS...
...AND COMPETING IS A DREAM FOR MANY MUSIC SCHOOL STUDENTS.
IT WAS IN THIS CONTEST
RUMBLE
RUMBLE
THEY SAID THAT CONTESTANTS HAD TO GET TOGETHER DURING LUNCH BUT...
A Gen Ed student?
MAIN CONFERENCE ROOM
I HATE COMING OVER TO THE MUSIC SCHOOL ...
SIGH...

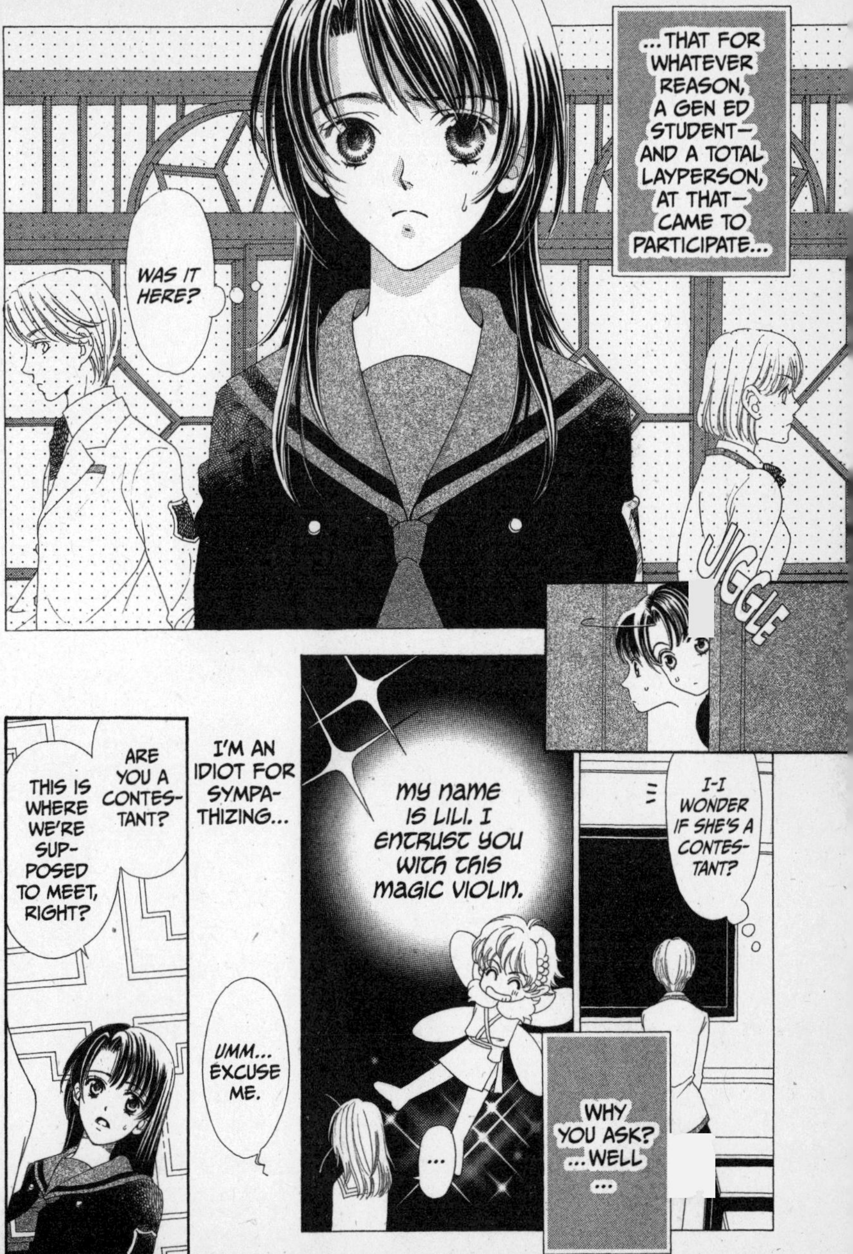
...THAT FOR WHATEVER REASON, A GEN ED STUDENT—AND A TOTAL LAYPERSON, AT THAT—CAME TO PARTICIPATE...
WAS IT HERE?
JIGGLE
I-I WONDER IF SHE'S A CONTESTANT?
WHY YOU ASK? ...WELL ...
my name is Lili. I entrust you with this magic violin.
...
I'M AN IDIOT FOR SYMPATHIZING...
ARE YOU A CONTESTANT?
THIS IS WHERE WE'RE SUPPOSED TO MEET, RIGHT?
UMM... EXCUSE ME.

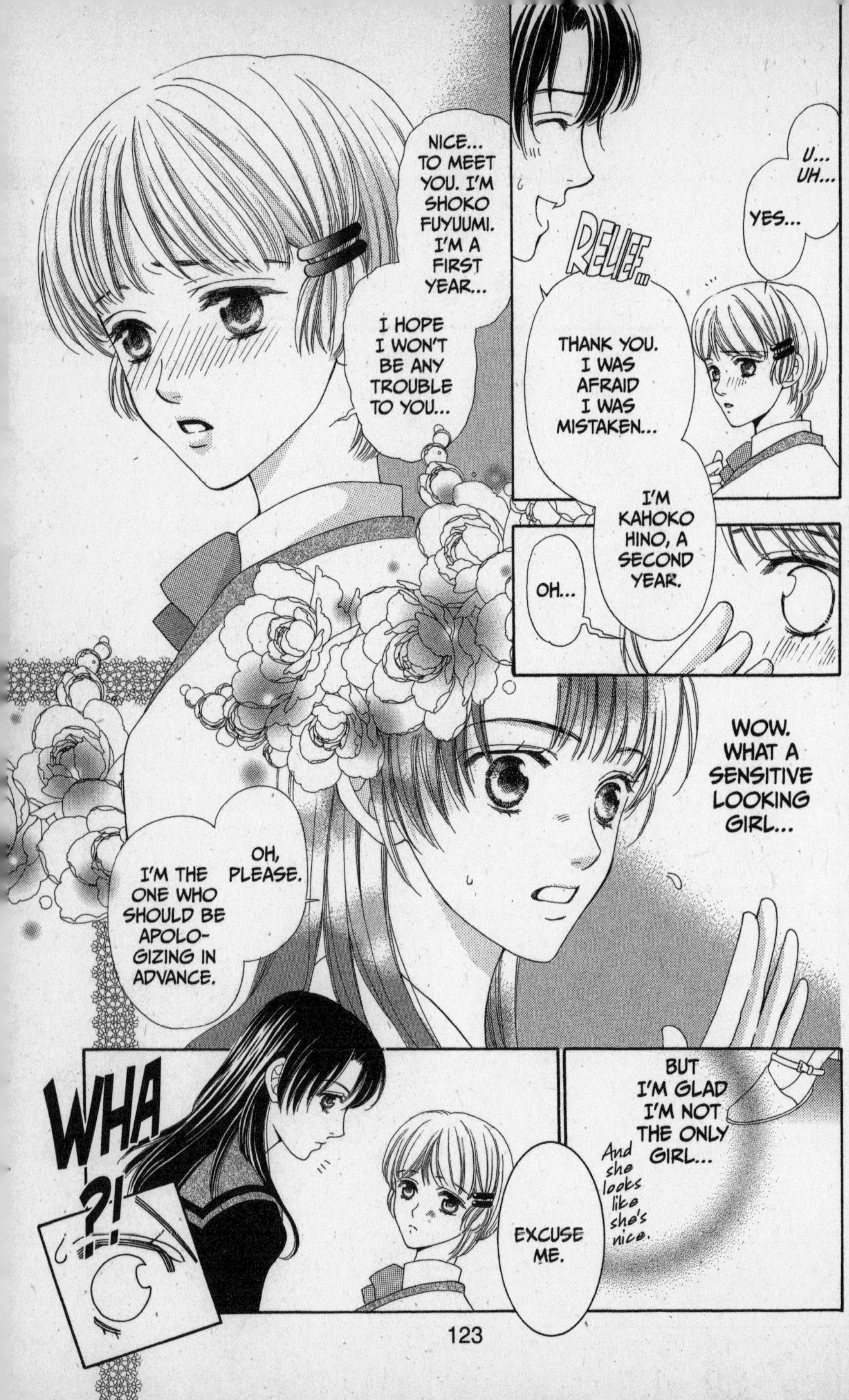
U... UH...
YES...
RELIEF...
THANK YOU. I WAS AFRAID I WAS MISTAKEN...
I'M KAHOKO HINO, A SECOND YEAR.
OH...
NICE... TO MEET YOU. I'M SHOKO FUYUUMI. I'M A FIRST YEAR...
I HOPE I WON'T BE ANY TROUBLE TO YOU...
OH, PLEASE.
I'M THE ONE WHO SHOULD BE APOLO-GIZING IN ADVANCE.
WOW. WHAT A SENSITIVE LOOKING GIRL...
BUT I'M GLAD I'M NOT THE ONLY GIRL...
And she looks like she's nice.
EXCUSE ME.
WHA ?!

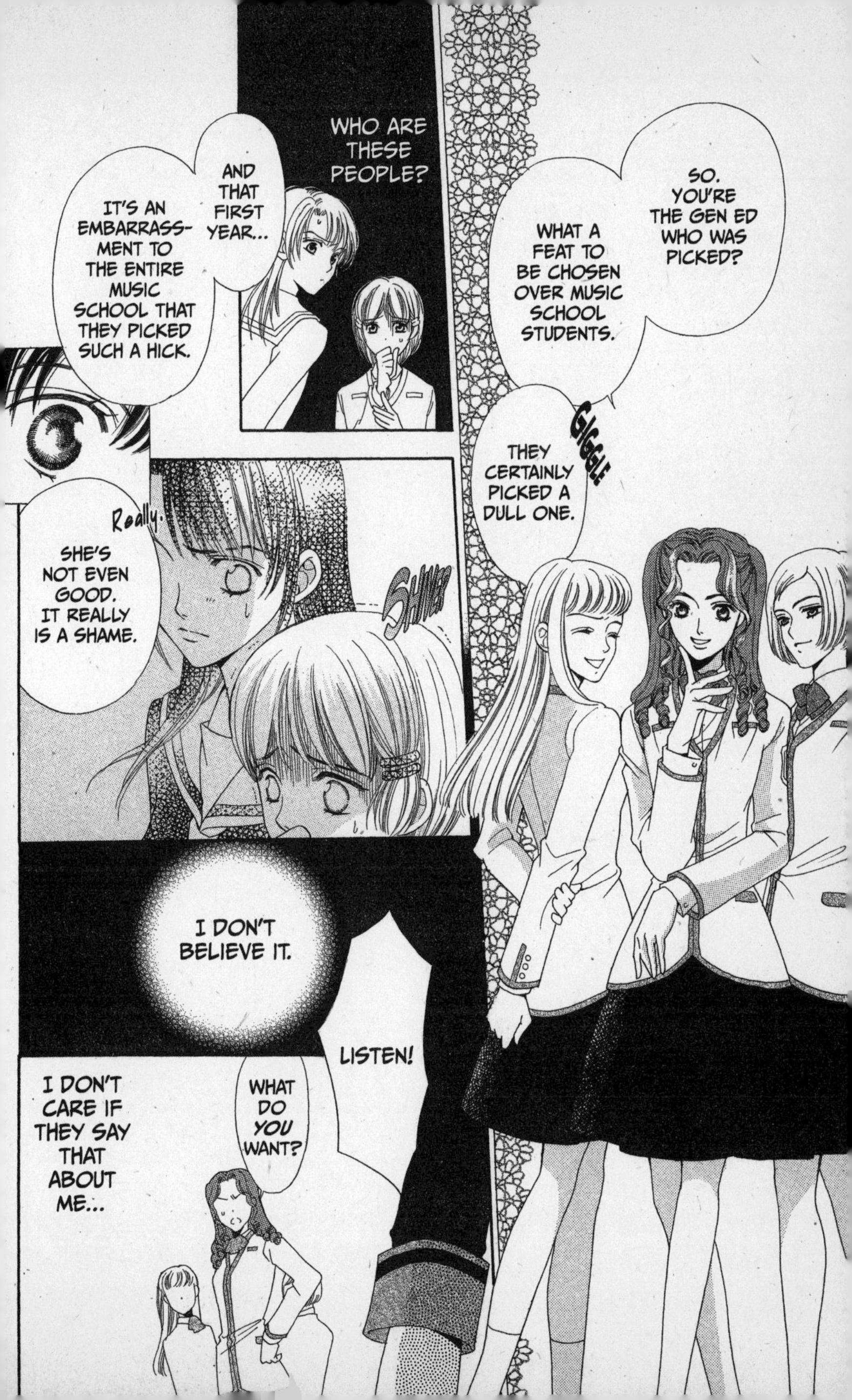

SO. YOU'RE THE GEN ED WHO WAS PICKED?
WHAT A FEAT TO BE CHOSEN OVER MUSIC SCHOOL STUDENTS.
GIGGLE
THEY CERTAINLY PICKED A DULL ONE.
WHO ARE THESE PEOPLE?
AND THAT FIRST YEAR...
IT'S AN EMBARRASSMENT TO THE ENTIRE MUSIC SCHOOL THAT THEY PICKED SUCH A HICK.
SHIVER
Really.
SHE'S NOT EVEN GOOD. IT REALLY IS A SHAME.
I DON'T BELIEVE IT.
LISTEN!
WHAT DO YOU WANT?
I DON'T CARE IF THEY SAY THAT ABOUT ME...

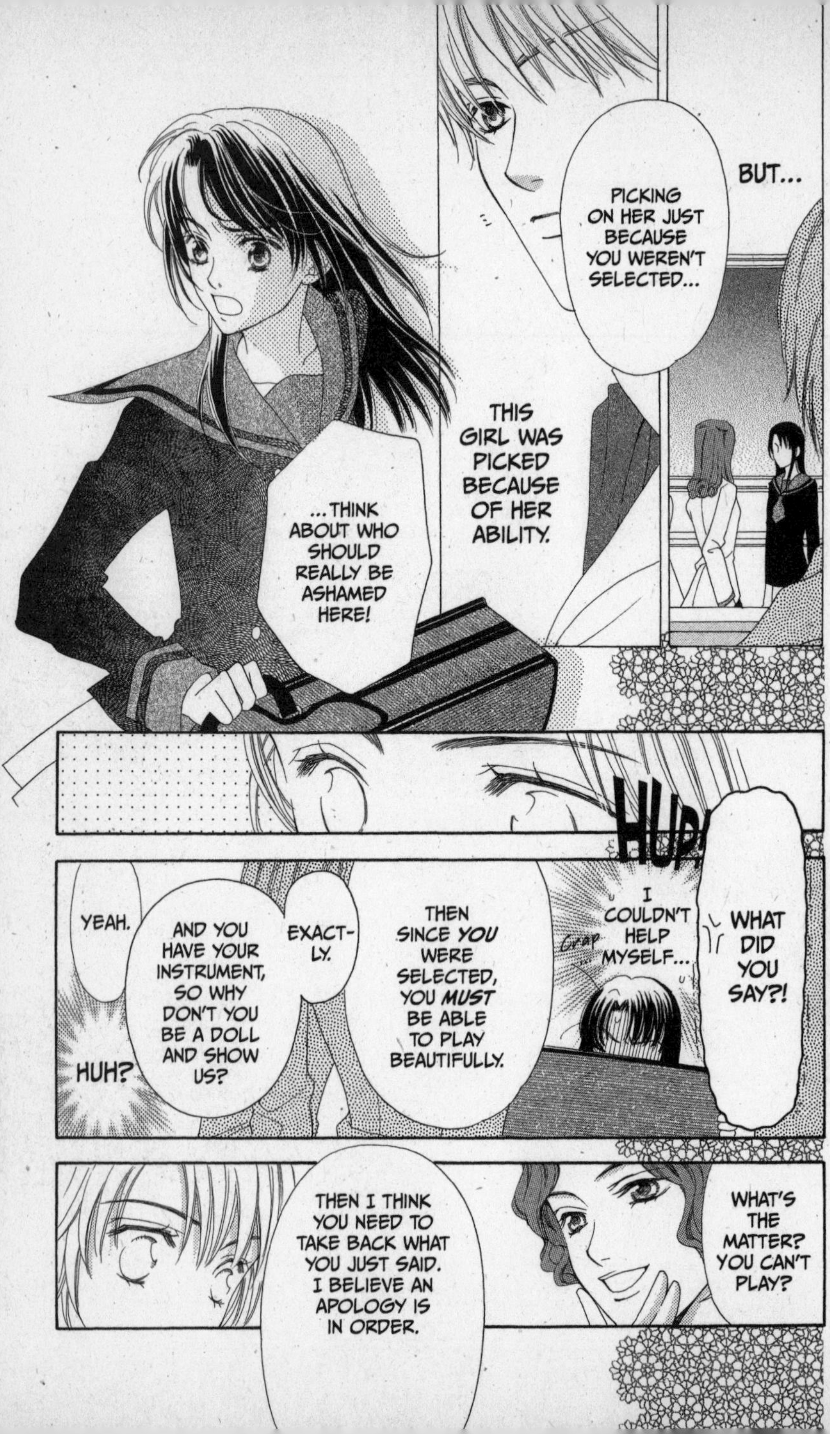
BUT...
PICKING ON HER JUST BECAUSE YOU WEREN'T SELECTED...
THIS GIRL WAS PICKED BECAUSE OF HER ABILITY.
...THINK ABOUT WHO SHOULD REALLY BE ASHAMED HERE!
HUH!
WHAT DID YOU SAY?!
I COULDN'T HELP MYSELF...
Grap...
THEN SINCE *YOU* WERE SELECTED, YOU *MUST* BE ABLE TO PLAY BEAUTIFULLY.
EXACT-LY.
AND YOU HAVE YOUR INSTRUMENT, SO WHY DON'T YOU BE A DOLL AND SHOW US?
YEAH.
HUH?
WHAT'S THE MATTER? YOU CAN'T PLAY?
THEN I THINK YOU NEED TO TAKE BACK WHAT YOU JUST SAID. I BELIEVE AN APOLOGY IS IN ORDER.

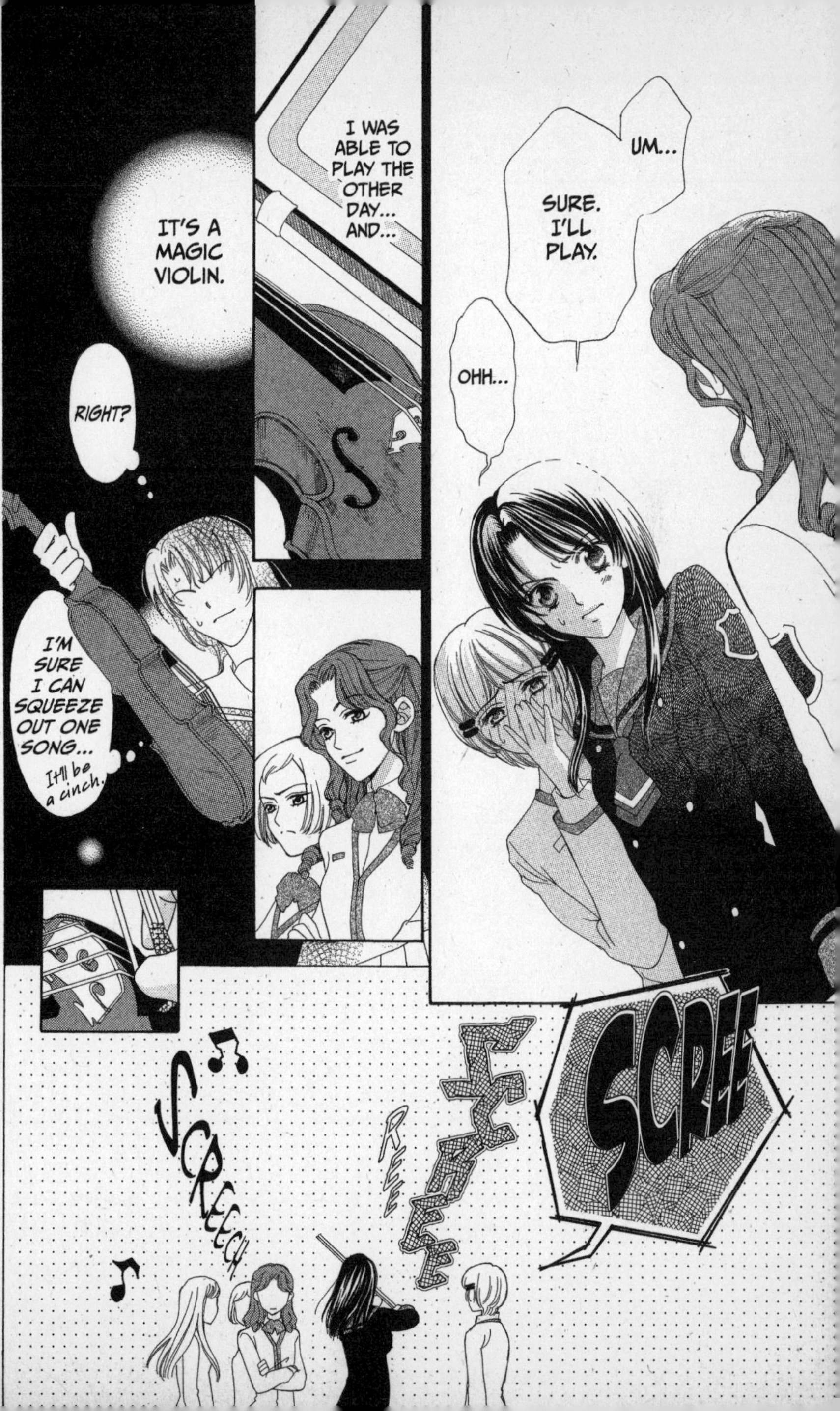
UM...
SURE. I'LL PLAY.
OHH...
I WAS ABLE TO PLAY THE OTHER DAY... AND...
IT'S A MAGIC VIOLIN.
RIGHT?
I'M SURE I CAN SQUEEZE OUT ONE SONG...
It'll be a cinch.
SCREE
REE
SCREECH

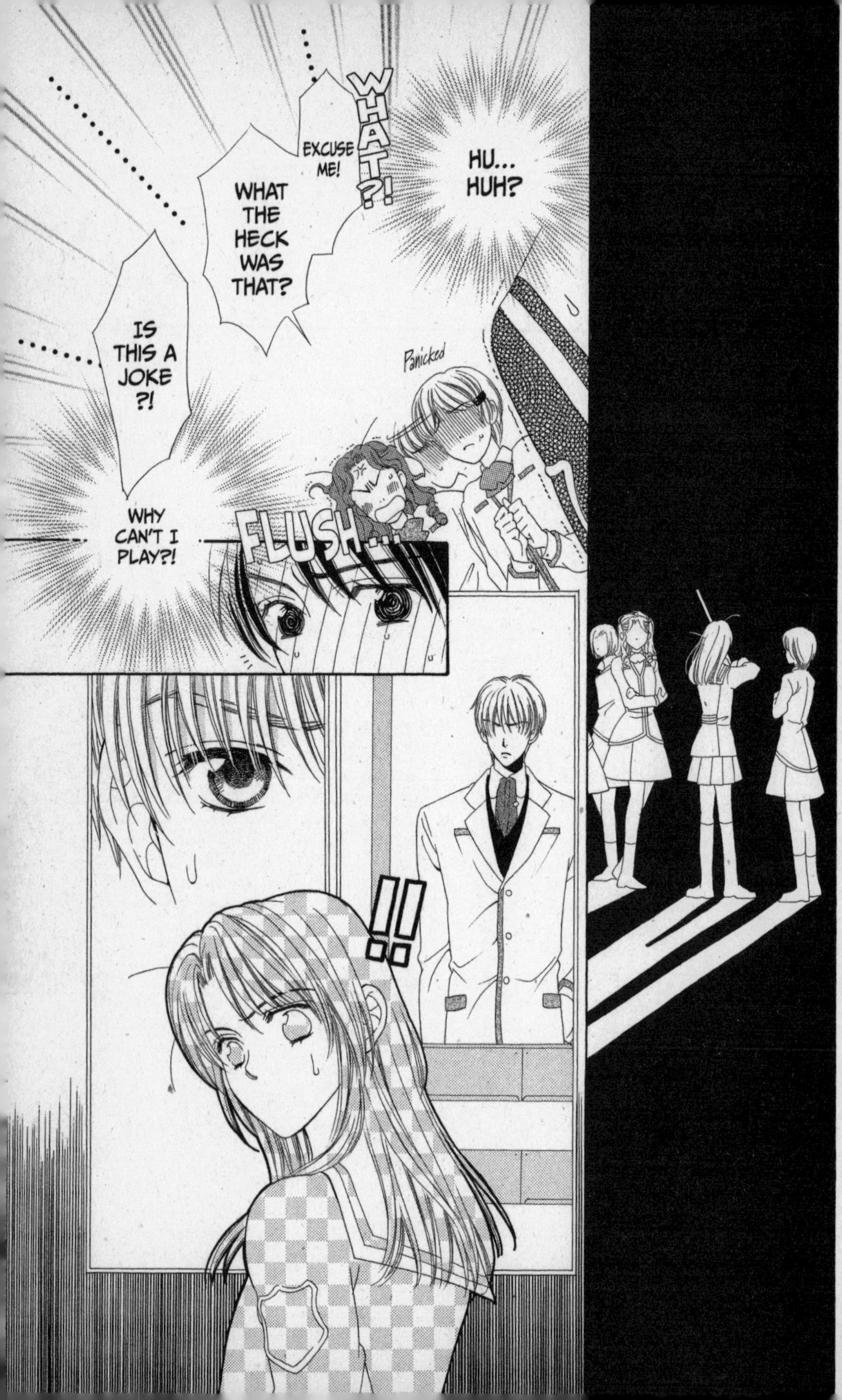
HU... HUH?
WHAT?!
EXCUSE ME!
WHAT THE HECK WAS THAT?
IS THIS A JOKE?!
WHY CAN'T I PLAY?!
Panicked
FLUSH...
!!

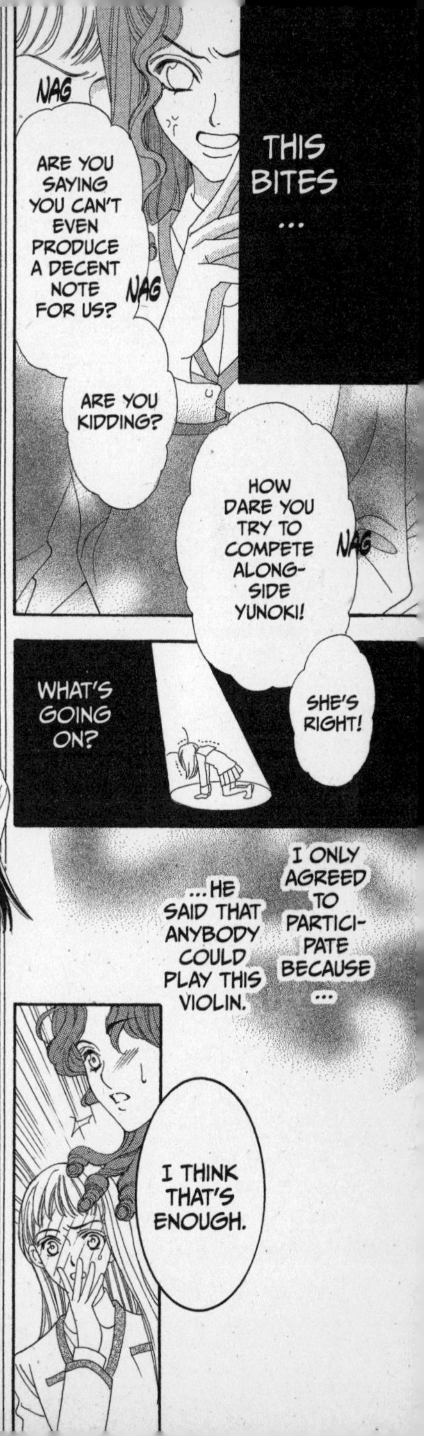
THIS BITES ...
NAG
ARE YOU SAYING YOU CAN'T EVEN PRODUCE A DECENT NOTE FOR US?
NAG
ARE YOU KIDDING?
HOW DARE YOU TRY TO COMPETE ALONG-SIDE YUNOKI!
NAG
SHE'S RIGHT!
WHAT'S GOING ON?
I ONLY AGREED TO PARTICI-PATE BECAUSE ...
...HE SAID THAT ANYBODY COULD PLAY THIS VIOLIN.
I THINK THAT'S ENOUGH.
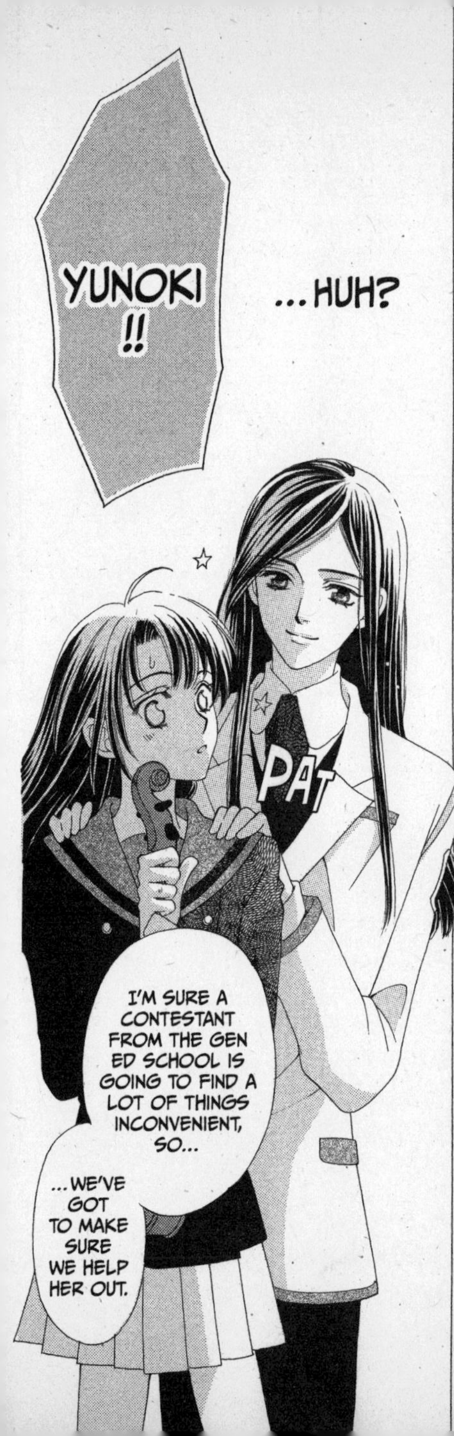
...HUH?
YUNOKI !!
PAT
I'M SURE A CONTESTANT FROM THE GEN ED SCHOOL IS GOING TO FIND A LOT OF THINGS INCONVENIENT, SO...
...WE'VE GOT TO MAKE SURE WE HELP HER OUT.

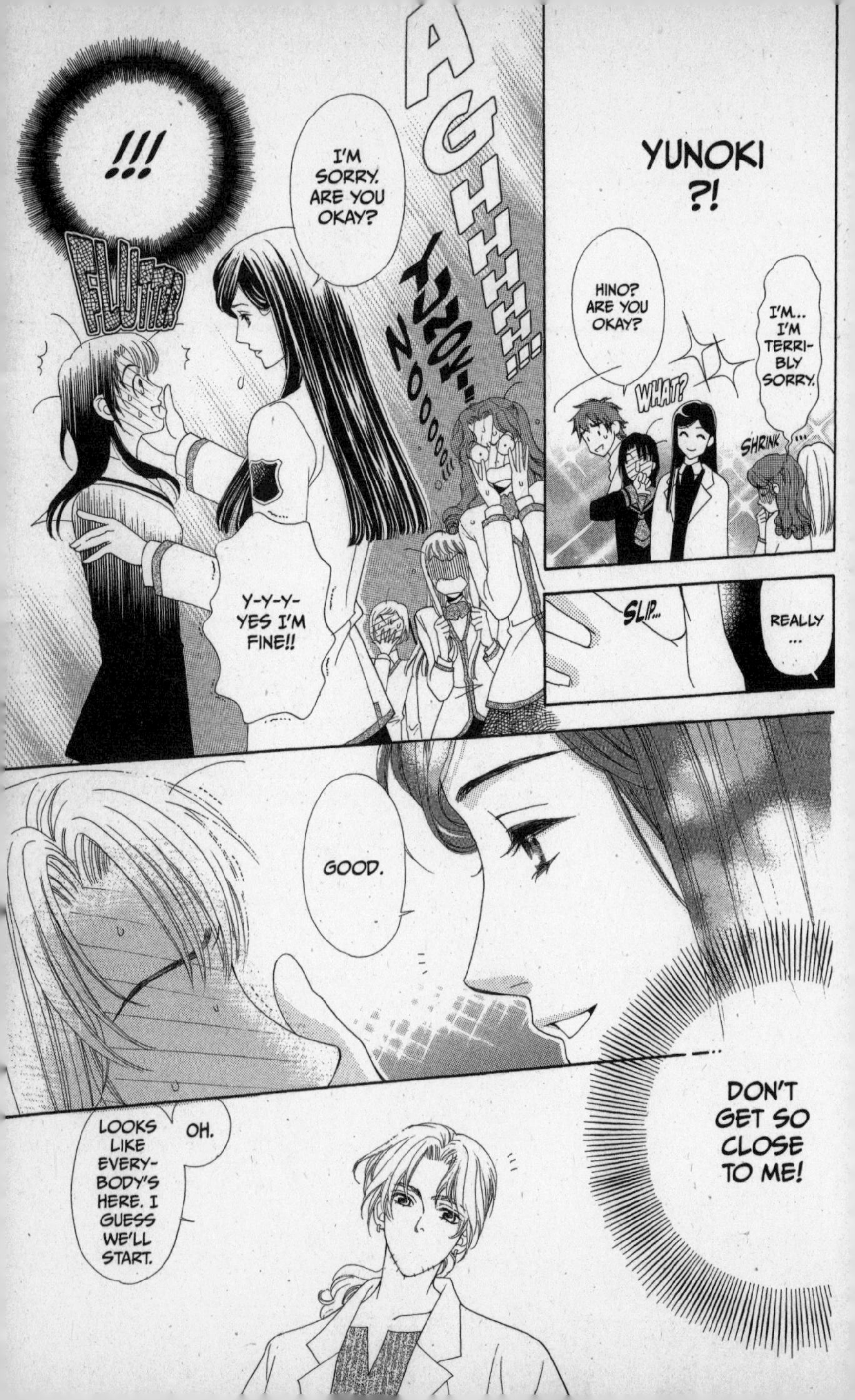
YUNOKI ?!
I'M.. I'M TERRI-BLY SORRY.
HINO? ARE YOU OKAY?
WHAT?
SHRINK
...
REALLY ...
SLIP...
AGHHHHHH!!!
I'M SORRY. ARE YOU OKAY?
!!!
Y-Y-Y-YES I'M FINE!!
GOOD.
DON'T GET SO CLOSE TO ME!
OH.
LOOKS LIKE EVERY-BODY'S HERE. I GUESS WE'LL START.

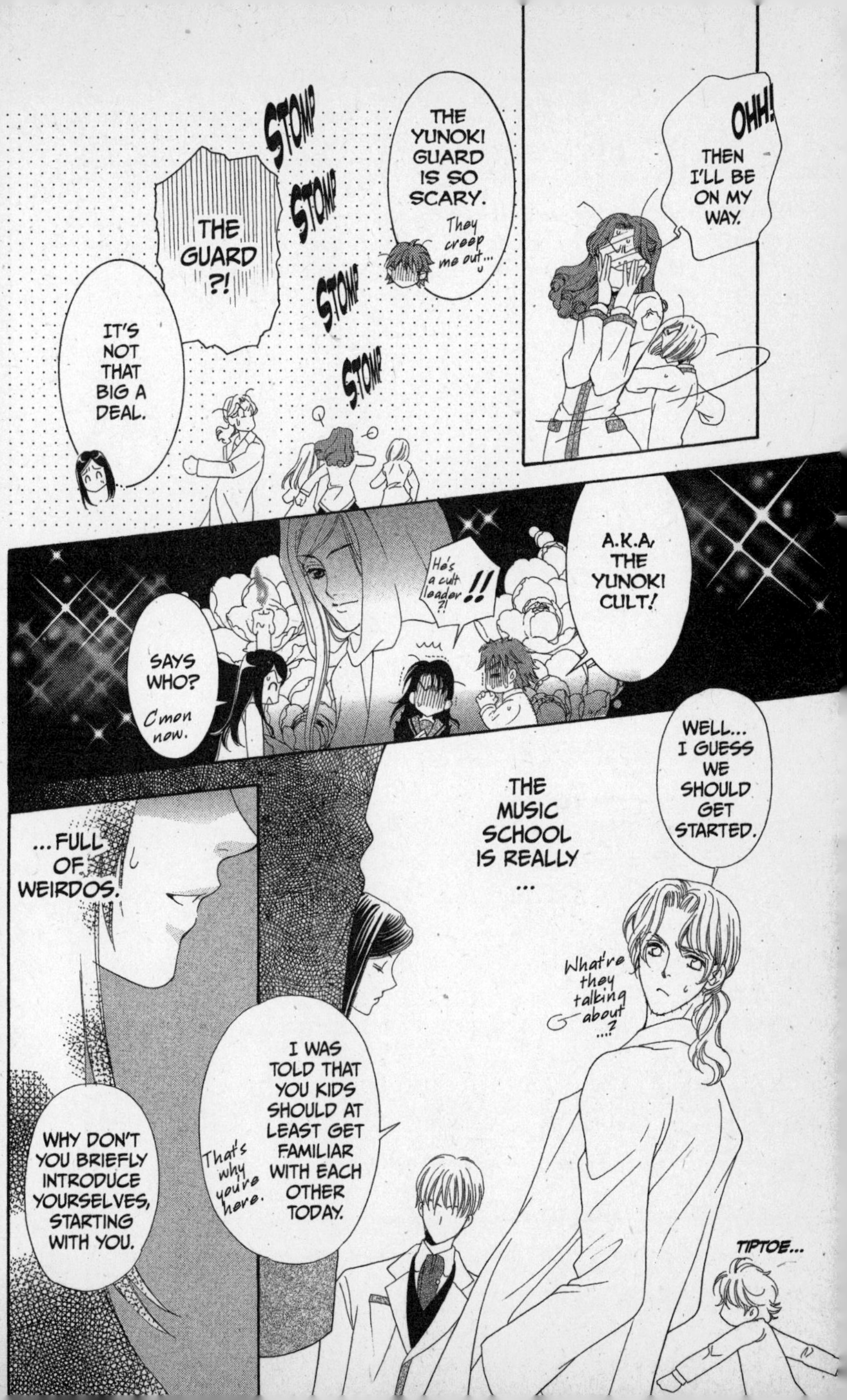
OHH!
THEN I'LL BE ON MY WAY.
THE YUNOKI GUARD IS SO SCARY.
They creep me out...
STOMP
STOMP
STOMP
STOMP
THE GUARD ?!
IT'S NOT THAT BIG A DEAL.
A.K.A. THE YUNOKI CULT!
He's a cult leader?!
!!
SAYS WHO?
C'mon now.
WELL... I GUESS WE SHOULD GET STARTED.
THE MUSIC SCHOOL IS REALLY...
...FULL OF WEIRDOS.
What're they talking about...?
I WAS TOLD THAT YOU KIDS SHOULD AT LEAST GET FAMILIAR WITH EACH OTHER TODAY.
That's why you're here.
WHY DON'T YOU BRIEFLY INTRODUCE YOURSELVES, STARTING WITH YOU.
TIPTOE...

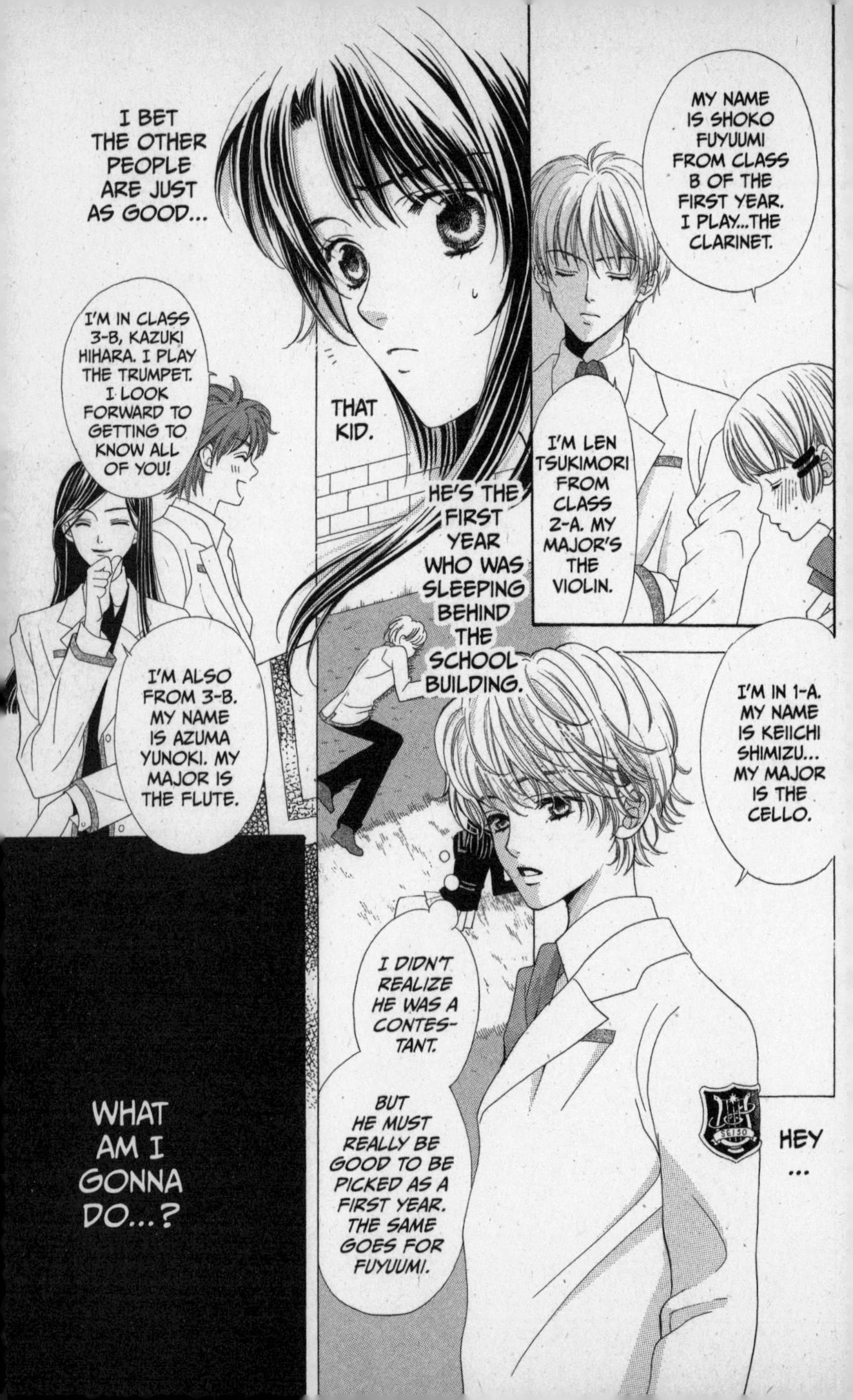

MY NAME IS SHOKO FUYUUMI FROM CLASS B OF THE FIRST YEAR. I PLAY...THE CLARINET.
I'M LEN TSUKIMORI FROM CLASS 2-A. MY MAJOR'S THE VIOLIN.
THAT KID.
HE'S THE FIRST YEAR WHO WAS SLEEPING BEHIND THE SCHOOL BUILDING.
I BET THE OTHER PEOPLE ARE JUST AS GOOD...
I'M IN CLASS 3-B, KAZUKI HIHARA. I PLAY THE TRUMPET. I LOOK FORWARD TO GETTING TO KNOW ALL OF YOU!
I'M ALSO FROM 3-B. MY NAME IS AZUMA YUNOKI. MY MAJOR IS THE FLUTE.
I'M IN 1-A. MY NAME IS KEIICHI SHIMIZU... MY MAJOR IS THE CELLO.
I DIDN'T REALIZE HE WAS A CONTES-TANT.
HEY ...
BUT HE MUST REALLY BE GOOD TO BE PICKED AS A FIRST YEAR. THE SAME GOES FOR FUYUUMI.
SEISO
WHAT AM I GONNA DO...?

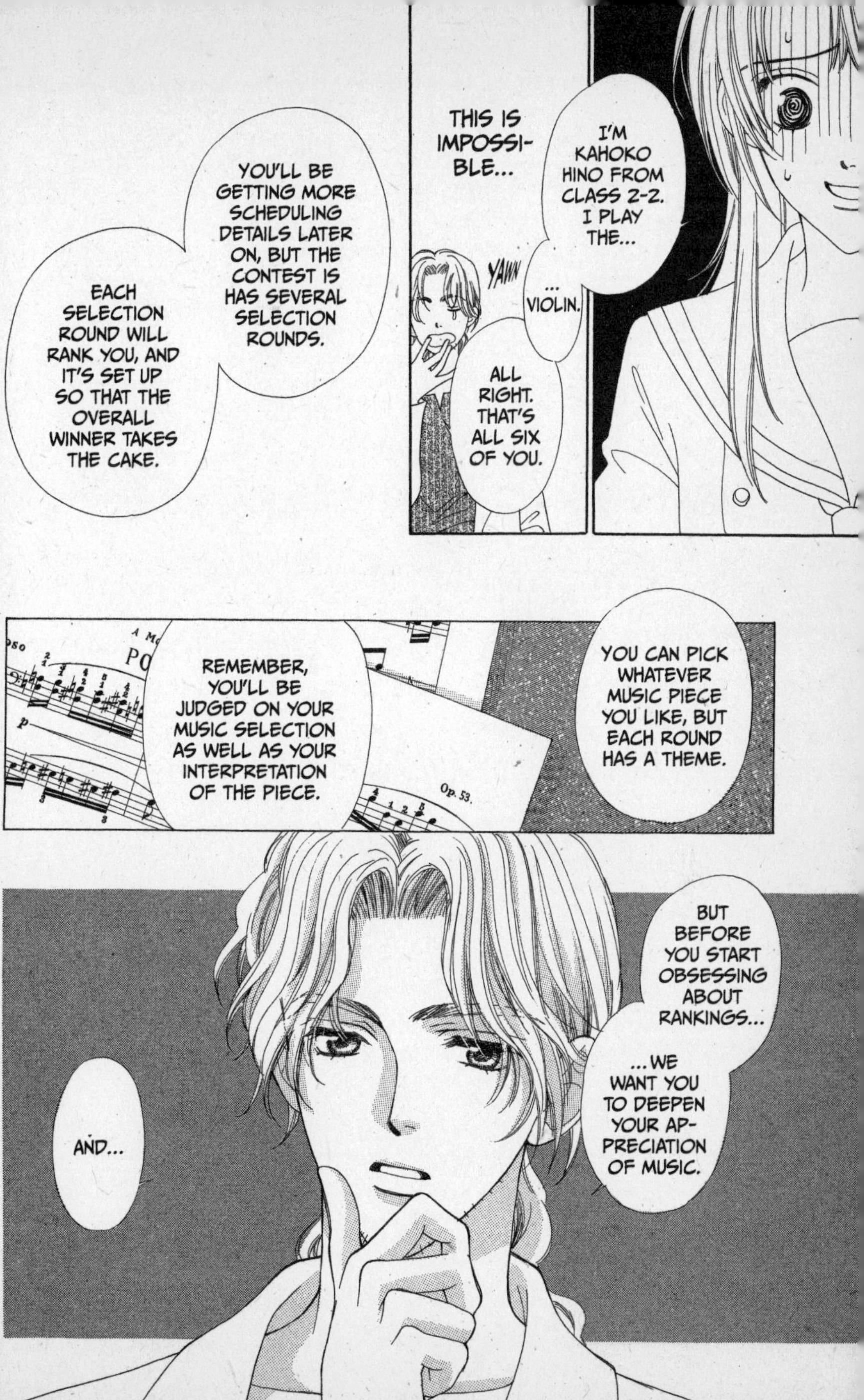
I'M KAHOKO HINO FROM CLASS 2-2. I PLAY THE...
THIS IS IMPOSSIBLE...
...VIOLIN.
YAWN
ALL RIGHT. THAT'S ALL SIX OF YOU.
YOU'LL BE GETTING MORE SCHEDULING DETAILS LATER ON, BUT THE CONTEST IS HAS SEVERAL SELECTION ROUNDS.
EACH SELECTION ROUND WILL RANK YOU, AND IT'S SET UP SO THAT THE OVERALL WINNER TAKES THE CAKE.
YOU CAN PICK WHATEVER MUSIC PIECE YOU LIKE, BUT EACH ROUND HAS A THEME.
REMEMBER, YOU'LL BE JUDGED ON YOUR MUSIC SELECTION AS WELL AS YOUR INTERPRETATION OF THE PIECE.
Op. 53.
BUT BEFORE YOU START OBSESSING ABOUT RANKINGS...
...WE WANT YOU TO DEEPEN YOUR APPRECIATION OF MUSIC.
AND...

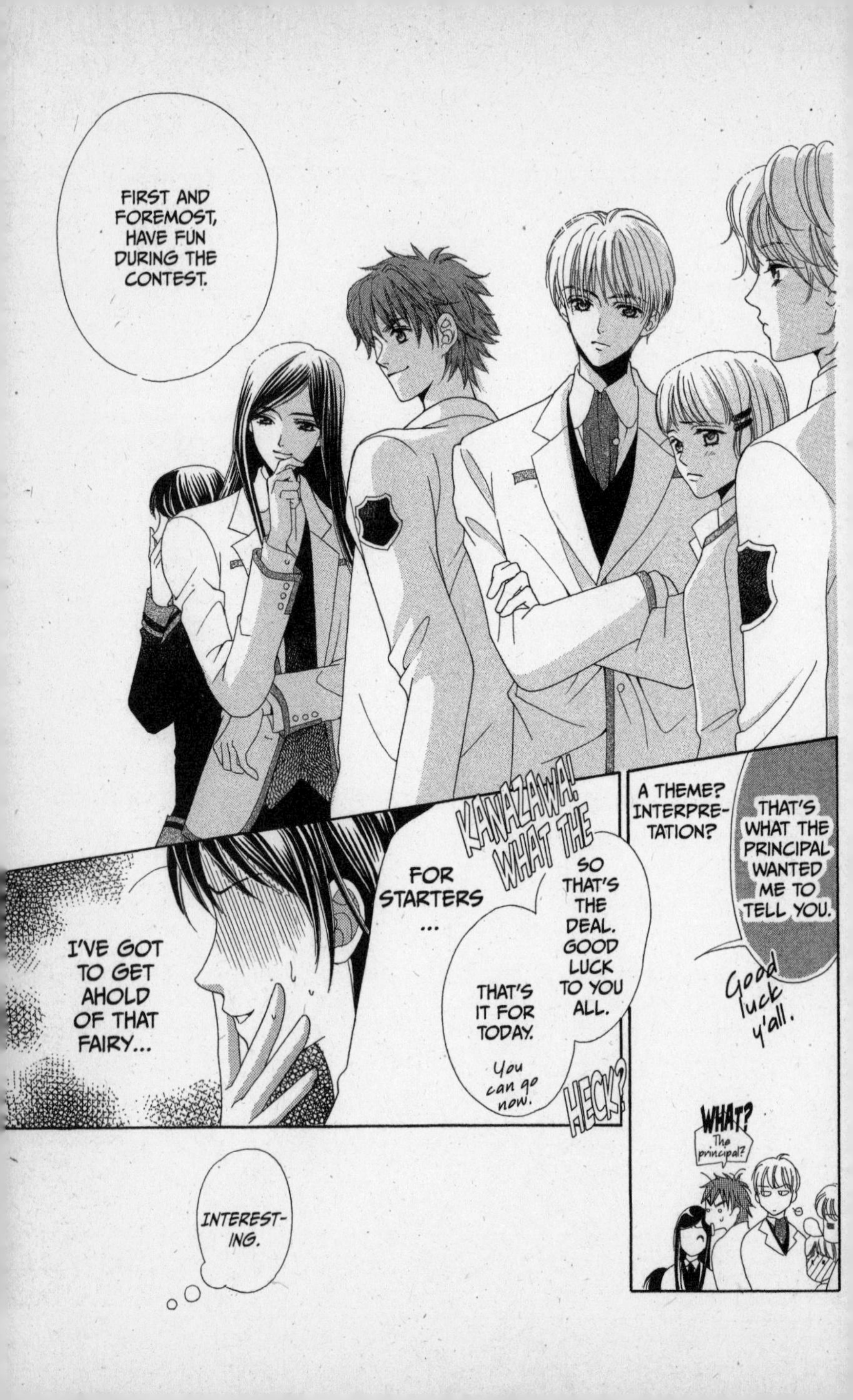
FIRST AND FOREMOST, HAVE FUN DURING THE CONTEST.
THAT'S WHAT THE PRINCIPAL WANTED ME TO TELL YOU.
Good luck y'all.
A THEME? INTERPRE-TATION?
WHAT?
The principal?
KANAZAWA! WHAT THE HECK?
SO THAT'S THE DEAL. GOOD LUCK TO YOU ALL.
THAT'S IT FOR TODAY.
You can go now.
FOR STARTERS ...
I'VE GOT TO GET AHOLD OF THAT FAIRY...
INTEREST-ING.

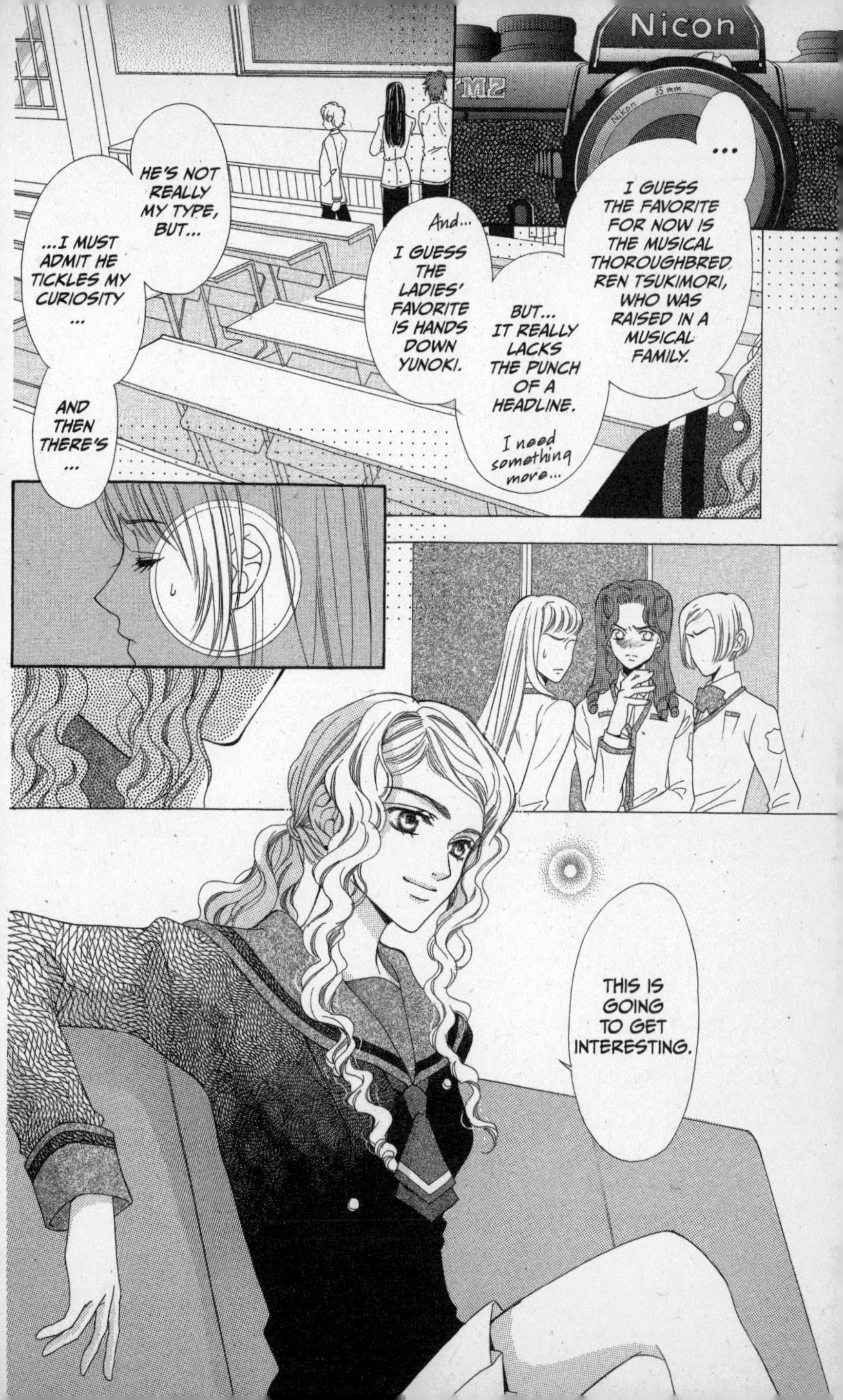
Nicon
...
I GUESS THE FAVORITE FOR NOW IS THE MUSICAL THOROUGHBRED REN TSUKIMORI, WHO WAS RAISED IN A MUSICAL FAMILY.
BUT... IT REALLY LACKS THE PUNCH OF A HEADLINE.
I need something more...
And... I GUESS THE LADIES' FAVORITE IS HANDS DOWN YUNOKI.
HE'S NOT REALLY MY TYPE, BUT...
...I MUST ADMIT HE TICKLES MY CURIOSITY ...
AND THEN THERE'S ...
THIS IS GOING TO GET INTERESTING.

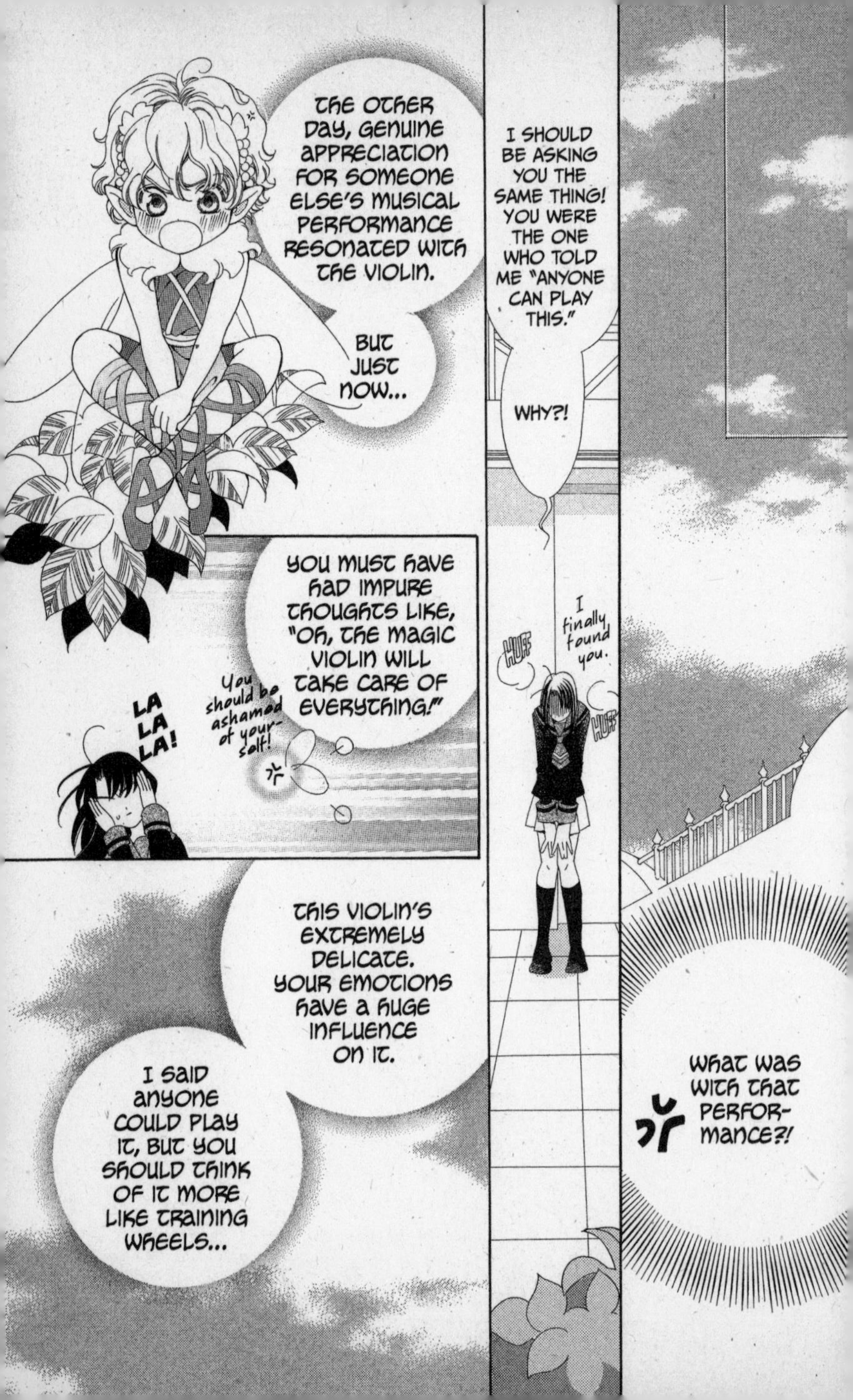
WHAT WAS WITH THAT PERFORMANCE?!
I SHOULD BE ASKING YOU THE SAME THING! YOU WERE THE ONE WHO TOLD ME "ANYONE CAN PLAY THIS."
WHY?!
I finally found you.
HUFF
HUFF
THE OTHER DAY, GENUINE APPRECIATION FOR SOMEONE ELSE'S MUSICAL PERFORMANCE RESONATED WITH THE VIOLIN.
BUT JUST NOW...
YOU MUST HAVE HAD IMPURE THOUGHTS LIKE, "OH, THE MAGIC VIOLIN WILL TAKE CARE OF EVERYTHING!"
You should be ashamed of yourself!
LA LA LA!
THIS VIOLIN'S EXTREMELY DELICATE. YOUR EMOTIONS HAVE A HUGE INFLUENCE ON IT.
I SAID ANYONE COULD PLAY IT, BUT YOU SHOULD THINK OF IT MORE LIKE TRAINING WHEELS...

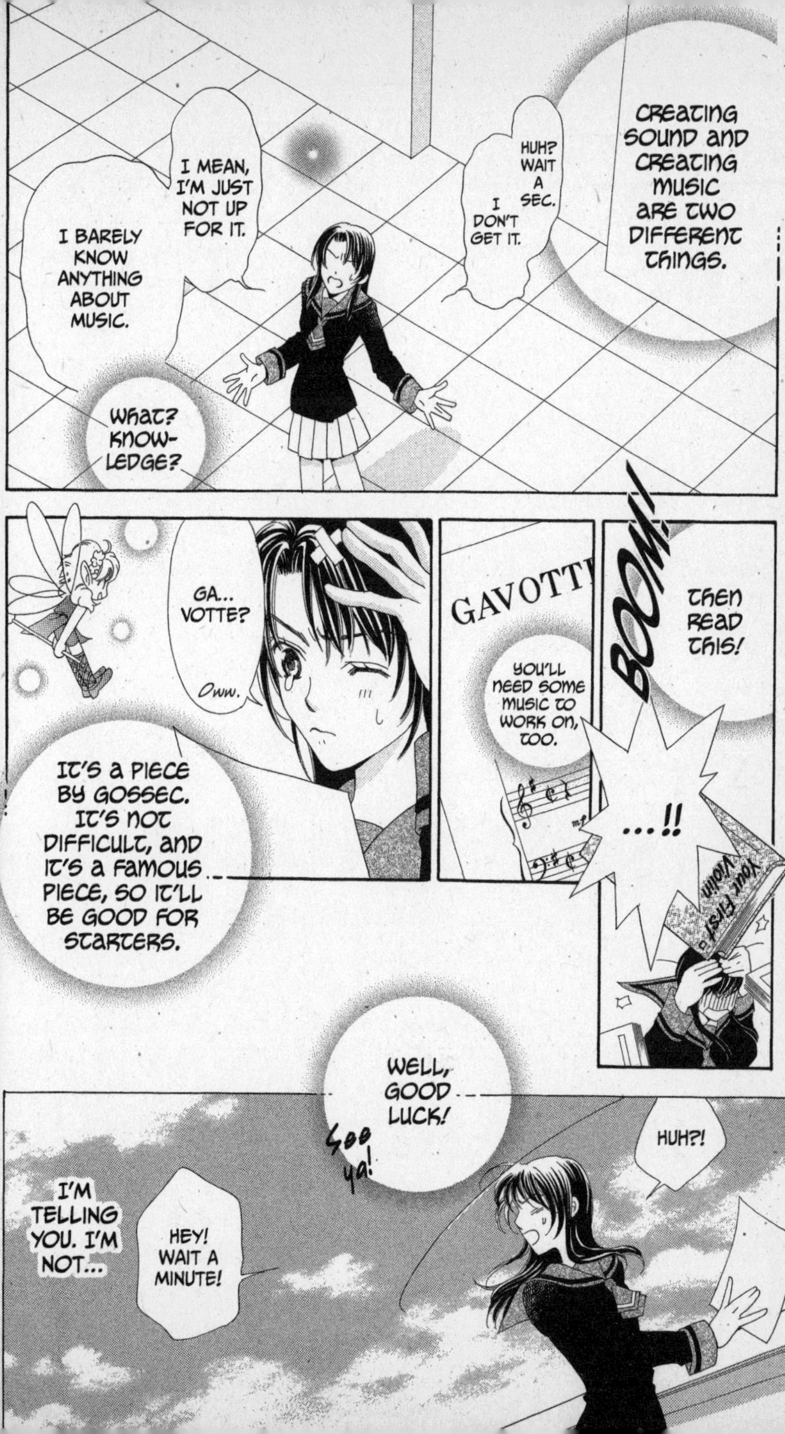
CREATING SOUND AND CREATING MUSIC ARE TWO DIFFERENT THINGS.
HUH? WAIT A SEC.
I DON'T GET IT.
I MEAN, I'M JUST NOT UP FOR IT.
I BARELY KNOW ANYTHING ABOUT MUSIC.
WHAT? KNOW-LEDGE?
THEN READ THIS!
BOOM!
...!!
Your First Violin
GAVOTT
YOU'LL NEED SOME MUSIC TO WORK ON, TOO.
GA... VOTTE?
Oww.
IT'S A PIECE BY GOSSEC. IT'S NOT DIFFICULT, AND IT'S A FAMOUS PIECE, SO IT'LL BE GOOD FOR STARTERS.
HUH?!
WELL, GOOD LUCK!
See ya!
HEY! WAIT A MINUTE!
I'M TELLING YOU. I'M NOT...

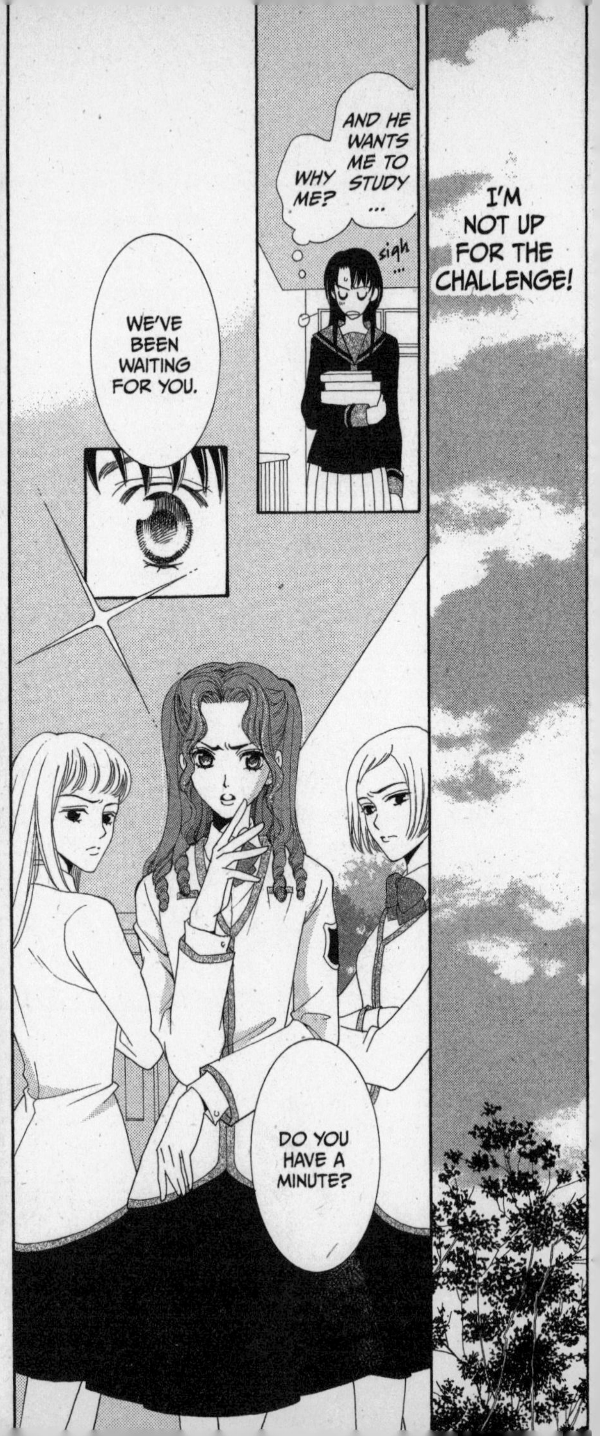
I'M NOT UP FOR THE CHALLENGE!
AND HE WANTS ME TO STUDY ...
WHY ME?
sigh ...
WE'VE BEEN WAITING FOR YOU.
DO YOU HAVE A MINUTE?

Lastly...

Given this opportunity, I wanted to take up an instrument (simpleminded I know...) and I thought for a moment that since my sister plays the flute, I could grab on to her coattails. But...the question remained whether someone like me, who gave up on music in elementary school when I couldn't play the recorder, could actually play the flute. I'm sorry to have taken up so much room with such boring babble, but I'm out of space now. I just wanted to thank you for reading this thus far.

Yuki Kure

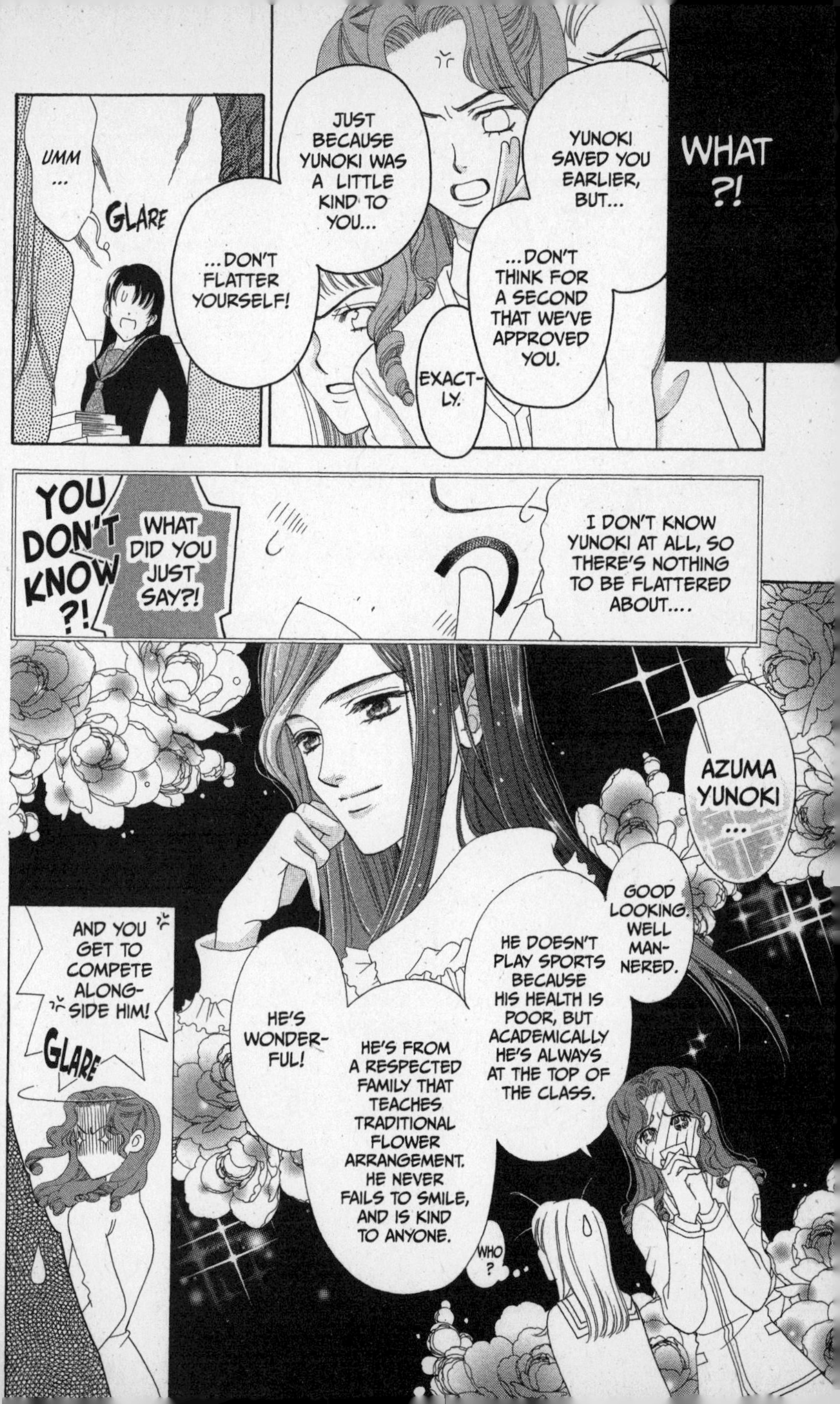
WHAT ?!
YUNOKI SAVED YOU EARLIER, BUT...
...DON'T THINK FOR A SECOND THAT WE'VE APPROVED YOU.
EXACT-LY.
JUST BECAUSE YUNOKI WAS A LITTLE KIND TO YOU...
...DON'T FLATTER YOURSELF!
UMM ...
GLARE
I DON'T KNOW YUNOKI AT ALL, SO THERE'S NOTHING TO BE FLATTERED ABOUT....
WHAT DID YOU JUST SAY?!
YOU DON'T KNOW ?!
AZUMA YUNOKI ...
GOOD LOOKING. WELL MAN-NERED.
HE DOESN'T PLAY SPORTS BECAUSE HIS HEALTH IS POOR, BUT ACADEMICALLY HE'S ALWAYS AT THE TOP OF THE CLASS.
HE'S FROM A RESPECTED FAMILY THAT TEACHES TRADITIONAL FLOWER ARRANGEMENT. HE NEVER FAILS TO SMILE, AND IS KIND TO ANYONE.
HE'S WONDER-FUL!
WHO ?
AND YOU GET TO COMPETE ALONG-SIDE HIM!
GLARE

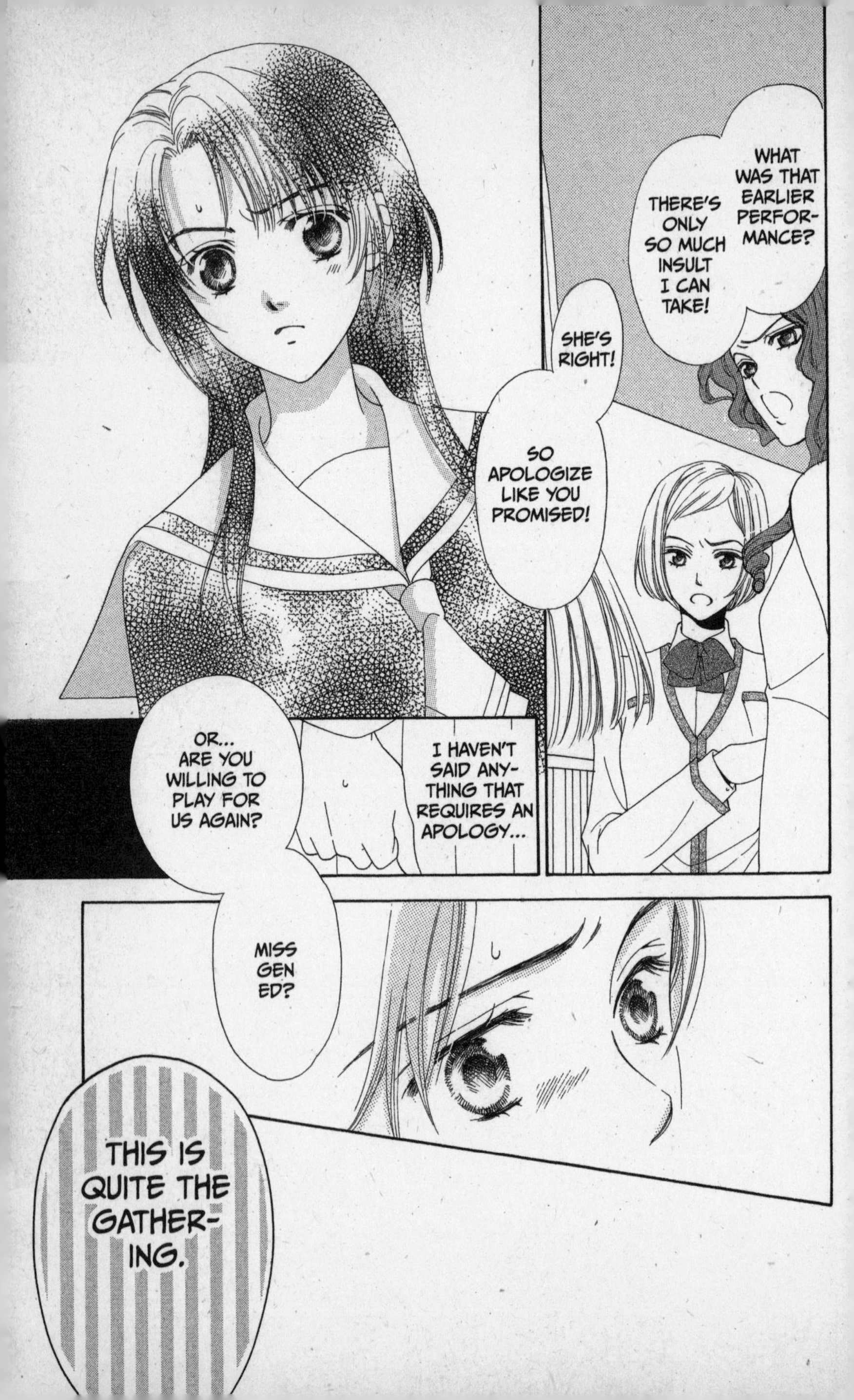
WHAT WAS THAT EARLIER PERFORMANCE?
THERE'S ONLY SO MUCH INSULT I CAN TAKE!
SHE'S RIGHT!
SO APOLOGIZE LIKE YOU PROMISED!
I HAVEN'T SAID ANYTHING THAT REQUIRES AN APOLOGY...
OR... ARE YOU WILLING TO PLAY FOR US AGAIN?
MISS GEN ED?
THIS IS QUITE THE GATHERING.

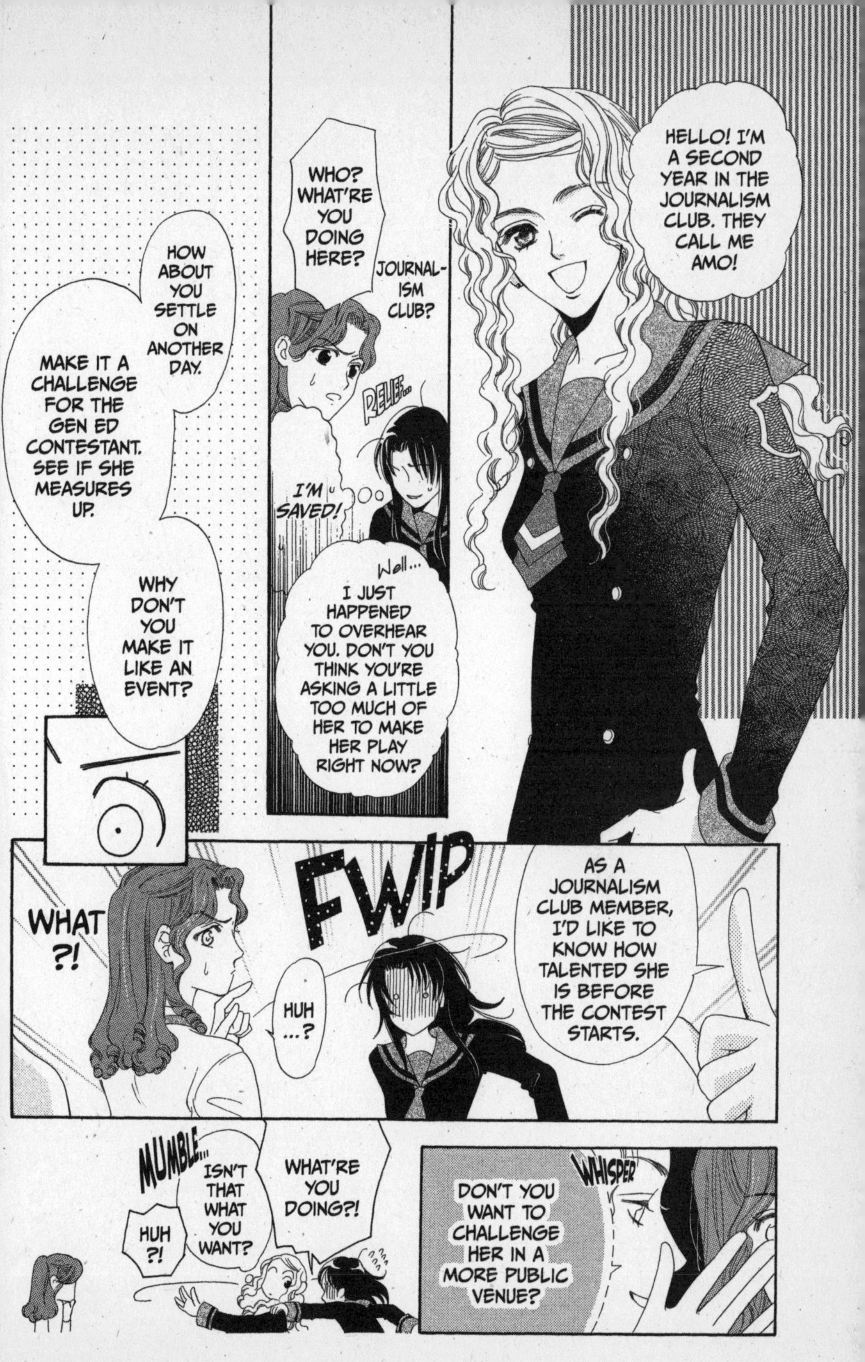
HELLO! I'M A SECOND YEAR IN THE JOURNALISM CLUB. THEY CALL ME AMO!
WHO? WHAT'RE YOU DOING HERE?
JOURNAL-ISM CLUB?
RELIEF...
I'M SAVED!
Well...
I JUST HAPPENED TO OVERHEAR YOU. DON'T YOU THINK YOU'RE ASKING A LITTLE TOO MUCH OF HER TO MAKE HER PLAY RIGHT NOW?
HOW ABOUT YOU SETTLE ON ANOTHER DAY.
MAKE IT A CHALLENGE FOR THE GEN ED CONTESTANT. SEE IF SHE MEASURES UP.
WHY DON'T YOU MAKE IT LIKE AN EVENT?
AS A JOURNALISM CLUB MEMBER, I'D LIKE TO KNOW HOW TALENTED SHE IS BEFORE THE CONTEST STARTS.
FWIP
HUH ...?
WHAT ?!
WHISPER
DON'T YOU WANT TO CHALLENGE HER IN A MORE PUBLIC VENUE?
WHAT'RE YOU DOING?!
MUMBLE...
ISN'T THAT WHAT YOU WANT?
HUH ?!

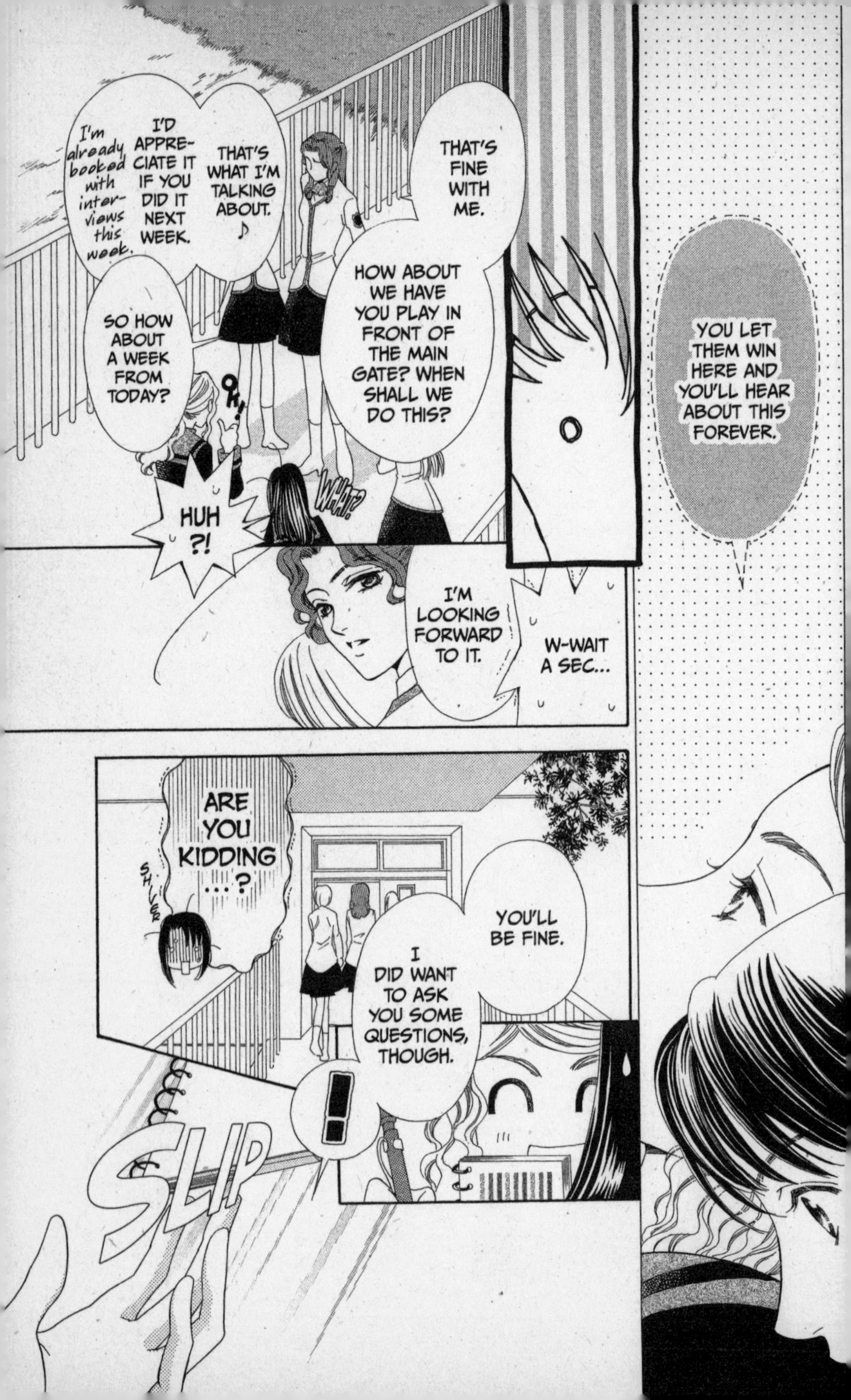
YOU LET THEM WIN HERE AND YOU'LL HEAR ABOUT THIS FOREVER.
THAT'S FINE WITH ME.
HOW ABOUT WE HAVE YOU PLAY IN FRONT OF THE MAIN GATE? WHEN SHALL WE DO THIS?
THAT'S WHAT I'M TALKING ABOUT. ♪
I'D APPRECIATE IT IF YOU DID IT NEXT WEEK.
I'm already booked with interviews this week.
SO HOW ABOUT A WEEK FROM TODAY?
OH!
WHAT?
HUH ?!
W-WAIT A SEC...
I'M LOOKING FORWARD TO IT.
YOU'LL BE FINE.
I DID WANT TO ASK YOU SOME QUESTIONS, THOUGH.
ARE YOU KIDDING ...?
SHIVER
!
SLIP

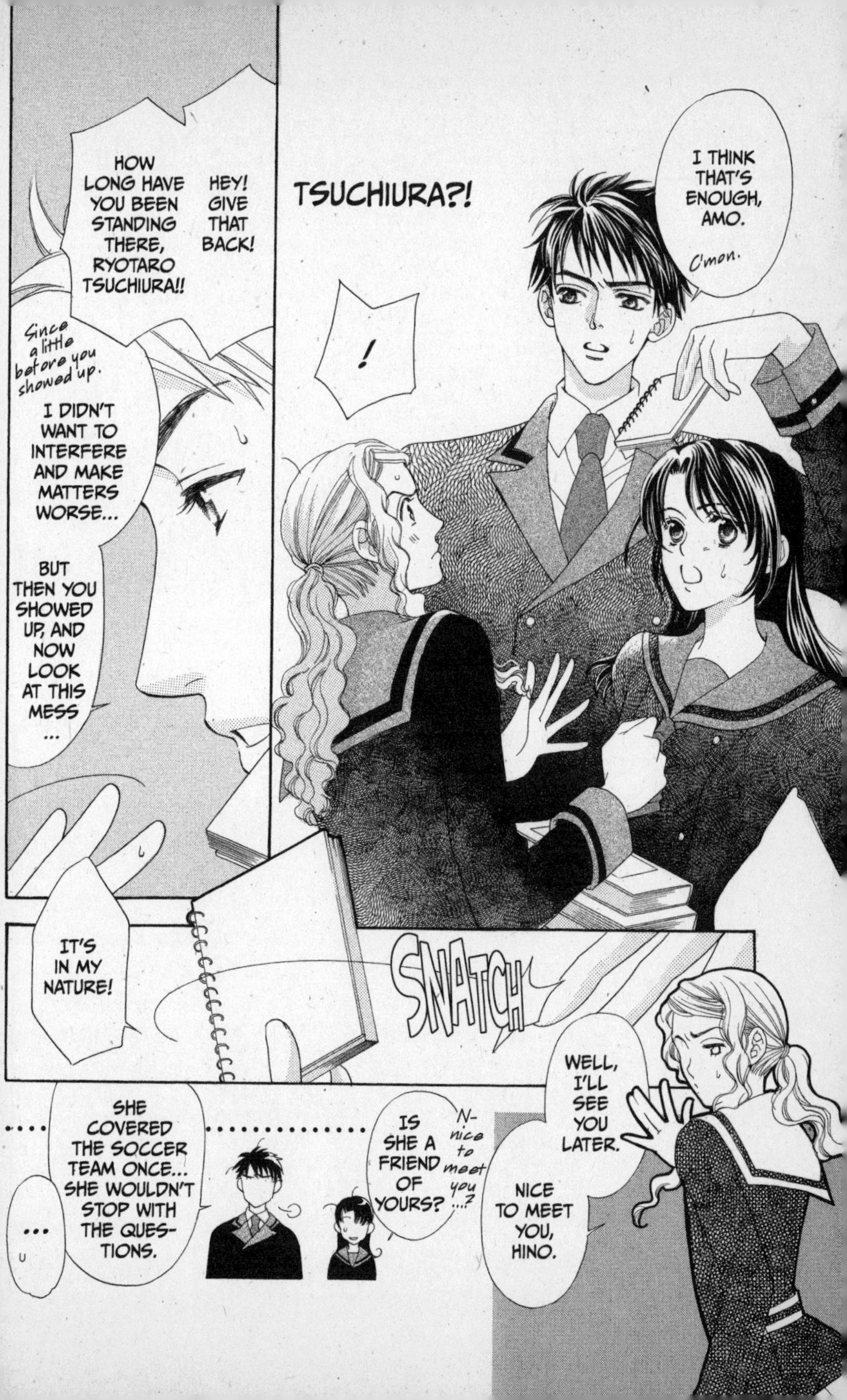
I THINK THAT'S ENOUGH, AMO.
C'mon.
TSUCHIURA?!
!
HEY! GIVE THAT BACK!
HOW LONG HAVE YOU BEEN STANDING THERE, RYOTARO TSUCHIURA!!
Since a little before you showed up.
I DIDN'T WANT TO INTERFERE AND MAKE MATTERS WORSE...
BUT THEN YOU SHOWED UP, AND NOW LOOK AT THIS MESS...
SNATCH
IT'S IN MY NATURE!
WELL, I'LL SEE YOU LATER.
NICE TO MEET YOU, HINO.
N-nice to meet you...?
IS SHE A FRIEND OF YOURS?
SHE COVERED THE SOCCER TEAM ONCE... SHE WOULDN'T STOP WITH THE QUESTIONS.
...

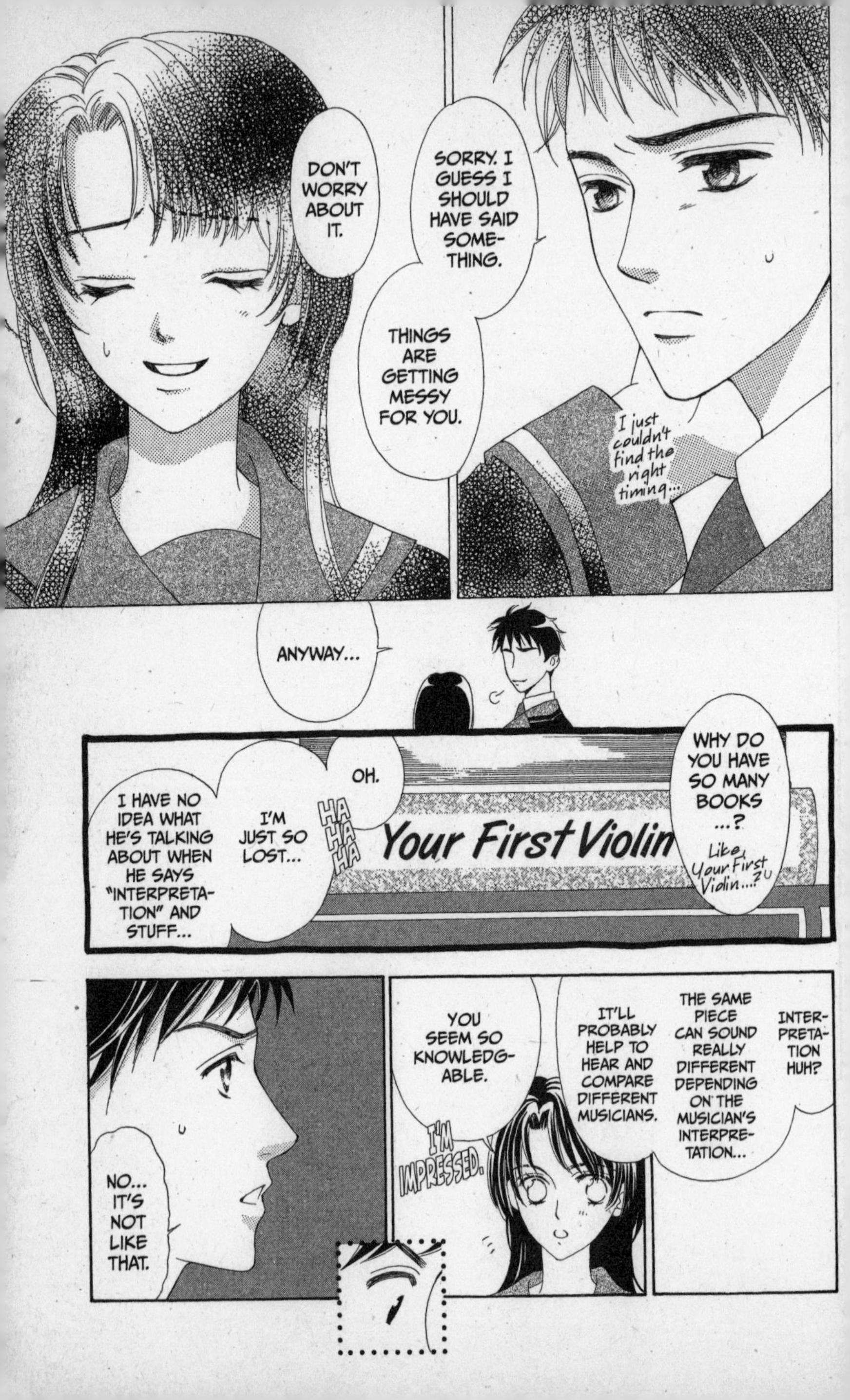
SORRY. I GUESS I SHOULD HAVE SAID SOME-THING.
THINGS ARE GETTING MESSY FOR YOU.
I just couldn't find the right timing...
DON'T WORRY ABOUT IT.
ANYWAY...
WHY DO YOU HAVE SO MANY BOOKS ...?
Like, Your First Violin...?
Your First Violin
OH.
HA HA HA
I'M JUST SO LOST...
I HAVE NO IDEA WHAT HE'S TALKING ABOUT WHEN HE SAYS "INTERPRETA-TION" AND STUFF...
INTER-PRETA-TION HUH?
THE SAME PIECE CAN SOUND REALLY DIFFERENT DEPENDING ON THE MUSICIAN'S INTERPRE-TATION...
IT'LL PROBABLY HELP TO HEAR AND COMPARE DIFFERENT MUSICIANS.
YOU SEEM SO KNOWLEDG-ABLE.
I'M IMPRESSED.
NO... IT'S NOT LIKE THAT.

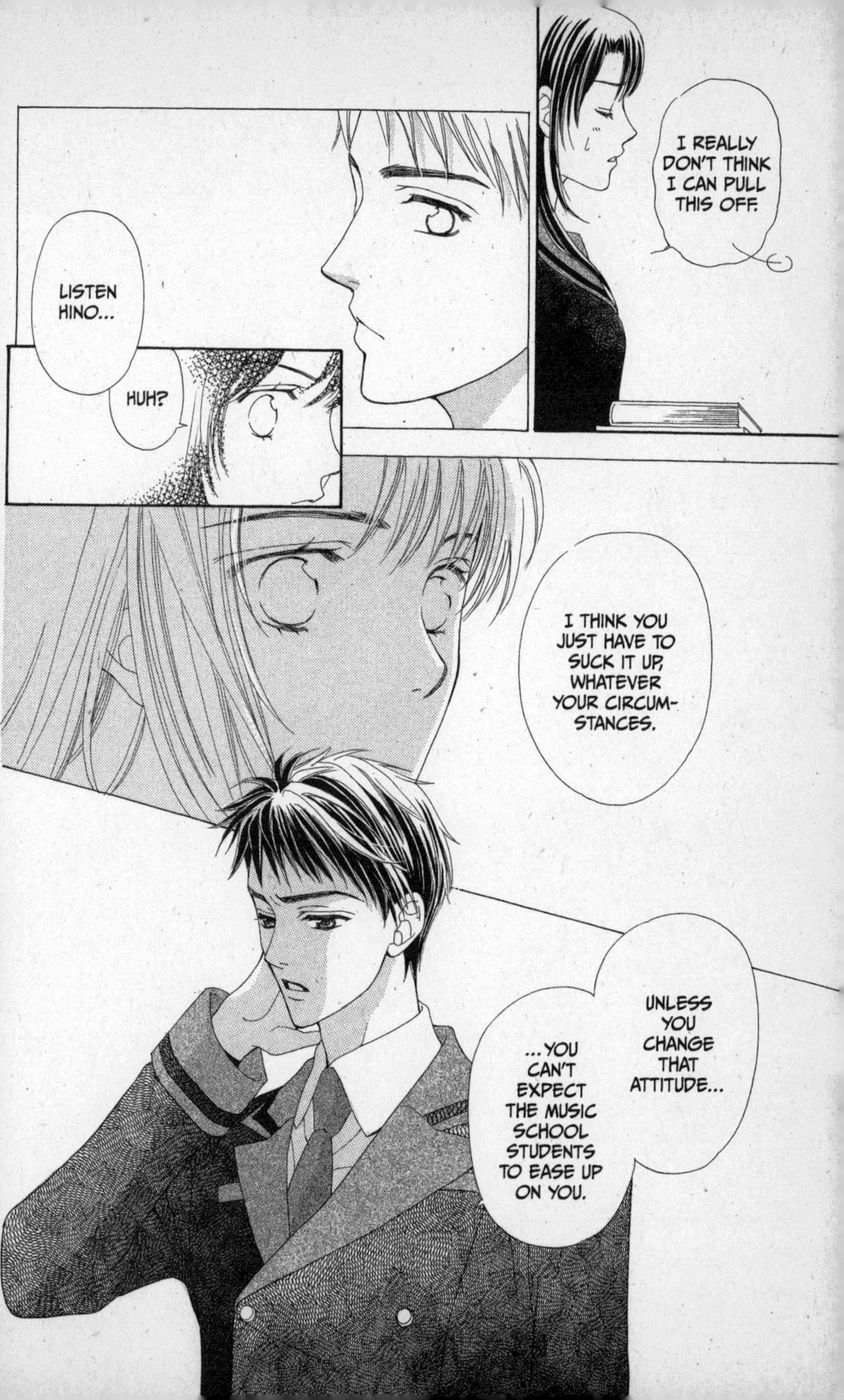
I REALLY DON'T THINK I CAN PULL THIS OFF.
LISTEN HINO...
HUH?
I THINK YOU JUST HAVE TO SUCK IT UP, WHATEVER YOUR CIRCUM-STANCES.
UNLESS YOU CHANGE THAT ATTITUDE...
...YOU CAN'T EXPECT THE MUSIC SCHOOL STUDENTS TO EASE UP ON YOU.

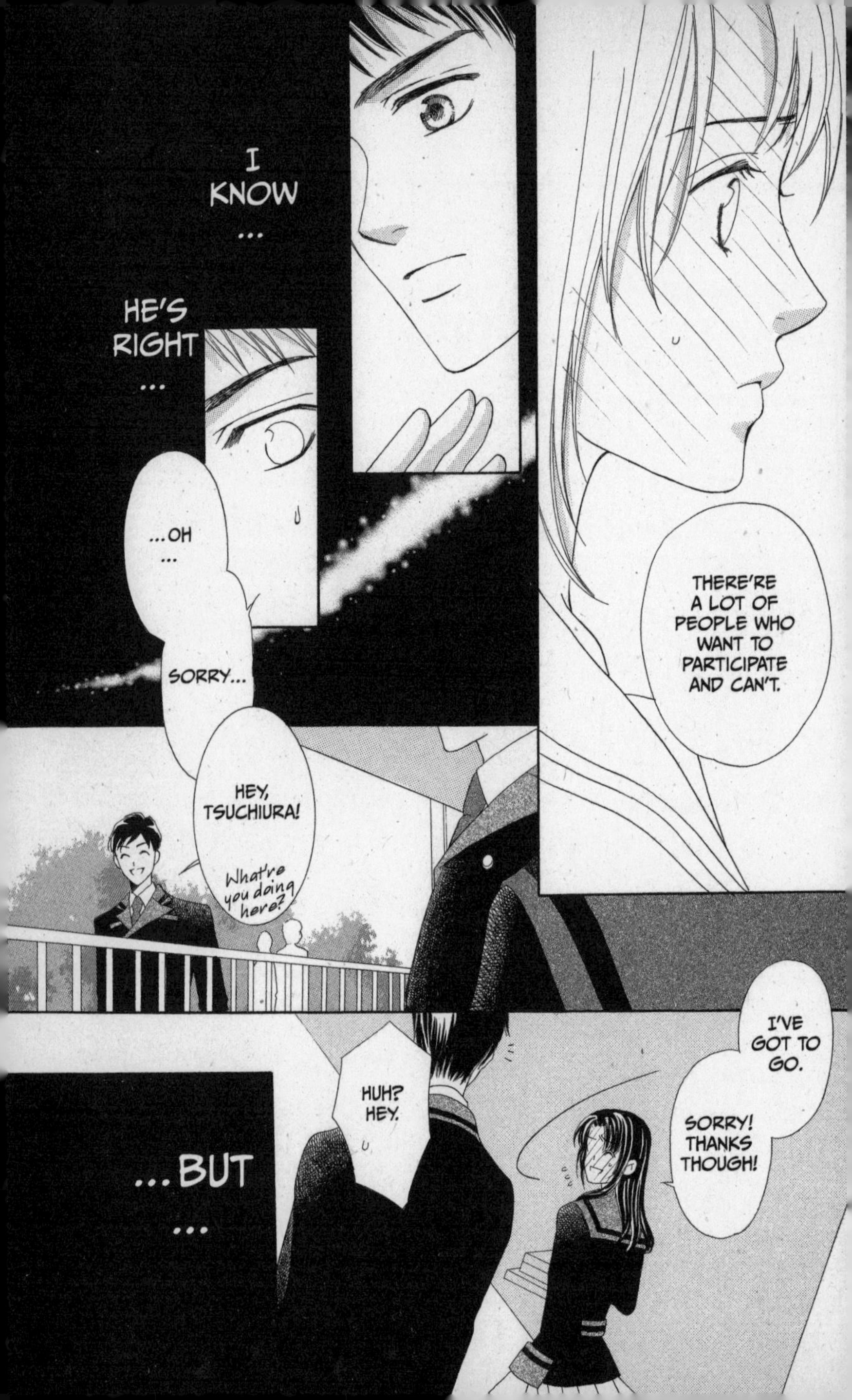
THERE'RE A LOT OF PEOPLE WHO WANT TO PARTICIPATE AND CAN'T.
I KNOW ...
HE'S RIGHT ...
...OH ...
SORRY...
HEY, TSUCHIURA!
What're you doing here?
I'VE GOT TO GO.
SORRY! THANKS THOUGH!
HUH? HEY.
...BUT ...

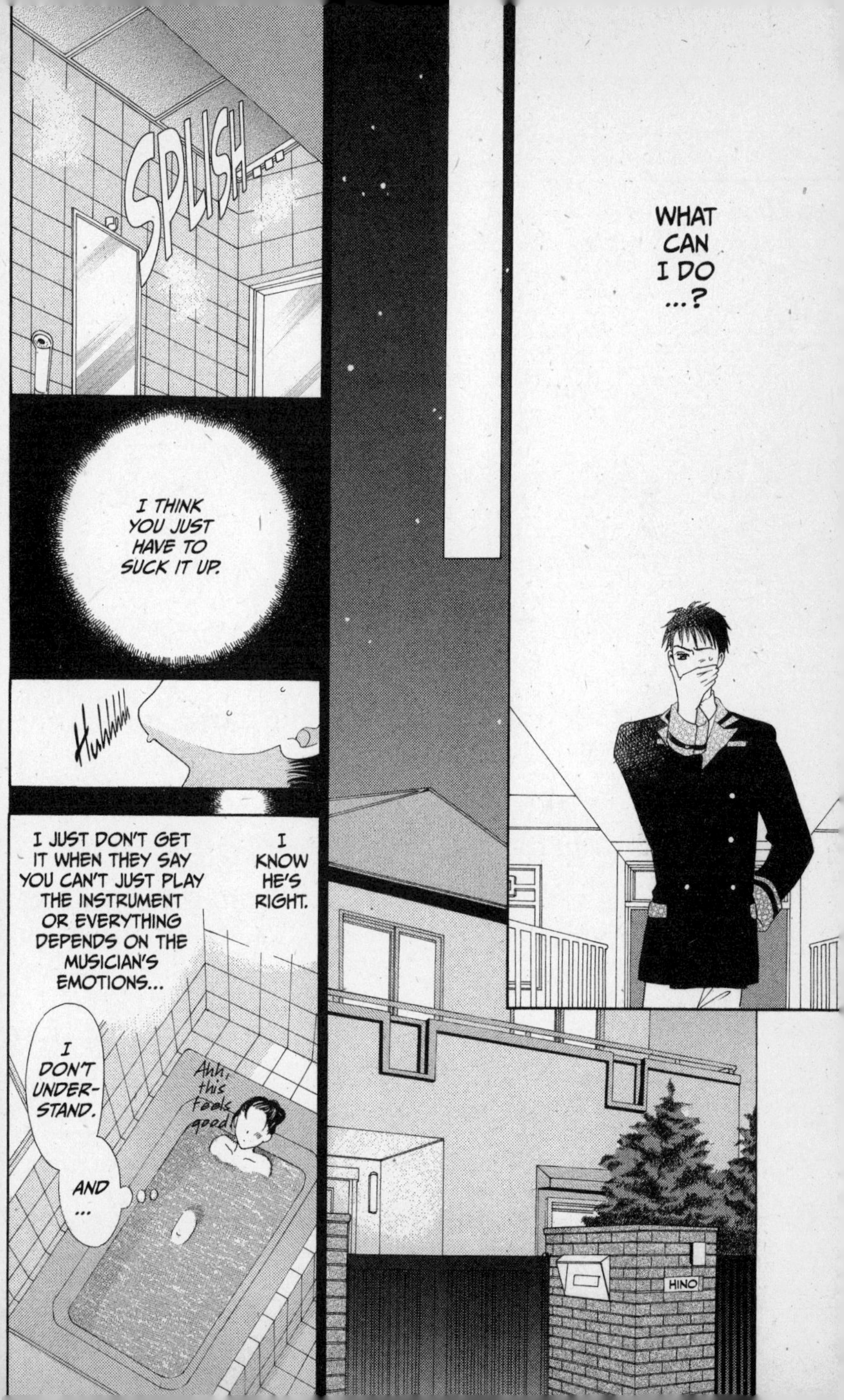
WHAT CAN I DO ...?
HINO
SPLISH
I THINK YOU JUST HAVE TO SUCK IT UP.
Huhhhhh
I KNOW HE'S RIGHT.
I JUST DON'T GET IT WHEN THEY SAY YOU CAN'T JUST PLAY THE INSTRUMENT OR EVERYTHING DEPENDS ON THE MUSICIAN'S EMOTIONS...
Ahh, this feels good
I DON'T UNDER-STAND.
AND ...

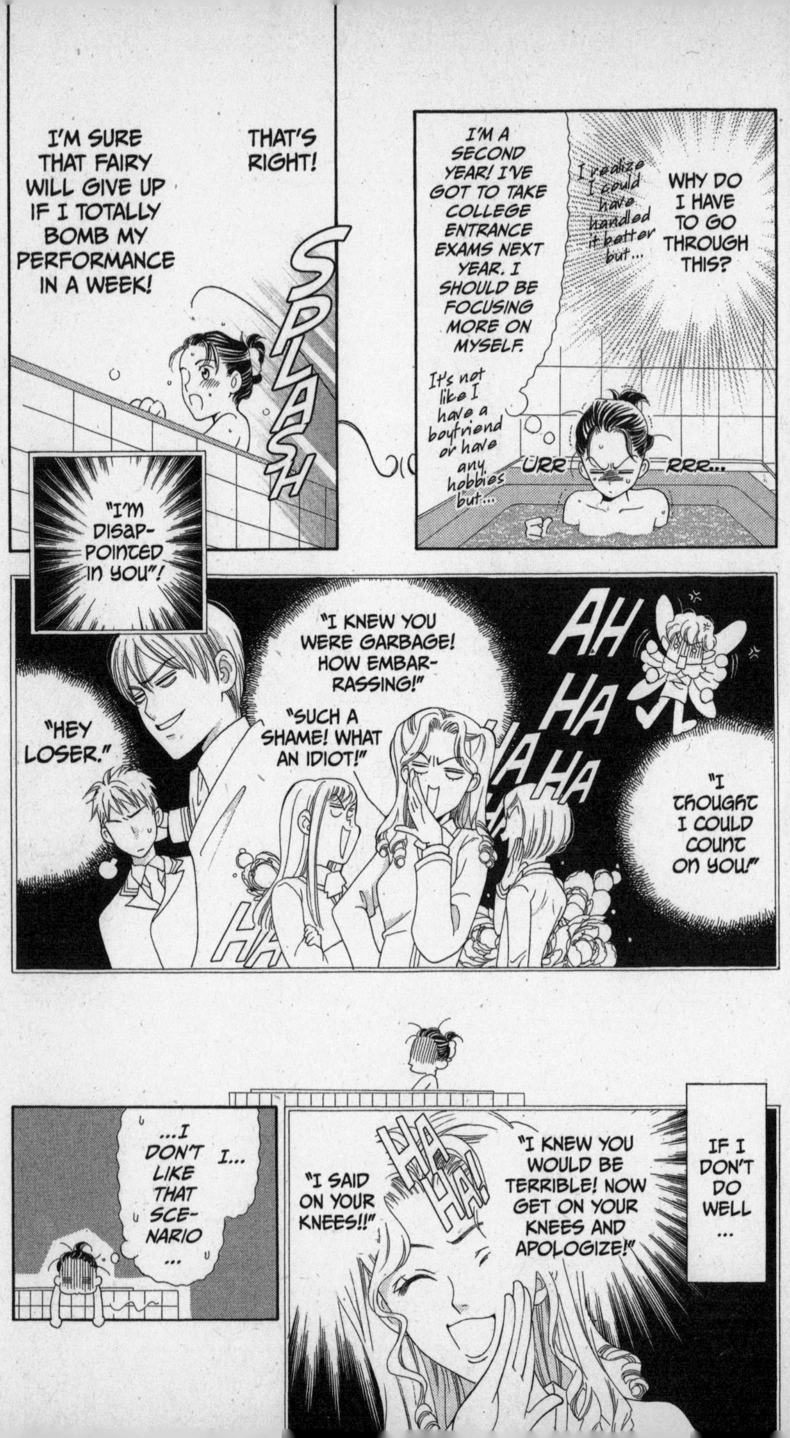
WHY DO I HAVE TO GO THROUGH THIS?
I realize I could have handled it better but...
I'M A SECOND YEAR! I'VE GOT TO TAKE COLLEGE ENTRANCE EXAMS NEXT YEAR. I SHOULD BE FOCUSING MORE ON MYSELF.
It's not like I have a boyfriend or have any hobbies but...
URR
RRR...
THAT'S RIGHT!
I'M SURE THAT FAIRY WILL GIVE UP IF I TOTALLY BOMB MY PERFORMANCE IN A WEEK!
SPLASH
"I THOUGHT I COULD COUNT ON YOU!"
AH HA HA HA HA
"I KNEW YOU WERE GARBAGE! HOW EMBAR-RASSING!"
"I'M DISAP-POINTED IN YOU"!
"SUCH A SHAME! WHAT AN IDIOT!"
"HEY LOSER."
HA
IF I DON'T DO WELL ...
"I KNEW YOU WOULD BE TERRIBLE! NOW GET ON YOUR KNEES AND APOLOGIZE!"
HA HA HA!
"I SAID ON YOUR KNEES!!"
I...
...I DON'T LIKE THAT SCE-NARIO ...

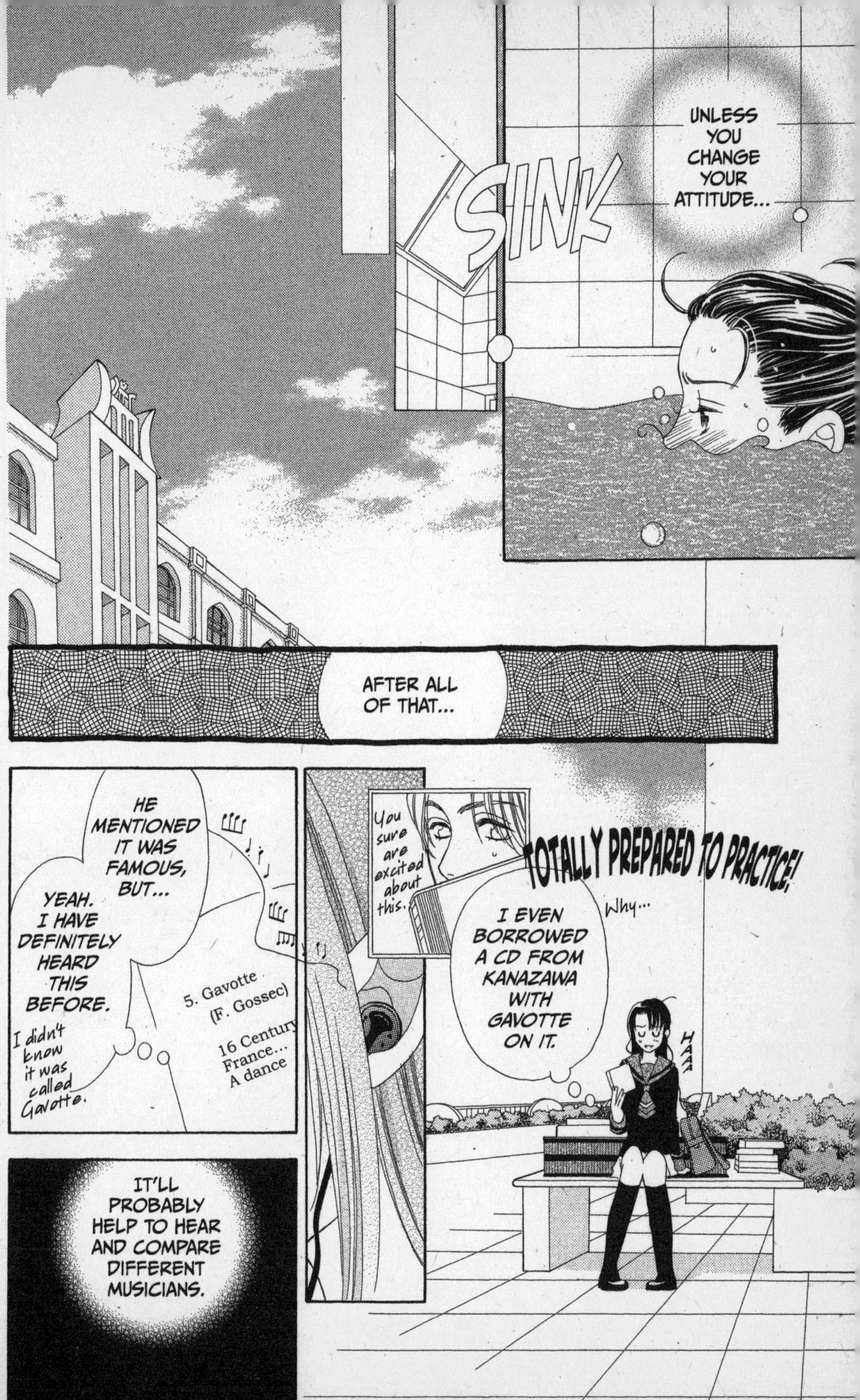
UNLESS YOU CHANGE YOUR ATTITUDE...
SINK
AFTER ALL OF THAT...
TOTALLY PREPARED TO PRACTICE!
I EVEN BORROWED A CD FROM KANAZAWA WITH GAVOTTE ON IT.
Why...
HAAA
You sure are excited about this.
HE MENTIONED IT WAS FAMOUS, BUT...
YEAH. I HAVE DEFINITELY HEARD THIS BEFORE.
5. Gavotte (F. Gossec)
16 Century France... A dance
I didn't know it was called Gavotte.
IT'LL PROBABLY HELP TO HEAR AND COMPARE DIFFERENT MUSICIANS.

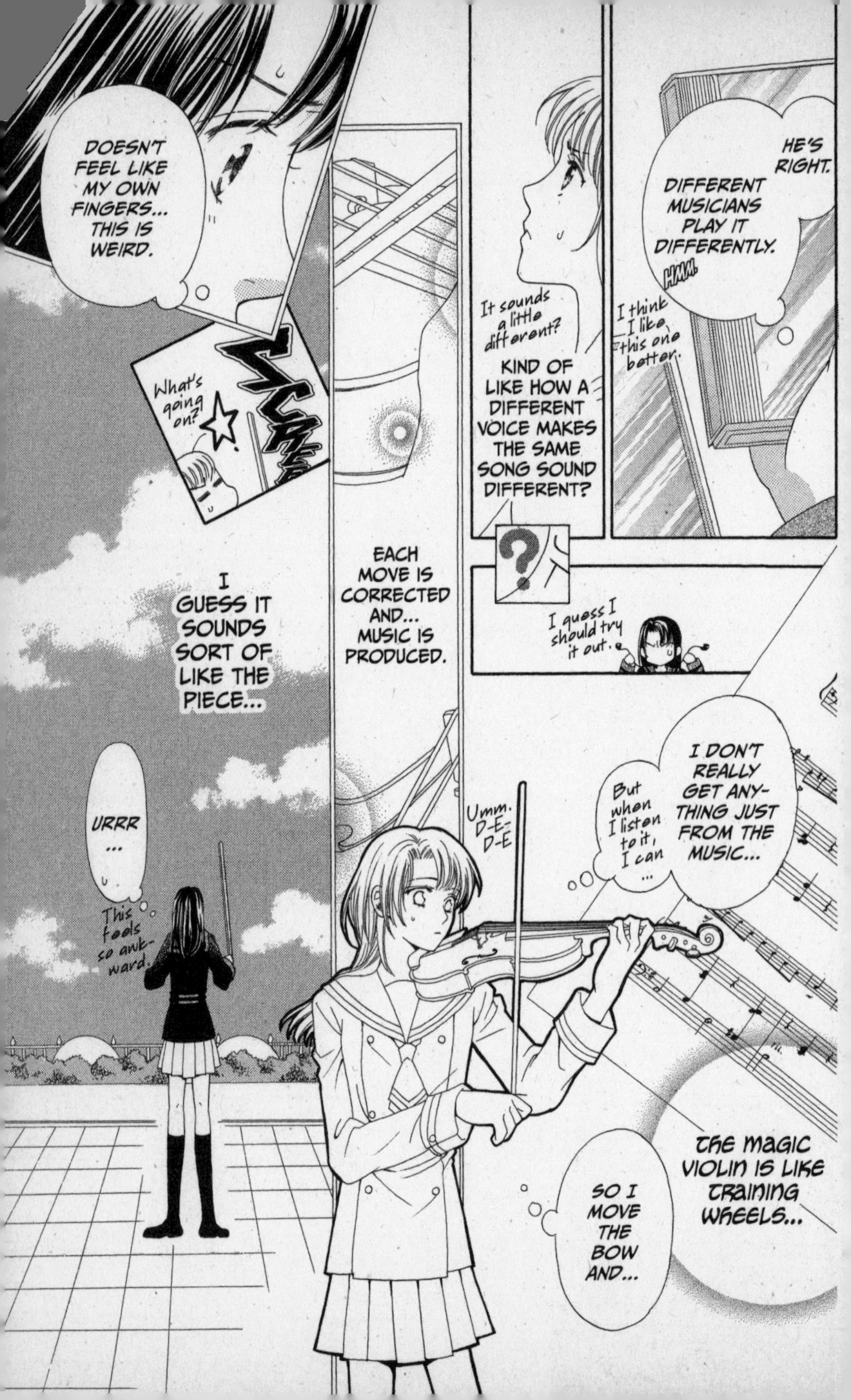
HE'S RIGHT.
DIFFERENT MUSICIANS PLAY IT DIFFERENTLY.
HMM.
I think I like this one better.
It sounds a little different?
KIND OF LIKE HOW A DIFFERENT VOICE MAKES THE SAME SONG SOUND DIFFERENT?
?
I guess I should try it out.
I DON'T REALLY GET ANYTHING JUST FROM THE MUSIC...
But when I listen to it, I can ...
Umm. D-E-D-E
THE MAGIC VIOLIN IS LIKE TRAINING WHEELS...
SO I MOVE THE BOW AND...
EACH MOVE IS CORRECTED AND... MUSIC IS PRODUCED.
DOESN'T FEEL LIKE MY OWN FINGERS... THIS IS WEIRD.
SCREE
What's going on?
I GUESS IT SOUNDS SORT OF LIKE THE PIECE...
URRR ...
This feels so awkward.

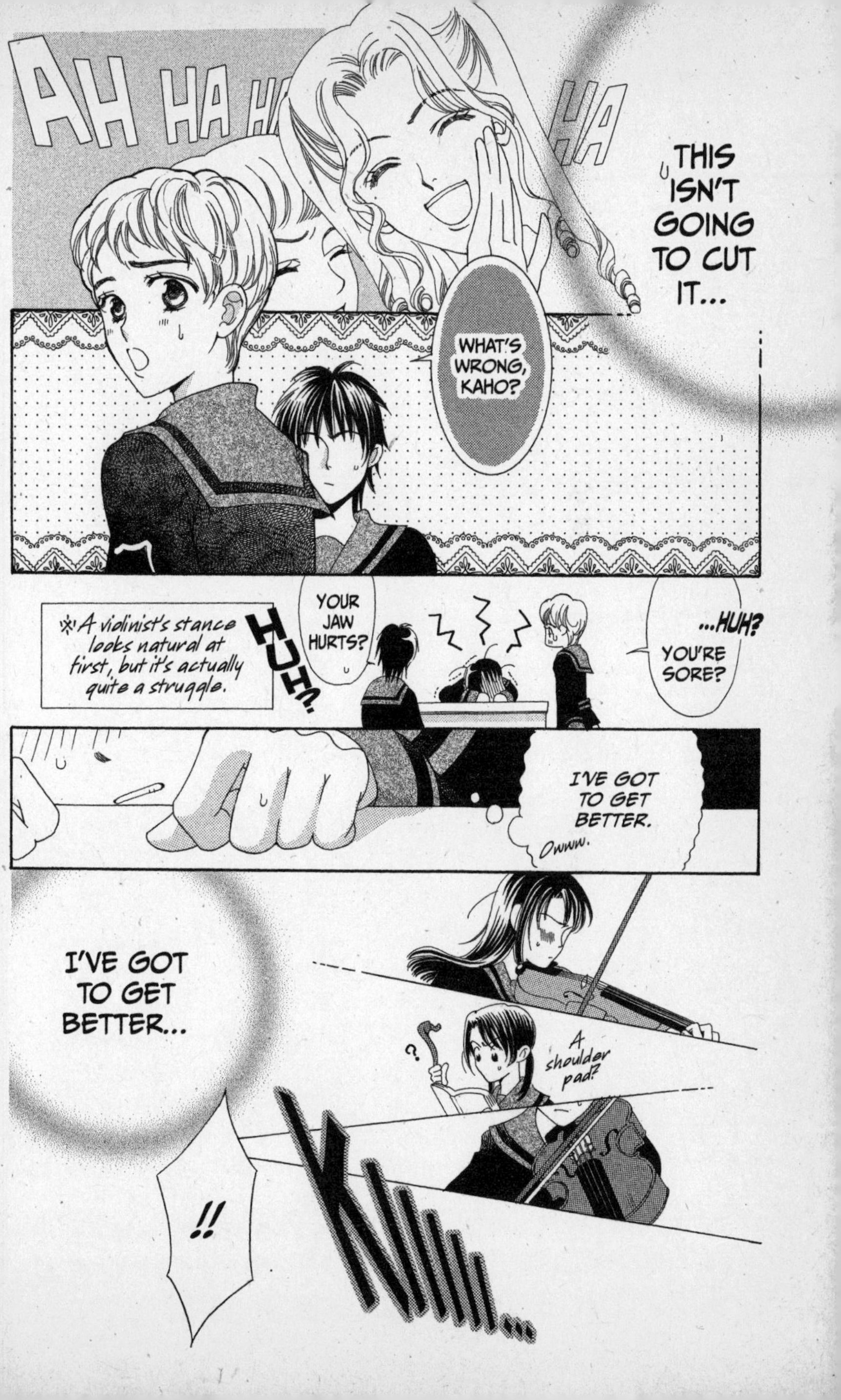
AH HA HA HA
THIS ISN'T GOING TO CUT IT...
WHAT'S WRONG, KAHO?
...HUH?
YOU'RE SORE?
YOUR JAW HURTS?
HUH?
※A violinist's stance looks natural at first, but it's actually quite a struggle.
I'VE GOT TO GET BETTER.
Owww.
A shoulder pad?
?
I'VE GOT TO GET BETTER...
!!

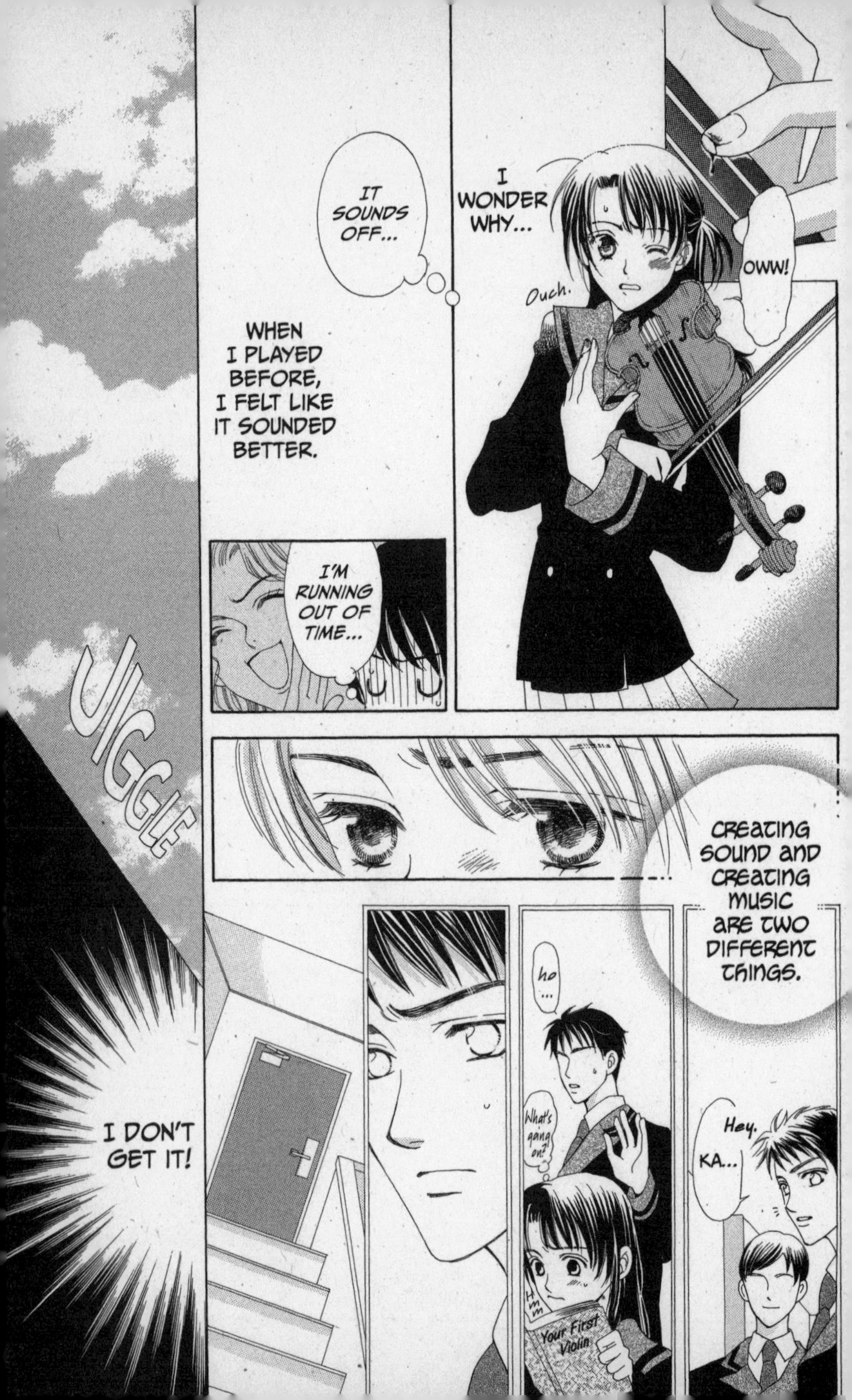
OWW!
Ouch.
I WONDER WHY...
IT SOUNDS OFF...
WHEN I PLAYED BEFORE, I FELT LIKE IT SOUNDED BETTER.
I'M RUNNING OUT OF TIME...
CREATING SOUND AND CREATING MUSIC ARE TWO DIFFERENT THINGS.
Hey.
KA...
ho...
What's going on?
Hmm
Your First Violin
JIGGLE
I DON'T GET IT!

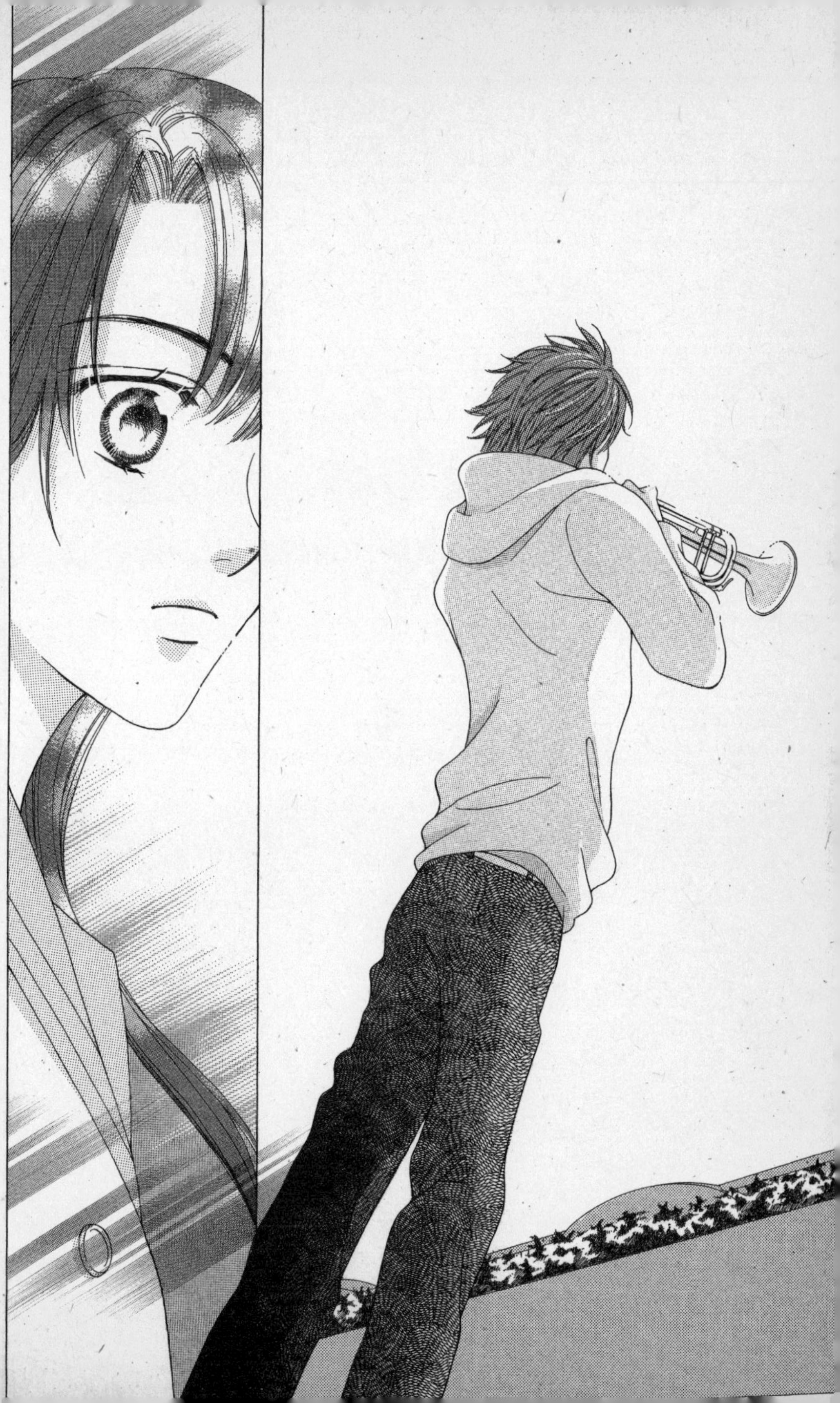

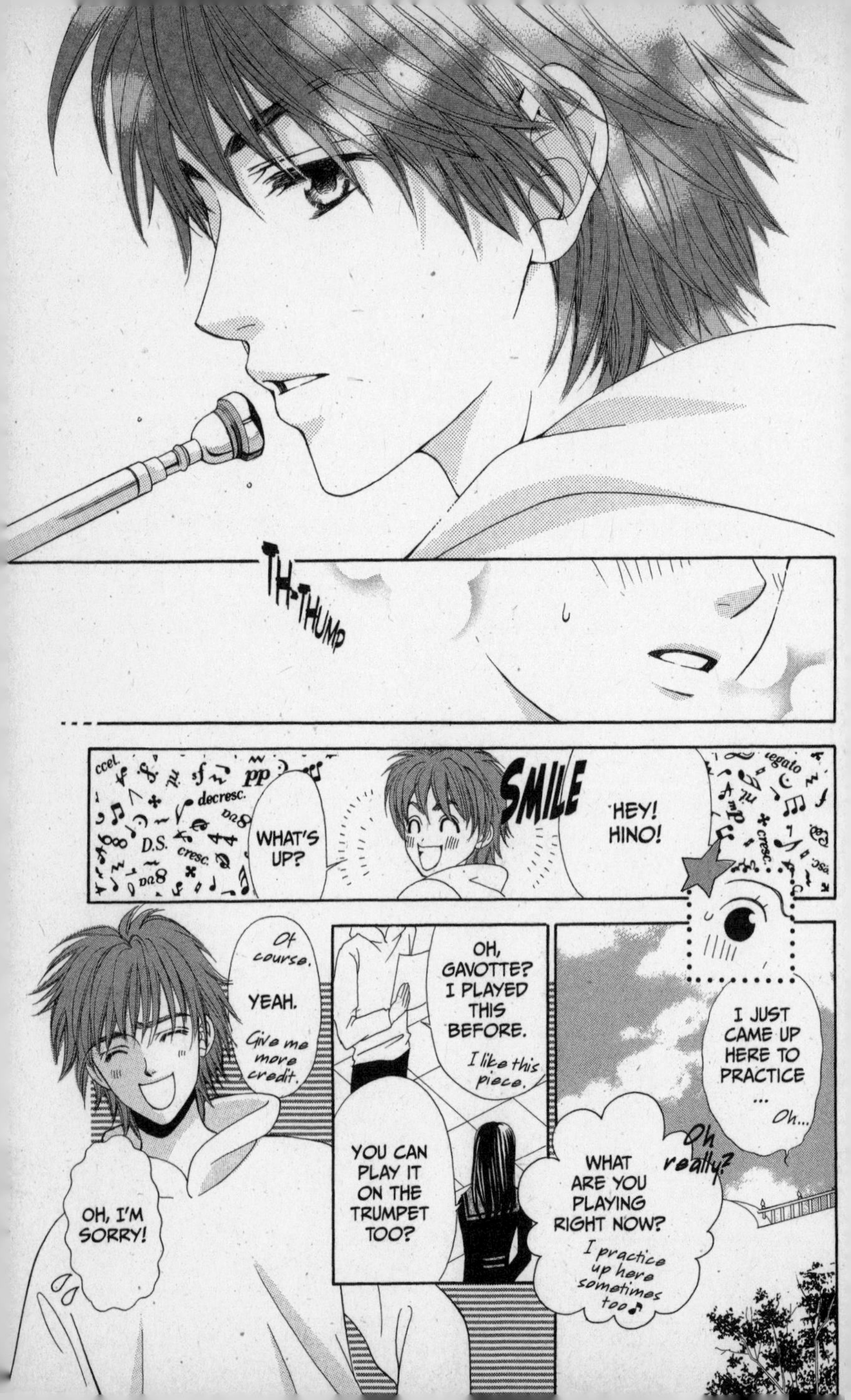
TH-THUMP
HEY! HINO!
SMILE
WHAT'S UP?
I JUST CAME UP HERE TO PRACTICE ...
Oh...
Oh really?
WHAT ARE YOU PLAYING RIGHT NOW?
I practice up here sometimes too♪
OH, GAVOTTE? I PLAYED THIS BEFORE.
I like this piece.
YOU CAN PLAY IT ON THE TRUMPET TOO?
Of course.
YEAH.
Give me more credit.
OH, I'M SORRY!

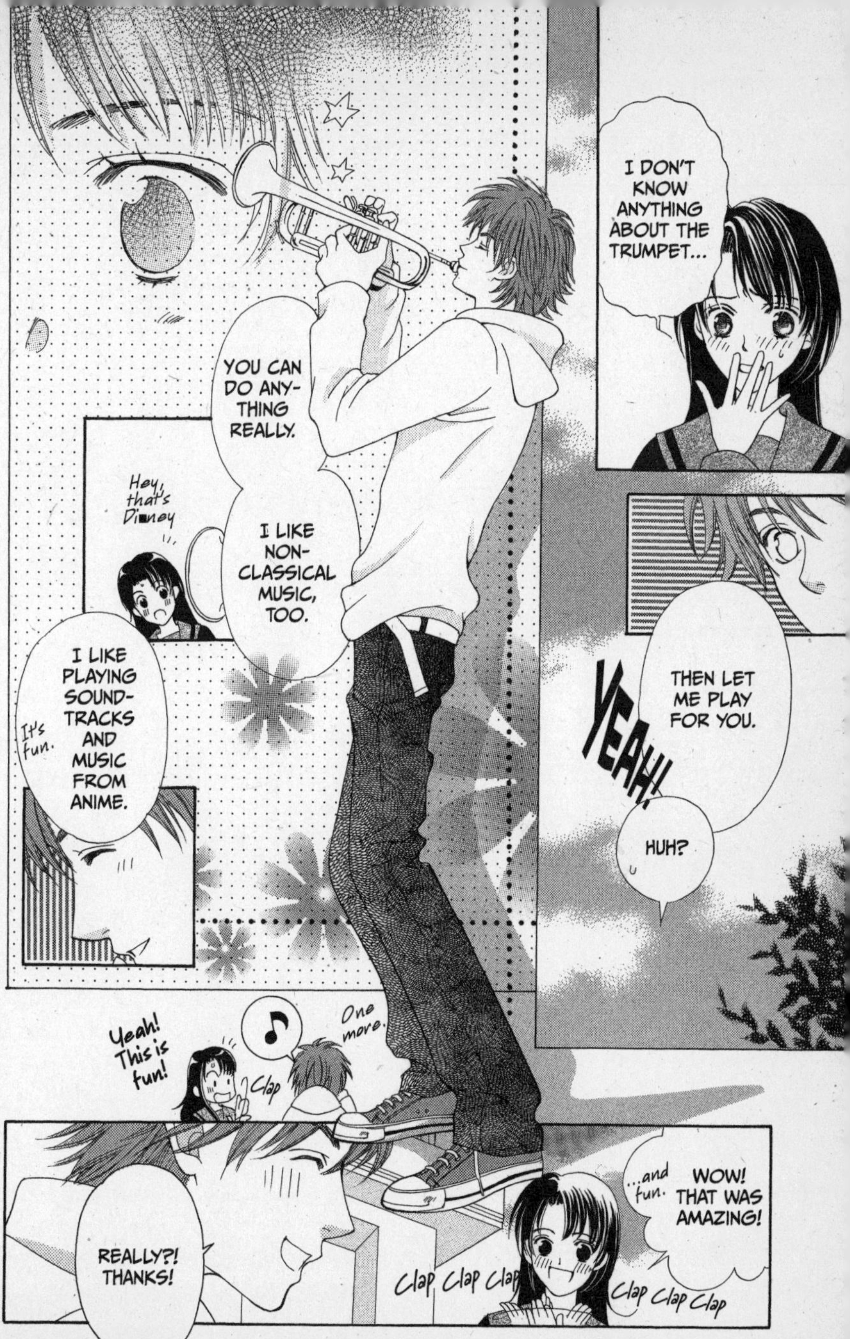
I DON'T KNOW ANYTHING ABOUT THE TRUMPET...
THEN LET ME PLAY FOR YOU.
YEAH!
HUH?
YOU CAN DO ANY-THING REALLY.
I LIKE NON-CLASSICAL MUSIC, TOO.
Hey, that's Di[redacted]ney
I LIKE PLAYING SOUND-TRACKS AND MUSIC FROM ANIME.
It's fun.
One more.
Yeah! This is fun!
Clap
WOW! THAT WAS AMAZING!
...and fun.
Clap Clap Clap
REALLY?! THANKS!
Clap Clap Clap

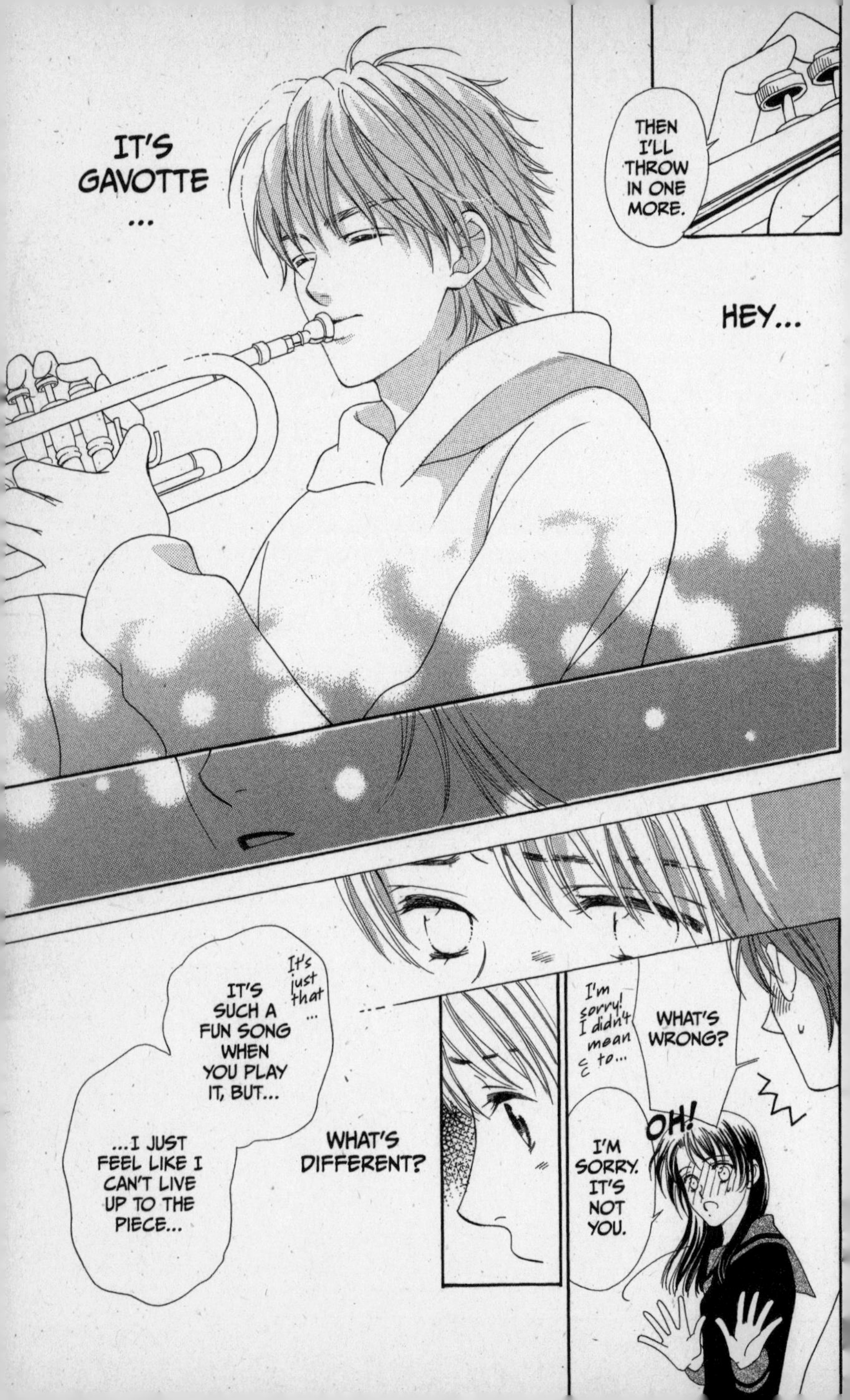
THEN I'LL THROW IN ONE MORE.
HEY...
IT'S GAVOTTE ...
WHAT'S WRONG?
OH!
I'm sorry! I didn't mean to...
I'M SORRY. IT'S NOT YOU.
WHAT'S DIFFERENT?
It's just that ...
IT'S SUCH A FUN SONG WHEN YOU PLAY IT, BUT...
...I JUST FEEL LIKE I CAN'T LIVE UP TO THE PIECE...

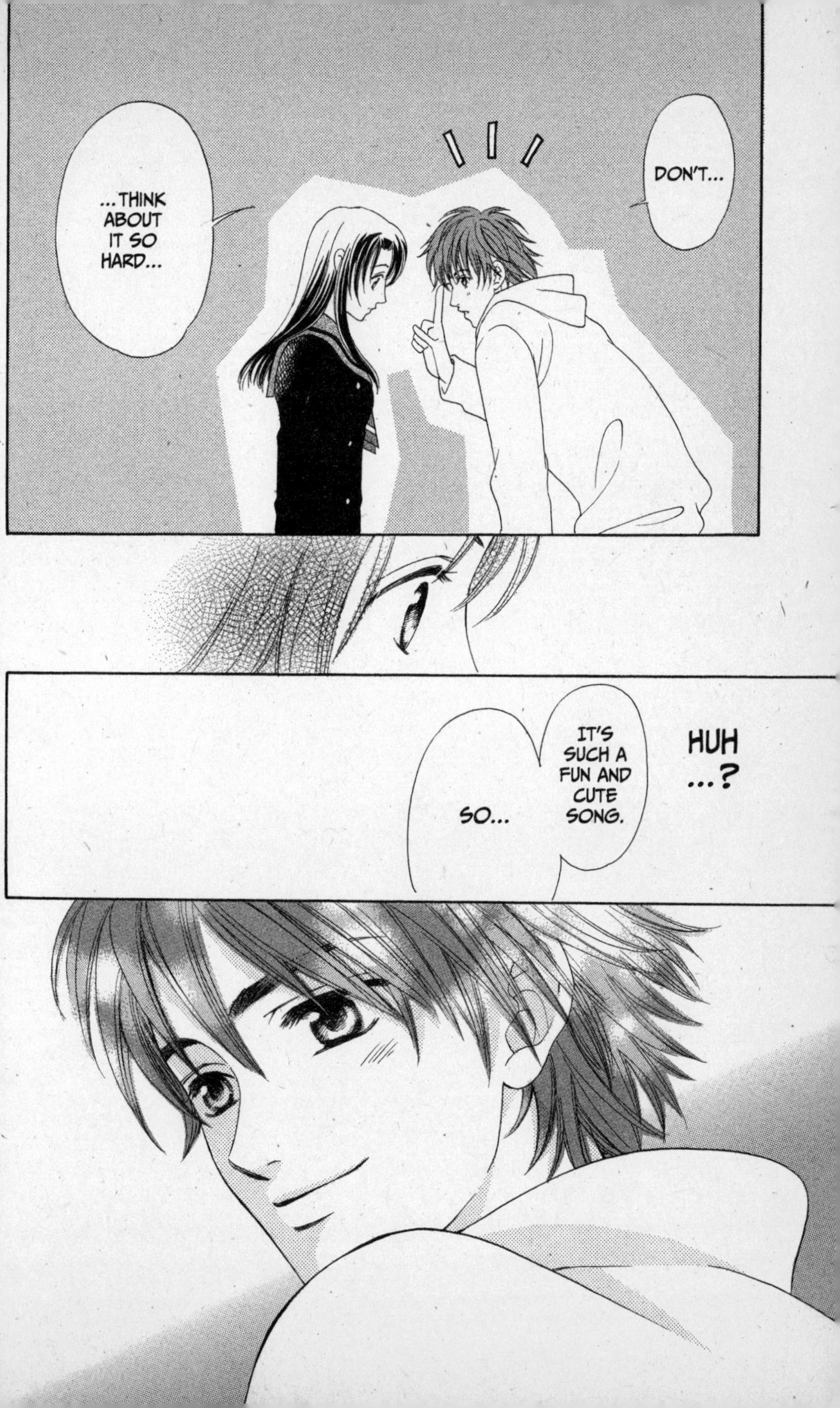
DON'T...
...THINK ABOUT IT SO HARD...
HUH ...?
IT'S SUCH A FUN AND CUTE SONG.
SO...

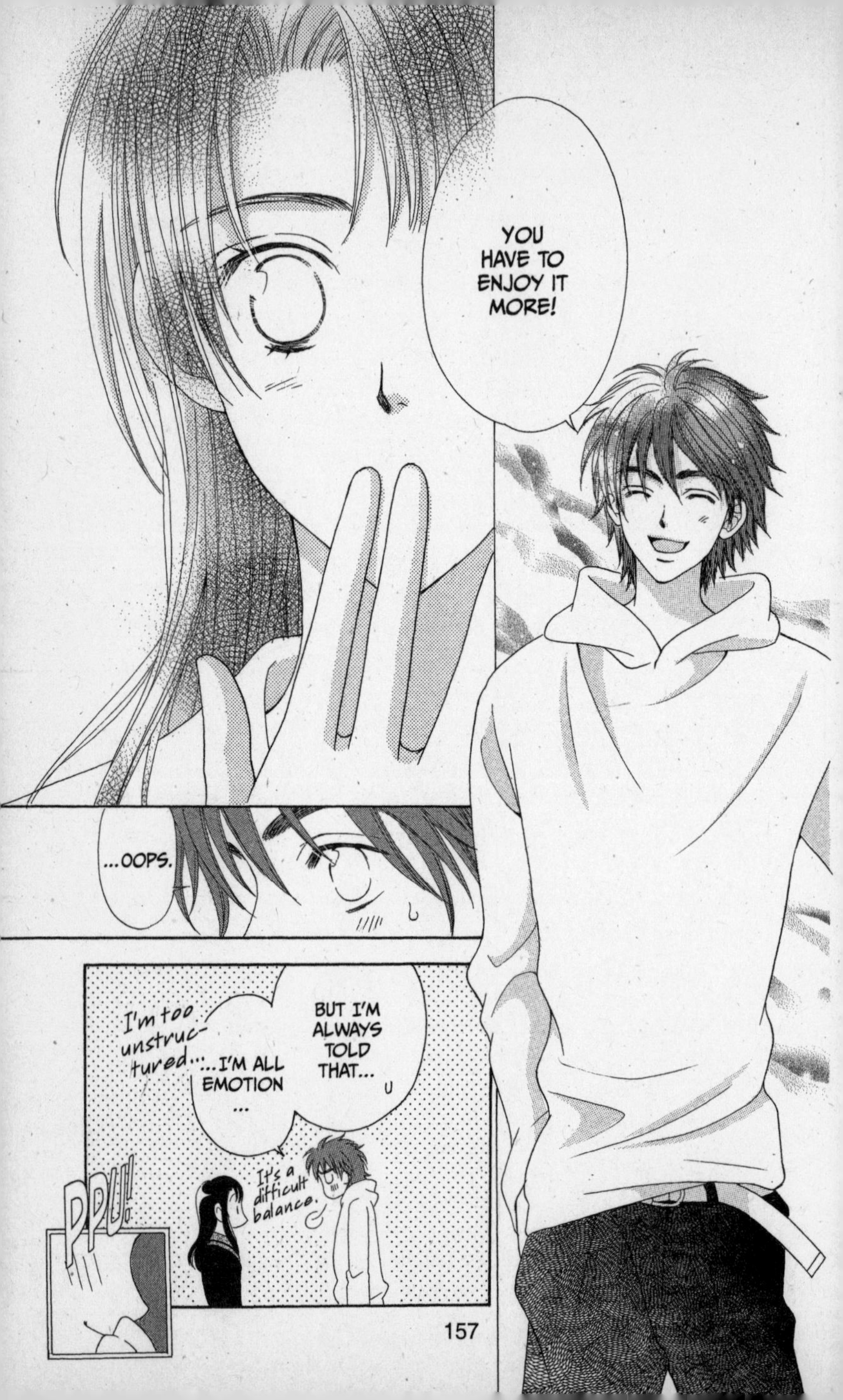
YOU HAVE TO ENJOY IT MORE!
...OOPS.
BUT I'M ALWAYS TOLD THAT...
...I'M ALL EMOTION ...
I'm too unstruc-tured...
It's a difficult balance.
PPU!!

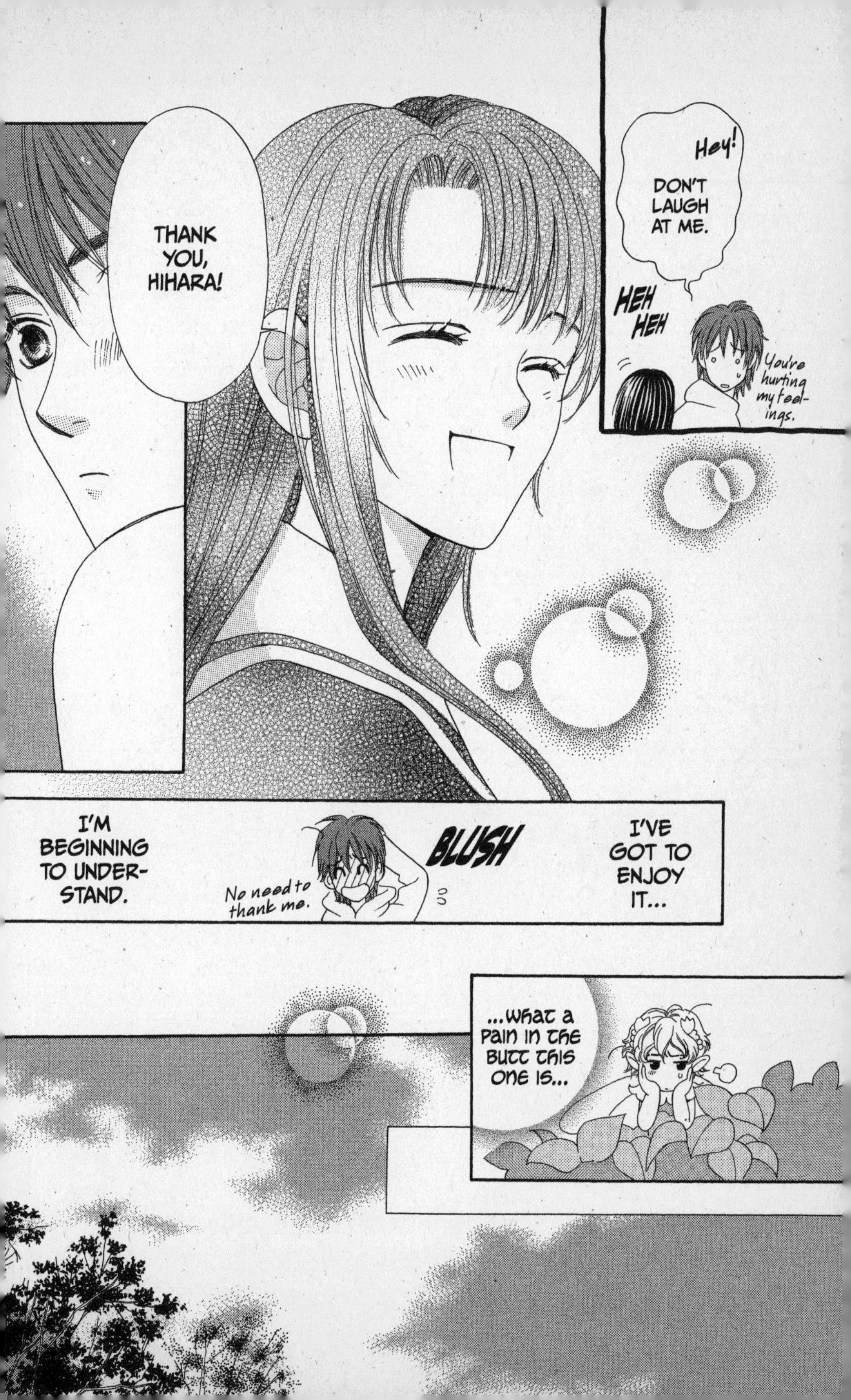
Hey! DON'T LAUGH AT ME.
HEH HEH
You're hurting my feelings.
THANK YOU, HIHARA!
I'VE GOT TO ENJOY IT...
BLUSH
No need to thank me.
I'M BEGINNING TO UNDERSTAND.
...what a pain in the butt this one is...

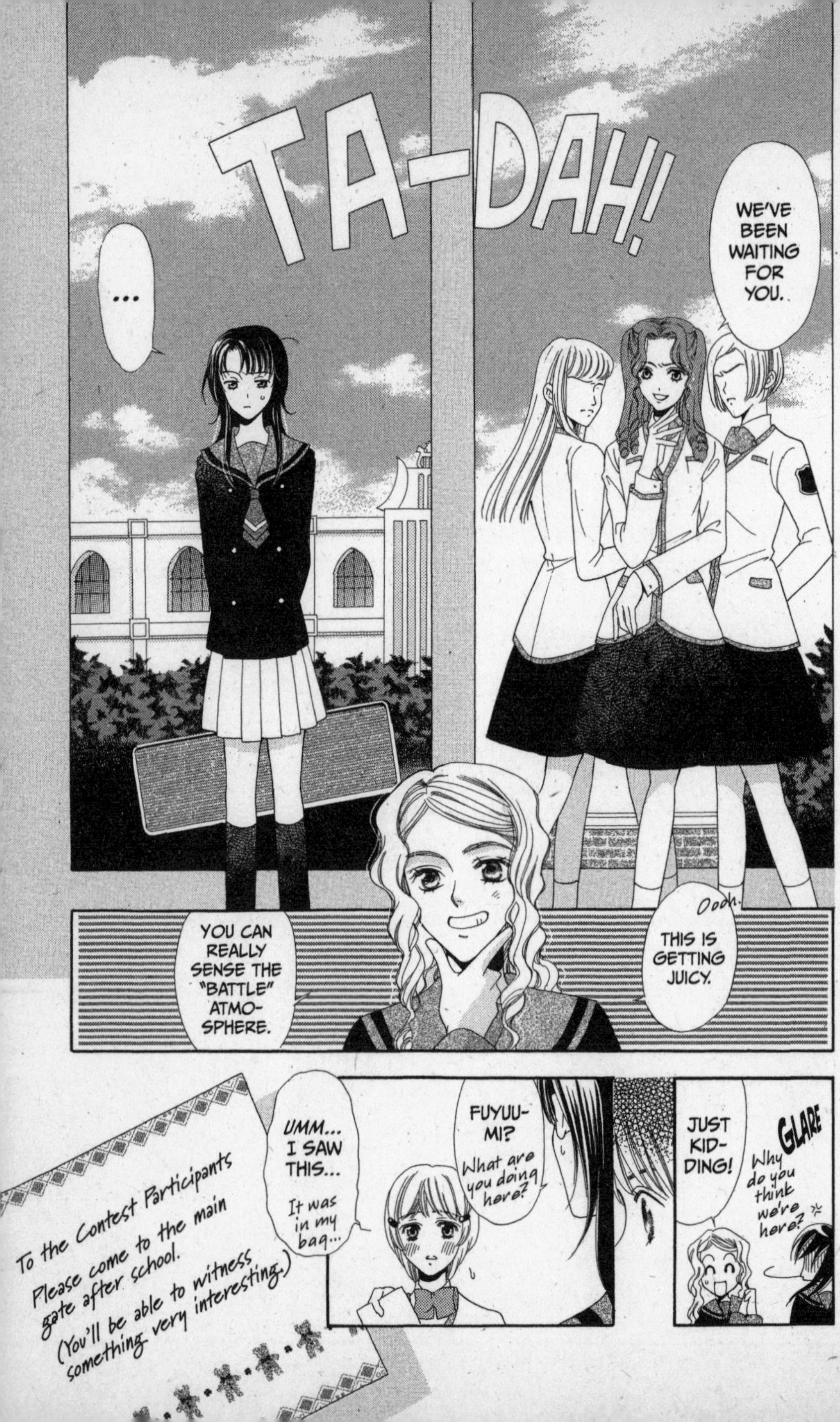
WE'VE BEEN WAITING FOR YOU.
TA-DAH!
...
Oooh.
THIS IS GETTING JUICY.
YOU CAN REALLY SENSE THE "BATTLE" ATMOSPHERE.
GLARE
Why do you think we're here?
JUST KIDDING!
FUYUU-MI?
What are you doing here?
UMM... I SAW THIS...
It was in my bag...
To the Contest Participants
Please come to the main gate after school.
(You'll be able to witness something very interesting.)

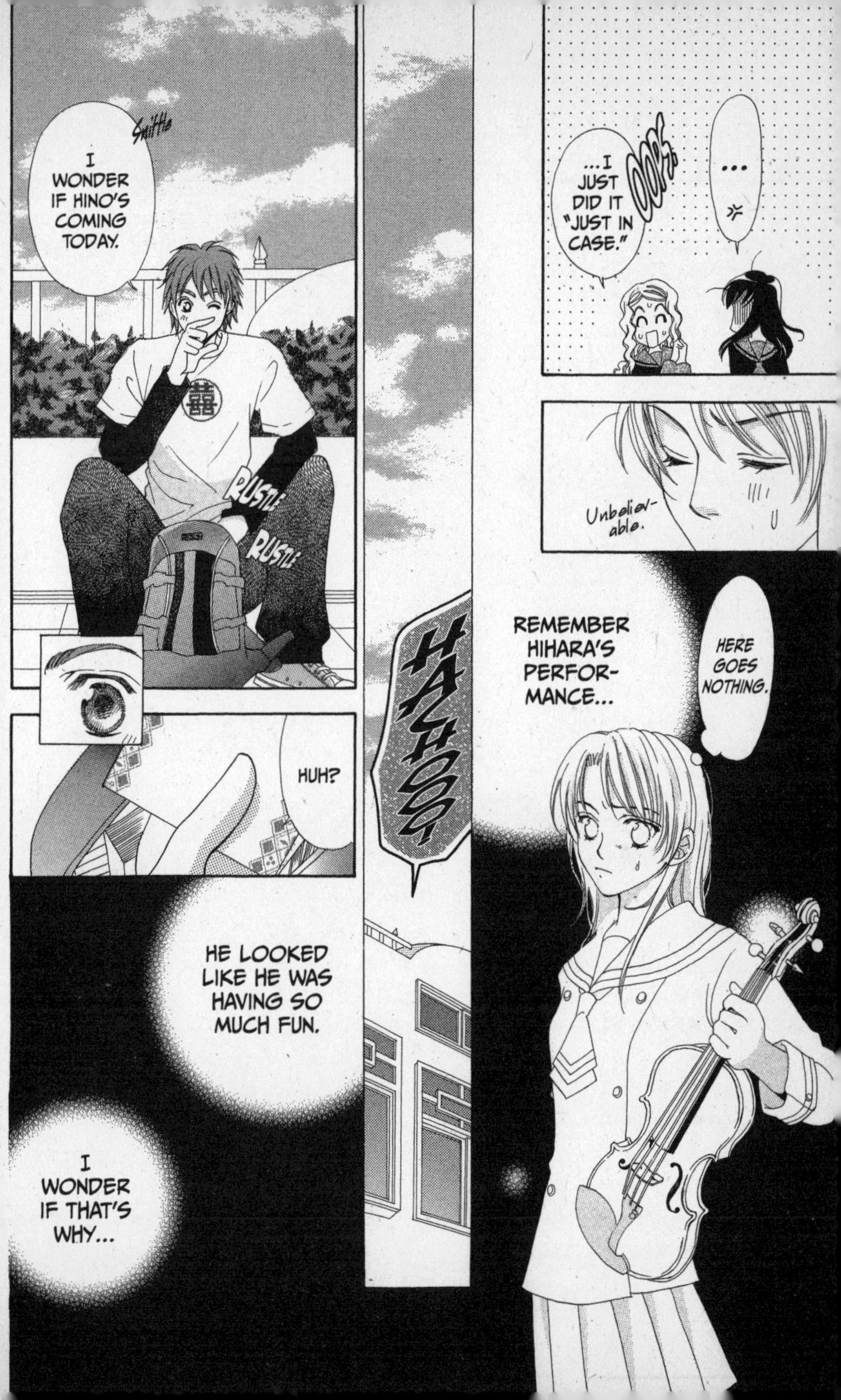
...
...I JUST DID IT "JUST IN CASE."
OOPS.
Unbelievable.
REMEMBER HIHARA'S PERFORMANCE...
HERE GOES NOTHING.
HAHOO!
I WONDER IF HINO'S COMING TODAY.
RUSTLE
RUSTLE
HUH?
HE LOOKED LIKE HE WAS HAVING SO MUCH FUN.
I WONDER IF THAT'S WHY...

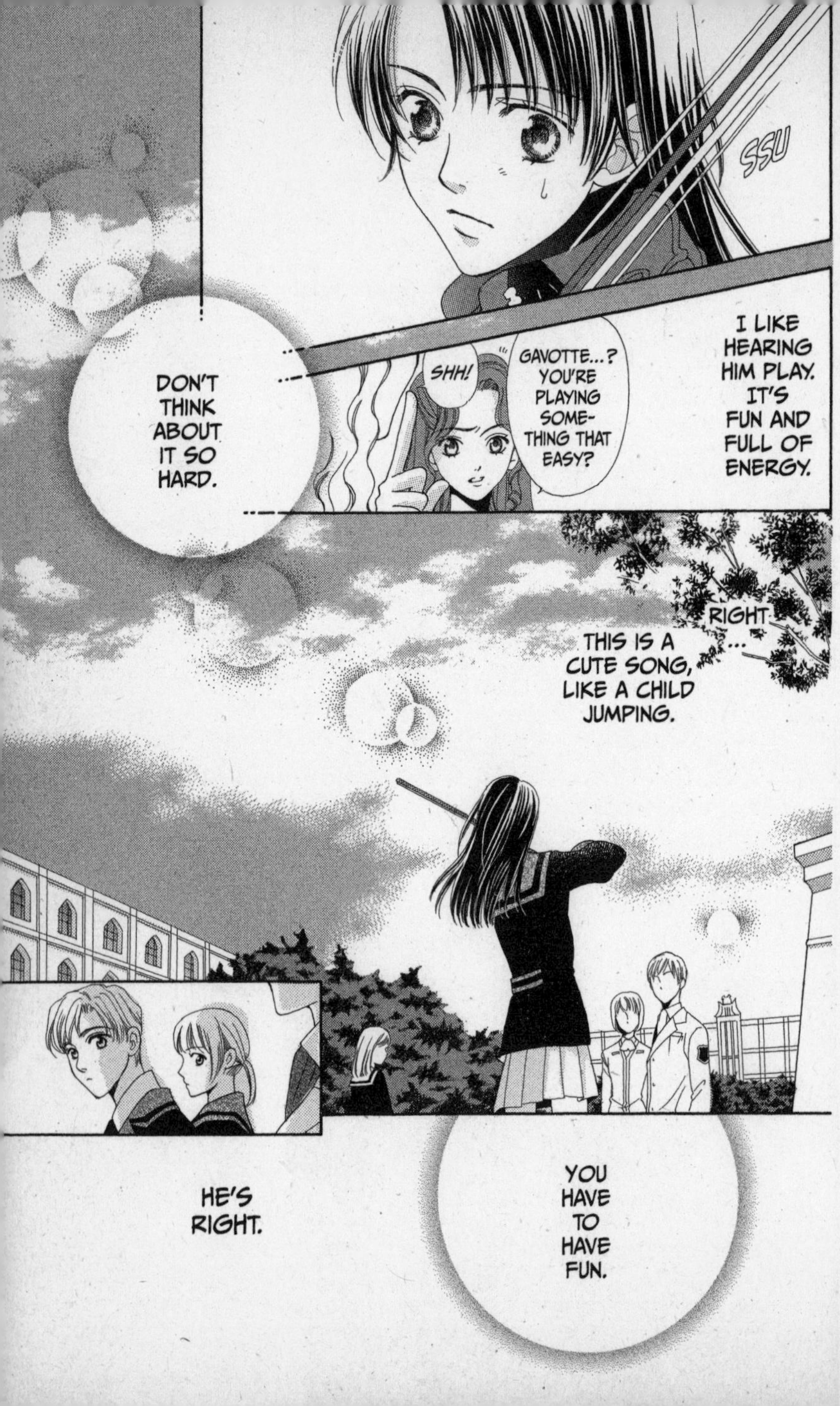
SSU
I LIKE HEARING HIM PLAY. IT'S FUN AND FULL OF ENERGY.
GAVOTTE...? YOU'RE PLAYING SOME-THING THAT EASY?
SHH!
DON'T THINK ABOUT IT SO HARD.
RIGHT...
THIS IS A CUTE SONG, LIKE A CHILD JUMPING.
YOU HAVE TO HAVE FUN.
HE'S RIGHT.

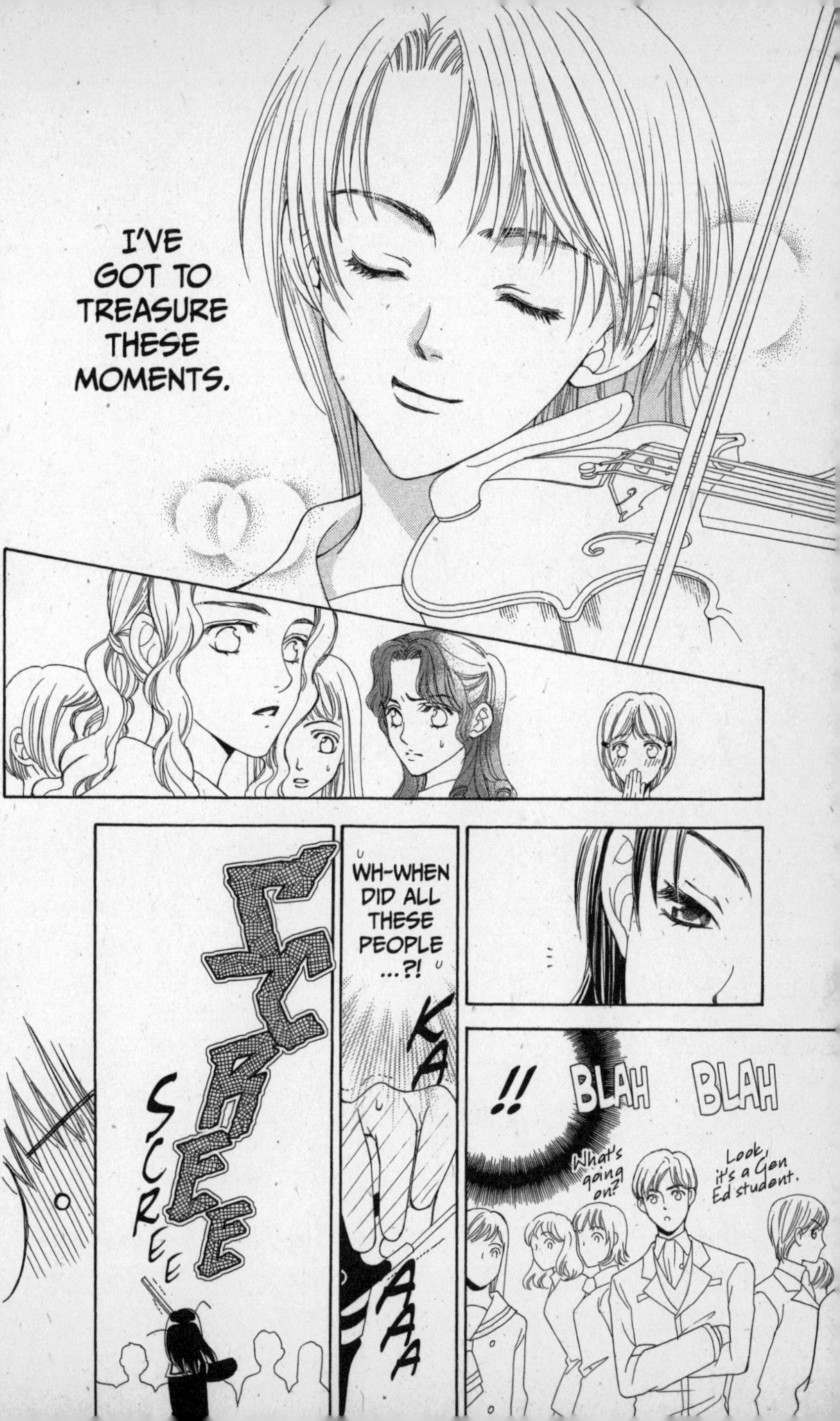
I'VE GOT TO TREASURE THESE MOMENTS.
BLAH BLAH
!!
Look, it's a Gen Ed student.
What's going on?
WH-WHEN DID ALL THESE PEOPLE ...?!
KAAAA
SCREE
SCREEE

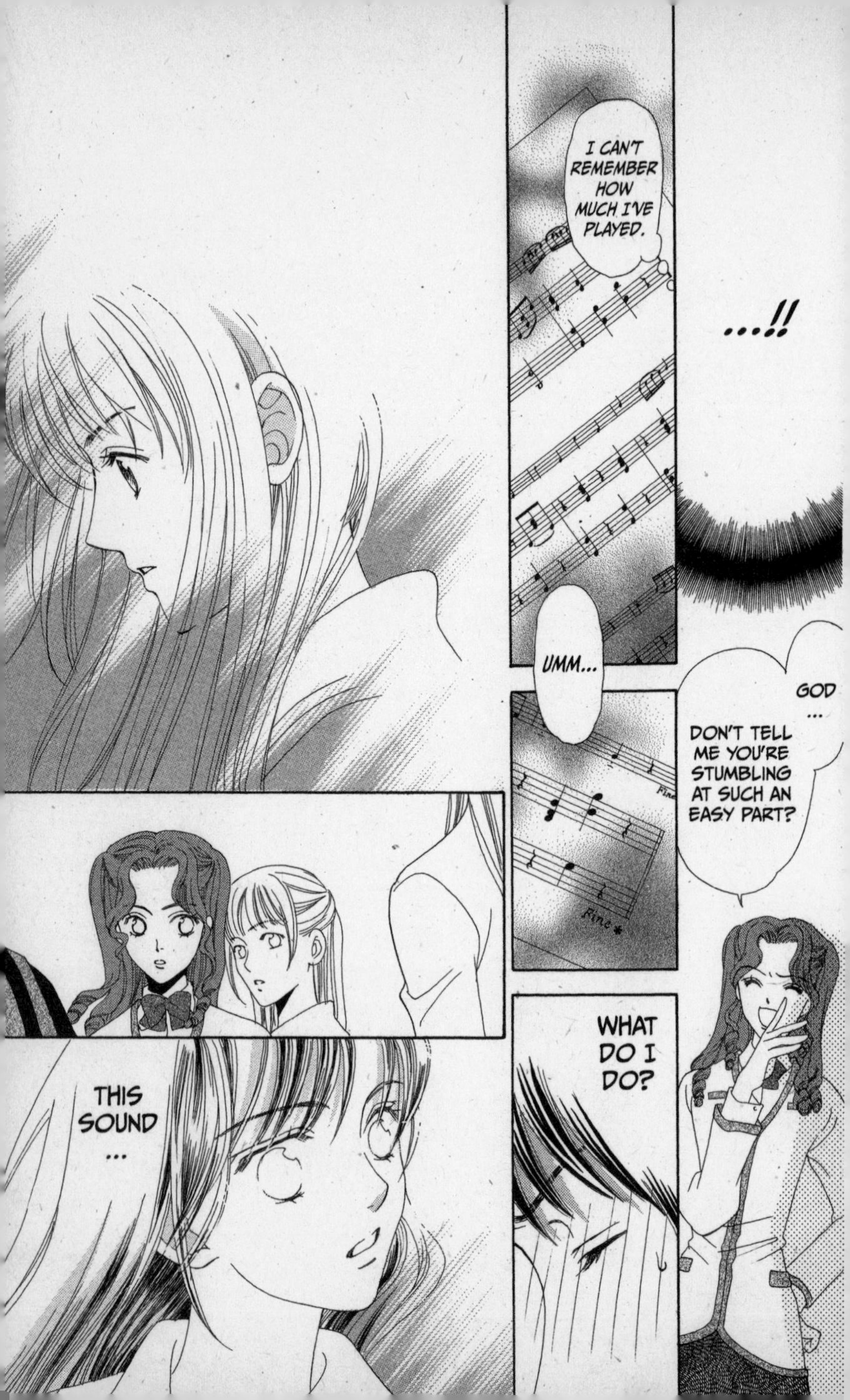

...!!
I CAN'T REMEMBER HOW MUCH I'VE PLAYED.
UMM...
GOD ... DON'T TELL ME YOU'RE STUMBLING AT SUCH AN EASY PART?
WHAT DO I DO?
THIS SOUND ...

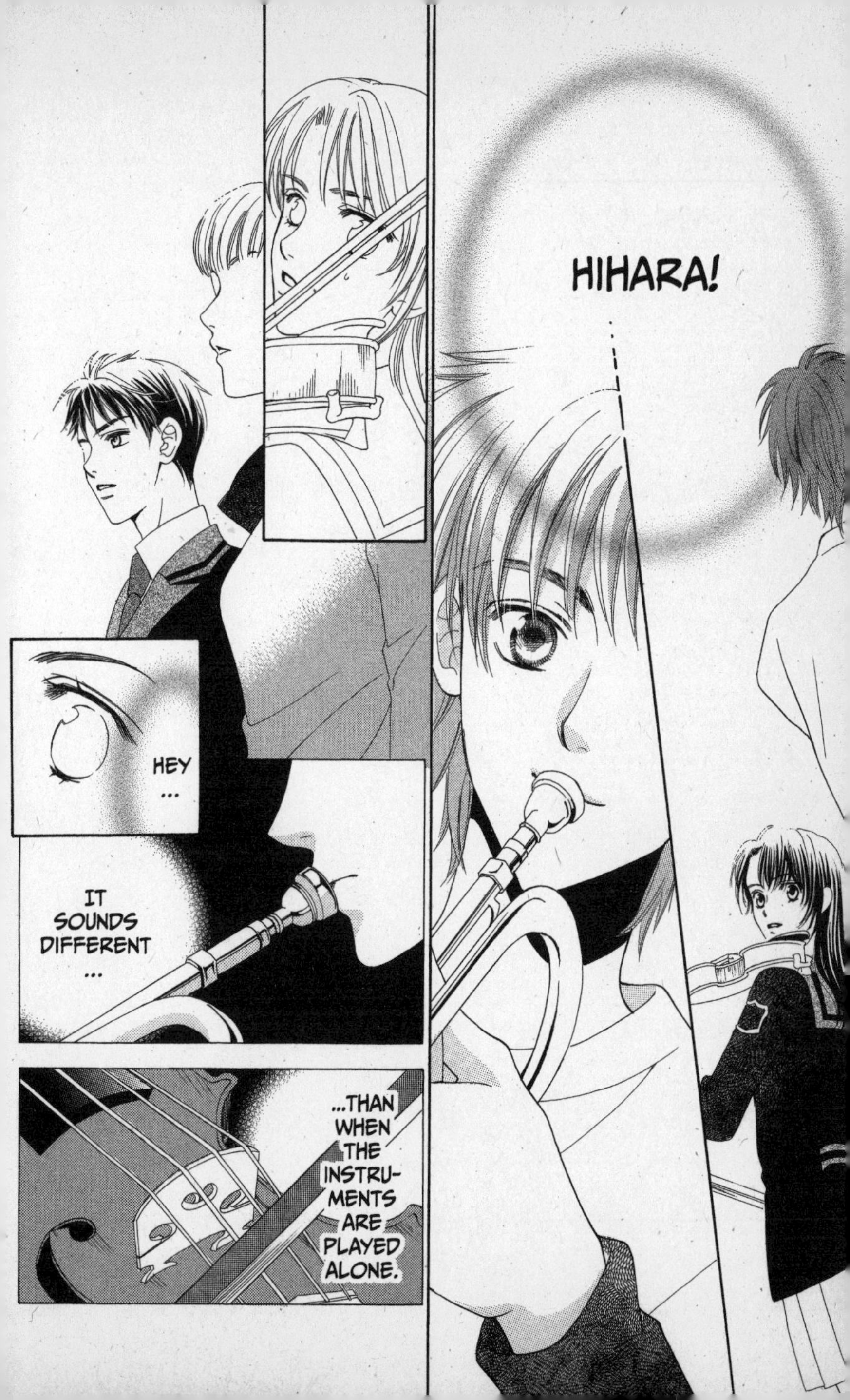
HIHARA!
HEY ...
IT SOUNDS DIFFERENT ...
...THAN WHEN THE INSTRUMENTS ARE PLAYED ALONE.

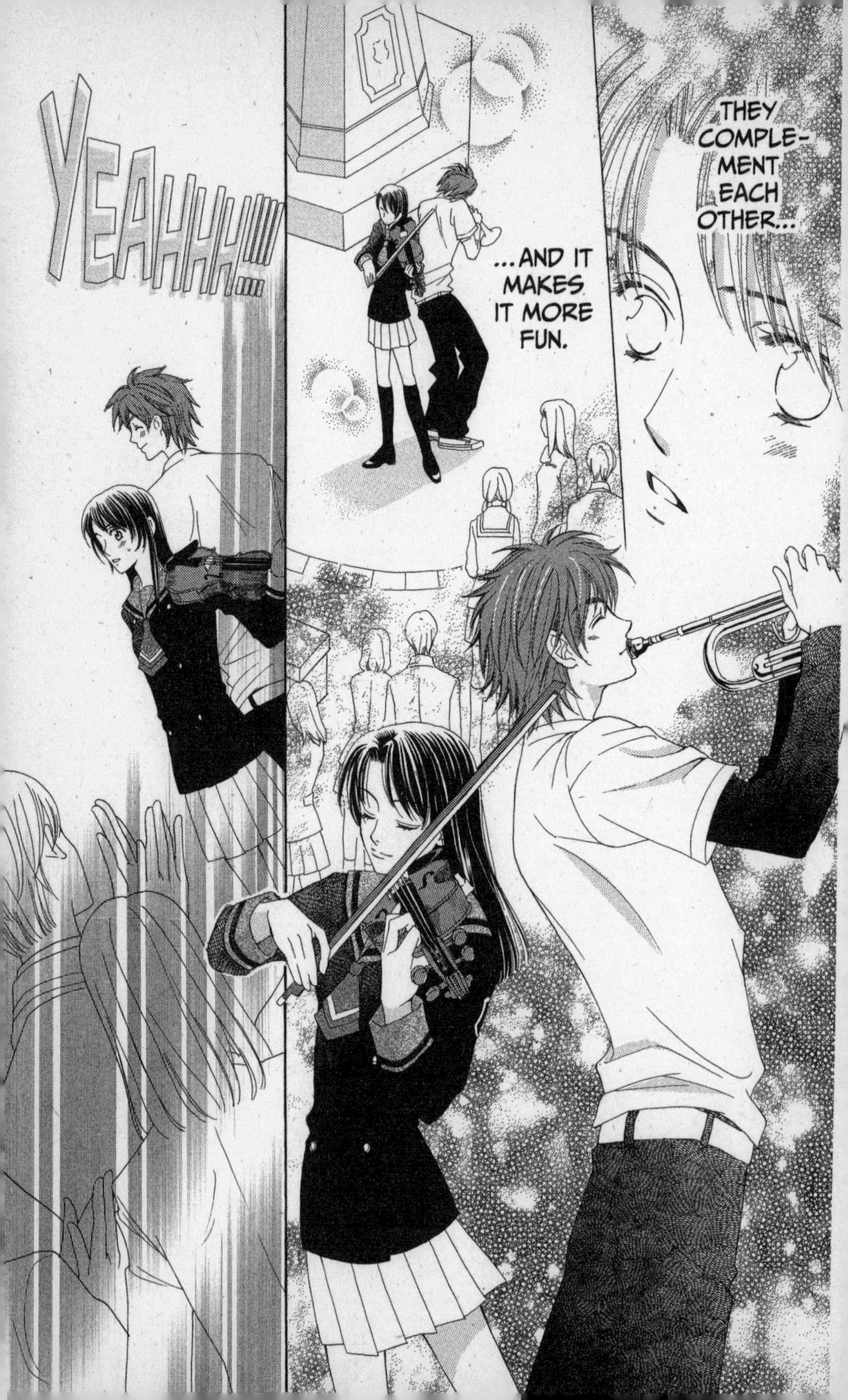
THEY COMPLEMENT EACH OTHER...
...AND IT MAKES IT MORE FUN.
YEAHHH!!!!

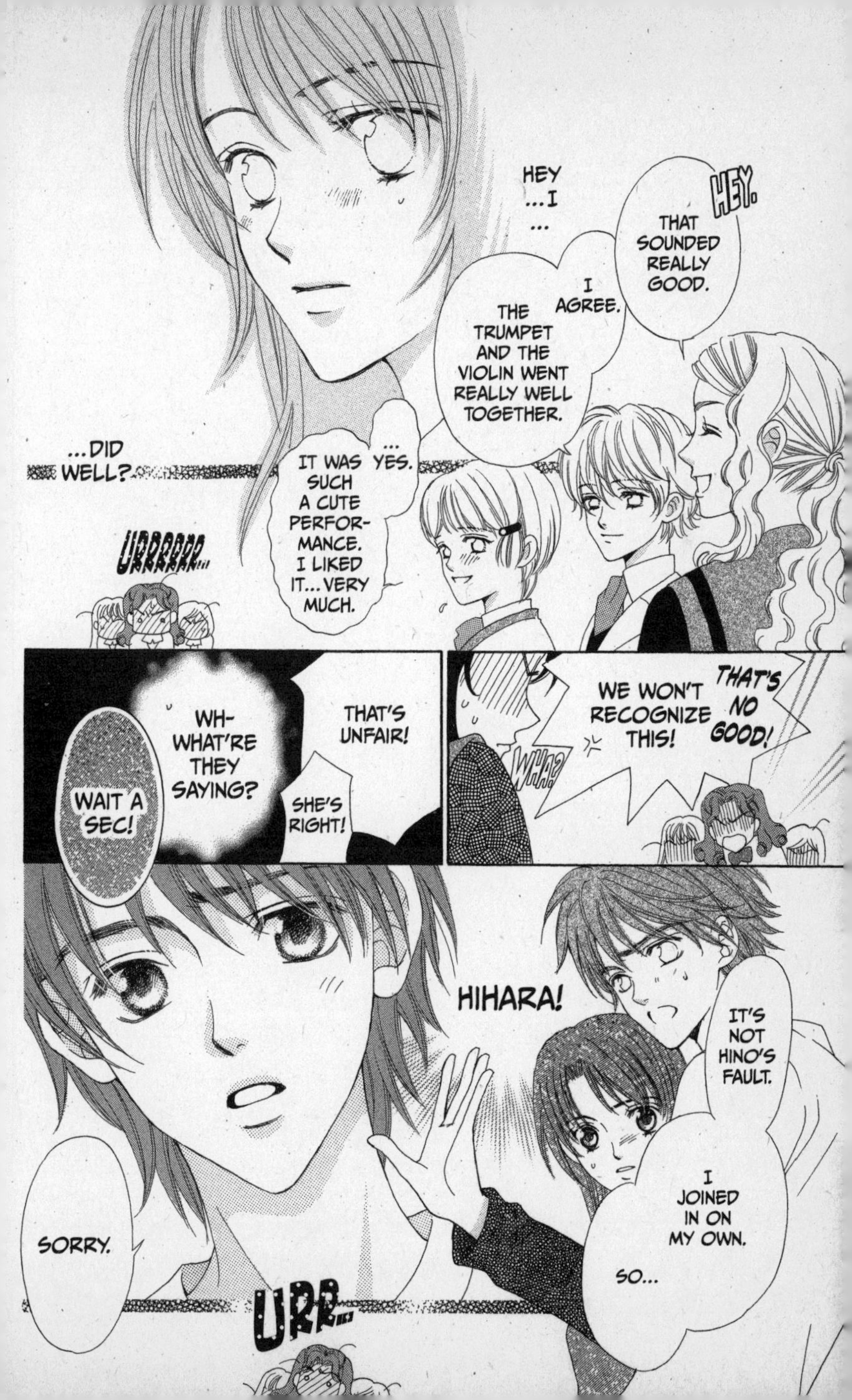
HEY.
THAT SOUNDED REALLY GOOD.
I AGREE.
THE TRUMPET AND THE VIOLIN WENT REALLY WELL TOGETHER.
HEY ...I ...
... YES.
IT WAS SUCH A CUTE PERFORMANCE. I LIKED IT... VERY MUCH.
...DID WELL?
URRRRRR...
THAT'S NO GOOD!
WE WON'T RECOGNIZE THIS!
WHA?
THAT'S UNFAIR!
SHE'S RIGHT!
WH- WHAT'RE THEY SAYING?
WAIT A SEC!
IT'S NOT HINO'S FAULT.
HIHARA!
I JOINED IN ON MY OWN.
SO...
SORRY.
URR...

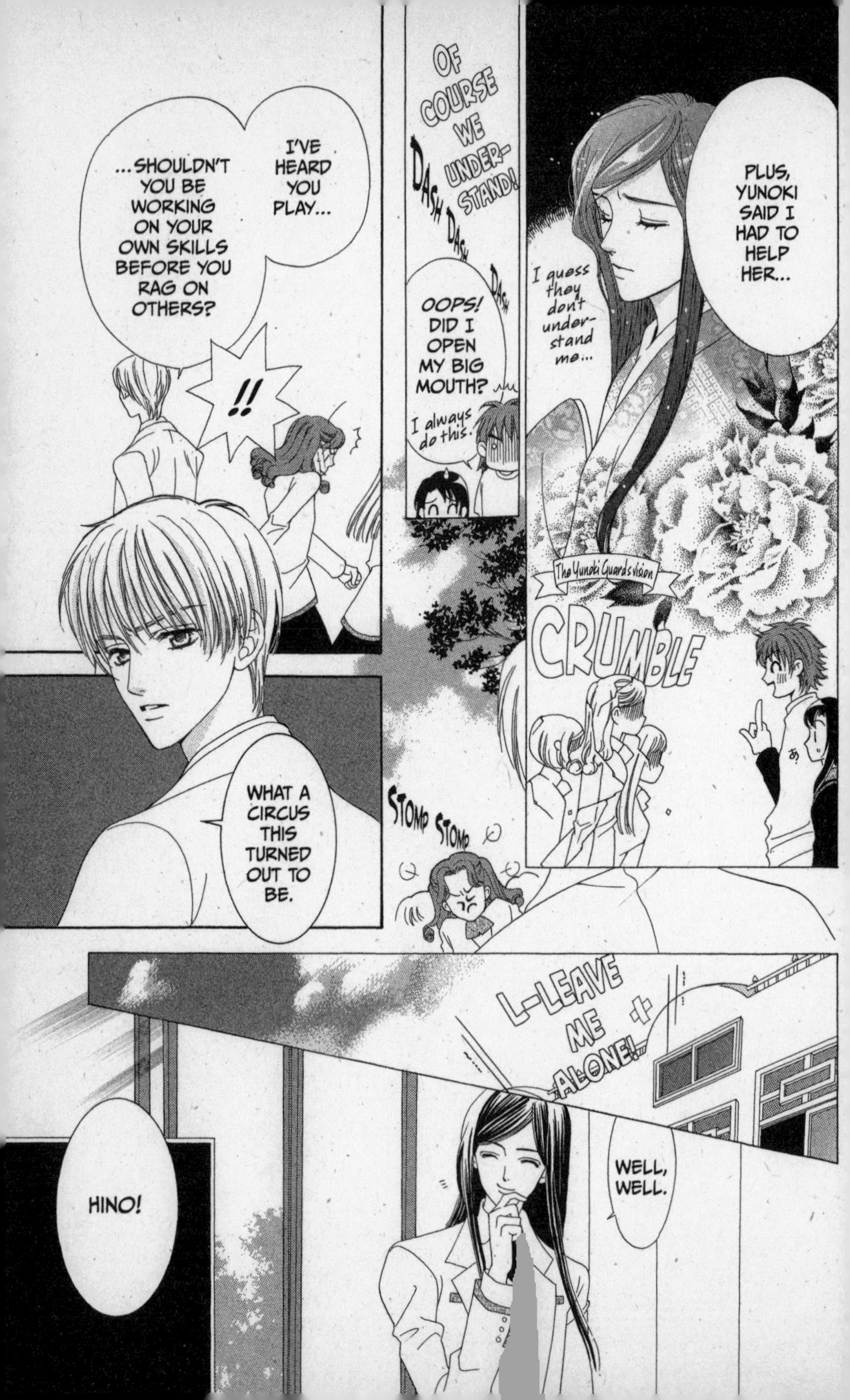
PLUS, YUNOKI SAID I HAD TO HELP HER...
I guess they don't understand me...
The Yunoki Guards vision
CRUMBLE
OF COURSE WE UNDER-STAND!
DASH DASH DASH
OOPS! DID I OPEN MY BIG MOUTH?
I always do this.
I'VE HEARD YOU PLAY...
...SHOULDN'T YOU BE WORKING ON YOUR OWN SKILLS BEFORE YOU RAG ON OTHERS?
!!
STOMP STOMP
WHAT A CIRCUS THIS TURNED OUT TO BE.
L-LEAVE ME ALONE!
WELL, WELL.
HINO!

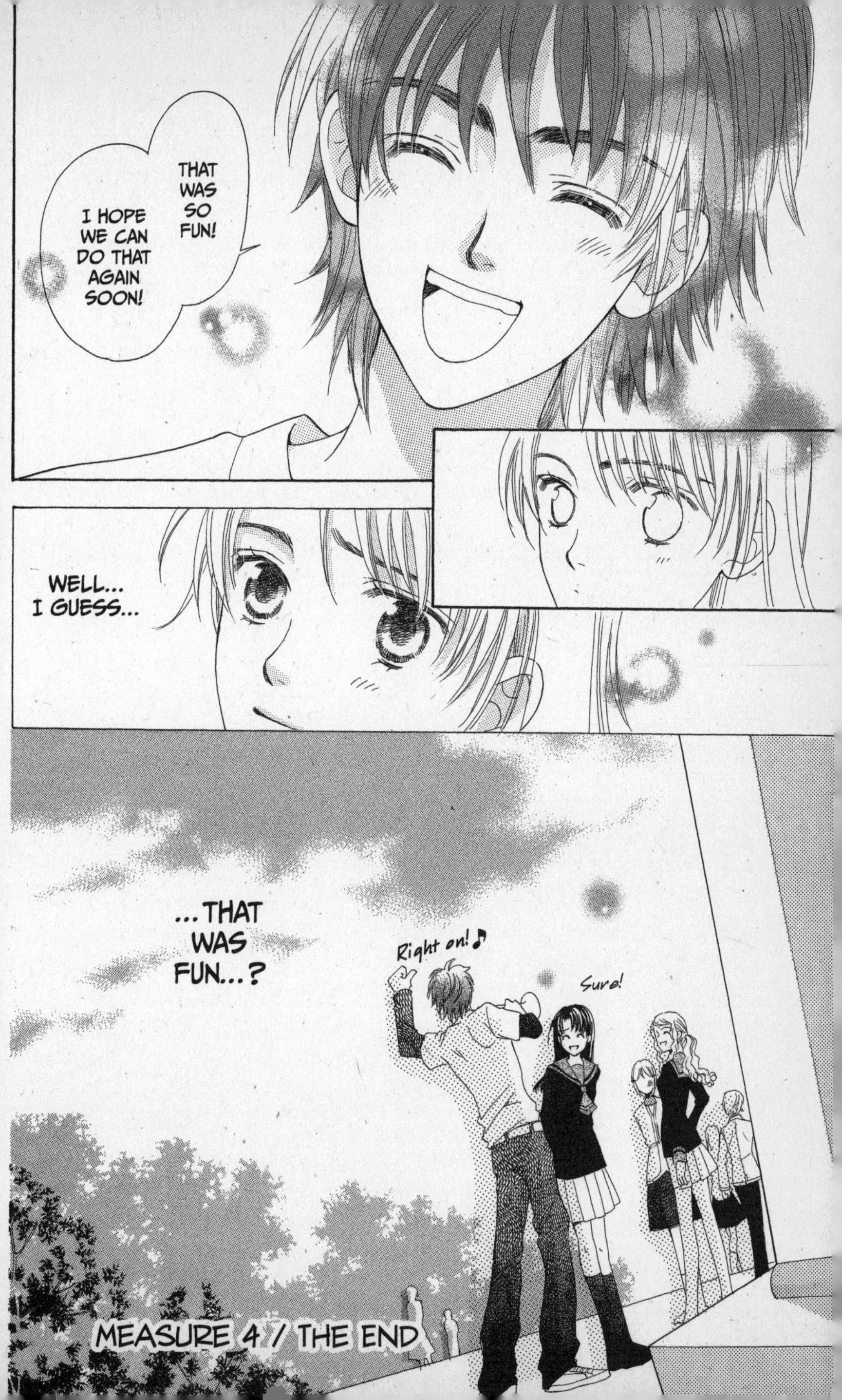
THAT WAS SO FUN!
I HOPE WE CAN DO THAT AGAIN SOON!
WELL... I GUESS...
...THAT WAS FUN...?
Right on! ♪
Sure!
MEASURE 4 / THE END

POSTSCRIPT

HELLO AGAIN.

I'D LIKE TO THANK YOU FOR TAKING THE TIME TO READ *LA CORDA D'ORO.*

Representative Hino

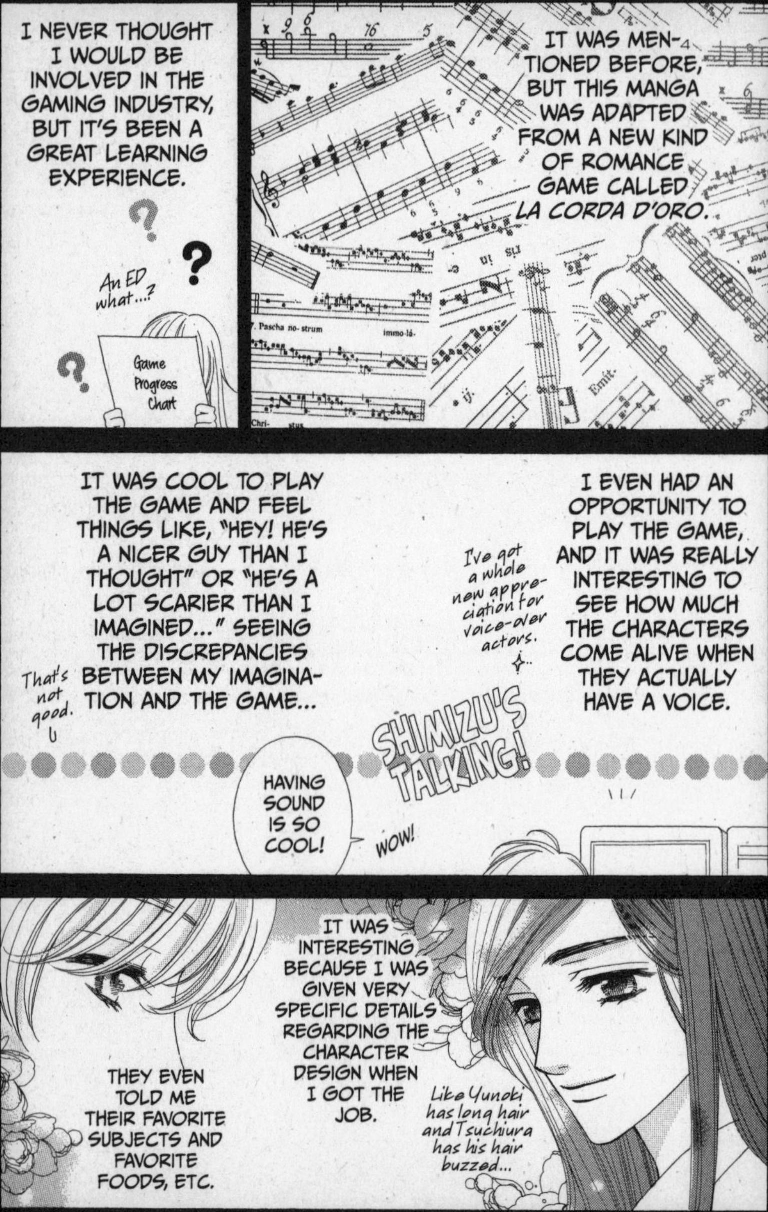
IT WAS MENTIONED BEFORE, BUT THIS MANGA WAS ADAPTED FROM A NEW KIND OF ROMANCE GAME CALLED LA CORDA D'ORO.
I NEVER THOUGHT I WOULD BE INVOLVED IN THE GAMING INDUSTRY, BUT IT'S BEEN A GREAT LEARNING EXPERIENCE.
An ED what...?
Game Progress Chart
I EVEN HAD AN OPPORTUNITY TO PLAY THE GAME, AND IT WAS REALLY INTERESTING TO SEE HOW MUCH THE CHARACTERS COME ALIVE WHEN THEY ACTUALLY HAVE A VOICE.
I've got a whole new appreciation for voice-over actors.
SHIMIZU'S TALKING!
HAVING SOUND IS SO COOL!
WOW!
IT WAS COOL TO PLAY THE GAME AND FEEL THINGS LIKE, "HEY! HE'S A NICER GUY THAN I THOUGHT" OR "HE'S A LOT SCARIER THAN I IMAGINED..." SEEING THE DISCREPANCIES BETWEEN MY IMAGINATION AND THE GAME...
That's not good.
Like Yunoki has long hair and Tsuchiura has his hair buzzed...
IT WAS INTERESTING BECAUSE I WAS GIVEN VERY SPECIFIC DETAILS REGARDING THE CHARACTER DESIGN WHEN I GOT THE JOB.
THEY EVEN TOLD ME THEIR FAVORITE SUBJECTS AND FAVORITE FOODS, ETC.

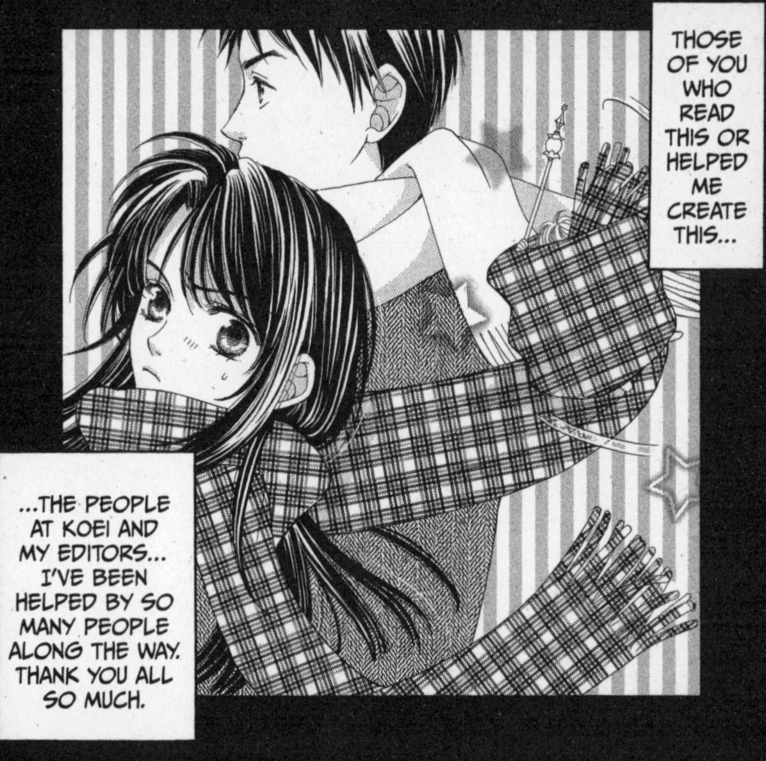
THOSE OF YOU WHO READ THIS OR HELPED ME CREATE THIS...
...THE PEOPLE AT KOEI AND MY EDITORS... I'VE BEEN HELPED BY SO MANY PEOPLE ALONG THE WAY. THANK YOU ALL SO MUCH.

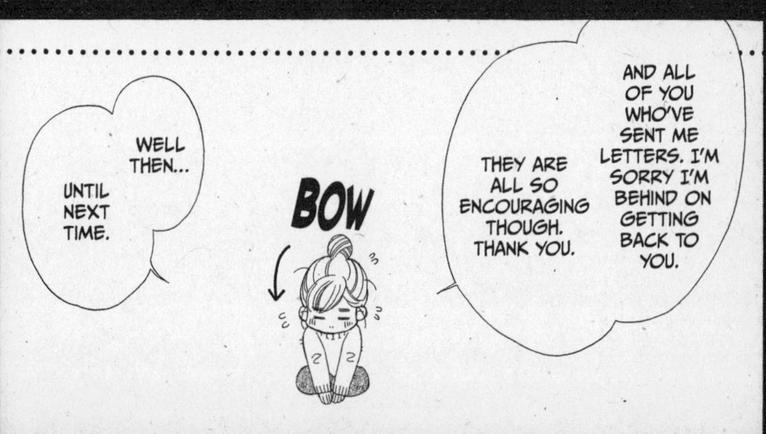
AND ALL OF YOU WHO'VE SENT ME LETTERS. I'M SORRY I'M BEHIND ON GETTING BACK TO YOU.
THEY ARE ALL SO ENCOURAGING THOUGH. THANK YOU.
BOW
WELL THEN...
UNTIL NEXT TIME.

SPECIAL THANKS

A.IZUMI
A.KASHIMA
M.SHIINO
S.MATSUOKA
Y.KOMURO
Y.URUNO

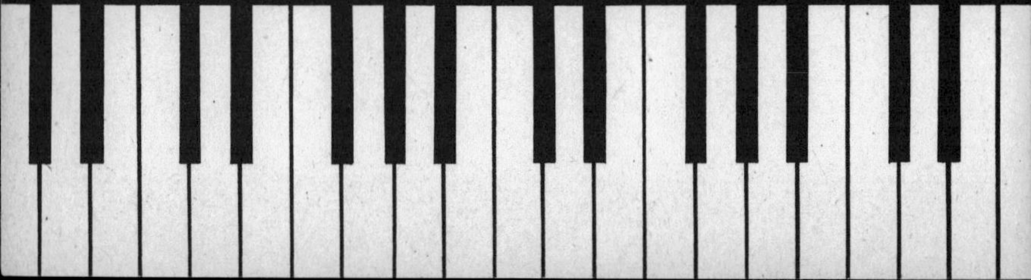

KAHOKO MAY HAVE A MAGIC VIOLIN,
BUT SHE NEEDS TO BE ABLE TO "FEEL"
THE MUSIC FOR THE MAGIC TO WORK. WITH
THE COMPETITION AROUND THE CORNER,
WILL KAHOKO MEASURE UP IN TIME?

LA CORDA D'ORO
VOLUME 2
ON SALE JANUARY 2007!

End of Volume Special, Part 1

PREMIER!

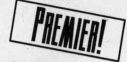

From the author's archives!

INITIAL ILLUSTRATIONS

AS A HUGE COLLABORATIVE PROJECT BETWEEN KOEI AND *LALA* MAGAZINE, *LA CORDA D'ORO* CALLED FOR THE CONCEPTUALIZATION OF THE CHARACTERS. SO HOW DID THESE CHARMING CHARACTERS COME TO LIFE? WE'RE PREMIERING YUKI KURE'S INITIAL ILLUSTRATIONS STRAIGHT FROM HER PERSONAL ARCHIVES! A TOKEN OF OUR APPRECIATION... HERE TODAY ARE KAHOKO, LEN AND RYOTARO! ♥

183
175
158
165
168
178
162
181
178
172

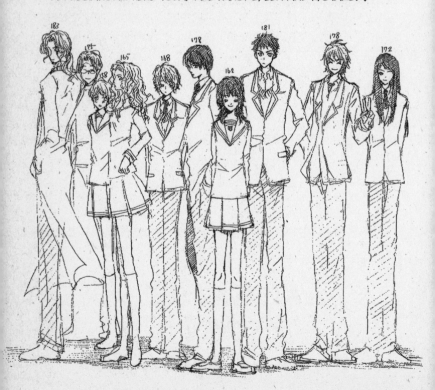

↑ AN INITIAL ROUGH DRAFT OF A GROUP SHOT. DO SOME CHARACTERS LOOK A LITTLE DIFFERENT...?

KAHOKO HINO

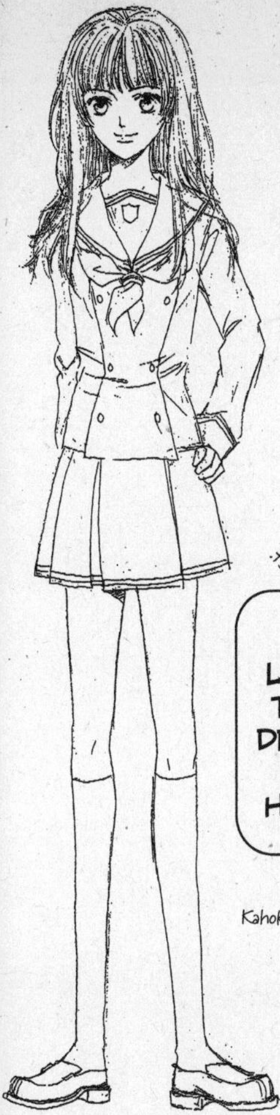

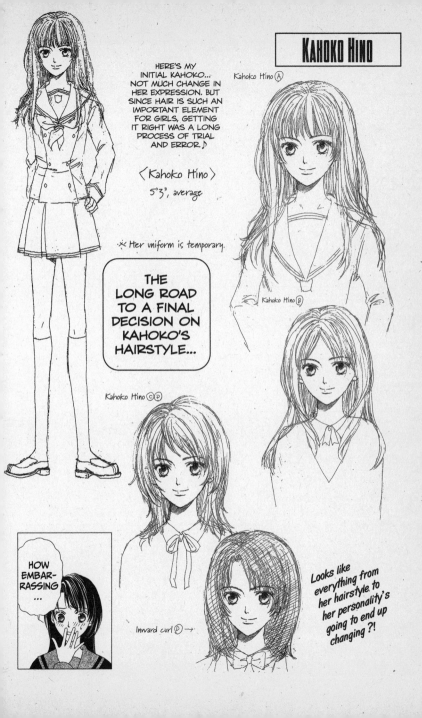

HERE'S MY INITIAL KAHOKO... NOT MUCH CHANGE IN HER EXPRESSION. BUT SINCE HAIR IS SUCH AN IMPORTANT ELEMENT FOR GIRLS, GETTING IT RIGHT WAS A LONG PROCESS OF TRIAL AND ERROR.♪

〈Kahoko Hino〉

5'3", average

※ Her uniform is temporary.

Kahoko Hino Ⓐ

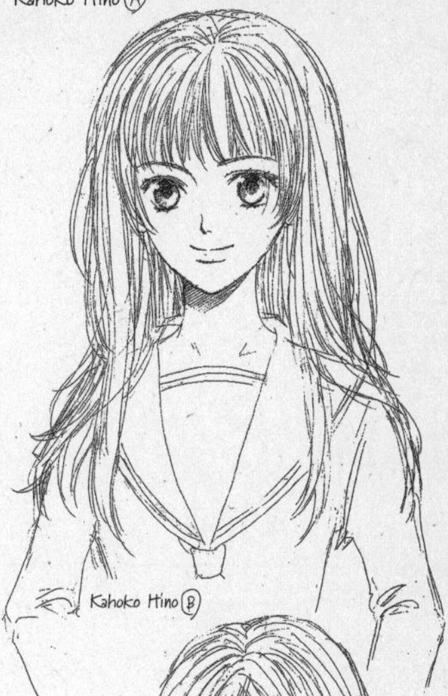

THE LONG ROAD TO A FINAL DECISION ON KAHOKO'S HAIRSTYLE...

Kahoko Hino Ⓑ

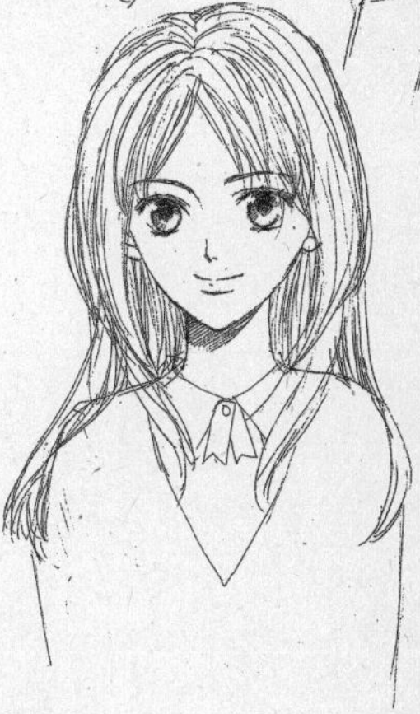

Kahoko Hino ⒸⒹ

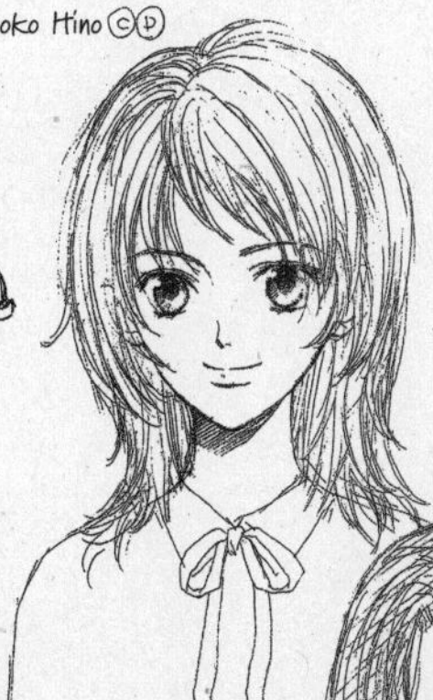

Inward curl Ⓓ →

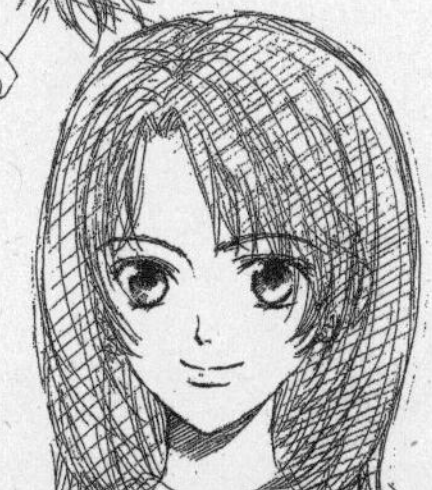

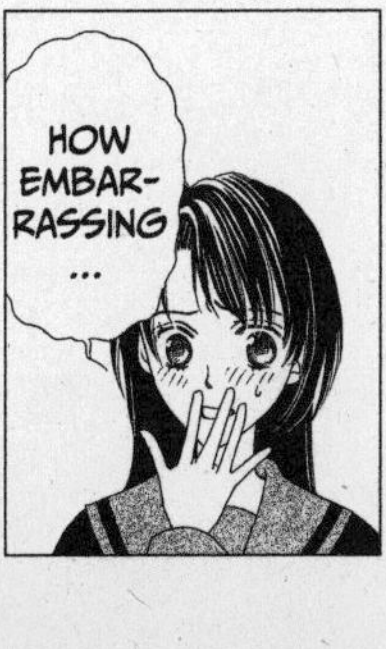
HOW EMBAR-RASSING ...

Looks like everything from her hairstyle to her personality's going to end up changing ?!

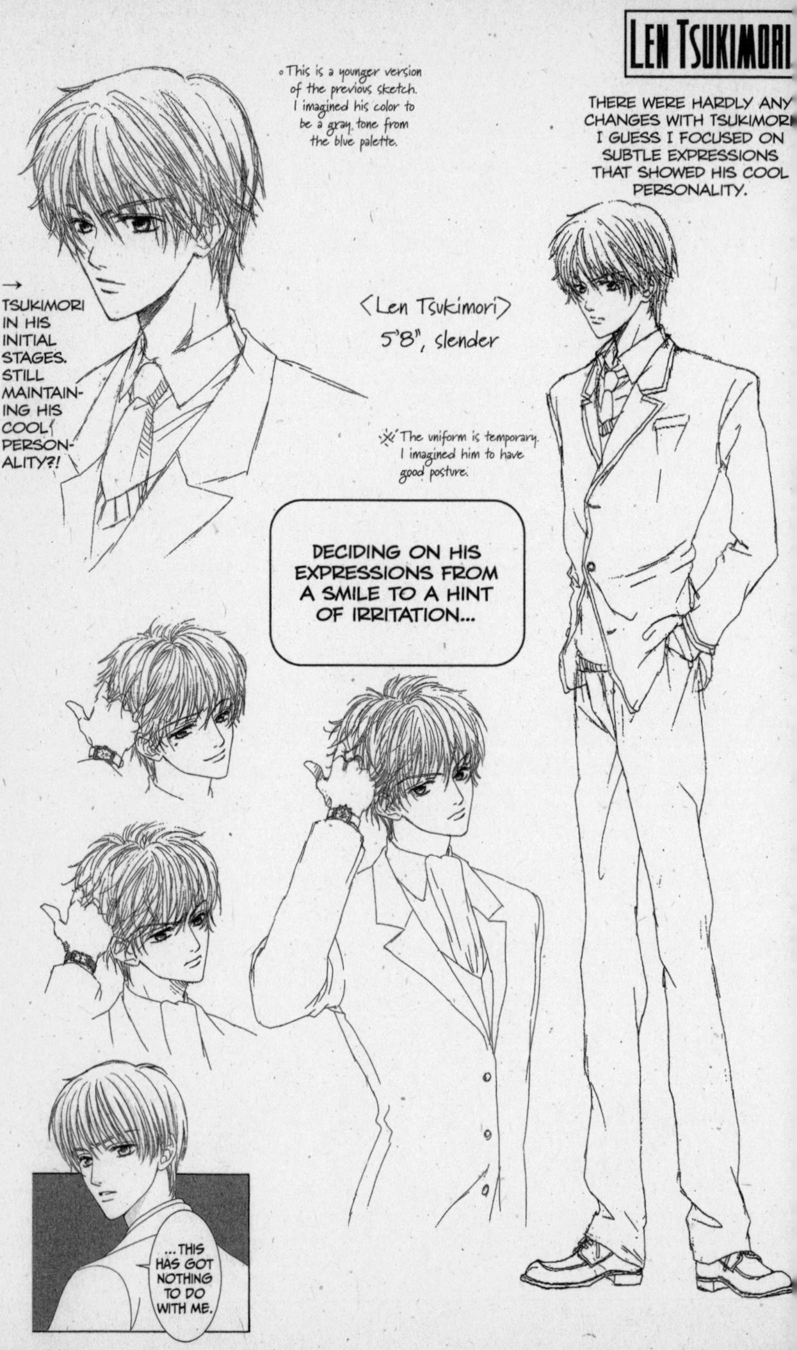
LEN TSUKIMORI
THERE WERE HARDLY ANY CHANGES WITH TSUKIMORI. I GUESS I FOCUSED ON SUBTLE EXPRESSIONS THAT SHOWED HIS COOL PERSONALITY.
∘This is a younger version of the previous sketch. I imagined his color to be a gray tone from the blue palette.
→ TSUKIMORI IN HIS INITIAL STAGES. STILL MAINTAINING HIS COOL PERSONALITY?!
〈Len Tsukimori〉
5'8", slender
※The uniform is temporary. I imagined him to have good posture.
DECIDING ON HIS EXPRESSIONS FROM A SMILE TO A HINT OF IRRITATION...
...THIS HAS GOT NOTHING TO DO WITH ME.

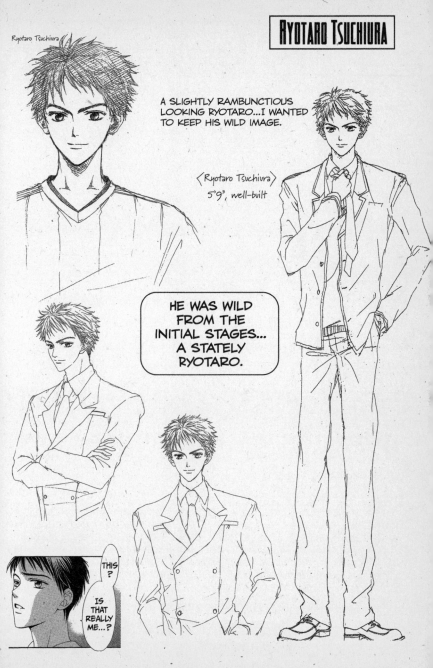

RYOTARO TSUCHIURA

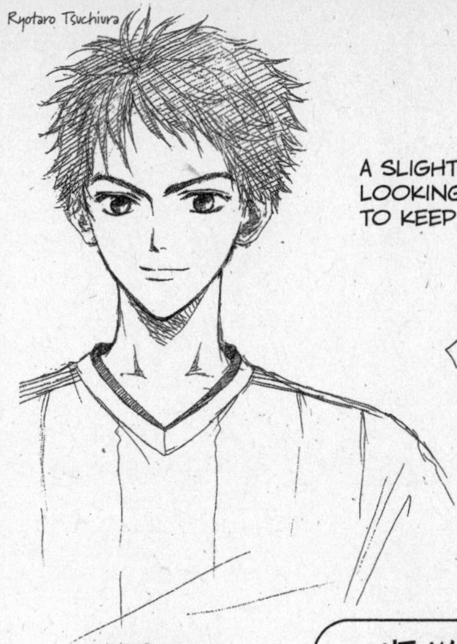
Ryotaro Tsuchiura

A SLIGHTLY RAMBUNCTIOUS LOOKING RYOTARO...I WANTED TO KEEP HIS WILD IMAGE.

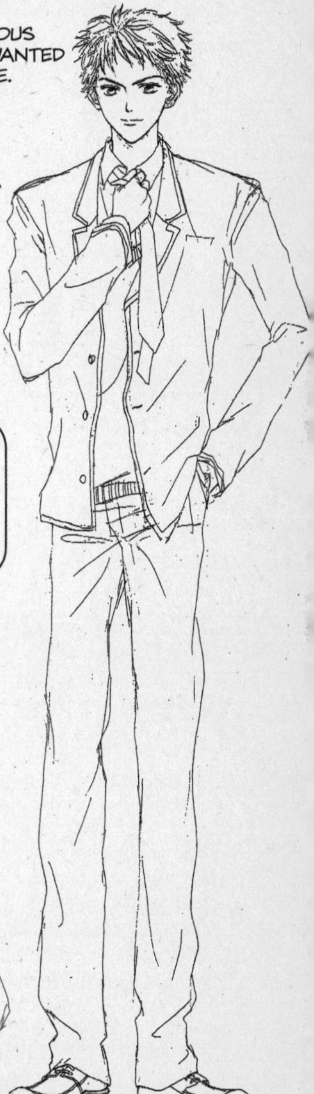

〈Ryotaro Tsuchiura〉

5'9", well-built

HE WAS WILD FROM THE INITIAL STAGES... A STATELY RYOTARO.

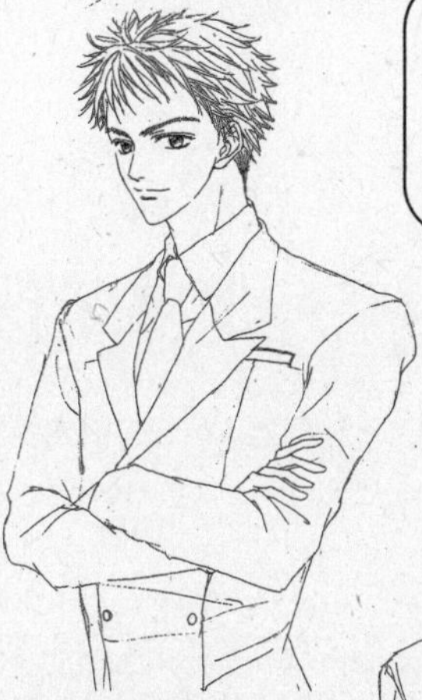

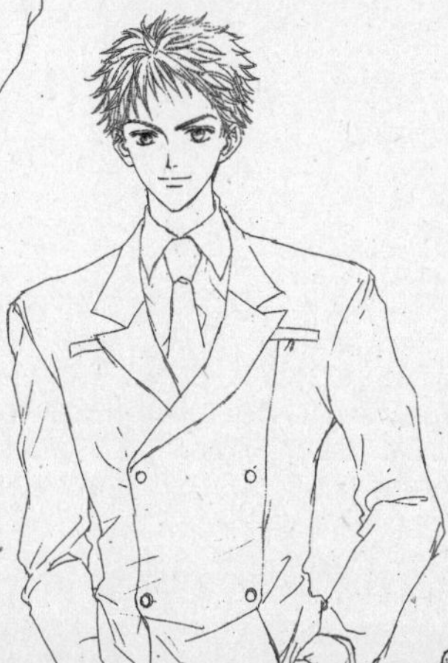

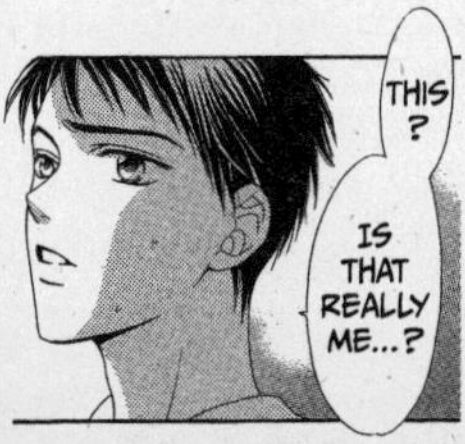
THIS?
IS THAT REALLY ME...?

I'LL INTRODUCE THE OTHER CHARACTERS NEXT TIME. ♥

End of Volume Special, Part 2

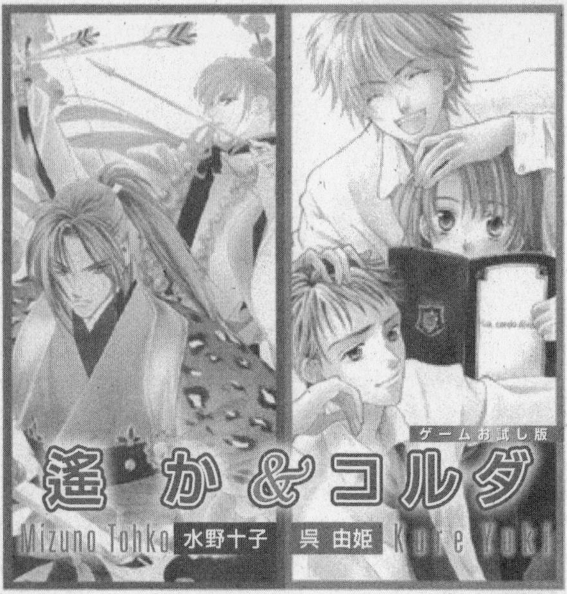
ゲームお試し版
遙か&コルダ
Mizuno Tohko 水野十子
呉 由姫

Haruka & Corda

All *LaLa* subscribers will receive a *Haruka & Corda* game trial version DVD/VHS

A sneak peek at a scene from the *La Corda* "Heart Throbbing Script Theater"

WELCOME TO THE END OF VOLUME SPECIAL, PART 2!
WE'LL BE PREMIERING A PART OF A SCENE FROM THE *LA CORDA* "HEART QUENCHING THEATER" FROM THE *HARUKA & CORDA* GAME TRIAL DVD/VHS THAT WAS ADVERTISED AS A SPECIAL GIFT TO ALL *LALA* SUBSCRIBERS. THE "HEART QUENCHING THEATER" IS A MINI-MOVIE VOICED BY REAL ACTORS THAT USES YUKI KURE ILLUSTRATIONS OF AN ORIGINAL SCENE MADE ESPECIALLY FOR THIS PROJECT. EIGHT MINI-MOVIES OF RYOTARO AND KAZUKI WERE MADE, AND THIS IS A SPECIAL PREMIER OF FOUR OF THOSE! WE HOPE YOU CAN GET A TASTE FOR THE ROMANCE!♥ ENJOY!★

※THIS SPECIAL SUBSCRIPTION OFFER ENDED IN MARCH 2004, AND WAS AVAILABLE IN JAPAN ONLY.★

THE RYOTARO TSUCHIURA EDITION, PART 1

IN THE NURSE'S ROOM ON THE DAY OF THE SCHOOL'S ANNUAL SPORT'S DAY.

K: I HEARD THAT YOU GOT HURT?!

R: YEAH, BUT DON'T TOUCH ME. I DON'T WANT TO GET YOU ALL BLOODY. THIS IS MORE LIKE A BATTLE THAN A SPORTING EVENT. I CAN'T BELIEVE I GOT HURT LIKE THIS.

K: THE NURSE ISN'T HERE. I CAN HELP YOU DRESS THAT WOUND.

R: HUH? DON'T WORRY ABOUT IT. I'M SURE YOU'VE GOT BETTER THINGS TO DO.

K: OH, SHUT UP AND SIT DOWN.

R: ...THANKS.

K: WOW! YOU REALLY GOT YOURSELF GOOD.

R: I ALREADY WASHED IT. IF YOU COULD JUST SPRAY ON SOME ANTI-SEPTIC AND SLAP A BAND-AID ON IT, THAT'LL BE MORE THAN ENOUGH.

K: IT'S GONNA STING. (SHE SPRAYS HIS WOUND.)

R: ...!!

K: DID IT HURT? I'M SORRY.

R: I'M FINE.

K: HERE, LET ME WIPE IT OFF AND GET THAT BAND-AID ON AND... THERE YOU GO. ALL DONE!

R: THANKS. YOU'RE A SAVIOR. I WENT TO THE FIRST AID STATION OUTSIDE AND CAME HERE CAUSE THE LINE WAS SO LONG, BUT I WAS ACTUALLY GETTING A LITTLE WORRIED CAUSE NO ONE WAS HERE.

K: HA HA HA. THEN I'M GLAD I CAME TO CHECK UP ON YOU.

R: THERE REALLY IS NO ONE AROUND. LET'S GET OUT OF HERE BEFORE SOMEONE THINKS WE'RE UP TO SOMETHING.

K: UP TO SOMETHING?

R: I-I MEAN...DON'T WORRY ABOUT IT. AREN'T YOU IN ONE OF THE EVENTS TODAY?

K: VOLLEYBALL. I DON'T MEAN TO BRAG, BUT I'M A GREAT RECEIVER.

R: WATCH YOUR FINGERS. I'LL CHEER FOR YOU AS A TOKEN OF MY APPRECIATION. YOU CAN SHOW OFF YOUR SKILLS TO ME THEN.

K= KAHOKO   R= RYOTARO

THE RYOTARO TSUCHIURA EDITION, PART 2

BAKING COOKIES IN HOME EC CLASS.

K: TSUCHIURA, CHECK IT OUT. LOOK AT HOW GOOD MINE TURNED OUT. (SHOWS HIM HER COOKIES.)

R: COOKIES? OH YEAH, I FORGOT YOU HAD HOME EC.

K: YEAH, YEAH. DON'T YOU THINK THEY CAME OUT GOOD?

R: THAT'S WHAT THAT SMELL WAS DURING CLASS.

K: YOU DON'T LIKE COOKIES?

R: NO, IT'S NOT THAT... I JUST GET HUNGRY WHEN I SMELL FOOD.

K: THEN HAVE THESE. I THINK THEY TASTE OKAY.

R: ...I CAN HAVE SOME? DON'T YOU HAVE SOME-ONE ELSE YOU NEED TO GIVE THEM TO?

K: UMM...YOU DON'T WANT THEM?

R: THAT'S NOT WHAT I SAID. DON'T PUT WORDS IN MY MOUTH. I WAS JUST WONDERING... (SOFTENS VOICE) IF I COULD HAVE THEM... THANKS.

K: WHAT?

R: NOTHING. THANKS A LOT. (HE EATS ONE.) ...IT'S REALLY GOOD. I'M RESERVING YOUR NEXT BATCH TOO, SO DON'T GO GIVING THEM TO SOMEONE ELSE.

K= KAHOKO R= RYOTARO

THE KAZUKI HIHARA EDITION, PART 1

HIHARA'S OUT WITH A COLD! GOING AND WISHING HIM WELL

H: (COUGHING) UGH... THIS SUCKS. I CAN'T BELIEVE I CAN'T GO OUTSIDE WHEN IT'S THIS NICE. WHAT CRAPPY LUCK... (COUGHS)

K: ARE YOU ALL RIGHT HIHARA?

H: ...I'M BEGINNING TO SEE THINGS... MY FEVER MUST BE....

K: YOU'RE NOT SEEING THINGS.

H: HUH? WH-WHA!! YOU'RE THE REAL THING! (COUGHS)

K: A-ARE YOU OKAY? HIHARA, PULL YOURSELF TOGETHER! (RUBS HIS BACK)

H: S-SORRY. I'M FINE. THIS IS NOTHING. I'M ALL BETTER NOW.

K: DON'T LIE. YOU LOOK HORRIBLE.

H: I'M SERIOUS. HEY, DO YOU WANT SOME TEA? I CAN'T BELIEVE NO ONE'S EVEN GIVEN YOU TEA. SORRY ABOUT THAT. (COUGHS)

K: DON'T GET UP. YOU NEED TO STAY IN BED.

H: ...YES MA'AM. I'LL STAY HERE. (GETS IN BED) UHH... THIS IS SO UNGENTLEMANLY OF ME...

K: YOU CAN'T BE WORRYING ABOUT BEING A GENTLEMAN WHEN YOU'RE SICK. YOU SHOULD ONLY BE THINKING ABOUT GETTING BETTER. RIGHT?

H: YOU'RE RIGHT. I'M GOING TO WORK ON GETTING BETTER. I WANT TO SEE YOU AT SCHOOL...BUT I'M SO HAPPY YOU CAME OVER. WILL YOU STAY A LITTLE LONGER?

K: OF COURSE. DO YOU WANT ME TO STAY UNTIL YOU FALL ASLEEP?

H: IF I FELL ASLEEP LIKE THIS, I FEEL LIKE I'D BE ABLE TO SEE YOU IN MY DREAMS. MAYBE THAT'LL HELP ME GET BETTER...

K= KAHOKO   H= HIHARA

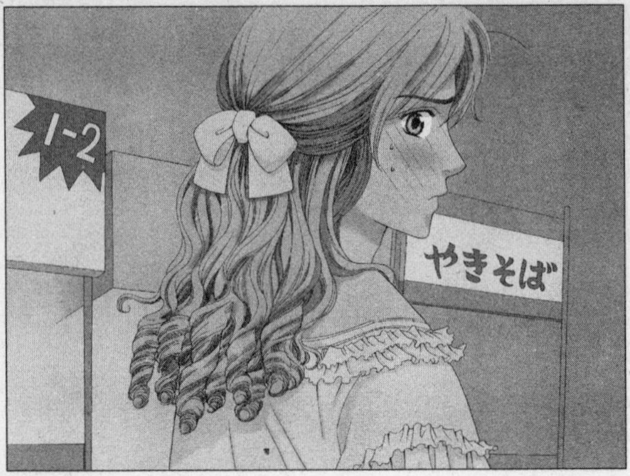
1-2
やきそば

THE KAZUKI HIHARA EDITION, PART 2

BUMPING INTO HIHARA AT THE SCHOOL FESTIVAL... WHY IS HE DRESSED THAT WAY...?!

K: HIHARAAA!
H: OH, CR...CRAP! SHE'S GONNA SEE...
K: WHY ARE YOU RUNNING AWAY?
H: (TOTALLY CAUGHT) H-HEY. I GUESS YOU FOUND ME...
K: WHAT'S WRONG? YOU LOOK SAD.
H: I DIDN'T WANT TO BE SEEN LIKE THIS. THE GIRLS IN MY CLASS GOT INTO IT, SAYING IT WAS OUR LAST SCHOOL FESTIVAL... I LOOK HORRIBLE IN A SKIRT.
K: W-WELL...
H: STOP RIGHT THERE! I DON'T WANT TO HEAR THE TRUTH, EVEN IF IT'S TO MAKE ME FEEL BETTER. I REALLY DIDN'T WANT YOU TO SEE ME LIKE THIS...CROSS-DRESSING. THESE ADORABLE CLOTHES ARE ONLY ADORABLE WHEN GIRLS WEAR THEM. ARG, I WISH YOU WERE THE ONE WEARING THIS AND NOT ME...
K: YOU LOOK GOOD, THOUGH.
H: IT SUCKS IF I LOOK BAD *OR* GOOD... LET'S TALK ABOUT YOU! WHAT'S YOUR CLASS DOING? YOU ON A BREAK RIGHT NOW?
K :WE'RE DOING A CAFÉ. I'M ON A BREAK, SO I'M GOING AROUND CHECKING THINGS OUT.
H: HEY, WHY DON'T WE GO AROUND TOGETHER? I WANT GO CHECK THINGS OUT WITH YOU.
K: SURE.
H: REALLY? YAY! THEN WILL YOU WAIT FOR ME FOR A SEC? I'M GOING TO GET CHANGED. I'LL BE RIGHT BACK SO STAY HERE!! (RUNS OFF IN A HURRY)

K= KAHOKO H= HIHARA

La Corda d'Oro End Notes

You can appreciate music just by listening to it, but knowing the story behind a piece can help enhance your enjoyment. In that spirit, here is the background information about some of the topics mentioned in *La Corda d'Oro*. Enjoy!

Page 72, panel 4: Fata
The Latin word referring to the mythological representations of fate, embodied by the Greek Moriae and the Roman Parcae or Fatae. These three women appeared on the third night after a child's birth to determine its fate. They were usually described as horrible old hags, much like the Weird Sisters in *Macbeth*. The Latin term Fata gave rise to the Italian fata, Portuguese fada, Spanish hada, Old French fée, and English fae or fairy. Popular perception of fairies has changed over the ages, and in our modern times many contrasting ideas exist.

Page 114, panel 6: Schubert's *Ave Maria*
Written by the Austrian composer Franz Schubert in 1825, when he was 25 years old. The original lyrics of the song were a German translation of an excerpt of Sir Walter Scott's poem, *The Lady of the Lake*. At some later date, the Latin version of the Hail Mary prayer (Ave Maria) was fit to the music, and is now the most commonly performed version of this song.

Page 136, panel 4: Gossec
Francois-Joseph Gossec was born in 1734 to a Belgian peasant family and displayed remarkable musical gifts. He moved to Paris as a young man and founded the Concert de Amateurs in 1769, and became the maître de musique of the Concert Spirituel in 1775. His *Gavotte* is often used as a lullaby.

Yuki Kure made her debut in 2000
with the story *Chijo yori Eien ni*
(Forever from the Earth), published
in monthly *LaLa* magazine.
La Corda d' Oro is her first manga
series published. Her hobby is
watching soccer games and
collecting small goodies.

LA CORDA D'ORO
Vol. 1
The Shojo Beat Manga Edition

STORY AND ART BY
YUKI KURE
ORIGINAL CONCEPT BY
RUBY PARTY

English Translation & Adaptation/Mai Ihara
Touch-up Art & Lettering/Gia Cam Luc
Design/Yukiko Whitley
Editor/Pancha Diaz

Managing Editor/Megan Bates
Editorial Director/Elizabeth Kawasaki
VP & Editor in Chief/Yumi Hoashi
Sr. Director of Acquisitions/Rika Inouye
Sr. VP of Marketing/Liza Coppola
Exec. VP of Sales & Marketing/John Easum
Publisher/Hyoe Narita

Printed in Canada

Published by VIZ Media, LLC
P.O. Box 77010
San Francisco, CA 94107

Shojo Beat Manga Edition
10 9 8 7 6 5 4 3 2
First printing, October 2006

store.viz.com

PARENTAL ADVISORY
LA CORDA D'ORO is rated T for Teen and is recommended for ages 13 and up. This volume contains mild violence.

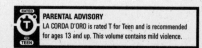

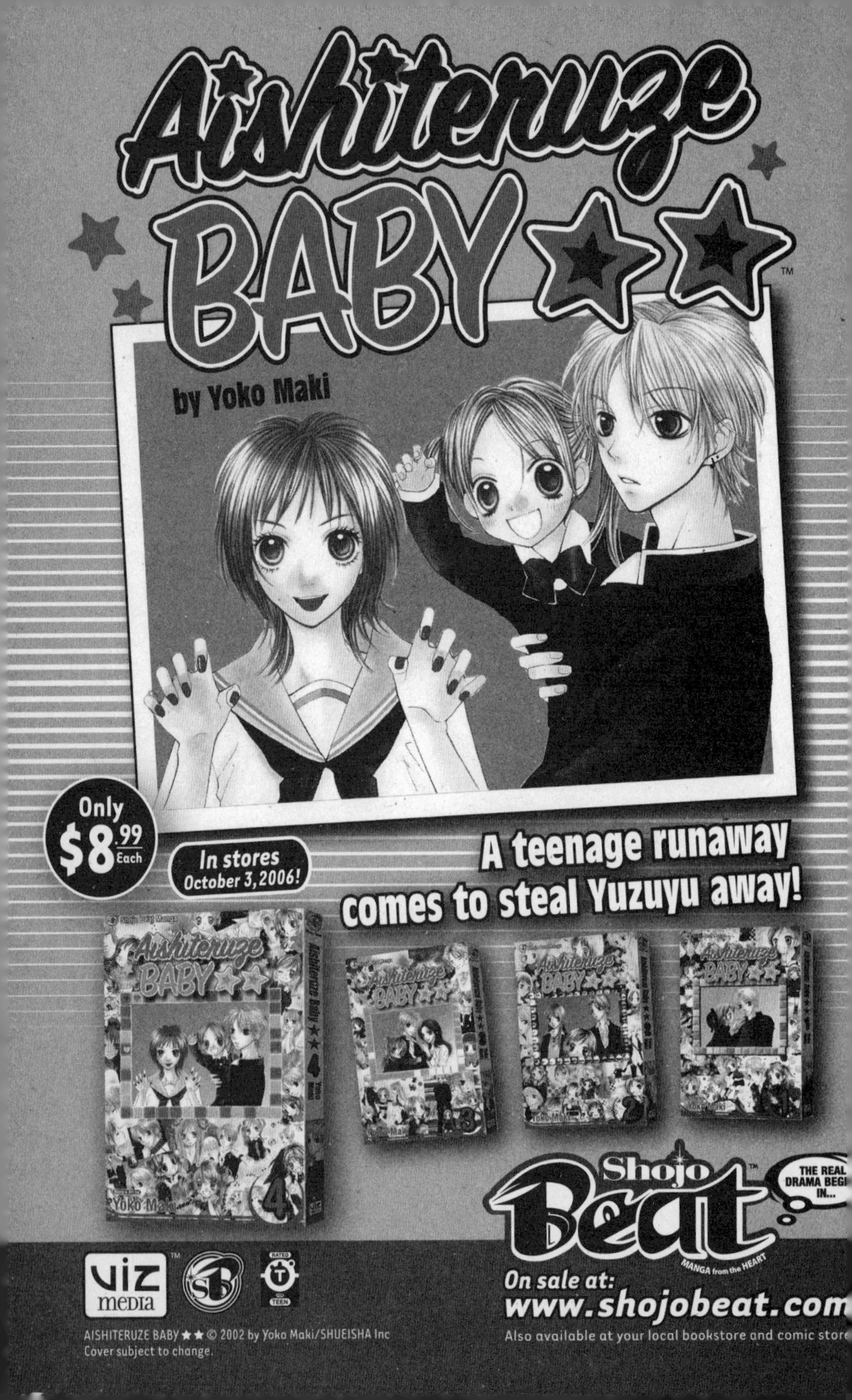

Aishiteruze BABY★★™
by Yoko Maki
Only $8.99 Each
In stores October 3, 2006!
A teenage runaway comes to steal Yuzuyu away!
Shojo Beat™ MANGA from the HEART
THE REAL DRAMA BEGI IN...
On sale at:
www.shojobeat.com
Also available at your local bookstore and comic store
AISHITERUZE BABY ★★ © 2002 by Yoko Maki/SHUEISHA Inc
Cover subject to change.

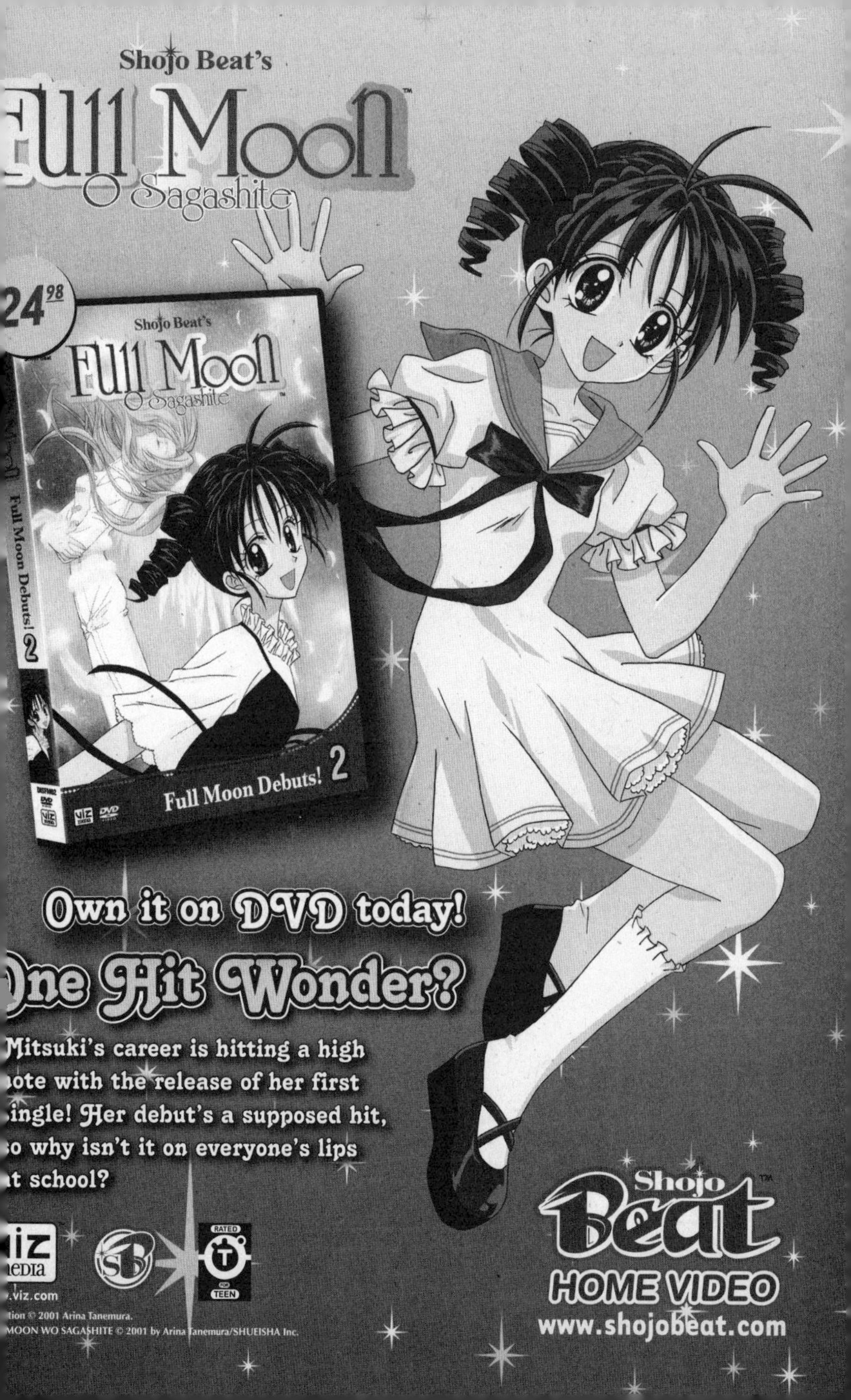
Shojo Beat's
Full Moon
O Sagashite
24.98
Shojo Beat's
Full Moon
O Sagashite
Full Moon Debuts! 2
Own it on DVD today!
One Hit Wonder?
Mitsuki's career is hitting a high note with the release of her first single! Her debut's a supposed hit, so why isn't it on everyone's lips at school?
viz media
.viz.com
RATED T FOR TEEN
Shojo Beat
HOME VIDEO
www.shojobeat.com
tion © 2001 Arina Tanemura.
MOON WO SAGASHITE © 2001 by Arina Tanemura/SHUEISHA Inc.

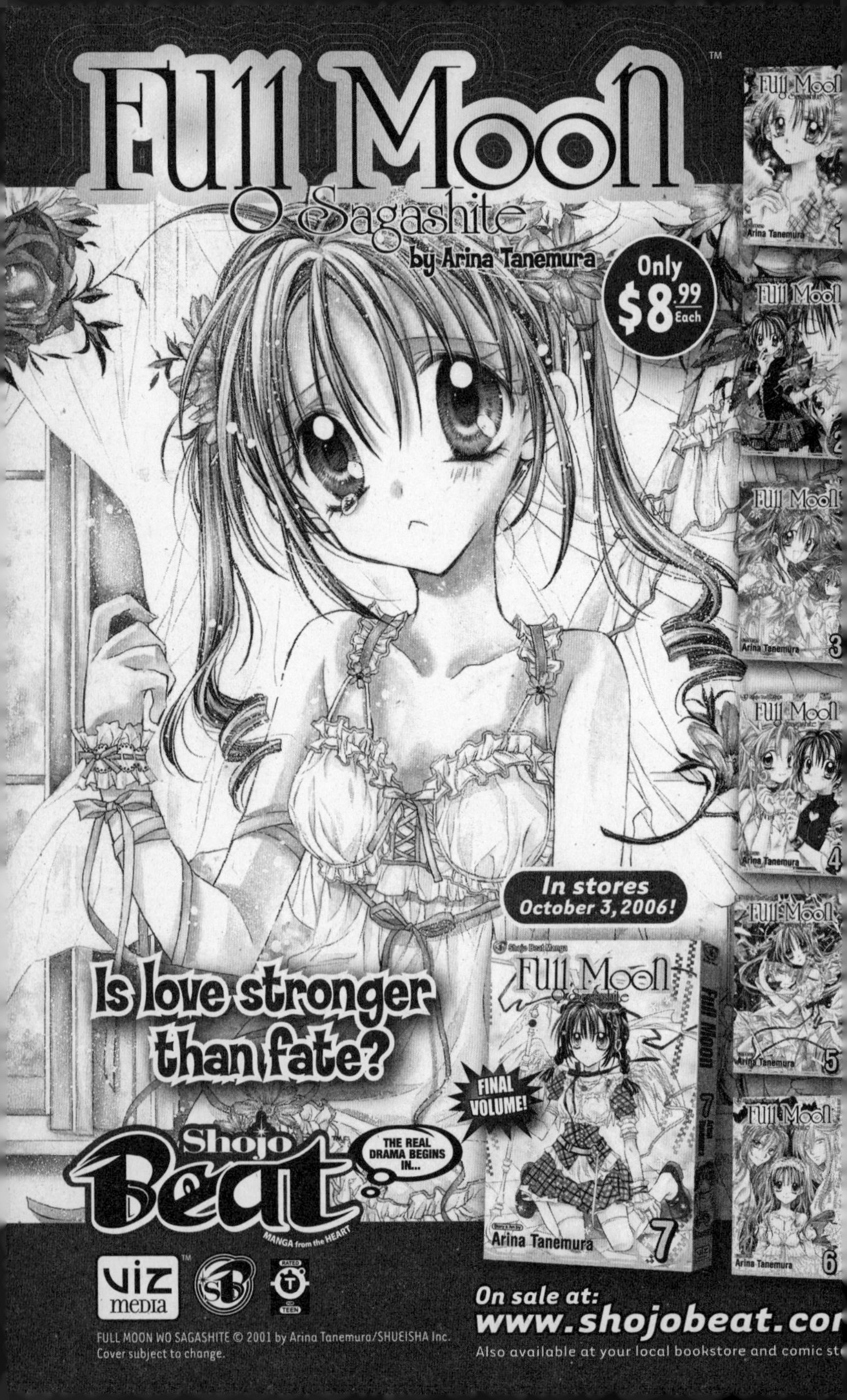

Full Moon O Sagashite
by Arina Tanemura
Only $8.99 Each
In stores October 3, 2006!
Is love stronger than fate?
FINAL VOLUME!
Shojo Beat
THE REAL DRAMA BEGINS IN...
MANGA from the HEART
viz media
On sale at:
www.shojobeat.com
Also available at your local bookstore and comic store.
FULL MOON WO SAGASHITE © 2001 by Arina Tanemura/SHUEISHA Inc.
Cover subject to change.

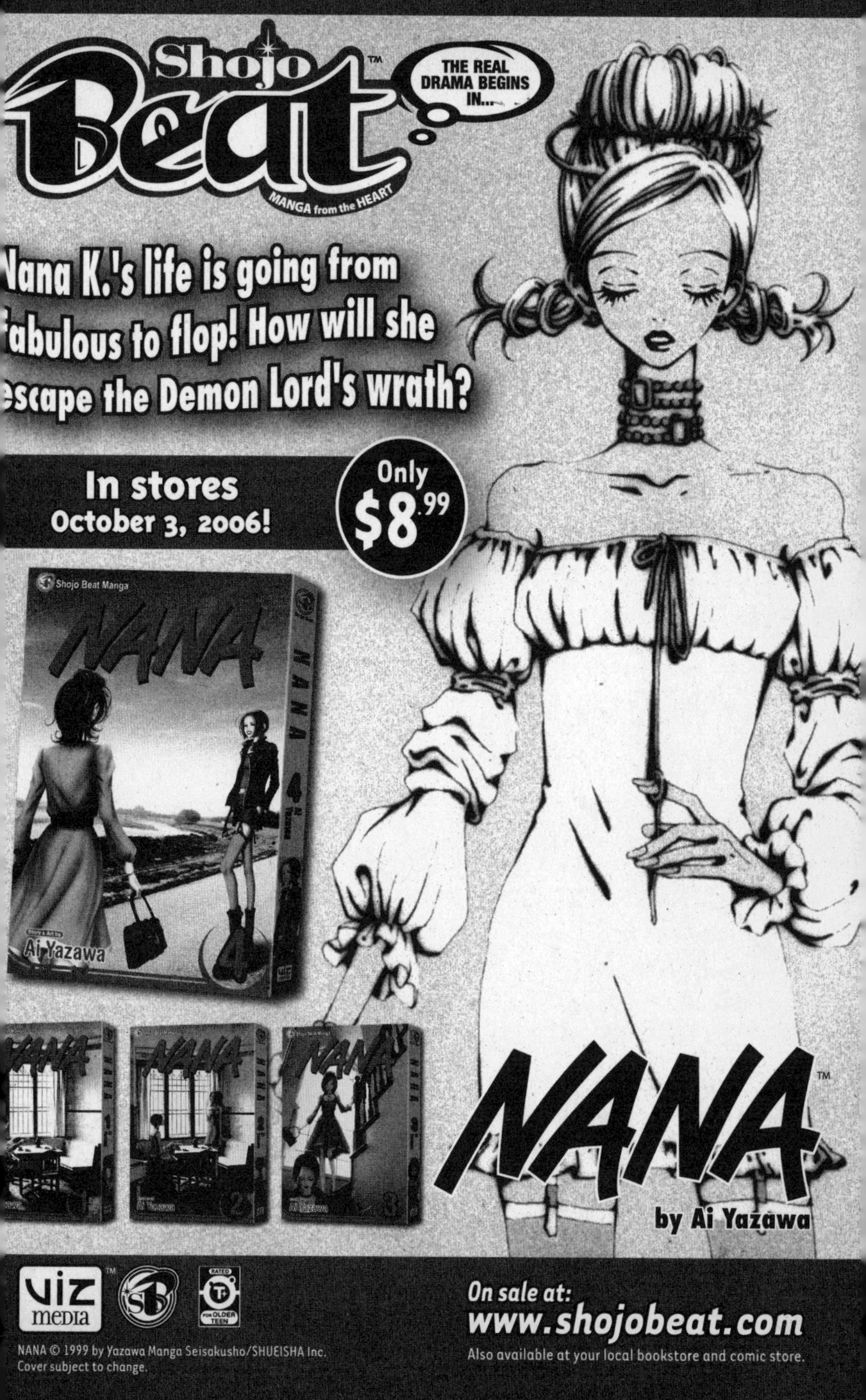
Shojo Beat™
MANGA from the HEART
THE REAL DRAMA BEGINS IN...
Nana K.'s life is going from fabulous to flop! How will she escape the Demon Lord's wrath?
In stores
October 3, 2006!
Only $8.99
Shojo Beat Manga
NANA
Ai Yazawa
NANA™
by Ai Yazawa
viz media
On sale at:
www.shojobeat.com
Also available at your local bookstore and comic store.
NANA © 1999 by Yazawa Manga Seisakusho/SHUEISHA Inc.
Cover subject to change.

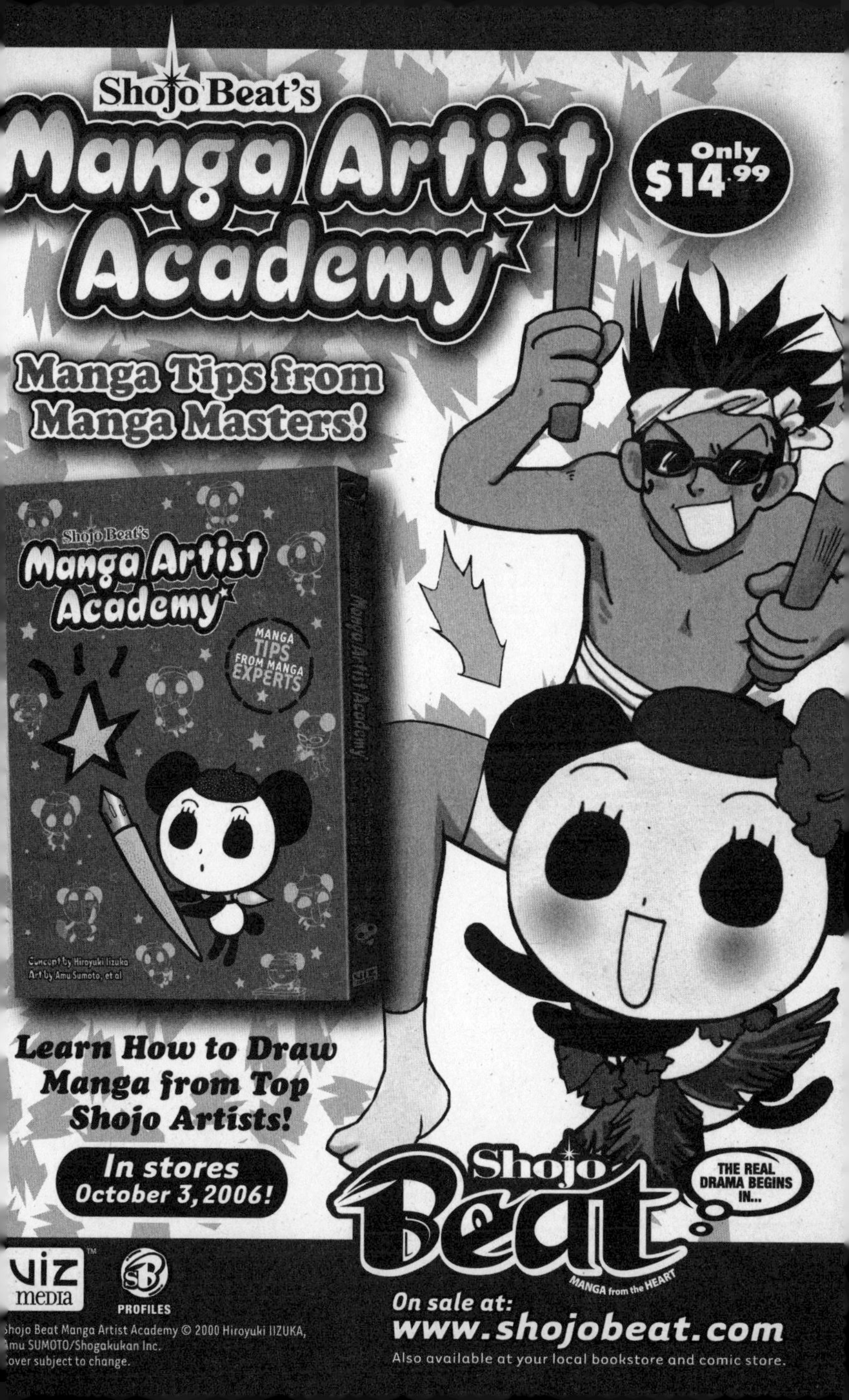

Shojo Beat's
Manga Artist Academy
Only $14.99
Manga Tips from Manga Masters!
Shojo Beat's
Manga Artist Academy
MANGA TIPS FROM MANGA EXPERTS
Concept by Hiroyuki Iizuka
Art by Amu Sumoto, et al
Manga Artist Academy
Learn How to Draw Manga from Top Shojo Artists!
In stores October 3, 2006!
Shojo Beat
THE REAL DRAMA BEGINS IN...
MANGA from the HEART
viz media
PROFILES
On sale at:
www.shojobeat.com
Also available at your local bookstore and comic store.
hojo Beat Manga Artist Academy © 2000 Hiroyuki IIZUKA,
mu SUMOTO/Shogakukan Inc.
over subject to change.

Find the Beat online!
Check us out at

www.shojobeat.com!

COMPLETE OUR SURVEY AND LET US KNOW WHAT YOU THINK!

☐ Please do NOT send me information about VIZ Media and Shojo Beat products, news and events, special offers, or other information.

☐ Please do NOT send me information from VIZ Media's trusted business partners.

Name: _____

Address: _____

City: _____ State: _____ Zip: _____

E-mail: _____

☐ Male ☐ Female Date of Birth (mm/dd/yyyy): ___ / ___ / ___ (Under 13? Parental consent required)

❶ Do you purchase *Shojo Beat* magazine?

☐ Yes ☐ No (if no, skip the next two questions)

If **YES**, do you subscribe?

☐ Yes ☐ No

If you do **NOT** subscribe, why? (please check one)

☐ I prefer to buy each issue at the store. ☐ I prefer to buy the manga volumes instead.

☐ I share a copy with my friends/family. ☐ It's too expensive.

☐ My parents/guardians won't let me. ☐ Other _____

❷ Which particular Shojo Beat Manga did you purchase? (please check one)

☐ Aishiteruze Baby ★★ ☐ Beauty Is the Beast ☐ Full Moon

☐ Fushigi Yûgi: Genbu Kaiden ☐ Kamikaze Girls ☐ MeruPuri

☐ Ouran High School Host Club ☐ Socrates In Love ☐ Tokyo Boys & Girls

☐ Ultra Maniac ☐ Other _____

Will/did you purchase subsequent volumes?

☐ Yes ☐ No ☐ Not Applicable

❸ How did you learn about this title? (check all that apply)

☐ Advertisement ☐ Article ☐ Favorite creator/artist

☐ Favorite title ☐ Gift ☐ Recommendation

☐ Read a preview online and wanted to read the rest of the story

☐ Read introduction in *Shojo Beat* magazine ☐ Special offer

☐ Website ☐ Other _____

4 Will/did you plan to purchase

☐ Yes ☐

If **YES**, which one(s) will/did you

☐ Absolute Boyfriend
☐ Godchild ☐ Kaze Hikaru

If **YES**, what are your reasons for purchasing? (please pick up to 3)

☐ Favorite title ☐ Favorite creator/artist
☐ I want to read the full volume(s) all at once ☐ I want to read it over and over again
☐ There are extras that aren't in the magazine ☐ Recommendation
☐ The quality of printing is better than the magazine
☐ Other _____

If **NO**, why would you not purchase it?

☐ I'm happy just reading it in the magazine ☐ It's not worth buying the graphic novel
☐ All the manga pages are in black and white ☐ There are other graphic novels that I prefer
☐ There are too many to collect for each title ☐ It's too small
☐ Other _____

5 Of the titles NOT serialized in the magazine, which ones have you purchased? (check all that apply)

☐ Aishiteruze Baby ★★ ☐ Beauty Is the Beast ☐ Full Moon
☐ Fushigi Yûgi: Genbu Kaiden ☐ Kamikaze Girls ☐ MeruPuri
☐ Ouran High School Host Club ☐ Socrates In Love ☐ Tokyo Boys & Girls
☐ Ultra Maniac ☐ Other _____

If you did purchase any of the above, what were your reasons for purchase?

☐ Advertisement ☐ Article ☐ Favorite creator/artist
☐ Favorite title ☐ Gift ☐ Recommendation
☐ Read a preview online and wanted to read the rest of the story
☐ Read introduction in *Shojo Beat* magazine ☐ Special offer
☐ Website ☐ Other _____

Will you purchase subsequent volumes, if available?

☐ Yes ☐ No

6 What race/ethnicity do you consider yourself? (please check one)

☐ Asian/Pacific Islander ☐ Black/African American ☐ Hispanic/Latino
☐ Native American/Alaskan Native ☐ White/Caucasian ☐ Other

THANK YOU! Please send the completed form to: **Shojo Survey**
42 Catharine St.
Poughkeepsie, NY 12601

VIZ media

All information provided will be used for internal purposes only. We promise not to sell or otherwise divulge your information.